Criss Cross

A Holly Novel

By: C.C. Warrens

Acknowledgements

To my amazing husband, who believed in me and encouraged me to write even when I had doubts.

To Joan Houghton, my favorite English teacher, who took time out of her busy schedule to give me advice and read my manuscript.

To the Adaptive Sports Program of Ohio for making a difference in the lives of disabled children and adults, and giving them the opportunity to play, compete, and challenge themselves.

Published April 2nd, 2017

1

The ominous sound of something scraping across the cement behind me raised the hairs on the back of my neck. I slid my fingers under the thick braided strap of my camera bag, preparing to use it as a weapon, as I paused to look behind me.

I'd stayed out too late photographing a young couple. The sun had dropped behind the horizon fifteen minutes ago, and it had been a long walk back from the park.

I scanned the dark streets. Light from the street lamps cast an orange glow over the buildings and sidewalks. A few female silhouettes haunted the corner, laughing and talking too loudly, and a taxi trolled slowly by.

I forced myself to breathe again and continued walking.

A tune I couldn't quite place drifted through my mind, distracting me from dwelling on the eerie street. I'd heard it somewhere before—something about someone saying hello and someone saying goodbye—and it was stuck in my head like a skipping record.

The faded yellow door of my apartment stood out in the darkness, and the sight of it sent a wave of relief through me. My living space wasn't technically an apartment; it was the unwanted, unkempt basement of an apartment complex that the owner had rented to me for dirt cheap. I couldn't afford much more than dirt.

I hurried down the two cement steps and thrust one of the keys into the first lock. Another chilling scrape came from somewhere behind me. I stiffened with my key poised over the remaining keyhole. The last thing I wanted to do was let a lunatic *into* my apartment.

If he made it into my apartment and locked us in, only the fire department could save me, and they would need to bring the Jaws of Life. This metal door would not budge otherwise.

Nope, getting attacked outside was much safer.

I glanced over my shoulder, but saw no one. I listened for the telltale scrape, but only the quiet crackling of tree limbs in the breeze and a distant siren broke through the silence. The city was quiet. Unnaturally so. That in itself was unsettling.

I slid the key into the lock, twisted it, and cracked the door just enough to slip through. I squeezed into my apartment and slammed the door behind me. I flipped all three dead bolts with practiced quickness and then dropped back against the door with a relief that made my knees weak.

The scent of must and lilac air freshener greeted me as I drew in a breath. No matter how often I cleaned, the musty aroma remained embedded in the walls and ceiling.

I shrugged my bag off on the kitchen counter immediately to my left, flipped the light switch that ignited the lone bulb over my kitchen table, and pushed away from the door.

My living space was a single L-shaped room with a quaint, if mismatched, kitchenette, a claustrophobic bathroom closet, and an alcove where my bed rested. I savored the openness. Small spaces brought back old memories better left forgotten.

A small chirp drew my gaze to the floor. A gray cat staggered around my ankles, his wide body throwing off his balance. Jordan looked up at me with crystalline blue eyes, pleading. I sighed and scooped him up with a grunt of effort.

"If I'd known you were going to be this chunky, I would've named you Sausage." I shifted his weight in my arms and he head-butted my chin affectionately. I really needed to put him on a diet. Would that be considered animal cruelty?

I grabbed the empty glass from the counter and filled it with water. A chunk of soggy cat food floated to the top of the glass and I set it aside with a frustrated sigh. "Really?" My cat blinked at me with wide, innocent eyes from the crook of my arm.

There were times when Jordan seemed confused about his species. He had an irritating habit of squirreling away his food anywhere he could find a spot: between couch cushions, in dishes, the silverware drawer . . . even the laundry hamper.

"I wasn't thirsty anyway," I grumbled.

I passed from the kitchen into the living room in four steps, and walked to the faded purple couch. I dropped Jordan onto the worn cushions and picked up the card-shaped envelope I had found taped to my door that morning. I hadn't had the opportunity to open it.

I sank onto the cushions beside Jordan as I examined the envelope. It was addressed simply to Holly, and the return address was 1288 Stony Brooke, Kansas.

I glanced at the battered silvery bracelet on my left wrist. It had begun to turn green around the edges a long time ago, and the letters engraved into the surface had all but faded away, leaving just a shadow of my name: Holly.

It was the only thing that had truly been mine when I drifted from one foster placement to the next, and I couldn't bring myself to part with it.

"Kansas," I said thoughtfully, letting the name roll around on my tongue. I didn't receive mail. I paid the landlord in cash for my utilities and rent, and I had no formal address. I glanced at my cat. "Do we know anyone from Kansas?"

My plump feline couldn't have looked more disinterested. I sighed and slipped my finger into the crease of the envelope, carefully tearing it open. There was a note card inside. Typewritten across the center of the card was the message:

Holly, come home.

An unexpected chill traveled down my spine. What was that supposed to mean? I had lived in a number of places in my twenty-eight years, but none of them had been in Kansas, and none of them had been home. At best they were rest stops, at worst . . .

I puffed out an anxious breath and flipped the card over. Except for the single phrase on the front, it was blank. There wasn't even a recipient address on the envelope, just my name.

The implications of that were terrifying.

Someone had tracked me down and taped it to the outside of my door. I moved through the world in the shadows, because that was the only way I knew how to survive, and this wasn't a good sign. I dropped the card on the couch as if it had singed my fingers, and stared at it warily.

I tapped an anxious rhythm on my thighs as I contemplated throwing what I could in a bag and running. Maybe I had stayed here too long; maybe I had become complacent.

I glanced at my cat when he bumped my leg with his head and purred. "Did he find us?" When I moved in a year ago, I had been determined to stay, to carve out a life for myself, but I'd known it was temporary. It was always temporary.

But this place was more a home to me than any other place I could remember. At times I even felt safe, and I wasn't ready to give that up. I had even adopted Jordan, and I couldn't abandon him; I wouldn't. I knew all too well how that felt.

I pulled him into my lap and stroked his head. His purr sputtered briefly before catching and deepening into a full-blown lawn mower vibration.

I can do all things through Christ who strengthens me. The verse fluttered through my mind, sparking hope. I could do this. Someone finding me was a complication I didn't need, but it was one I could handle. I had Jesus, and I had chocolate.

I stood and walked to the kitchen. I dragged a folding chair over to the counter and climbed on top of it. I fished a chocolate bar out of the back of the cupboard. I love the kind of bitter dark chocolate that makes you shiver with surprise when it first hits your taste buds.

I plopped onto the counter and unwrapped the long slender bar. The first bite was heavenly. I savored the bittersweet flavor as it melted over my tongue. I took another bite. I should really stop there and tuck the rest back into its hiding spot. I stared at the chocolate, feeling conflicted.

"Eh," I muttered with a shrug. I was going to eat the whole bar. I was stressed.

I slid off the counter and strode to my bed. Jordan trotted behind me, anticipating cuddle time. He bounced up and down on his hind legs a few times, too fat to scale the bed, and then sat down in defeat. He let out a wail that should be reserved for wounded or dying animals, and I took pity on him. I dragged him onto the bed next to me.

I flopped back on the blankets and grabbed the notebook and pen from the top of the cardboard box that served as my nightstand. I released a heavy breath as I uncapped the pen and opened the book.

It was my nightly tradition. In a life of chaos, it was easy to be swallowed by despair and pain, so I had decided to be thankful for at least one thing every day. I pressed the pen to the page tentatively.

This was the first time fear hadn't sent me running, a decision I hoped wouldn't be an awful mistake, and I considered the reasons for that. I glanced at the purring bundle against my side and started to write.

Dear Jesus,
    Today I'm thankful for Jordan. And for chocolate.

2

Breath rushed in and out of my lungs with the rhythm of my shoes on the pavement. Autumn had come a few weeks early this year, and dry leaves stirred around my feet.

Some of the trees bloomed with richly colored leaves, which resembled jewels as the sunlight filtered through them, while others clung to their green leaves rebelliously despite the cooling temperatures.

Autumn was beautiful in its own way, but it was my least favorite season. The crunch of dead leaves beneath my feet, the sound of gnarled, naked tree limbs knocking together in the breeze, candlelit pumpkins with twisted faces . . . it always left me feeling rattled.

My gait faltered when something orange smashed into the pavement a few feet in front of me and exploded. I barely avoided being splattered in pumpkin goo. I glanced up at the two adolescent boys who leaned out of an upstairs apartment window and laughed at the remains of the pumpkin.

I hated October.

I hopped over the pumpkin and finished my lap around the block at a brisker pace than usual. It helped me to evade the fellow jogger who always managed to overlap my jogging path and insisted on trying to flag me down with a wave. I considered changing my route just to avoid him, but this was my time.

I tried never to miss my 7:00 a.m. run, even if it was a crisp thirty-something degrees, like this morning, because it afforded me a steady routine that my unpredictable life didn't.

Someone was on the sidewalk outside of my apartment when I turned onto my street. I slowed to a cautious walk. I wasn't expecting company. A shock of black hair frosted with blue identified my visitor.

Jace.

She lived in one of the upstairs apartments, which was technically not connected to my underground basement, and she was the closest person I had to a friend. She was never up this early.

Jace was tall and slender, and her wild hair and slightly Asian eyes made her look like a character from an anime cartoon. She'd been able to walk for most of her life, but I met her after a car accident left her bound to a wheelchair.

"Hey," I said between heavy breaths. I strode up behind her with my hands on my hips. My sides ached from pushing myself harder than usual. "How are you even alive at seven thirty in the morning?"

Jace spun her wheelchair around to face me. She lifted a paper coffee mug and grinned, "Caffeine and sugar. Liquid magic." She held up a second cup. "I brought you one too."

I regarded the offering warily. "It's not another cinnamon spice latte, is it?"

She looked offended. "I only made that mistake like two, maybe five times. It's hard to remember. Normal people like cinnamon." She dangled the cup in front of me tauntingly. "It's hot cocoa."

"With marshmallows?" I asked hopefully as I took it from her. I'd been fantasizing about marshmallows since I jogged past the pastry shop.

"They were out. Extra whipped cream, though."

I popped the lid and drew in the sweet, chocolaty aroma. "You . . . are my favorite person in the whole world," I declared.

"Wow," she said flatly. "If I wasn't the only person you spoke to *in the whole world*, that might mean something."

I smirked as I took a sip of the warm drink. Apart from the occasional word exchanged with my landlord when I dropped off my rent, and the information gathering from my customers, she really was the only person I spoke to. I was certain she knew deep down that I kind of liked her.

"Can we go inside? It's cold and I can't feel my toes," she

9

announced, completely deadpan.

I laughed. Her toes had been numb since the accident; it had absolutely nothing to do with the cold. I hopped down the steps and unlocked the door. I flung it open and grabbed the slab of wood that rested against the side of the building. There was no ramp or elevator to my apartment, so we had to make do. I laid it over the steps and backed into the apartment to give her room.

She cruised down the board and maneuvered over the dip at the bottom and into my apartment.

"What . . . what is this hideously inconvenient lump on your floor?" Jace demanded as her casual glide through the doorway was abruptly halted when the front wheels of her wheelchair collided with the rug.

"It's called a rug," I replied evenly as I took another sip of my hot chocolate.

"I'm sorry, you said death trap?" Jace asked with a painfully serious expression. She spun her wheels, but the bunched-up rug moved with her, forcing her into a slow circle. "I feel like I'm in a tailspin here." She sighed and stopped struggling. Her blue eyes met mine. "Can I burn it? Pretty please with sprinkles?"

I smiled and set my cup down so I could untangle the rug from her wheels. I tossed it aside. She sped across the tile and spun in a deliberate circle in her chair.

"Oh yeah, smooth sailing." She popped a wheelie in her chair and somehow managed to maintain the precarious position. I was pretty sure if I tried that I would tip backwards and crack my head open like that pumpkin I saw hit the pavement. "The next time you try to redecorate, buy a pillow. Pillows are fantastic."

"Fine, no more rugs," I agreed as I dropped onto the couch. I folded my legs beneath me and grabbed one of the brown pillows to put in my lap. "So what brings you to my door at the crack of dawn with a bribe?"

Jace locked her wheels and folded her arms over her legs as she leaned forward. "I need a favor."

I twirled my hand in a gesture for her to continue.

10

"I have a date," she said.

I wasn't sure what the appropriate best-friend response to that news was supposed to be—seeing as I'd never had a best friend before—so I just nodded and said, "Have fun?"

Jace stared at me.

Okay, apparently "have fun" wasn't the right response. I racked my brain for something better. "Is he . . . cute?" That was normal, right? I could do normal. I took a casual sip of my hot chocolate as if it hadn't taken me ages to think of that *normal* question.

"Yes. Absolutely."

I waited for more, but she offered nothing. *Crap, is it my turn again?* "I assume he has a face and it looks like . . . something."

Jace rolled her eyes and said with exasperation, "Yes, he has a face. A cute face. *And* he has an accent."

"Southern?"

"English," she said, grinning. "Although Southern would be delicious."

I wasn't particularly drawn to a person because they had an accent, but I had to admit that English accents were interesting, and Southern accents, depending on what part of the South they were from, could be downright soothing to listen to. But delicious?

"I'm assuming he doesn't have a criminal record."

Jace grimaced. "I didn't ask. You don't just *ask* things like that, Holly."

It was absolutely a question I would ask, right after "why are you speaking to me?" I frowned at her as I said, "But it's important."

"Not really."

I groaned and rubbed my head. My brain was starting to hurt. "Did you at least get his name?"

"Gale."

"Does Gale have a last name?"

Jace puckered her lips inward in reluctance. "Doe" finally popped out.

"Seriously?"

Jace straightened and her tone was mildly defensive. "Yes, seriously. It's more real than Smith, so don't even . . ." She slapped a hand over her mouth, and her eyes widened in shock and horror.

I forced a thin smile. "It's fine, Jace. It's not like I just realized my last name isn't actually Smith." I doubted it was the surname I'd been born with, but it was the one assigned to me by the state when I was twelve.

Before that day, I didn't officially exist. My first memory was of waking up in a cabin with a strange woman and her husband when I was ten. They clothed me, fed me, gave me chores to do, and to the best of my knowledge we were a family. Until their cabin was raided by the police two years later and I was removed. My "family" went to prison, the state assigned me an identity, and I was chucked unceremoniously into the foster care system.

In all that time, I had never managed to build a trusting relationship with another human being, and sometimes I questioned letting Jace in. I had only shared a few details about my past with her, and it was still more than I'd shared with anyone. Ever.

I had rebuffed her multiple times when we first met, and even flat out told her to take a hike, to which she mockingly replied, "I can't hike; I'm in a wheelchair." She was one of those frustratingly determined people.

I cleared my throat. "So about that favor . . ."

"Right, the favor," she muttered. "I don't know what to wear. I could um . . . use a little help tracking down an outfit."

I pursed my lips. "You want me to go shopping." I abhorred shopping.

"If we go super early when the stores just open, there won't be many people." She gazed at me with wide, pleading eyes.

She wanted me to go with her badly enough that she'd forced herself out of bed hours before she usually did in an effort to make me more comfortable with the idea. And she brought me hot chocolate. How could I say no? I sighed and said, "Fine. But I have a photo shoot at four this afternoon, and I will *not* model clothing with you in front of the mirrors."

"Just one outfit?"

"No."

"Shoes?"

"I will wheel you out that door and leave you on the sidewalk," I threatened.

Jace grinned. "Okay fine, no modeling. I'm ready when you are."

"Just gimme a second to change." I dragged myself off the couch and over to the nook where my bed was. There wasn't room for a dresser, so I hung my clothes on a curtain rod mounted to the ceiling above my bed. I tugged the heavy purple drapes closed between the bed and the couch to give myself some privacy and stripped out of my sweat-dampened clothes.

I sat on the edge of the bed and pulled off my socks and shoes. My feet ached, though I expected the pain resonated more from my memories than from the scars that covered the bottoms of my feet. The wounds were old enough that the scars had faded to white.

I wiggled my feet into a fresh pair of socks before the old wounds could stir up frightening memories. I was tugging a thin white sweater over my purple long sleeved T-shirt when Jace asked, "Holly, what is this?"

I poked my head through the curtain. She was studying the note card I'd left sitting on the couch for the past few days. "Mail," I replied dismissively.

Her heavily lined eyes narrowed. "You don't get mail. And it says it's from Kansas."

"I know nothing about Kansas." I teetered precariously on one leg as I tried to shove my other foot into a stubborn brown boot. Who ever thought it was a bright idea to make a boot without a zipper?

"That you remember," she insisted. "You can't remember anything before the age of ten. For all you know you could have been raised in Kansas."

Fair point.

"This could be from your family. Your *real* family."

If my biological family had managed to track me down, which was incredibly unlikely, then I was genuinely offended that all they left behind was a cryptic message typed on a note card. Surely after all these years I at least deserved a face-to-face "this is why we didn't want you" explanation.

Like any other child who was discarded into the foster care system, I had thought about my family every day. No one could even tell me their names. Someone said once that you can't miss something you never had. I didn't have a single memory of my family, but I missed them.

Eventually I decided that if they existed—if they had even a glimmer of love for me—they would never have left me in some of the "homes" where I was placed.

"I don't have a family," I replied flatly.

"That you remember," she repeated with emphasis. She rotated her wheelchair to face me. "People don't just forget ten years of their lives, Holly. That doesn't just happen."

Except it did.

My brain wasn't broken; the state had sent me to various hospitals to have brain scans done when I was a child, but there was no evidence of physical trauma to my brain, which left one possibility.

"Maybe you were abducted, maybe something bad happened that made you wanna forget everything," Jace continued.

And that was the other possibility. No amount of therapy had helped me to regain those lost memories, so I couldn't say one way or another if my memory loss was due to psychological trauma.

I folded my arms and gazed at her from behind the small opening in the drapes. "I don't wanna talk about this anymore, okay? Let's just go shopping."

Jace sighed in defeat and dropped the note card back onto the couch. If I would rather go shopping than discuss my family, she knew the conversation was utterly hopeless.

3

"Move a little to your left," I suggested. I watched through the camera lens as the couple shifted under the orange-and-yellow oak tree. The light captured their faces perfectly, and I snapped a few quick shots before stepping to my right to adjust my angle.

I tried to avoid taking photos straight on despite what my customers requested; it was the angle and the lighting that gave a picture life.

A gust of wind sent orange leaves showering down around the couple, and I snapped the picture just as they both looked up in laughter. That would be a keeper. When I lowered the camera and scrolled through the last few photos to be certain I liked the quality, something odd caught my attention.

I zoomed in on a dark blur in the background of the last photo. It was a human figure standing in the shadow of a tree. It was too dark to tell, but he appeared to be looking in our direction. Frowning, I slowly scrolled back through the photos. The figure was present in every single picture for the past hour.

Unease fluttered through my stomach. I looked up and gazed into the distance, but I couldn't see anything but trees. I lifted the camera and zoomed in.

Whoever had been standing there was gone.

"Is everything all right with the pictures?" the woman asked.

I lowered the camera and looked at the couple. "I think you'll like them. I would take a few more but the lighting's shifted too much. I'll develop a few of the better ones in a couple days and let you take a look. If you don't like any of them, we can set up another appointment."

The woman smiled. "Okay. Thanks, Holly."

The man intertwined his fingers with hers, and they strode off toward the road. I tucked my camera safely into the bag and slung the strap over my shoulder. I usually crossed it over my body, but that just wasn't comfortable tonight. I wound the purple scarf around my neck to stave off the chill of evening.

I turned toward the trees that divided the park from the inner city and then paused, reconsidering. I glanced back at the tree where the mysterious figure had been standing. I couldn't help but wonder if it had been pure chance or if he'd been spying on one of my clients. A quick glimpse of the receding sun told me I had about an hour before nightfall.

This is a dumb idea.

I sighed and walked toward the tree. As I drew nearer, my steps became more cautious. If someone was hiding behind the tree, I didn't want to risk being jumped.

I gave the area a wide berth as I circled it. The shady photobomber was nowhere to be seen, but I found the impressions of his boots in the moist grass. I would have guessed it was a man from the height and shape of him in the photos, but I hadn't been sure until now.

I placed my foot next to his footprint. I wore a size 6 shoe, and this print was a little more than double the size of my foot. It was definitely a man, and a large one. That kind of unnerved me a bit. I had my fair share of run-ins with creepers, but none of them hid in the trees and watched people.

"You're a special kind of weird, aren't you?" I murmured to the man who had left these prints.

I pulled out my camera and snapped a picture of my foot next to the footprints. I doubted anything bad would happen to the young couple, but if I knew anything about the nature of human beings, it was that they were just as prone to outbursts of violence as they were to unexpected kindness. It was always better to err on the side of caution. And if anything did happen to the couple, I could at least provide the police with a direction.

I wasn't particularly fond of the police. Not only had they snatched me out of the first place I could identify as a home, but they had hunted me down every time I fled from one of my foster homes. If I ran, it was for a good reason, but none of them had bothered to listen. To them, I was just another troubled child looking for attention. They threw me right back into the situation I had worked so hard to save myself from.

Sometimes it was hard not to see them as the enemy. But they had a purpose, and I knew that many of them were heroes and wonderful people. Why couldn't I have met some of those?

I slid the camera back in my bag and headed through the trees toward the street. There was something about wooded areas that made me anxious, but the trees in the park were typically far enough apart that I didn't feel the need to pant hysterically into a paper bag.

No matter how sparse the trees, though, I walked on egg shells until I cleared them. Leaves rustled above me, and I scanned the thinning canopy warily. A squirrel bounded from one tree and onto another, sending leaves fluttering down around me.

Quiet crunching came from behind me, and anxiety flared in my stomach. I glanced over my shoulder, but there was nothing behind me but more trees.

If creepy noises were going to become a regular soundtrack when I was walking home, I was going to have to invest in a can of mace and some bricks. Just in case the mace didn't put a lunatic down, I could beat him over the head with a bag of bricks. That worked on anyone.

I was going to freak myself out if I kept thinking about men lurking in the shadows. That man in the photos had unnerved me more than I thought. I tried to ignore the sounds of nature around me as I walked toward the eastern edge of the park.

A loud whistling tune shattered the quiet and I jumped. I turned in a frantic circle before realizing the sound was coming from the pocket of my coat. My phone was ringing. I sighed in exasperation of my own reaction and grabbed my phone.

Jace's name flashed across the screen. I flipped it open and pressed the phone to my ear. "So either you're excited to tell me the details of your date or it went horribly wrong and you're calling because we're about to have a very late night full of ice cream and frosted brownies."

Jace scoffed. "You're hilarious. We had to reschedule. Something came up with his mother or something. I wanted to see if you wanted to grab some Italian or Mexican on the way home."

I paused for a beat. "That's called kidnapping, Jace."

She laughed loudly through the phone, and I had to pull it away from my ear. "Cute," she said. "I meant food."

"I am craving breadsticks slathered in butter." I had planned on becoming acquainted with an old generic can of beef ravioli I had stashed in the cupboard, but I wouldn't say no to real Italian food.

"Good. I'll order and pay over the phone, and you can pick it up on the way home. It's on your way, right?"

"Yep. I'll be home in about thirty minutes."

"Cool. See ya then."

I disconnected the call and slipped the phone back into my coat pocket. I could see the abandoned playground several hundred feet ahead through the sparse trees. I was almost out of the woods. Literally.

Musical whistling filled the air again, and I fished my phone out of my pocket. I wondered if Jace had changed her mind already. The phone screen was blank. I froze and looked up, tracking the sound of the whistling.

A man stepped out from between the trees ahead of me. He whistled softly as he dragged his feet leisurely through the leaves. He stopped directly between me and the path to the playground and cocked his head. "Catchy tune."

His lips were curved into a thin smile, but there was something about his eyes that sent a tingle of warning across all my nerve endings.

I made an effort to appear casual as I took a slow step back. The man's gaze flickered to my feet and then back to my face. I recognized the shine of amusement in his eyes, but I couldn't decide if it was me that amused him or my fear.

He plucked a leaf from one of the low-hanging limbs and

turned it over thoughtfully in his large hands. "Having dinner with your friend, huh? Italian?"

Not only had he imitated my ringtone perfectly, but he had eavesdropped on my conversation? That wasn't creepy at all.

He lifted his gaze to mine and flicked the leaf away carelessly. "I hate to break it to you, but you won't be making it to dinner."

Fear twisted through my stomach, and I backed away from him. I flipped open my phone and punched in 9-1-1. Maybe I would meet some of the hero cops after all.

"It's Friday night in the city." He made a show of glancing at the expensive watch on his wrist. I had a feeling he'd stolen it from some other poor soul who wandered through here. "Cops are busy. That gives us plenty of time."

Plenty of time for what?

My heart hammered in my ears, and I barely heard the 9-1-1 operator pick up the call. "9-1-1, what is your emergency?"

A second man dropped out of one of the trees beside me, and I sucked in a startled breath as I stumbled backwards over my own feet. He landed in a crouch and stood slowly, brushing the dirt and bark from his hands.

"Hi there," he said. He plucked the phone from my fingers, snapped it shut, and tossed it over his shoulder into the grass.

"Pretty little thing, isn't she?" the Whistling Man commented. "I've always had a thing for redheads."

The second man's dark eyes took me in with one long, lingering sweep before he grunted, "Eh."

My gaze shifted between the two of them as I slowly backed away. "I don't have anything to give you." I hated the quiet tremor in my voice. "I don't have any money or valuables." All I had was my camera and my worn bracelet. I'd heard about drug deals and muggings in the park before, but that was usually after nightfall. I still had an hour of sunlight left.

"We don't want your money," the Whistling Man declared.

"Or your valuables," the second man added.

19

Nausea crawled the walls of my stomach as their words sank in. This wasn't a mugging then. The only two things remaining that they could possibly want from me I wasn't willing to give.

God, I begged silently. I couldn't form the thoughts I needed, but I knew He would understand.

I expected panic to set in, but a familiar icy resolve slid beneath my skin. It had been my armor as a child—a barrier that protected me when the pain and fear became too much. I had learned that sometimes the only way to survive was to feel nothing. And I did whatever I could to survive.

I studied the two men as they closed in around me. There was no way I was going to be able to skirt past them to the street. Even if I managed to escape the park, there was nothing to stop them from catching me and dragging me back inside.

I knew my chances of escaping unscathed were virtually impossible. The dark-eyed man was the smaller of the two, and I might be able to fend him off, but the Whistling Man was probably a foot taller than me—six two, maybe—and he moved like an athlete.

I had to accept the fact that they were going to hurt me. I would escape if I could—I would survive—but if nothing else, I would do my best to make them regret choosing me.

"I have a feeling she's gonna rabbit," the dark-eyed man observed. "She looks cagey."

"Don't do this," I pleaded, and my voice came out far steadier than it had moments ago.

Painful memories and emotions pressed against the barrier I had erected, but I held them back by sheer force of will. I needed my mind to be sharp. I backed away and discretely slid my fingers under the strap of my camera bag. I was suddenly grateful I hadn't slung it across my body like I usually did.

"I promise it won't hurt," the dark-eyed man said.

Someone should let him know he was a really bad liar. "You're a terrible liar," I blurted. May as well be me.

The dark-eyed man grinned. "Yeah?"

He stretched out a hand to touch me, and I slid the strap off

20

my shoulder and swung the bag in one swift movement. The bag smashed into his face, and I heard the lens of my camera shatter against his nose. The man let out a string of curses as his hands flew to his face.

I swung the bag at the second man, but he jumped back to avoid it. I lost my grip on the strap and let it hurdle through the air toward him as I pivoted on my heel and ran. I dashed through the park at full speed.

I trained every day so that when I came face to face with my fears again, I could outrun them.

"She broke my nose!" the man bellowed, his voice muffled by the hands he had cupped over his face. A small sense of relief flickered through me. I knew from experience that blinding tears were welling in his eyes and streaming down his cheeks, and it would slow him down.

An eerie feeling of deja vu crept over me as I darted through the trees, trying to outrun the heavy footsteps that nipped at my heels. My foot hit a patch of damp leaves, and I grabbed a branch to catch myself before my legs could slide out from under me. I slipped and skated down a small wet slope and then picked up the pace again.

"There's nowhere to run!" the Whistling Man called out.

Every step led me deeper into the park. There was another playground at the opposite end, but I didn't want to endanger children. The nearest walking path was empty, and there was no one I could ask for help. I just needed to reach the street.

Fear pounded violently against the emotional barrier I had erected, sending hairline cracks through it. Something old seeped through—like a memory of terrifying, debilitating fear—and it threatened to consume me.

I tried to push it away, but it clung tighter with every breath. It was suffocating. I ducked behind a patch of bushes whose leaves had begun to fade into fiery red and sank to a crouch.

Something was wrong with me. I was so terrified that my body was trembling, and tears pooled across my vision. I hadn't been this frightened in two years, and those circumstances had been far more dire. These men hadn't even touched me yet. I covered my mouth to quiet my gasps, and closed my eyes. I needed to control myself.

Unbidden scenes flashed behind my closed eyelids.

I tried to melt into the tree behind me and disappear as I listened to the heavy footsteps snapping through the brush behind me. I bit down on my lips to keep my teeth from chattering as the cold air whipped through my nightgown.

Another snap brought him closer. He was going to find me. Fear stole my breath, and I wrapped my arms around myself as I began to tremble. I mouthed the prayer Mom had made us memorize in case we were ever lost or afraid:

> *Jesus, sir,*
> *I come to thee*
> *And ask you please*
> *Watch over me*
> *Keep me safe*
> *Dry my tears*
> *Protect me from*
> *The things I fear*

My eyes snapped open as the scene dissolved. For a moment I'd been there in those woods, shivering in a nightgown as someone hunted me. I shuddered. It had felt so real.

I heard a heavy thump, followed by a string of violent curses. The Whistling Man had found the small slope I had skated down, but his descent hadn't been as graceful.

I needed to move. He was too close. I slunk around the bushes and kept low to the ground until I was sure he couldn't see me from the spot where he'd landed.

He was dragging himself to his feet and grumbling under his breath. His head lifted and his eyes scanned the area for me. My heart hammered in my chest as his gaze glossed over the small tree I hunkered behind.

"There's nowhere to hide," he shouted. "You're not gonna reach the sidewalks. No one's gonna help you."

He was probably right. People were selfish creatures. Most would probably walk by a guy bleeding to death on the street because they were late for an appointment. Or because they just didn't want to get involved. But really, just because no one would help me didn't mean I was going to roll over and offer myself up as their evening entertainment.

"Stop playing with her and just grab her!" the dark-eyed man shouted from somewhere in the distance. "Or is a hundred-pound girl too hard for you to handle?"

"I'm not the one with the broken nose!" the Whistling man shouted back. He swatted the nearest bush in irritation, and then swore at it when the rough stems cut his palm.

He walked forward slowly, and I shrank down. If I moved, he would see me, and if I stayed, he would find me in a matter of seconds, but then it would be too late to run.

Running at least gave me a chance. I shot to my feet and bolted.

"Found her!" he shouted before launching after me. "She's on the move again!"

On flat ground his long stride gave him an advantage. I had no doubt I could tire him out if I could just stay ahead of him, but he was gaining on me. He stretched out an arm to grab me, and I swerved, narrowly avoiding the tips of his fingers. He stumbled as he reached for me the second time and missed.

I spotted a figure in the distance. Someone had appeared on one of the walking paths that wound through the park. "Help!" I cried out. I had no idea who it was or if he would even help me, but I had to try to reach him.

I screamed when a heavy force slammed into my back and tackled me to the ground, knocking the breath from my lungs. I coughed and clawed at the grass as I tried to pull myself out from under my attacker.

"No, you don't," he grunted, as he dug his fingers into my

23

hips and dragged me back.

I searched desperately for something to hold onto, but there was nothing. My fingertips brushed a thick branch, and I grabbed it. I twisted and swung it with as much force as the awkward position allowed. It thumped the man across the side of his head.

I hit him again and he recoiled, raising his hands to shield his face. I scrambled forward a few feet before he grabbed a fistful of my jacket and tried to drag me back. My cold fingers fumbled hastily with the zipper. I twisted out of the sleeves and nearly fell forward from the sudden lack of resistance. The man threw my coat aside with a growl of frustration and lunged after me.

I skirted around a tree in my path, and he cut me off on the other side. I screamed as he locked an arm around my waist and heaved me off my feet.

He clamped a hand over my mouth to silence me. "Got her!" he hollered over his shoulder. I squirmed against his hold. I needed to get away from him. I had to fight harder than this.

God, please don't let this happen.

"Let's go somewhere a little more private," he suggested, as he carried me toward a thicker patch of trees.

Panic threaded through me. It made me want to scream and fight, but I couldn't fight him. Even if I managed to kick him or hit him, he would put me down with a single blow. I had to find another way to get free.

I stopped fighting. I let my body go limp, and I dropped like a sack of bricks, which I could really use right now, and took my captor with me.

"What the . . . ," he exclaimed, as my sudden drop threw him off balance. He'd expected squirming and flailing, but 115 pounds of dead weight were more difficult to maneuver.

He uncovered my mouth to wrap his other arm around my stomach and heaved me up. I took advantage of his confusion and let out a scream shrill enough to reverberate through the entire park. He slapped his hand back over my mouth. "Shut up."

I thrashed violently as he lifted me up, and the moment he

adjusted to carrying me, I let my body go limp again. He nearly dropped me. I was going to make this process as frustrating as possible for him.

"'Riley! Stop!'" someone shouted in the distance.

The sound of something or someone racing across the grass through the dead leaves made the man holding me stiffen. "What is that?" he muttered to himself.

I squinted against the fading light at the blur cutting through the park too quickly to be a person. It hunkered low to the ground, and the color of its fur nearly blended into the fall background.

"Is that . . . a dog?" he asked, and there was fear in his voice. A German shepherd bared down on us, his muzzle contorted in a snarl. I tried to shrink away as the predator leaped toward us. The dog slammed into my attacker, sending both of them tumbling into the grass. The German shepherd growled and ripped into the man's arm.

"Get it off me! Get it off!" the man screamed.

I scrambled backwards through the leaves as the fight between my attacker and the dog came closer. The man balled his fist and hit the dog in the side of the head. The German shepherd whimpered and reared back.

The man stumbled to his feet and fled through the park, running as fast as he could with his injuries. The dog gave chase, and I had no doubt he would catch him. I couldn't find it in my heart to feel sorry for him.

A third man lumbered over on my left, and I gathered my legs under me to run. He plodded to a stop a few feet from me, bent over to grip his knees, and gasped, "My dog . . ."

I froze where I crouched. I noticed he was carrying half of a leash that had been snapped in two. He'd called after his dog when he broke the leash and came for my attackers. This was the man from the walking path.

He was a round man pushing sixty, and he was in no shape to be running. He wheezed as he stood up, and his face was an unhealthy shade of red. "Riley," he managed to squeeze out.

Too stunned to do anything else, I pointed in the direction the dog had run. The man sighed heavily and hung his head. "He'll come back." He dropped onto the ground where he stood. He examined me with a quick thorough glance. "Were you the girl who was screaming?"

I watched him warily, unsure what to make of the situation. "That was your dog?" When he nodded, I said, "I don't understand. Why did he chase that man off?"

The man drew another heavy breath and let it out. "Riley is a retired police dog. He has PTSD. Gunfire and screaming set him off. His former partner was a female officer, and I guess something happened to the two of them. I don't know all the details. I do know he gets me in a lot of trouble when we go walking. Someone is always screaming, and it's like it's programmed into his head to help them . . . but half the time it's just some kid playing. At least this time he was right, huh?" He looked down at his broken leash and tossed it aside with an unhappy grunt. "Third one this month. I'm gonna go broke."

There was nothing I could say to express the awe and gratitude that flooded through me. I had prayed for help, and God had sent Riley.

4

I studied my broken, ragged fingernails as I sat on the curb. Blood and dirt were caked beneath what remained of them; I hadn't paid much attention to the pain when I was trying to claw my way out from under my attacker, but now they throbbed.

If these were the worst of my injuries, though, I couldn't complain.

"Ms. Smith?"

I flinched at the male voice that came from my left. I looked up to see a lean, forty-something man standing next to me. His face was serious and tired, but his green eyes were warm.

A quick scan of his attire told me he wasn't a member of the police force or the medical personnel. He wore a pair of dark jeans and a threadbare brown suit jacket. Beneath the jacket was a bulge that suspiciously resembled a gun.

My eyes darted to the ambulance and police cars, but no one seemed alarmed by his presence. He must have noticed my wariness, because he peeled his jacket aside slowly with two fingers and showed me the badge attached to his belt.

"I'm Detective Richard Marx." He had a slow, gentle voice with a touch of Southern. He certainly hadn't grown up here.

I hoped he didn't expect a badge to make me like him more, because it didn't. But it did settle some of the anxiety in my stomach.

"Holly," I corrected. I hated to be addressed as Ms. Smith.

"How are you doin'?"

"I've had worse days," I answered with a shrug.

The detective blinked, clearly unsure how to take my response. Ha. I'd stumped a seasoned detective in four words. That had to be some kind of record. He looked as if he wanted to ask for an explanation, but he didn't.

"Did you find my camera?" I asked, hopeful. I doubted I

could afford to repair the lens right now, but that would be better than having to replace the entire camera.

"We did." He gestured to the curb. "Do you mind if I sit?"

I hesitated at the thought of him sitting next to me, but it was public property and I couldn't really tell him to go find his own curb to sit on. I scooted over, allowing for about five feet of space between us.

The barely perceptible arch of his eyebrow told me the amount of space I deliberately put between us was not lost on him, but he chose not to comment. He was careful not to invade that space as he sat down.

"Is my camera okay?"

"For the most part. The lens is damaged, but the memory card and display are intact. I skimmed through a few of the photos. One of them seems a little out of place. Would you mind explainin' it to me?"

Realizing that some stranger was snooping through the photos on *my* camera made me cranky. Other than my bracelet, my camera was the only material possession I treasured. If they had asked, I might have given them the memory card. But they hadn't asked.

"I want my camera back," I said, and I couldn't completely keep the irritation from my voice.

"It's evidence."

"Why?"

"Accordin' to the statement you gave the officer first on scene, you struck one of your attackers with it . . . in the face. Broke his nose." He flipped absently through the notepad in his hands but didn't appear to read it.

"Why does that matter?"

He drew in a careful breath before saying, "Because he's dead."

The news hit me like a punch to the stomach, and my voice came out breathless. "What?"

Detective Marx raised a hand to calm me. "Don't worry.

28

You didn't kill him with the camera."

I slumped forward in relief. Regardless of what the man's intentions had been, I hadn't wanted to kill him. "How did he die?"

"Throat was cut," he answered calmly. I imagined he saw a great many awful things in his line of work, but the dispassionate calm in his voice as he spoke about someone's murder was a bit . . . disconcerting.

"Someone slit his throat?"

"Seems that way."

I swallowed the bile that brushed the back of my tongue.

"I need you to tell me about the last time you saw or heard from him."

I thought back on the events of the night. I had been so busy trying to stay ahead of the Whistling Man that the dark-eyed man's absence hadn't even registered. "He was . . . pretty far off, I guess. The last time I saw him was when I hit him."

Detective Marx jotted down my answers. "And when was that?"

"About . . . 5:10 or so. I already told all this to the other cop. The short guy who looks like a Keebler Elf."

His lips curved into a small smile. "I'm sure he'd be delighted to hear your description of him. And I understand that you already spoke with him, but I need to hear the details for myself, if you don't mind."

I did mind. I was exhausted and sore, and I just wanted to go home and take a shower. I glanced in the direction of home and fear clenched low in my stomach. I wasn't sure how I was going to get there; I usually walked, but . . . what if he was still out there? What if he came after me again while I was walking home? I didn't have money for a cab.

Detective Marx asked me a question, but I was too distracted to catch anything more than the tail end of it. "After that?"

I dragged my gaze away from the sidewalk and blinked at him. "What?"

29

His gaze flicked toward the sidewalk I'd been staring at and then back at me. "The man who died. You said the last time you saw him was around 5:10. Did you hear him at all after that?"

"Oh, um . . ." I looked down and rubbed at the dirt on my fingers. "Just once."

"And when was that?"

"I don't know," I shrugged. "He took my phone, and I don't have a watch."

"What did he say?"

"He was taunting the man who was chasing me, asking if . . . if I was too much for him to handle."

I looked over to find the detective assessing me with cautious interest. "I have to be honest, Ms. Smith—"

"*Don't* call me that."

"Holly," he amended. "I'm not sure I quite understand how you got away. The man we found was pretty fit, and the second man you described"—he considered his words carefully—"well, he sounds formidable." He met my gaze, and I saw the uncertainty and doubt in his eyes. "You're, what, five-foot, hundred pounds?"

"Five-two and hundred and fifteen."

He lifted a skeptical eyebrow, and I wondered if he could tell that I was rounding up on the inches. If he could, he chose not to comment. "Okay, but my point is, it's unusual for someone of your . . . size . . . to be able to defend herself against two well-developed males. So what I'm wonderin' is, did you have help?"

I frowned. "I already told the police. Riley."

"Right. The dog." He sighed and rubbed his forehead. "I don't suppose you know what happened to this dog?"

"No," I admitted, as I tugged the blanket the paramedics had given me tighter around my shoulders. The owner had called the police despite my objections and then gone in search of his dog when he didn't come back, and neither of them had returned.

Detective Marx grunted thoughtfully. "I'm thinkin' you had help of a human persuasion, and I'm wonderin' if they might have been carryin' a knife."

I gaped at him in disbelief. "You think a friend of mine slit that man's throat?"

"Well, he did have ill intentions toward you."

I almost choked. *Ill intentions.* Well, that was one way to put it. "My only friend is about four feet tall," I snapped. "So, unless he willingly got on his knees in front of her or suffered from a sudden case of dwarfism, she didn't slit his throat."

"It's just a workin' theory," he explained.

"Well, it's not working very well. Find another one." I stood and stripped out of the warm blanket. The cold night air passed straight through my layered shirts. I held out the blanket to the detective, and he took it reluctantly as he stood with me.

"Look, Ms. Holly, I'm not the enemy. I'm just tryin' to put the pieces together." His warm eyes implored me to understand. "I know you had a rough night and I promise I'm not tryin' to make it worse."

I folded my arms over my chest and willed my body not to shiver from the cold. I would feel ridiculous if I asked for the blanket back.

Detective Marx sighed at my stony expression and draped the blanket over one arm. "We're not gettin' off to a good start."

"That could be because you're accusing my friend of murder."

"I didn't say the killer was your friend."

"I'm guessing—and this is just a *theory*—that he was involved in some other criminal activities. Maybe it was an associate of his who killed him. Maybe he forgot to pay his drug dealer."

"Those are all possibilities, but I have to investigate every angle," he explained calmly. His calmness grated on my frayed nerves. "I know this is an inconvenience, but a man is dead, Ms. Smith." I parted my lips to snap at him, but he quickly corrected himself. "Holly."

He tapped his pen against his notebook as he watched me, like a person waiting patiently for an icicle to thaw. I glared at him.

"You're angry," he said.

"You're intuitive." My tone was frosty. Anger was more bearable than fear or pain, and I savored the warmth it lent me.

Detective Marx smiled slightly. "You don't much like cops, do you, Ms. Holly?" He studied my face, and I suddenly felt like he was trying to pick through my brain for answers like my state-assigned therapists used to do. He was trying to puzzle me out. Well, I wished him luck with that. I hadn't even figured me out. "Judgin' by the way you're lookin' at me, I'm guessin' you had some bad experiences with law enforcement."

"I'm not a criminal."

"I didn't say you were," he replied patiently. "I realize that just because somebody's a cop, it doesn't mean they're a good person. It also doesn't mean they're automatically trustworthy." He'd nailed that one. "I don't expect you to trust me right away. That's somethin' that should be earned. But I am askin' you to give me a chance to earn it. Let me help you."

I curled my toes under my feet as the cold from the pavement leached into my boots. I knew I was being unfair to him. He wasn't one of the officers who had helped to wreck my childhood. I closed my eyes and sighed. "No one I know did this."

"Okay."

I looked at him in surprise.

He smiled. "I'm not a disagreeable know-it-all. I can listen." He offered me the blanket as he said gently, "I do have a few more questions, though, and then I'll have someone take you home."

I stared at the blanket as stubborn refusal warred with the desperate need to be warm. I'd begun to shiver. I accepted the blanket begrudgingly and wrapped it around my back. "I don't know what more I can tell you." I plunked back down on the curb.

The detective crouched beside me, and I drew my knees to my chest beneath the blanket to put some space between us. "For starters, I'd like you to tell me about the photo."

"It was just . . ." I trailed off when I saw two men carrying a stretcher out of the park. A black body-shaped bag was belted to the gurney, and I watched them load the body into the back of a van.

The detective had told me the dark-eyed man was dead—murdered—but somehow seeing the body bag made it that much more shocking.

"Ms. Holly."

I watched the van drive away, and somewhere in the back of my mind between the confusion and anxiety, I was grateful the man was dead. If someone hadn't slit his throat, I couldn't help but wonder if . . .

I swallowed uneasily and pushed those thoughts away. A man was dead, and I had no right to be relieved about that. Human life was precious.

"Ms. Holly," Detective Marx said again, drawing me out of my thoughts. He cocked his head to meet my eyes, and his expression was patient and understanding despite how easily distracted I was. "I know you have a lot on your mind, and you're probably not quite sure how to feel about the fact that one of your attackers is dead, but that means you don't have to worry about him anymore. And I will do everythin' in my power to find his friend. Everythin' will be okay."

I shifted uncomfortably under his sympathetic gaze. "Do you know who they are?"

He considered me for a moment and then nodded. "The deceased is Jimmy. We've had a few complaints about him loiterin' in the park harassin' people for the past few months. A few women have mentioned that he made them uncomfortable, but if he ever crossed that line, no one has come forward."

"And the other one?"

"Given your description of him, I have an idea who he might be. He . . . has a history." He sank a lot of meaning into that word, and I shuddered inwardly.

Detective Marx tapped his pen on the notepad as he continued, "Now, I'm gonna say this knowin' full well from our brief interlude that you are—as people call it these days—*independent* and you'll do what you want. But until we catch the other man who assaulted you, don't walk around the city alone. And for the love of all things holy, don't go near the park."

That was going to put a real cramp in my photography. I needed to call that couple and let them know we would have to reschedule their photos. Except . . . I no longer had a phone to call them with . . . or a camera. I released a frustrated sigh.

"Can you tell me about the photo?" Detective Marx requested.

"I noticed a shadow in the background of every photo I took this afternoon. Nearly an hour's worth of pictures, and someone stood there in the background the entire time, watching."

"What happened when you noticed this person? Did they leave?"

"I decided to ask them what they were doing if they were still hanging around, but they left before I even noticed them in the pictures. I thought maybe they were spying on one of my clients, so I took a picture of the evidence just in case something happened."

Detective Marx's eyes squinted. "You thought somebody might be spyin' on your clients and you thought it was a good idea to approach that person alone?"

I'd known it was a dumb idea when I did it, but I glared at him anyway. I was really trying to be courteous with him, but I had a serious urge to flick him in his squinty eyeball. "What do the footprints matter to you anyway?"

"Because it was the last picture you took before bein' assaulted," he pointed out.

"Maybe I like shoes," I countered, but he didn't look amused.

"I might have dismissed the boot prints until you told me that man stood there and watched you with that couple for an hour. Shortly after they leave, you're attacked, and some mysterious individual slits your attacker's throat? I might just be tired, Ms. Holly, but that doesn't seem like a coincidence to me."

I shifted uneasily. I didn't like the direction his theory was taking.

"Do you have any more memory cards at home or your place of business?" he asked.

"Yes," I answered, unsure of where he was headed. I kept a small memory card for each of my customers in case they needed duplicates or replacements.

"I would like you to go through them and see if you notice any more mysterious shadows in the background. If this person was just loiterin' or watchin' your current clients, then he won't be there."

"And what will that prove?" I asked.

"If he's present in the older photos, it will prove he has another interest entirely," he replied. "So will you look and get back to me?" He pulled a card from his pocket with his name and number on it and handed it to me. I decided not to point out that I no longer had a phone to call him with even if I found something.

"Sure."

"Just one more question and then we'll call it a night," Detective Marx said. "Has there been anyone in your life recently—intimate partners, acquaintances, clients—who've made you uneasy? Anythin' that might have set off warnin' bells?"

I considered the question carefully. His phrasing gave me a bit of wiggle room to answer without having to lie or give away any of my secrets. "There was an ex-boyfriend who followed one of my clients to her photo shoot about three months ago. I think she had a restraining order against him." Not that it had done her much good.

"Did you have any interaction with this man?"

I shrugged. "I told him to leave."

"And how did he react?"

I thought back on that afternoon for the exact conversation, and then decided I really didn't want to repeat the words he'd used. "He creatively told me to mind my own business."

"Did he threaten you in any way?"

"Not really. He seemed more interested in patching things up with his ex-girlfriend."

Detective Marx scribbled on his notepad. I leaned over to peek at his notes and scrunched my nose. I was pretty sure he'd written: *popsicle possessed ex-boyfriend of Clint.* Best guess: *possible obsessed*

"Do you . . ." The detective paused when he noticed me studying his notes. He smiled and said, "I know. I'm a terrible writer. My ex-wife calls it chicken scratch."

"I think I've seen chickens do better."

His smiled broadened. "Of that I have no doubt. Do you happen to remember the name of this client or her ex-boyfriend?"

"Helen. I don't remember her last name. I can check my files."

"All right then. Let's get you home." He stood and offered his hand to me, but I declined help to my feet. "Officer," he called, and a young woman hurried over.

"Detective," she chirped. She was a slender woman in her thirties with blond hair tucked up beneath her hat.

"Could you see that this young lady gets home safely?"

"Of course."

Detective Marx flipped his notebook closed and slid it into an inside pocket of his suit jacket along with his pen. "I'll be in touch, Ms. Holly." He gave me a tired, warm smile before heading back to his car.

I stood slowly and remembered I had a question. "Detective."

He stopped and turned to face me, giving me his full attention.

"You said he might have another interest entirely. If he's not watching my clients, what's your theory?"

His expression turned grim. "That he was watchin' you, Ms. Holly."

5

A loud banging reverberated through my apartment, and I shot upright in bed, my heart pounding heavily. Jordan scampered off the bed and took refuge beneath it.

I stared blankly at the nearest window until my mind registered the golden morning light filtering in through the dingy glass. I'd fallen asleep while sifting through old photos after my shower. As fruitless as I thought the effort would be, I had promised the detective I would take a look.

I looked down at my open laptop on the bed and popped the memory card out of it, tucking it securely back into its Ziploc bag. Since I was a freelance photographer, my filing system consisted of sandwich baggies labeled in permanent marker under my bed.

Someone knocked again. Now that I was awake, it didn't sound like an elephant kicking my front door. I cast a longing glance toward the bathroom as I slid off the bed. Despite the fact that I was perfectly clean, I had the urge to take another shower to try to scrub away the old memories last night's events had unearthed.

Maybe later.

I tugged on a sweatshirt over my tank top and slid my feet into a pair of fuzzy green slippers to protect them from the cold of the cement floor before walking into the kitchen.

I didn't have a peephole in my door, so I dragged one of the metal chairs over in front of the sink and climbed on top of it to peer out the window. Whoever stood at my front door was too close to the building for me to see.

Irrationally, my palms began to sweat. I seriously doubted the second man from the park was on the other side of my door. He had no way to find me, and I had a feeling I'd been more of a convenience than a target.

"Who is it?" I called out nervously.

"Detective Marx."

I dropped my head and groaned as I climbed down off the chair. I was not awake enough to carry on a conversation with him. In fact, I would probably fall asleep sitting up halfway through the conversation and start drooling.

I rubbed my tired eyes and shuffled to the door. I unbolted it and wrenched it inward a few inches. I kept one hand on it in case I felt compelled to slam it shut in his face for one reason or another, and tried to arrange my displeased grimace into something mildly welcoming.

"Detective."

Detective Marx smiled at my exasperated tone. "Ms. Holly." His attention slid from my face to the door, and he commented with mild interest, "Three dead bolts and a metal door."

"I didn't choose the door."

"Just the dead bolts."

I lifted my chin to meet his eyes. "Is there a point to this line of questioning, or can I go back to bed?" I glanced at the microwave. It was 7:55 a.m. Ordinarily, I would be out for my morning jog, but after the incident in the park last night, I was a little more jittery than usual. It would take me a few days to find my balance again.

"May I come in?"

My grip on the door tightened. I knew inviting a person into your home was common courtesy, but this was my place, and it was the only place I felt safe. The only person I had ever allowed in was Jace.

I assessed the man on my doorstep carefully as I tried to decide whether or not he was a threat. He hadn't made me so nervous last night when there were plenty of other people around. But now that he was at my door, I couldn't help but notice that he was fit for a man in his forties, and if he wasn't six feet, he was just shy of it.

The gun on his hip didn't exactly put me at ease, and then there was the fact that he was probably trained to restrain a person in his sleep.

No, he's not intimidating at all, my mind offered up sarcastically.

His green eyes glinted with amusement, as if he knew I was sizing him up. I pushed the anxiety back into its box and stepped aside, widening the door for him. I was not going to be a chicken.

Detective Marx stepped through the doorway and stopped just inside the kitchen to take in my humble living arrangements. His gaze absorbed every detail, and I saw a question flicker behind his eyes.

My home was not what he'd expected. It wasn't embellished with bright, colorful things and family photos. To him it must have seemed cold and sparse.

"I don't do frilly things," I stated simply.

"I see that."

Don't get me wrong, I love frilly things: colors, patterns, sparkles. But what was the point? Even if I could afford them, I couldn't stuff them in a bag and take them with me.

Detective Marx noticed the chair I'd pushed up against the kitchen cupboards to see out the window, and asked, "May I?" I nodded and he sank down with a tired sigh.

"I don't have any coffee to offer you," I said. "But I have some fruit punch and chocolate milk." I wasn't used to having guests, but I was pretty sure offering refreshments was the socially acceptable response.

"Chocolate milk would be lovely, thank you," he said. "Did you get much sleep last night?"

"Probably more than you." If the dark circles under his eyes and the shadow of stubble across his jaw were anything to go by. I deliberately left the front door open as I walked around the table to the refrigerator. "I'm guessing it was a long night?"

He smiled tiredly. "It certainly was. I haven't actually slept yet."

I felt a twinge of guilt for being the cause of his exhaustion. How long had he searched for my attacker last night? I set a glass of chocolate milk on the table in front of him.

He looked into it, and a wrinkle of interest creased his forehead. "There are . . . things floatin' in my chocolate milk."

I frowned at the note of distaste in his voice. "They're called marshmallows." I always had marshmallows in my chocolate milk. And my hot chocolate, and my cereal, and occasionally by themselves in a bowl. Did that count as an addiction?

Detective Marx's lips quivered slightly as he suppressed a smile. "Thank you." He set the glass aside on the counter without trying it. He glanced at the open door. "Are you sure you wanna leave the door open? It's lettin' the heat out."

"It's fine. The fresh air is nice." *And freezing.* But I wasn't about to shut the door and trap myself in here with him. I took a sip of my chocolate milk and chewed on a spongy marshmallow before asking, "How did you find me?" I made it a point not to leave a trail. And yet . . . there he sat.

"Well, you certainly didn't make it easy, considerin' you didn't leave an address with the interviewin' officer, and there's no Holly Smith in the phone book that's even remotely close to your description." There was an unspoken question in his eyes.

I ignored it.

He pulled an evidence bag from inside his brown suit jacket. A small, gray flip phone rested in the bottom of the bag. "We recovered your phone. It's been processed, so I thought you might like it back. I spoke to an *effervescent* young lady named Jace last night, and she told me where to find you."

I gritted my teeth. I was going to have to have a conversation with her about sharing my personal information.

"She was a bit distressed at not havin' heard from you. Is there any particular reason she might think you were abducted?"

I smirked behind my cup. I could be five minutes late and Jace would think I'd gotten lost. Considering I had missed dinner and then forgotten to assure her I was all right, it didn't surprise me

40

that she thought I'd been abducted. If I didn't call or pop in by noon, she would think I was dead.

"She's . . . protective."

"I noticed. I was on the phone with her for an hour before she talked herself into exhaustion and fell asleep."

"What did you tell her?" I worried.

"That you lost your phone and I wanted to return it to you." He pulled my phone out of the bag and offered it to me. "I took the liberty of puttin' my number in there for you."

"How thoughtful," I said dryly as I accepted the phone.

His eyes twinkled with amusement. "I do try."

I flipped open my phone. There he was: DET Marx. And then there were five unopened voice mails from Jace as well as nine hysterical text messages.

Oh boy.

"Thank you for finding it for me." At least I wouldn't have to buy a new phone. "I looked into those photos for you. There were no mysterious shadows or figures. Not even a suspicious-looking tree."

I went to grab the box of memory cards from the bed and then set them on the table. I rifled through the box and plucked out a bag containing the memory card he'd asked about last night. "Helen Holcomb," I said, showing him the label. "She's the woman with the restraining order and the angry ex-boyfriend. I took a picture of them arguing, so the boyfriend's picture is on there too. But I can't imagine why he would've been there last night, because she wasn't."

A line of concern formed between Detective Marx's eyebrows. "Not that I don't appreciate the photo, but you have a tendency to take pictures of things you should be avoidin', Ms. Holly. And it's a bit unnervin'."

I lifted my chin. I didn't need a lecture from some detective I'd known for less than twenty-four hours about the dangers of taking pictures. "Are we done?"

41

"Not quite. I do have a few follow-up questions." He retrieved the spiral notebook and pen from the inside pocket of his suit jacket.

I sighed and melted into the chair on the opposite side of the table. I just wanted to go back to bed. I pulled my feet up onto the edge of the folding chair and tapped my fingers impatiently on my glass. "Do you ever actually run out of questions?"

"Typically, the answers run out first." He flipped through his notebook, extracted a folded sheet of paper and pushed it across the table. "I need you to look at this picture for me."

I unfolded the paper cautiously. My breath hitched for just an instant, and then I forced myself to breathe normally as I met the detective's eyes. "That's the second man from the park."

"I thought as much. He and Jimmy were practically joined at the hip. His name is Cambel." I slid the picture back to him, and he tucked it back into his notebook. "How tall would you say the shadowy figure by the tree was?"

I shrugged. "I'm a terrible judge of height unless someone is standing right next to me."

"How tall would you say I am?"

"Maybe six feet?"

"I'm five-ten. Was the shadow taller or shorter than me?"

I puckered my lips in thought. "Taller."

"Given your two-inch margin of error, is it safe to assume he was somewhere between six and six-four?"

I narrowed my eyes. "Where are you going with this?"

"Just tryin' to determine if it might have been Cambel watchin' you by that tree. It's possible he targeted you before you ever made it to the edge of the park."

"But he didn't kill his friend."

"Like I said, I'm considerin' every angle."

I sighed. "So now are we done?"

"If I didn't know better, I would think you were eager for me to leave, Ms. Holly." He regarded me with a small smile. "Just a couple more questions, if you don't mind."

I pressed my lips together.

"I spoke with the officer first on scene a bit more after you left just to compare notes."

And why does that sound ominous?

"The Good Samaritan who placed the 9-1-1 call described the victim of the assault as a petite, red-haired woman. No jacket, despite the weather, covered in grass stains with bloody fingers."

Yeah, that sounded like me. I took a slow, cautious sip of my chocolate milk and waited for him to continue. I was sure there was more to this retelling of events than just my description.

"So, when the first officer on scene approached you, fully aware that you matched the description given, and asked you what happened, you responded with 'I have nothin' to say'." He looked at me and I arched my eyebrows at him.

"There wasn't actually a question in there," I pointed out.

"Why were you so reluctant to give your statement?"

Ah, there it was. Tense shoulders were difficult to shrug, but I managed it. "Because there wasn't really anything to report. I'm fine." Well, except for some very colorful bruises.

"Fine," he repeated evenly. "Ms. Holly, you've kept at least three feet of distance between you and me since we met last night, and I'm pretty sure I saw fear in your eyes when I asked to come inside. That doesn't exactly coincide with *fine*."

"That has nothing to do with—" I bit off the rest of that sentence before I could say more. My mouth had started speaking before my exhausted brain caught up and realized I shouldn't say that. He arched an eyebrow at my tight-lipped expression, and I realized I'd already said too much. "I like my personal space."

"Mmm hmm," he grunted, and I didn't think he could lace that sound with any more skepticism if he tried. "I think you're scared of somethin'. Either more happened last night than you're tellin', and we need to take you to the hospital to be examined, or somethin' else is goin' on. I just haven't figured out which."

I squirmed uncomfortably under his probing gaze. Last night had left me off balance, and I knew I'd made a mistake by giving my statement to the police. I just hadn't figured out how to fix it yet.

I forced a calm breath through my nose and asked, "Am I under investigation, Detective?"

"No."

"Then I think we're done here." I unfolded myself from the chair, concentrating on keeping my movements slow and relaxed, and walked to the front door. I gripped the edge of it, silently inviting him to leave. "Thank you for bringing my phone back."

He sighed and stood, returning the chair to the table. He tucked his notebook and pen back into his pocket before meeting me at the door. "Ms. Holly . . ." He glanced at the locks on my door and then back to me. "Who's responsible for the dead bolts on your door?"

I stiffened.

He couldn't possibly be that insightful. I tried to keep the fear from my voice as I said, "Have a nice day, Detective."

6

I bounced my leg as we sat at the cafe table outside the coffee shop. It was a bright autumn day, and there was a steady stream of people passing by. I watched their faces, half expecting to see the man from the park among them. I wasn't sure what I would do if I saw his face in the crowd.

"Would you sit still?" Jace asked. "You're twitchier than a crack addict in withdrawal."

I realized I was also tapping my gloved fingers against my cup of tea in an anxious rhythm. I forced my nervous tics to still and took a deliberate sip of my tea. "Sorry, I have a lot on my mind today," I admitted.

Jace's shoulders hunched and she muttered, "Is this about the cop? I said I was sorry. I won't give anyone else your address. I didn't think you would mind since he was bringing your phone back, which you really should be more careful with, by the way. What if you lose it and there's an emergency?"

Oh, if she only knew.

"And besides, that cop sounded totally trustworthy. That soothing Southern drawl. Is he single, do you know?"

"Ew. He's like . . . forty-five."

"Holly, I'm thirty. My face is starting to melt. Soon I'm gonna look like a bloodhound with saggy jowls and wrinkles deeper than the Grand Canyon."

I laughed so hard that tea almost came out of my nose.

"Excuse me, miss," a polite male voice called. I looked up to see a waiter hovering nearby. "The gentleman two tables away asked me to deliver this to you."

He set a plump chocolate muffin in front of me. I stared at it in confusion and then looked across the sidewalk at the man who had sent it over.

It took me a moment to recognize him without his sweat stained T-shirt and mussed hair. It was the man who frequented the same jogging route as mine. He was dressed in jeans and a red button-up shirt.

He flashed me a charming smile.

Well, great. Now what was I supposed to do? As tasty and tempting as the muffin looked sitting in front of me, accepting it would give the man the wrong impression, and returning it would be rude.

I leaned across the table and whispered, "Is there some kind of etiquette for this? Because I'm not sure what to do."

"Eat the tasty free muffin and thank the gorgeous man with your number," Jace suggested. At my scowl, she said, "Oh, you meant something *you* would do. Chuck the muffin at his head and tell him to take a hike."

My mouth fell open. "I am not that bad."

Jace arched an eyebrow at me. "When was your last date?"

I pursed my lips to keep from saying something snippy. I pushed back my chair and stood up. "I'm taking it back."

"Oh, come on. I was kidding. At least let me eat it," Jace whined as I walked past her toward the man's table.

Butterflies swarmed my stomach. I couldn't remember the last time I'd had a normal conversation with a man that didn't involve the question "Paper or plastic?" or an interrogation.

All right, mouth, don't say something stupid.

"Hi," I said with a small, tense smile.

He stood to greet me with another blinding smile. What was he, a toothpaste model? "Hi. I hope the muffin isn't too forward. I recognized you from when we cross paths jogging and I've always wanted to introduce myself. I've tried a few times, but you jog pretty quick."

Ha. Guy didn't get the hint, I guess. Apparently, my efforts to avoid him hadn't been obvious enough. "I appreciate the muffin, but I'm not really hungry."

His smile didn't even dim. "It was just an introduction, really.

46

I'm Luke."

I hesitated before giving him my name. "Holly." He was handsome in a way, but I didn't feel any more attracted to him than I did a bottle of nail polish.

"Why don't you have a seat? Share a drink with me."

"I'm in a relationship," I blurted. *With Jesus*, but he didn't need to know that.

"Oh." He blanched. "I mean, of course you are. Is it serious?"

"Very."

He looked a little disappointed. "Ah," he said. "I'm sorry if my offer causes any friction between the two of you. If I'd known—"

"It was thoughtful." I set the plate down.

"If anything changes between you and him, you know where to find me," he added quickly.

I gave him a tense smile and felt relief crest over me as I walked away. I had managed not to bungle the interaction or freak out for what appeared to be no apparent reason. I dropped back into my chair and wrapped my fingers around my tea.

"Is he crying?" Jace asked.

"Why on earth would he be crying?"

"Because a beautiful woman just returned his please-pay-attention-to-me gesture and then told him she's not interested. What's to be sad about?"

I scrunched my nose at her. "That doesn't even make sense."

She glanced over her shoulder, and I followed her gaze. The man had slipped away, and the lonely muffin sat in the center of an otherwise empty table.

"Quick, go grab the muffin," Jace whispered.

I laughed. "I am not going back for the muffin."

"Fine, I'll grab the muffin." She weaved through the tables and chairs and plucked the chocolate muffin off the empty table. I bit down on my lips to keep from asking if she'd lost her mind. She parked back at our table and grinned before taking a huge bite and asking something that sounded like, "Do Jews have any pants to play?"

I frowned. "I'm sorry, I don't speak muffin."

She gulped it down and repeated, "Do you have any plans today?"

"Nope." Not until I got my camera back. I was wishing I'd hit the man in the face with a rock instead of my camera. "So, where are you and Mr. Doe going to lunch?" I asked casually.

"Papa Gio's. You know, the place I bought Italian from Friday night and you forgot to pick it up."

So she was still upset about that. That was okay. She would be more upset if I told her the truth. "Did you do a background check on him yet?"

She rolled her eyes. "Of course. I tried to google him and all that came up were articles about dead guys. It's the last name. And he doesn't have a Facebook. The guy's forty. He's not a dinosaur. Who doesn't have a Facebook?" Then she paused and looked at me. "Oh. Right."

Yeah, aside from an anonymous email account to connect with new clients, I avoided the Internet like a contagious disease. "Does he have one of those Twinner things?"

"Twitter, Holly. *Tuh.* They're t's, not n's. And the only Gale Doe I found on Twitter is a guy who knits doll booties for his doll collection, so I really hope he doesn't. And before you ask about Misplace, it's actually called *MySpace*, and no, no one really uses it anymore."

I smiled behind my cup of tea.

A shrill whistling pierced the murmur of voices outside, and I nearly jumped out of my chair.

"It's just your phone, Holly," Jace pointed out with a perplexed expression.

Right. I was going to have to change that ringtone. I pulled the phone from my bag with shaky fingers, and fear stiffened my spine as I stared at the blank screen. This couldn't be happening again.

"Holly, what's wrong?"

"It's not my phone," I mumbled absently as my gaze flickered over the faces in the cafe, seeking the one from the park.

The whistling abruptly stopped and then started up again a moment later. It *was* a phone. It just wasn't *my* phone.

"Sorry, that's me," a woman muttered to her friend behind me. She rummaged around in her purse until she found her phone. The whistling grew louder as she pulled it out. She tapped the screen and the sound died. I breathed a mental sigh of relief and slid down in my chair.

Jace was watching me closely. "What was that?" At my blank stare, she explained, "That phone went off and you went white. I thought you were gonna pass out."

I shrugged mutely and held my tea a little tighter.

Jace's phone rang, and the death march filled the air. She glanced at me as she fished it out of her purse. "Well, at least mine didn't startle you into a full-on seizure." She had one of those smart phones the size of a giant chocolate bar, and it took up the entire right side of her face when she pressed it to her ear. I heard her mutter a few words to the person on the other end, but I was too lost in thought to follow her conversation. "Holly," she said after a moment, and her tone suggested it hadn't been the first time.

"What?" I asked blankly.

She frowned at me and said, "I have to go to the library. Terry got sick. It's just a five-hour fill-in shift, but I have to hurry. They're about to open. Are you okay walking home?"

A little spark of fear kindled in my stomach but I smothered it. I was a grown woman. I could handle walking home alone. "Yep, I'm good."

"Cool. I'll call you after my date." She plopped her purse in her lap, gave me a little wave, and headed off to her car.

I sank lower in my chair and flipped open my phone. I needed to figure out how to change the ringtone. I didn't want to lose it every time my phone rang, which, admittedly, wasn't often. I was still fumbling my way around the menu several minutes later when someone screamed.

Another scream and then chaos erupted around me. People clambered over chairs and tables, and glass shattered on the pavement. Someone shouted, "Call for help!"

What on earth?

I stood up and tried to see what was happening. A tall man with wavy blond hair was visible above the crowd, and people parted around him. When he came into view, cold fear flooded my extremities.

He was paler than I remembered, and something red tinged his parted lips, but I recognized the Whistling Man's face. He staggered through the cafe on stiff legs, and bright red blood spilled down the front of him.

His eyes locked on me and he changed direction. I stumbled backwards over my chair until my back hit the glass window of the coffee shop. The man's mouth spasmed like a suffocating fish as he tried to speak.

"Me," he managed to say.

He reached out a hand toward me, and I tried to shrink away, but there was nowhere to go. He stumbled into the chair and lost his balance. He fell to the pavement and took the table with him. I didn't scream. I wasn't sure I could make a single sound as I gazed at him in horror.

He lay on his back at my feet, dying on a sidewalk full of people who crowded around to watch. His eyes met mine, and I saw his terror and desperation. "Help . . . me."

I froze. He wanted me to help him. Of all the people at this cafe, he'd fallen at *my* feet. I didn't want to help him. But I didn't want to watch him die either.

God, what do I do?

I wrestled with my choices until one finally won out. He was still a human being. I pulled the scarf I had borrowed from Jace over my head and sank to my knees beside him.

I pressed the wadded-up scarf to the wound on his abdomen

50

and leaned down. He gasped in pain. I hoped someone had called an ambulance, because the scarf was saturated in seconds.

7

I sat against the front window of the coffee shop with my legs drawn to my chest. In some part of my mind I was aware of people moving around me and murmuring, but I just stared at my palms.

The man's blood had soaked through the sleeves of my shirts and into the knees of my pants. I had peeled off my saturated gloves and thrown them aside, but it had already touched my skin. This wasn't the first time I'd seen my hands covered in blood, but it had been darker then.

I remembered the slick feel of it between my fingers and the way it had glistened in the moonlight. I had tried to rub it off on my nightgown. I remembered knowing that it belonged to someone I knew, but I couldn't remember who or when.

A familiar Southern voice broke into my thoughts. "I received a call about one of my suspects."

"We're pretty sure the deceased is the man you were looking for in connection to your recent assault case," another male voice explained.

"Cambel Broderick?"

My ears followed the conversation—drawn to the gentle cadence of that familiar voice—but my mind drifted between fragmented thoughts and memories.

"And then there's the matter of the young woman covered in blood."

"What young woman?" Detective Marx demanded.

"She's approximately five-one, red hair, brown eyes," the man explained.

"You've got to be kiddin' me," Detective Marx groaned. "Is she all right?"

I could smell the damp forest around me, and feel the

painful prick of twigs and weeds beneath my cold bare feet as I gaped at my hands. The echo of someone's scream rang in my ears—a child's scream. No, that wasn't right. I could hear Detective Marx's voice, and he wasn't in the forest.

A figure crouched down in front of me, and the sun vanished behind him. "Why am I not surprised to find you out and about in the city alone?" Detective Marx asked, but there was no bite to his tone.

I dragged my eyes away from my hands to look at him. Worry was etched across his face. I blinked, but I couldn't gather enough of my senses to form a coherent sentence. I looked past him to the body lying on the pavement.

"He's dead," I said after a long moment.

"I see that," Detective Marx replied softly.

My brain felt confused and sluggish, and I couldn't seem to put my thoughts in order. "Someone died."

"Yes, somebody did," Detective Marx said with practiced patience. But he didn't understand. I didn't mean the man on the pavement. "Can you tell me what happened?"

I had tripped and fallen in the blood and there was so much of it on my hands. I needed to get it off. I tried to wipe it off on my clothes like I'd done once before.

"Holly," Detective Marx scolded as he caught my forearms. "Stop it. That's evidence." I tried harder, desperate to get it off, but he held my arms away from my body.

"Don't touch me." I twisted my arms from his grip, and he made no effort to hold me. I crossed them over my chest and tried to scoot closer to the wall. I didn't like him in my personal space.

"Okay." He raised his hands slowly and moved back. "Hands to myself. You have my word."

I watched him warily until I was certain he intended to keep that promise. I relaxed a little and looked around at the overturned chairs and tables and at the police uniforms that swarmed the area. I was at the café where I'd been having tea with Jace.

The sounds and smells of the forest faded to the back of my

mind, returning to whatever mysterious place they had come from, but my hands were still wet with blood. It wasn't hers. *Hers.* My mind tried to wander down that slippery path, but I wrenched it back.

My eyes drifted back to the man's body on the pavement. "Why is he dead?"

"Because somebody killed him," Detective Marx stated matter-of-factly. He motioned one of the officers over and ordered, "Cover that body before any more of these vultures snap photos. The Medical Examiner should be here soon."

"But . . . why is he dead?"

"I don't know why, Ms. Holly."

"But you have a theory."

The worry I had glimpsed in his face when he arrived only deepened. "Why don't you just tell me what happened?"

I knew there was a reason I shouldn't tell him what had happened, but it took me a moment to find it in the confused haze of my mind. I'd already made the mistake of giving my statement once, and I knew it would probably cost me.

I shook my head and he frowned.

"Why are you shakin' your head at me?"

"I have nothing to say."

He narrowed his eyes at my response. "I find it interestin' that—considerin' you're not a suspect of a crime—you frequently have *nothin' to say*, Ms. Holly. So let me explain how this works: whether you speak to me or not, a police report will be filed, and because you're a participant in this . . . unpleasant mess, your name and any evidence collected from your person will be included in that report."

A fresh wave of fear washed over me.

"If you're concerned about the media or some other party gainin' access to your statement, don't be. Our database has never been breached, and we're not in the habit of sharin' our records with the public."

"Detective," a woman called. Our attention shifted to the

young, blond woman crouched next to the body. She was dressed in normal attire, but the badge hanging around her neck on a lanyard identified her as a deputy medical examiner. She held up one side of the sheet with a gloved hand. "You may want to see this."

Detective Marx sighed. "We're not done with this conversation, Ms. Holly. Don't you move."

I lifted my hands. "Can I—"

"Not yet. We need to collect the evidence." He waved over an older woman with a tackle box. She weaved around the police tape that cordoned off the body and approached us. "Could you take care of Ms. Holly, Jeanie?"

"I'd be delighted," the plump older woman declared with a sweet smile. With her short, curly gray hair and small glasses, she looked like the stereotypical grandmother who should be home baking cookies with a flowery apron on, not scraping DNA out from under someone's fingernails.

"I'll be right over here," Detective Marx said, gesturing to the body. "And try to be gentle with her."

Jeanie looked stricken at the suggestion she might do things any other way, and she sputtered, "Well, of course, Richard." But I was pretty certain his parting comment had been meant for me.

Jeanie pulled a chair over and sat down in front of me. She opened her tackle box to reveal various swabs, gloves, bags, and canisters. She snapped on a pair of purple gloves and grabbed a long cotton swab.

That cotton swab reminded me of another time and place, and I fought to shut out the gut-twisting memory. This was a completely different situation.

"Now then, let's have a look at those fingernails," she said. When I lifted my hands, she gasped, "Oh, don't have many of those left, do you?"

I blinked at her bluntness and glanced past her at Detective Marx. Maybe I'd been wrong and his parting comment *had* been for her. He flashed me a smile before crouching down next to the body alongside the medical examiner.

"You really shouldn't chew your nails, dear. It's an unsanitary habit." Jeanie continued. She took samples from my palms and beneath my nails. "Now, I need your clothes."

"Excuse me?"

"Your clothes are covered in trace evidence, and I'll be needing them. Up you get, let's go."

I frowned and pushed myself to my feet. I certainly hoped she had something else for me to wear.

She gathered up her tackle box and declared, "Follow me."

My eyes snagged on Detective Marx as we passed by. The grim expression on his face left me wondering what else lay beneath that sheet. He shifted his weight to get a better angle, and I could see the tension in his body. He exchanged a few hushed words with the medical examiner.

Jeanie led me to the restroom and set a pair of clean scrubs on the corner of the sink. She stepped out of the room when I refused to change in front of her, but ordered me to leave the door cracked. If I intended to destroy evidence by putting it in the sink or toilet, she would see me before I had the chance to do so.

I rolled up the legs of the scrubs until I could see my feet. I looked ridiculous. I wadded up my clothes and stepped out of the bathroom. Jeanie held out an open evidence bag with a sweet smile, and I shoved my clothes into the bag.

Detective Marx was leaning against the wall next to her. His expression was guarded, and two uniformed officers stood to his left.

"What's going on?" I asked warily.

Detective Marx pushed away from the wall and said, "Let's get you home, and we'll discuss it there."

8

I paced anxiously from the foot of my bed to the outside bathroom wall as I stole glances of the three police officers in my small apartment. Their presence made my home feel cramped and smothering.

The uniformed officers tried to be invisible as they stood close to the door, but Detective Marx leaned against the kitchen table, his fingers tapping the edge as he watched me pace.

His expression was firm but patient. I had a feeling he was waiting for me to calm down, but if so, he would be waiting for quite some time.

"You're gonna make yourself dizzy, Ms. Holly," he said.

I was already dizzy, but I couldn't bring myself to sit. "Why are they here? Do they have to stand right in front of the door?" It was my only exit, and having it cut off wasn't helping my nerves.

Detective Marx twisted to see the two officers. "Would the two of you mind steppin' out for a moment?" The two officers nodded and obediently filed out the front door before closing it behind them. "You're not trapped, Holly, but I do need you to stay here with me."

"Why?"

"Because it's safer than talkin' on the street, and I thought you'd be more comfortable here than at the precinct."

I stiffened. "I didn't do anything. You can't arrest me."

He rubbed the back of his neck tiredly and mumbled, "I have no intention of arrestin' you. But we need to talk about the man who killed your attackers from the park."

"You know who killed them?"

"I think *you* know who killed them."

My pace slowed and I stared at him. "I told you. I don't know anyone who would do something like this." The disbelief I saw reflected in his eyes bothered me. I wouldn't lie, especially about something as important as a human life.

"Well, let me tell you what I know, and maybe it will jog your memory." He pulled out his notebook and dropped it on the table beside him. "Jimmy Miller was murdered Friday night in the park shortly after threatenin' you. Cambel Broderick disappeared Friday night after assaultin' you. He shows up three days later outside a cafe where you just happen to be, seeks you out of the crowd to ask you for help, and then falls down dead."

He flipped the pages of his notes absently and asked, "Are you with me so far?"

I scowled at his condescending tone.

"Given the extent of Cambel's injuries, he was incapable of walkin' to the cafe. Somebody dropped him off. Witnesses saw him step out of a white vehicle before it drove away. Who would drop off a dyin' man at a café? And what criminal in his right mind would seek out one of his victims for help when he has the option of a hospital? With exception of you, Ms. Holly, that's a surefire prescription for suicide."

He folded his arms and looked at me as if he expected me to have some sort of insight on the matter, but I had nothing to give him. I didn't even understand what was happening.

"Accordin' to the medical examiner, the knife that slit Jimmy's throat looks like the same knife used to disfigure and kill Cambel. Whoever killed Jimmy Friday night tracked Cambel down, tortured him, and then sent him into that café to find *you*. The killer knew you were there and he sent Cambel with a message."

"All he said was, 'Help me.' What kind of message is that?"

Detective Marx drew in a deep breath and let it out slowly. If a seasoned detective was having difficulty putting the details into words, I wasn't sure I wanted to hear them. "The message was on his body. Carved into his chest and abdomen."

I was suddenly grateful I hadn't eaten. "He was alive when . . ."

Detective Marx's jaw clenched. "Yes. And I imagine every

58

letter was agonizin'."

I sank down onto the edge of my bed and took a few deep breaths to try to keep my stomach where it belonged. No one, no matter what evil they had committed, should have to endure that much suffering.

Detective Marx stepped away from the table and came to sit on the arm of the couch. "I'm not sayin' Cambel deserved to die the way he did, but you should not feel guilty."

"You're telling me that someone killed those two men to . . . what, protect me?" The slight pinching of his lips told me I hadn't gotten it quite right. "How can I not feel responsible for that? For whatever reason, they're dead because of me."

"Unless this killer is attached to strings and you are the puppet master, Ms. Holly, these deaths are not on your hands."

I pulled my legs onto the bed and huddled behind them as if they might somehow shield me from whatever he would say next.

"I know this isn't easy for you," he began. "But I need you to set your misplaced feelin's of guilt aside and try to stay with me on this. The man who killed them and the man watchin' you in the park are likely the same person. Aside from that night, can you think of any other time you felt watched or followed?"

"Last Monday," I said as I stared at the blanket beneath me. "I was coming home late from a photo shoot, and I thought I heard scraping sounds—like footsteps on the pavement."

"Did you see anybody?"

"No, it was more of a feeling."

He tapped his fingers on his knees as he regarded me. "I'm gonna ask you this again, and I need you to be honest with me this time. Has anyone threatened you or made you feel uneasy?"

"Aside from *you* with your questions?"

His lips curved into a thin smile. "Aside from me."

"No, no one around here makes me uneasy. This has to be some kind of mistake."

"It's not a mistake."

"Why?" I asked irritably. "Because coincidences make you

uncomfortable?"

"No, because you are the common factor."

"There were plenty of people at that café."

"All of whom he bypassed to get to you."

"No," I argued. I slid off the bed and glared at him. "He was dying. Maybe he just happened to fall at my feet. It's not like dying people really get to decide which way they fall."

Detective Marx gave me a sympathetic look that only fueled my anger. "You're graspin' at straws."

"You're wrong. All you have are theories."

"And twenty-five years of experience," he added with a modest shrug. He had almost as many years of experience as I had of life. Okay, that was hard to refute.

"What about Helen? Did you find her ex-boyfriend? Maybe it was him. Or maybe it was someone watching my clients that day. Did you even talk to them?"

"Of course I talked to them. Helen and her ex-boyfriend mended their relationship, and he has an alibi durin' the time of your assault. As for your clients in the park that night, they can't think of anybody who would do somethin' like this, and neither of them have felt followed or watched at any point. This isn't about them. This is about you."

I began to pace again, the rapid movement pumping warmth back into my icy body. This couldn't be happening. I already had one person determined to hunt me down; I didn't need another one. "I don't understand why this is happening. Why did he kill those men?"

He exhaled a frustrated breath and folded his arms. "Because he's insane. I'm not a forensic psychologist, Holly. I can't offer you some childhood trauma story that led him to kill people and engrave creepy cryptic messages on their bodies. I can tell you that it had nothin' to do with protectin' you. It also had nothin' to do with love. And if he's been followin' you, and it seems he has, then he has an obsession with you. My best guess: in his mind, the two of you share some kind of connection. And I'm hopin' the

60

message he left for you might help you to identify him."

I regarded him warily.

"He carved two words into that man's body and sent him to deliver them upon his death." He watched me carefully for a reaction as he recited, "Come home."

Any hope that this was all a mistake evaporated, and I felt suddenly faint. My legs gave out and I dropped onto the side of the bed. My fingers shook as I plucked the note card off my cardboard side table and stared down at the message: *Holly, come home.*

If I'd found those words unsettling before, they were downright chilling now. I tried not to imagine them being carved into human flesh.

"Ms. Holly," Detective Marx said. I looked up to find him standing at the foot of the bed, watching me with a glimmer of worry in his eyes. I offered him the card reluctantly and without explanation. He skimmed the contents before looking at me. "When did you get this?"

"It was taped to the outside of my door last Monday morning."

"Do you know who sent it? Do you recognize the address?"

I shook my head.

He stared at the card thoughtfully for a long moment before saying, "We need to talk about the man you're hidin' from." I wasn't sure what he saw in my face, but his expression softened. "This isn't my first day on the job, Ms. Holly. I recognize the signs. You've got no state ID. No driver's license. No official home address. No work history that I could find. Your cell phone is a pay-as-you-go. Hardly anybody in your contact list. You live in a bunker."

I tried to swallow the lump of dread forming in my throat.

"And when you were assaulted in the park, you didn't wanna give a statement because it could be logged. You didn't wanna go to the hospital where there would be a record of your visit." He laid the note card on the foot of the bed and looked at me. "You told me there's nobody who makes you uneasy, but I know for a fact that whoever is responsible for the three dead bolts on your door does exactly that. And I'm not talkin' about the locksmith."

"You don't know anything," I said, but I couldn't keep the faint tremor of fear from my voice.

Detective Marx crouched down beside me, and I drew my feet onto the mattress and scooted across the bed to put some much-needed space between us. "I've worked with a lot of different kinds of victims—"

"I am not a victim," I snapped.

He exhaled patiently. "Survivors, then. And if nothin' else, it's obvious to me that you're hidin' from somebody, and that *somebody* terrifies you." His eyes reflected an emotion I couldn't quite identify as he watched me. "We need to talk about that man."

I clenched my fingers into fists and wrapped my arms around my stomach protectively as I shook my head.

"Is he still in the picture?" he asked.

This was a part of my life I couldn't afford for him to investigate. If he dug too deeply, he would leave a trail of bread crumbs right to my front door.

"Was it an abusive relationship?"

"We weren't in a relationship," I spat before I could think better of it.

Detective Marx cocked his head thoughtfully. "Acquaintance? Family? Foster family?" He studied me for a moment and then said with more certainty, "Foster family. So you lived together then. For how long?"

I pinched my lips together. I had no intention of giving him any more information than he'd already gleaned from my face. He didn't understand the danger he was putting me in by digging into my past.

"When was the last time you saw him?" At my refusal to answer, he continued, "A person graduates from the foster system when they turn eighteen. If you'd managed to elude him for ten years, you wouldn't still be this scared. He caught up to you at some point." He tilted his head to catch my gaze. "What did he do when he caught up with you?"

My heart thumped too heavily in my chest and I was breathing too quickly. I couldn't conceal my fear no matter how hard I tried. "I don't . . . wanna talk about this."

"The killer we're lookin' for sent you two messages to *come home*, and the man you're hidin' from shared a foster home with you. If he's been lookin' for you for ten years, he's obsessive if not possessive. How can you be certain he didn't step back into your life without you knowin' and kill those two men?"

I knew it was only a matter of time before he caught up to me again; he was far too resourceful and intelligent to let me stay hidden for long. But I'd been so careful this time. He couldn't possibly have found me already, could he?

"Please stop digging," I pleaded.

"I need his name."

"I can't," I said as I fumbled off the other side of the bed. I wasn't having this conversation. He discovered the answers to his questions whether I spoke or not, and I couldn't let that happen.

I grabbed the box of Lucky Mallows off the counter, snagged my fat cat off the couch, and scampered into the bathroom. I slammed the door and sat down against it, barricading it with my body.

I heard Detective Marx puff out a heavy breath. "Well, that could've gone better."

9

I tried to tune out the quiet voice that didn't belong in my apartment as I picked through the box of cereal, sorting the marshmallows by shape. The entire edge of the tub was covered in clusters of rainbows, stars, and unicorn horns.

Some people had expensive therapists to help them work through their anxiety and fears; I had cereal. Sorting the marshmallows distracted me from all the worries and frightening theories fluttering around inside my head.

Detective Marx's voice grew agitated as he tried to speak quietly into his phone, "Yes, sir, I understand that I can and probably should arrest her for withholdin' vital information, but . . ." There was a long pause as he listened. "Bringin' her in would be a mistake." Another pause. "Because I think she'll completely shut down." His voice faded and returned as he paced the length of my small apartment. He released an exasperated sigh. "Yes, sir, I understand."

I heard the snap of his phone as he ended the call. He grumbled something under his breath. There was a thump against the wall at my back and the sound of someone sliding to the floor. I listened to the quiet breathing on the other side of the wall, waiting for someone to speak.

A quiet rap of knuckles against the plaster made me jump.

"What?" I asked curtly.

"Are you gonna hide in there all afternoon?" Detective Marx asked.

I exhaled in exasperation. "Why won't you leave?"

"I'm sorry if I made you uncomfortable earlier. That wasn't my intention."

Uncomfortable. Apparently, we defined that word differently. To me, *uncomfortable* didn't result in OCD marshmallow sorting in a bathroom. He'd stirred up a frightening array of emotions, the least of which was *uncomfortable*.

"Holly," he prompted.

"I'm trying to think of a snippy retort. Be quiet for a minute." Nothing came to mind. I was certain I heard him chuckle quietly to himself on the other side of the wall.

"I have a few more questions. You mind comin' out so we can talk?"

Of course he did.

"You've been in there for two hours," he pointed out.

I glanced around the confined bathroom that made it difficult to breathe if I gave it too much thought, and decided it was still preferable to talking to him. "I think I'll stay here."

"It's hard to have a conversation with a wall in the middle."

"The wall doesn't do that creepy mind-reading thing you do with my face."

He sighed, and I heard the muffled thump of his head resting back against the wall. "I need answers, Holly. As much as I wanna give you time, we just don't have it. My captain is pressurin' me to take you in for questionin'."

My stomach clenched at the thought of being taken to the police station. They would take my photo and document everything about my life. "I won't go," I told him firmly.

"You won't go *willin'ly*," he clarified, and he sounded no happier about that scenario than I did. "But if push comes to shove, that flimsy bathroom door won't put up much of a defense." After a beat of silence, he said, "I'd rather it not come to that."

I rolled a piece of cereal between my thumb and forefinger as I considered his words. "So, if I don't give you his name, you'll arrest me?"

"More or less."

I gritted my teeth.

"Ms. Holly, the last thing I wanna do is handcuff you and take you to jail."

"So don't."

He grunted in frustration. "It's not that simple. I have a chain of command. And if I defy my superiors, they will likely remove me from this case and assign somebody else. And that somebody else might not be as lenient with you."

I threw the box of cereal across the bathroom. I had no good options.

"Ms. Holly—"

"Just . . . gimme a minute," I interrupted. I propped my elbows on my knees and dropped my head into my hands. The thought of sharing any of the secrets I had guarded so closely for all these years made me feel physically ill. It went against my every instinct for survival. "You don't know what you're asking."

"I know you're terrified of him, but I promise you I will not let him hurt you."

"You shouldn't make promises you can't keep." My voice sounded as bleak as I felt. I ran my fingers through my hair and released a heavy breath. "I'll give you one question, but I won't tell you his name."

"I need more than one question. Gimme at least three."

"One," I insisted.

"One and a follow-up question for clarification," he countered.

I sighed. Two questions wasn't an unreasonable request. "Fine."

He barely needed a moment to consider his first question. "The man you're hidin' from—was he a younger foster brother, older foster brother, or your foster father?"

"Older," I said without hesitation. He'd just turned eighteen when I was placed in the same foster home at fifteen. All the other children were younger, and he'd been overjoyed by my placement. It wasn't long before I realized why.

Detective Marx took a moment longer to consider his second question. He spoke carefully. "What did he do to you to make you so afraid of him?"

I'd hoped he wouldn't ask that one.

Painful memories gathered like storm clouds in my mind. No matter how hard I tried to forget them, they refused to fade away. I could conceal the physical scars, but it was the invisible ones that haunted me the most: the memories of screams and tears— some of them my own, some of them belonging to younger children—of pain, of not being able to breathe.

If there was such a thing as living darkness, it wrapped itself in his skin. There was nothing human about him. He fed off the suffering of others; it fueled him, excited him.

Nausea swept over me, and I scrambled to the toilet just in time to throw up the few pieces of cereal in my stomach. I heard once that vomiting was the body's way of expelling things that were harmful to it. Maybe one day I would be able to think about those memories without my body trying to regurgitate them.

Someone pulled my hair away from my face as I dry heaved into the toilet, but it was too late to save it. I sat there for a moment, winded, before dropping back against the wall and drawing my knees to my chest. I wiped at my face with the sleeve of the scrubs as I glanced warily at Detective Marx, who was crouching next to the tub.

My small bathroom was not made for two.

He moved back and sat against the far wall, leaving the doorway open without me having to ask. "I suppose that wasn't the best question," he said, sounding apologetic.

My voice came out a little hoarse. "Well, you could've asked something simple like my favorite color. It's purple, by the way."

"I saw the purple couch," he replied with a strained smile. "You all right?"

I tried to ignore the hint of concern in his eyes. "I guess all that sugar didn't set well with me."

"Mmm hmm."

I cleared my throat. "I owe you one more question." I didn't want to answer any more, but I had agreed to two questions, and I had no intention of answering his last one.

He tapped the ring finger of his left hand absently as he

regarded me. I remembered him mentioning an ex-wife, but he still wore the ring. Maybe he hadn't quite fallen out of love with her. "I won't ask you for the details. But if you can tell me, I would like to know: when was the last time he caught up with you?"

I swallowed and dropped my head. "Two years ago, when I was waitressing in Pennsylvania."

"And he hurt you when he found you."

I tried to keep the painful memories from haunting my voice. "Is that a question, Detective? Because you're out of questions."

"No, Ms. Holly, unfortunately that is not a question." He stood and walked out of the bathroom without another word.

I closed my eyes and sighed. It was over. No more questions. At least for a while. I rested for a moment before pushing myself to my feet and turning on the faucet. I splashed my face with water and rinsed out my mouth to erase the bitter taste of bad memories.

Bickering voices rose from somewhere nearby, followed by a loud, reverberating clang. I flinched.

"What in the name of all that is holy," Detective Marx grumbled. My kitchen window let out a loud shriek as it popped open. "What is goin' on?" he demanded.

A voice I didn't recognize replied hastily, "There's an angry woman out here. She demanded we step aside and we asked her to leave. She picked up a large stick and started spearing the door."

Another deafening clang. "Let. Me. In!"

I recognized Jace's voice instantly. She was furious. She hit the door again with increasing force. Good grief. She was going to dent my door.

I stepped out of the bathroom to see what was happening. The younger of the two officers was crouched outside the kitchen window, and Detective Marx was watching the situation through the screen with a bemused expression.

"You should probably lower the drawbridge and let her through before she starts spearing *people*," I suggested.

Detective Marx glanced back at me. "You know this young lady?"

"That'd be Ms. *Effervescent.*"

Recognition dawned on his face, and he gave the officer a small gesture. The officer disappeared, and the front door opened a second later.

One of them must have tried to help her down the steps, because she snapped, "Don't touch my wheelchair."

"Ma'am, we're just trying to—"

"If you like your fingers, keep them to yourself," she warned.

She must have poked at the nearest officer with her stick, because Detective Marx groaned and rubbed his forehead. "Disarm her before we have to arrest her for assault."

I bit down on my lower lip as I tried not to laugh. If these men couldn't handle a woman in a wheelchair armed with a stick, I didn't have much confidence in them fending off a psychotic killer.

"Hey!" Jace shouted when they wrenched the stick away from her.

Detective Marx frowned. "How exactly does she get down the steps?"

I smiled and shrugged. It was more amusing to watch them figure it out themselves. Detective Marx gave me an unhappy look and peered back out the window. "Gentlemen," he said, tapping on the window frame. "The board." He had finally noticed it resting against the side of the building.

I heard the board smack down a moment before Jace came rolling into the apartment. I stepped into the kitchen to meet her and had to leap back to protect my toes when she barreled into me. The force of her impact knocked me back a step, but she still somehow managed to wrap her arms around my waist in a freakishly tight hug.

I stiffened for an instant before patting her awkwardly on the back. "I'm fine, Jace." She grumbled obscenities against my stomach. I glanced at Detective Marx, who was watching the display with mild curiosity. I arched my eyebrows at him.

Yes, I had friends. Well, one.

Jace pulled back as abruptly as she'd grabbed me, and I stumbled to find my balance again. Her relief at finding me alive gave way to a rush of anger and fear. "I drove past the café and there were police, and police tape, and there was blood on the patio where I left you. I thought . . . I thought something really bad happened and . . . I called you, and I heard your stupid whistling ringtone. Your phone was still there on the patio." She was so angry with me that she was shaking. "Did we not just talk about this phone thing!?"

I winced at the shrillness of her voice.

"I thought you died!"

Well, I'd stepped up from being abducted then.

"I wasn't kidnapped and the police aren't drawing a really unflattering chalk outline of my body on the pavement," I said. "Everything is okay."

She puffed out a breath, and as her nerves began to settle, I noticed the sparkle of clarity return to her eyes. Jace was sharp when she wasn't frightened. She took in my appearance with brisk efficiency. "Okay? Really? Because you weren't wearing scrubs when I left you at the café. And your hands . . ." She snatched one of my hands before I could react and examined my scabbed and bruised fingertips. "What happened?"

I tugged back my hand and curled my fingers into fists before folding my arms uneasily. "It's not a big deal."

"Not a big deal?" she asked hotly. "You look like you got in a fight with a nail file and lost, and there are cops *guarding* your front door. You're not telling me something."

"I don't tell you a lot of things."

"Please, Holly."

I shifted guiltily under the weight of her gaze. I had tried to protect her by keeping her in the dark, but in hindsight that really hadn't been my decision to make. I looked at Detective Marx.

He gave a small shrug. "It's your decision, but if she's your friend, it's probably safer if she knows."

Jace froze at the sound of his voice, and her eyes widened to the size of golf balls. "Sexy accent guy?" she whispered to me.

Detective Marx overheard the comment, and a very peculiar expression crossed his face. Jace gave him a quick once-over before returning her attention to me. I had a feeling we would be having a very disturbing conversation about him later.

10

Three uneventful days passed, and I felt like I was going to crawl out of my skin. I hadn't left my apartment, and I was beginning to doubt the detective's theory of a stalker.

I leaned against the kitchen counter as I sipped my hot tea and finished my plate of scrambled eggs. I tapped my fork against my lips and watched the officer on the front lawn through the kitchen window. Despite my vehement objections, Detective Marx had assigned two officers to watch over me: one during the day and one at night.

We'd bickered in circles for nearly an hour about whether or not they would protect me from inside my apartment. It was my home and he couldn't legally force his officers inside if I didn't want them. And I didn't want them.

I had a one-bedroom apartment with a curtain instead of a door. I would never be able to relax, let alone sleep, while a strange man sat in my kitchen or lounged on my couch.

But apparently I had no say in whether or not they stood watch outside. Detective Marx had informed me that it wasn't my property, and he could post his officers on the premises without my permission. He could be insufferably pushy.

The officer outside now was young, but his age was difficult to gauge. He was probably in his twenties, but he had a baby face that made him look eighteen, and his big brown eyes were full of innocence. I was pretty sure his name was John. No, that wasn't right. James, Jobe, Jack . . . Jacob, that was it.

The officer who worked the night shift looked Hispanic, but he didn't sound Hispanic. Sam, I think. He was probably the most boring individual I had ever met. He almost seemed robotic in the way he spoke with scarcely any inflection, and he had a very limited range of facial expressions: mostly he was just a big wall of blank. He was nice enough, though, so I couldn't really complain.

He'd brought my phone back last night when he came on shift, so at least I could text Jace when it felt like the walls were closing in. I was honestly surprised she was still talking to me. She hadn't taken the news of my attack in the park well, and she was even more upset that I'd kept it from her.

She'd stopped by every day to check on me and to make sure the officers were doing their job. She had texted me earlier this morning: "Library is a snooze. Visiting Scott later. Wanna come?"

Yes, yes, I did. It was pathetic that going to the hospital would be the highlight of my day. Jace tried to visit her brother every week, and I knew how much she hated to go alone.

I noticed Jacob shiver a little in the front yard, and guilt gnawed at me. It was a bitter autumn day; I could feel the cold air seeping through the old seals of the windows. I set my tea on the counter and fixed him a mug of hot chocolate. I wished I had coffee or pastries to give him, but this would have to do.

Icy air cut through my jeans and hoodie when I opened the front door, and it was almost enough to make me burrow back into my *bunker*, as Detective Marx had so eloquently described my home. I clenched my teeth so they wouldn't chatter and walked up the steps onto the lawn.

The corners of Jacob's lips dipped into a frown when he saw me. "Is everything all right?" I hadn't come out in days, so it was no wonder he thought something was wrong.

"Fine. Here," I said stiffly. I held out the cup of hot chocolate.

His face brightened. "Thanks. I could use a little warming." He took the hot mug and clamped it between his red fingers.

If I were kind, I would invite him inside so he could keep warm, but he would have to settle for hot chocolate. "How much longer before Detective Marx accepts that he's wrong and pulls you and Sam off protection detail?"

Jacob smiled and bounced a little to warm his cold arms and legs. "You really don't want us here, huh?"

No, I didn't. I had finally managed to scrape together some semblance of a normal life for myself, and I didn't want my every movement shadowed and my every decision scrutinized. "Not particularly, no."

His smile broadened, accentuating the boyishness of his features. "Yeah, I get that. But we're not here to make things difficult for you. Marx will catch your stalker-slash-killer. We're just making sure nothing happens to you in the meantime."

"He's wrong about the stalker."

Jacob considered it a moment before shaking his head. "Marx isn't often wrong. Don't tell him I said that, though."

I folded my arms as the cold air sucked away my body heat. "Nothing's happened."

"I read the report. From what I understand, you're pretty lucky to be standing here."

"I meant lately."

"One of your attackers just died three days ago. I'm not sure what you consider lately, but that seems pretty recent to me."

I sighed in exasperation. "I don't need bodyguards."

He smiled as he took a sip of his hot chocolate. "You mean you don't *want* bodyguards." At my flat look, he grinned. "You made Marx really cranky when he suggested protection detail and you lifted your chin and declared 'I don't want them here.' He grumbled for hours. It was actually pretty hilarious."

I blushed with embarrassment. I hadn't realized we'd argued loudly enough for the officers to hear us from outside the apartment.

"I can take care of myself," I explained. Although recent events contradicted that statement, I was going to stick with it. It made me feel better.

Jacob cocked his head, considering. "Maybe, but it's safer this way."

"I can't hide until Detective Marx finds this guy. I won't do it." I'd spent too many years in hiding, and I just wanted to live my life.

"No one said you had to hide. Just limit your extracurricular activities and take Sam or me with you for protection."

"I don't want anyone else dying because of me."

"I'm sure we can all agree on that."

A silver Prius skidded up to the curb in front of us and parked. Jacob's free hand went to his gun. Surely, he recognized Jace's car by now, but he kept a hand on his weapon until she rolled down the window and he could see her face.

"You ready?" she shouted.

Jacob glanced at me.

"We're going to the hospital to visit her brother. He's in a coma," I explained. Scott, her older brother, had been mugged two years ago, and the men had beaten him and left him for dead.

"I'll follow you."

We spent the evening at the hospital, and I lingered awkwardly in the back of the hospital room as Jace held her brother's hand and filled him in on the events of her week.

She told him about my stalker and the cute police officers, who had stepped up to protect me. I was pretty sure I saw Jacob blush and grin in the doorway before he melted back into the hall to stand guard.

Scott looked thinner and weaker than he had last week, and it pained me to see how his body was withering with time. I was afraid Jace would lose him completely in the near future, so I never begrudged her the visits that stretched well into the night. The nurses all knew her by name now, and they let her stay as long as she wanted.

It was nearly midnight before I arrived home. I crawled beneath my covers with a tired yawn and drifted easily to sleep.

11

Something roused me a couple hours after I fell asleep. I blinked groggily at the purring bundle of fur on the pillow beside me until a strange tapping sound drew my attention. It sounded like a tree branch bumping against a window.

I sat up reluctantly and rubbed the tiredness from my eyes. One glance at the windows told me something wasn't right. Moonlight should have been filtering into the apartment, but there was an irregular line of darkness that bisected each one of the windows.

I threw back the covers and slid out of bed. My bare feet hit the cold cement and a shiver passed through me. I staggered to the kitchen and flipped on the overhead light.

My breath caught.

Photographs were arranged across the rear windows like a film strip. They hadn't been there when I'd fallen asleep.

I fumbled blindly with the silverware drawer at my back until I found the handle of my knife. I gripped it with shaking fingers as I crept slowly forward. Horror and fear twisted through me as I recognized the faces in the photographs.

The first photo was of me asleep in bed in my tank top and pajama pants from the night before. The second was of me stepping out of the bathroom with a towel wrapped around me. I was almost afraid to look at the other pictures. I saw myself frozen in a tank top and jeans as I brushed my hair, wrote in my journal, and mused about the officer in the front yard, sipping my morning tea.

My entire morning routine was captured in five chilling photographs. The sixth was of Jacob and me talking on the lawn. I followed the sequence of events to the hospital, where there were snapshots of Jacob and me in the hall, of Jace . . .

A tremor of fear made me take a step back.

Someone had followed us every step of the way, and not one of us even had an inkling he was lurking in the background. The pictures were taped to the outside of the windows, which brought me some small comfort. Whoever had taken them hadn't been inside my home.

There was another quiet tap, and my gaze flickered over the windows frantically. The tap grew louder, and I followed it until I pinpointed the sound near my bed. I stood on my tiptoes to see through the sliver of uncovered glass.

A gloved fingertip tapped the window in front of me, and I screamed involuntarily. I fell back on the bed and scrambled hastily off the other side. I skidded into the front door as loud, urgent pounding erupted on the other side.

"Ms. Smith! Is everything all right?" It was Sam.

"There's someone outside my window."

"I'll check it out. Stay inside and keep the doors and windows locked," Sam's muffled voice replied. I heard him mutter something into a radio before his voice faded away into the night.

I huddled in the small corner between the counter and the door and watched the windows warily. The knife in my hands grew slippery as my palms began to sweat. I was safe in my apartment. I was *perfectly* safe.

I listened for the sound of a fight or gunshots, but all I could hear was my own irregular breathing. The seconds dragged into minutes, and then I heard the sound of footsteps on the patio. I waited for Sam to announce that it was all clear, or that there was no sign of danger, but no one spoke.

The quiet scrape of a key in the lock sent my pulse skittering. The officers didn't have keys to my door. No one should've had keys to my door. I shot to my feet and backed away through the kitchen.

The first dead bolt snapped open.

I looked around desperately. There was nowhere to hide. As Detective Marx had pointed out, my bathroom door was too flimsy to protect me. I had never planned for this scenario, because no one should've been able to get in.

I grabbed my phone off the nightstand and dropped to my stomach on the cement floor. I shoved the knife and phone under the bed and wriggled after them.

Sometimes being petite had its advantages; I managed to squeeze under the low twin bed frame where most people couldn't. It was hard to breathe, and panic gnawed at the edges of my mind. I hated small spaces.

They reminded me too much of the box. Only a single hole to breathe and not enough room to move. Like a coffin. I shoved that memory out of my mind before it catapulted me into a full-on panic attack under the bed. I could curse my foster brother for his sadistic games later.

I gripped the knife and phone so tightly in my hands that the bones in my fingers ached.

The front door opened with a metallic creak, and I held my breath. Heavy, slow footsteps echoed through the apartment, and I had to resist the urge to shrink closer to the wall. Even the smallest movement would draw attention.

I watched a pair of black boots slowly cross the apartment, hesitate, and vanish from sight in the direction of the bathroom. A warm glow spilled out across the floor as the man flipped on the light. An intimidating shadow stretched out behind him, and I gulped down the whimper that climbed up my throat.

Tricks of the light, I reminded myself. He could be five feet tall and his shadow might still appear massive. I heard the screech of the shower curtain being drawn back. He was looking for something.

I wondered if I could make it to the front door before he noticed. But then I remembered how difficult it had been to get *under* the bed. Getting out would be just as slow and challenging.

I wasn't even sure why I had bothered to grab my phone. Even if I could figure out how to silence the chirp of the buttons as I dialed 9-1-1, the dispatcher's voice on the other end would seem like a shout in this otherwise silent room. It would be impossible to miss.

Sam would come back. He had to come back.

The man's boots came back into view, and my ears picked up a strange sound that seemed to move with him. It reminded me of change jingling in a pocket. He walked slowly toward my side of the apartment and paused less than a foot from my bed. I tried not to breathe and prayed he couldn't hear the deafening drum of my heartbeat.

He turned in a slow circle. I stared at his shoes—the only piece of him I could see—and tried to memorize every detail: black carpenter boots, worn to the point that the laces had begun to fray at the tips. There was a splotch of yellow paint on the sole of his left boot. I mentally prepared myself to stab him in the foot if he came any closer.

"NYPD. Put your hands on your head and turn around," a Southern voice instructed.

A small spark of hope ignited in my chest. The man in front of my bed gasped, and a thick ring of keys dropped from his hands and clattered on the floor. They were the source of the jingling I'd heard as he walked. I stared at the keys with a vague sense of recognition.

"Get on your knees and interlock your fingers behind your head," Detective Marx instructed. I saw his feet as he closed in on the intruder. I heard a pitiful whimper before the unmistakable snap of handcuffs.

"Please, I was just trying to help," the intruder whined.

"You have the right to remain silent, so shut up until I ask you a question. Holly?" He sounded worried.

"Here," I croaked as I sent the knife and phone skidding across the floor ahead of me. I wiggled out from under the bed with some difficulty.

"How on earth did you get under there?" He holstered his gun and reached down to help me up.

I would've objected, but he had his hand under my arm and was pulling me to my feet before I could react. I sank onto the foot of the bed and wrapped the blanket around my bare shoulders. I wore only a tank top and pajama pants; I wasn't exactly dressed for company.

I gaped in confusion at the scene in front of me. Detective Marx stood over an older man, who knelt on the cold floor in gray sweatpants, a house coat, and black boots. The old man's wrinkled face was twisted with fear.

"Mr. Stanley?" I glanced between the intruder and Detective Marx, unsure what to make of the situation. My fear dwindled to confusion.

"Oh, thank goodness, Holly," Mr. Stanley gasped. "Tell him I'm not a criminal. Tell him I haven't done anything."

He leaned toward me in desperation, and Detective Marx put a hand on his shoulder and wrenched him back. "Sit still."

"Stanley is my landlord."

Detective Marx's expression changed to one of suspicion. "Do you frequently let yourself into young women's apartments in the middle of the night, Mr. Stanley?"

Stanley looked mortified. "No, never!" He started to shake, and I wasn't sure if it was from the cold drifting through the open door or the shock of the situation he found himself in.

"To my knowledge, he's never done this before," I offered. Stanley was often a grumpy, if not rude, old man, but he'd never struck me as creepy. He might have been my intruder, but he hadn't plastered the photos across the outside of my windows. And I doubted he'd been the one tapping on the glass.

Detective Marx pulled Stanley to his feet, and the old man struggled to find his balance on stiff knees. "You better have a good reason for lettin' yourself into this young woman's apartment, Mr. Stanley."

I saw the moment he realized the cranky old man wasn't the only thing out of place in my apartment. Something shifted in his expression when he saw the pictures on the windows. "Holly, shut the door. Lock it."

The gravity in his voice had me off the bed and across the room instantly. I closed the door and flipped the dead bolts. He studied the pictures carefully from the center of the room. "When did this happen?"

"I don't know. They weren't there when I went to sleep."

Detective Marx's gaze slid to Stanley, and he took him by the elbow and led him to one of my kitchen chairs. He pushed him into it a little more forcefully than necessary and planted both of his hands on the table so that he leaned face to face with the older man "Mr. Stanley, have you been scrapbookin' on the windows?" He nodded to the windows behind him, and Stanley paled as he looked over his shoulder.

"No. I didn't do anything. All I did was let myself in."

"I'm ready to hear that good reason now."

Mr. Stanley's eyes shifted between me and the detective who stood uncomfortably close to him. He looked so shaken that I considered asking Detective Marx to back off, but I was pretty sure that request would fall on deaf ears. "Because Holly was hurt."

Detective Marx glanced at me, taking a quick inventory of my condition. Everything was still attached; I didn't even have a scratch to complain about. "Hurt how?"

"She was passed out on the floor."

Detective Marx arched his eyebrows at me in question, and I shook my head. I had no idea what Stanley was talking about. "Just how much have you had to drink tonight?"

Stanley sputtered indignantly as he tried to straighten up in the chair. "I'm not drunk. I didn't hallucinate."

"As you can clearly see, Ms. Holly is in good health. And she's been that way all evenin'. You're gonna have to try better than that."

Stanley lifted his chin and tried to look down his bird-beak nose at Detective Marx. "Don't speak to me like I'm an imbecile. I see that she's fine now. But he said . . ." He glanced at me with uncertainty, and I cocked my head. "He said, 'I think Holly's hurt. I'm going to call the police. Unlock the door. She might need CPR,' so I came to check."

81

"*He*," Detective Marx repeated, latching onto that one word. "Who is *he*?"

Stanley shrugged. "I don't know. I've never seen him before. I just assumed he was a boyfriend."

"What did he look like?"

Lines of concentration formed around Stanley's eyes. "Tall, six three or six four. Dark hair. Beyond that he was a bit of a blur."

It wasn't enough detail to draw a stick figure, let alone a police sketch.

"A blur," Detective Marx repeated flatly.

"I seem to have misplaced my glasses."

Mmm, I wasn't sure glasses were the issue. Standing close to him now, I could smell the alcohol on his breath. I wondered why someone would create such an elaborate charade if they didn't intend to take advantage of it. Mr. Stanley was barely functional after his evening dance with the bottle, and they could've simply followed him in or knocked him out and taken the keys.

I glanced at the key ring across the room. There were probably fifty keys on it, one for every apartment. "Why do you have keys to my apartment?"

When I moved in, I had paid to have two extra dead bolts added to my door. Mr. Stanley had agreed to the renovation so long as he didn't have to foot the bill and I gave him the keys before moving out. I was supposed to be the only person with the keys until that time. I wasn't aware that arrangement had been changed.

Mr. Stanley hesitated. "I . . . asked for them. When the locksmith added the extra locks, I told him I wanted an extra set of keys in case you . . . left unexpectedly or there was an emergency."

I folded my arms. "I paid for them."

"It's my property!" he protested.

I gritted my teeth. Detective Marx didn't look pleased that I had derailed his interrogation with a side question, and he gave me a quelling look before asking Stanley, "Did you see which way the man went?"

"It was dark."

"Is that a no?"

Mr. Stanley nodded. A loud knock on the door made me jump. Apparently, all my nerves hadn't quite settled down.

"It's Sam," a male voice called out before I could ask who was there. I unbolted the door and opened it. Sam did a quick visual assessment of me and the apartment before stepping inside. He spotted the old man sitting in my kitchen chair with his wrists cuffed behind his back. "What happened? I thought I told you to lock the door."

"I did," I replied defensively.

"Mr. Stanley let himself in," Detective Marx explained. "*Apparently*, he has keys."

I scowled at his mocking tone.

"Are you all right?" Sam asked me.

"Yeah . . ." My voice trailed off as I leaned out the doorway to see flashing red and blue lights . . . at 3:00 a.m. Awesome. Not only were we holding my landlord hostage, but my neighbors were all going to wish me dead. I closed the door. "What's with all the cars?'

"I trailed a suspect from the back of the apartment complex for two blocks. I lost track of him, but I called in backup and they're searching for him now. I doubled back to make sure you're okay," Sam explained.

Ah. A manhunt for the dark-haired blurry giant. That was going to be fruitful.

"Did you get a good look?" Detective Marx asked.

"No, he was dressed in black. I can tell you he was tall, but not much more than that."

Mr. Stanley shifted anxiously in the chair as he looked at each of us. His gaze finally settled on Detective Marx. "Are you gonna arrest me?"

"No, you're not under arrest." Detective Marx removed the handcuffs, and Mr. Stanley rubbed his wrists as he rose from the chair. "Take your keys and get out."

Mr. Stanley plucked the key ring off the floor with quivering fingers and hurried toward the door. I opened it to let him escape, but he froze on the doorstep when Detective Marx called, "And Mr. Stanley . . . knock next time." The older man nodded anxiously before disappearing up the steps.

Detective Marx gripped the back of the chair. He looked as tired as I felt. "Somebody tell me what happened."

Sam described the events from his perspective, and then Detective Marx looked at me for more information.

"I woke up to a strange sound. He was tapping on the window, like he wanted me to notice him."

"Because he knew you would tell the officer at the front door, and he could draw away your protection. And then he mixed your landlord up in this mess. Why?" His eyes grew distant as he tried to work it out. "We're missin' somethin'."

"Maybe he just wanted to scare her," Sam offered.

Detective Marx pushed off the chair and crossed the room. He walked along the wall, absorbing the photos from beginning to end. I fidgeted when he walked back and started again, his eyes studying the first few pictures.

It was unnerving enough to think that whoever had taken those photos had crouched outside my window and watched me as I slept and changed my clothes; I didn't want other people looking at them.

"In most of these pictures you're with other people, but these here. . ." Detective Marx gestured to the photos of my morning routine. "These are more intimate. Just you."

"He obviously watched her get dressed, but she's decently covered in all the photos," Sam observed.

"I've no doubt he took photos of her in between these, but I'm guessin' he knew we would be examinin' them, and he's possessive enough that he doesn't want anybody else lookin' at her."

My stomach lurched.

"Why plaster them on the windows?" Sam asked.

"Because he wants her to know she's vulnerable, that he's watchin' and he can get to her whenever he wants. If he hadn't intentionally woken her up, we would never have even known he was outside the window."

"What does he want from me?" I asked. I had nothing of any value, and I'd never done anything to anyone that might inspire a desire for revenge.

Detective Marx looked at me and frowned, but he kept whatever he was thinking to himself. "I don't know. And until I figure out how to put a stop to this, you need to work with me."

"I haven't shoved you out the door yet," I pointed out with a hint of irritation. "What more do you want from me?" I wished I could take the words back the moment they left my lips. I hadn't meant to sound so snotty.

Detective Marx cocked an eyebrow at me. "You know, you have a very big attitude for such a small person."

I pressed my lips together.

"And as for what I want, I want a name for the man who did this, but we both know how pointless that conversation is. And I want you to be smarter."

I glared at him as my temper flared. "I'm not stupid."

"I didn't say you were stupid." He sighed and scrubbed a hand over his tired face. "Look, I know you're stressed, you're scared, and you're not fond of cops—for whatever reason—and you're havin' a hard time with this, but we're on the same side, Holly."

I clenched my teeth and made an effort to control my attitude, which had been sharpened to a fine point by both fear and exhaustion, and asked as reasonably as I could manage, "What do you want me to do, Detective?"

"For one, quit callin' me Detective. You can call me Richard or Marx, whichever you prefer. And second, I need you to understand that the more risks you take, the more danger it puts you and my officers in. I will do everythin' in my power to keep you safe, but no more spontaneous trips to the hospital without givin' us a heads up." He gestured to the photos taken at the hospital. "No goin' for runs or walks around the city. If you need to go out, we need to know in advance so we can plan accordin'ly."

I wanted to tell him no, but I couldn't ignore the fact that this stalker scared me. I was afraid of what might happen if I ran into him alone.

"Okay," I agreed reluctantly.

He tapped a finger on the handle of the kitchen knife now lying on the table. "And none of this. We're here to protect you, so the moment you feel threatened by anythin' or anyone, tell us immediately. Please . . . do not grab a kitchen knife and investigate it yourself first."

"I'm not . . ."

He arched an eyebrow, and I clamped my mouth shut to avoid rudely reminding him I wasn't helpless and incapable. I desperately needed to sleep before I said something I would regret.

When I remained silent, he said, "Let's get these windows covered. If he enjoys watchin' you while you sleep, the least we can do is disappoint him."

We blacked out the rear windows of the apartment with bath towels, and my apartment quickly transformed into a dungeon.

12

I closed the front door before dropping back against it with a shaky breath. It was five a.m. and I was exhausted after a fitful night of sleep, but I couldn't bring myself to crawl back beneath the covers.

Nothing but nightmares waited for me there.

Most of my nightmares were tolerable—vague images and feelings I could shake off when I woke—but some clung to me for hours after waking. It hadn't been my own screams that woke me tonight, but Sam pounding frantically on the door.

Apparently, I had sounded like I was being murdered—brutally—and after my stalker's visit the other night, Sam wouldn't accept my explanation that it had only been a nightmare without seeing for himself that I was all right. So I had dragged myself out of bed and wrenched open the front door to show him that I was still in one rumpled, shaky piece.

I combed back my damp hair with my fingers and went into the bathroom to clean up. I showered and changed into fresh clothes, and I felt marginally human again.

I plopped onto the end of my bed and glared at the towels and blankets that covered my windows. One lone light bulb on the ceiling did little to illuminate my dungeon. Maybe I should invest in torches. At least that would improve the ambiance.

I picked up my notebook and stared down at the entry I'd started last night.

Dear Jesus,
Today I am thankful for . . .

So much had gone wrong lately that I struggled to find something to be grateful for. God understood the unrest I was feeling, so I didn't really feel the need to write it out.

I picked up my pen and wrote a single word: *You*.

I closed the notebook with the pen still between the pages and set it aside. Jordan hopped up and down by the end of the bed, and I dragged the tubby beast onto the mattress with me. He chortled and dropped a soggy blob of cat food onto my notebook.

Lovely.

I'd found a piece in my slipper earlier. I shook the cat food off onto the floor and rubbed his head. He couldn't help that there was a wire crossed in there somewhere.

I stood and stretched. I needed to do something to take my mind off the nightmares that left my insides feeling like a twisted-up slinky. A run wasn't an option; even if it weren't pitch black outside, Marx would lose his Southern cool if I deliberately ignored his warnings.

Something to do . . .

I paused in front of the couch and stared at the ghastly yellow wall. It reminded me of . . . pee . . . and Cheerios, but I wasn't really sure what the connection was there.

I had a few partial tubs of paint that I had picked up here and there, and I was pretty sure I had . . . I rummaged under the sink . . . yep, a paint roller and paint tray.

I dragged everything I needed over into the living room. I squeezed between the wall and my couch and tried to move it with my hips. It slid inch by agonizingly slow inch. Good grief, it was heavy.

Free of the couch, I propped my hands on my hips and gazed at my hideous yellow canvas. My paint options weren't ideal: moss green, Care Bear purple, and hot pink . . . which terrified me a little. I chewed on my lip as I considered the options.

Care Bear purple. It was the least offensive. I poured it into the pan and dove headfirst into my project. Projects were a good distraction from the troubles of life.

I quickly realized I was too short to reach the highest part of the wall, even with my folding chair. I stretched on my tiptoes and wound up with a funky purple zigzag across the top of the wall.

Voices penetrated the quiet. At this time of morning, the city was still a little sleepy, and there weren't many people out. I hopped down and pulled my chair over to the kitchen window to get a view of what was going on outside.

A man in a ball cap stood on the sidewalk with a medium-sized cardboard box in his arms. He looked like he was a whopping four inches taller than me. Definitely not the killer. "I'm supposed to deliver this," he said a little nervously.

"To whom?" Sam demanded.

The man looked down at the box and then around the front of the apartment with a confused expression. "It doesn't say. He just told me to give it to the pretty redhead in the overalls."

My heart beat a little faster as I glanced down at my paint-splattered overalls. He was watching me. My gaze flitted over the empty streets, searching every shadow and window for a face, but there was no one.

"Who gave you the box?"

"Some guy. I didn't get a good look at his face. He was tall, spoke kinda soft-like. He paid me fifty bucks to bring it over."

"When?"

"Uh . . . maybe ten minutes ago?"

"Which building?" Sam demanded.

"That one." He directed Sam's attention to the condemned factory directly across the street. If the killer had binoculars, he could probably see straight into my front window from the second floor.

Sam called for backup, but I suspected we both knew the man was no longer there. There were any number of exits he could've taken without being seen.

"What's your name?" Sam demanded.

"Ty."

"Ty, set the box down very gently and step over there." Sam gestured toward the steps of the main apartment complex. The young man put the box down carefully and backed away.

I waited for Sam to collect the package, but he didn't move. Did he think it might be a bomb? That didn't make sense. After everything, would my stalker really just . . . blow me up?

I sat down on the edge of the sink when waiting grew tiresome and glanced at the clock on the microwave. Ten minutes crawled by before I heard a car door slam. I popped up to see Marx walking down the sidewalk and then shrank down a little. If he saw me, he would tell me to get out of the window.

"Where's Holly?" he asked as he pulled on a pair of rubber gloves.

"Inside," Sam answered. "She's safe."

"Has anybody touched it?"

Sam gestured to Ty. "Just him. Should we call the bomb squad?"

Marx shook his head as he crouched beside the box. "He's not interested in killin' her yet, and when he is, he won't do it with a bomb."

That was a reassuring thought.

Marx pulled a knife from his pocket and sliced open the tape across the top. He peeled open the flaps carefully and peered inside. I saw the subtle hardening of his jaw as he looked up from the box.

"Did the man say anythin' when he gave you this box?" he asked Ty.

"Just that it was a gift for the pretty redhead in overalls. That's it. I swear."

Marx tapped his fingers on the outside of the box as he glanced back inside. It must not have been what he expected it to be. "Sam, get this young man's fingerprints and statement and then go home."

"But what about—"

90

"Officers are canvasin' for the suspect," Marx interrupted. "I'll stay here with Holly so you and Jacob can get a little rest."

"You think he's watching?"

"Oh, he's watchin'. He wants to see her face when she opens his *gift*," Marx explained. He stood and picked up the box. He knocked on my door but didn't wait for an invitation before coming inside. Without even looking my way, he said, "Holly, get out of the window."

He'd known I was watching the entire time. And here I thought I was being stealthy. I hopped down and slid my hands into the back pockets of my overalls as I stared cautiously at the box in his arms. "What is it?"

He set the box on the table and slid it toward me. "Have a look, and then you tell me."

I approached the table slowly and glanced into the box. Wrapped in a clear plastic bag was a white stuffed rabbit, a child's toy, and one side of it was stained with something dark. My throat tightened and I suddenly couldn't breathe.

I knew that rabbit.

I backed away from the box and groped for the counter to steady me. Another fragment of memory sliced through my mental barrier, and my mind instinctively tried to pull away from it to protect me.

I padded down the hallway in my bare feet, holding my rabbit snugly under one arm. There was a noise in the room down the hall. I should've been sleeping, but I'd been thirsty . . . and I was curious now. I walked on my tiptoes so no one could hear me sneaking, but I slipped on something warm and wet just inside the room.

I tried to catch myself as I fell on top of something lumpy, and my rabbit tumbled into the dark puddle on the floor. I tried to push myself up but my hands kept slipping in the wetness. The moon peeked out from behind the clouds and white light filtered through the window, highlighting the dark red liquid that coated my hands . . .

"Holly," Marx called, but his voice sounded distant. I felt warm hands cupping my face. "Come on, Holly, breathe."

As the memory faded, I found myself lying flat on the floor. The tight muscles in my body relaxed, and I drew in a deep, much-needed breath.

Marx removed his hands from my face and sat back on his legs beside me. When I took another normal breath, he visibly sagged in relief. He dragged a hand over his face and pleaded, "Don't ever do that to me again."

"Do what?" I asked, and my voice sounded hoarse. "Why am I on the floor?" My arms felt weak and shaky as I pushed myself up against the cupboards and away from the man sitting too close to me. My face was damp with tears I didn't remember crying, and I wiped them away with my hands.

Not again, I thought with frustration.

"I'm not a doctor, but if I had to guess, that was a panic attack," he explained. He watched me carefully, as if he expected something more to happen. "You were tryin' to breathe, but it just wasn't workin'."

I remembered not being able to breathe and the feeling that my heart was about to pound out of my chest. Unfortunately, it was a familiar experience. "I was looking at the box . . ." I tried to get up to see what was inside of it, but Marx put up a hand to stop me.

"You're done with the box," he said firmly.

I dropped back against the cupboards without argument. I felt completely drained, and I just wanted to lie down. "What's in it?" I asked a little reluctantly.

Marx frowned as he considered my question. "A stuffed rabbit."

I closed my eyes against the memory that had found its way to the surface. "A white one . . . with blood on it."

"Appears that way."

I sighed. "It's mine."

"You wanna run that by me again?"

My brain felt fuzzy as it tried to sort current reality from memory. "It's my rabbit. From when I was a little girl."

"How did this man get your stuffed rabbit from when you were a kid?"

I shrugged, and even that small movement felt exhausting. "I don't know."

"Whose blood is on it?"

"I don't know."

Marx huffed in exasperation. "You're not givin' me much to work with, Holly."

"I know." I refused to apologize for something I couldn't control. The few memories I had from before I was ten made little to no sense. I had no more information than he did.

13

I jotted down the sporadic memories of my childhood in the back of my notebook. None of the memories that had surfaced were happy; none of them were even complete. The only common thread between them was fear.

One of my many state-appointed therapists had suggested that my memory loss might be due to psychological trauma. But no one could tell me what had happened or even who I was, so there wasn't much hope of picking up the pieces.

The ten-year-old girl I used to be had erected a nearly impenetrable mental barrier to protect herself from memories too frightening for her to bear. They were my memories, but I couldn't figure how to reach them.

I must have made a sound of frustration, because Marx asked from the kitchen, "Everythin' all right in there?"

I tossed the notebook aside. "My head is a scrambled egg."

"I don't find your head to be particularly egg shaped," he replied seriously.

I flopped back on the bed and rubbed my face. I heard the quiet shuffle of Marx's footsteps as he approached the purple drapes I'd drawn shut to separate my bed from the rest of the apartment. It was as close to privacy as I could get without hiding in the bathroom.

"I would knock, but . . ."

I sighed and sat up. "It's fine."

He pushed open the drapes, and I scooted to the head of the bed to put a few extra feet of space between us. "I have two more questions to ask you."

I shifted uneasily. This didn't work out so well for me last time.

"I promise I won't ask anythin' along the lines of what you're worried about," he assured me. "If it makes you too uncomfortable, then pass and I'll ask another question."

I considered it. If I got to cherry-pick the questions, it gave me a bit more control over the flow of information. "Okay." I wrapped my arms around my legs to brace myself.

"What does your foster brother look like?"

My insides twisted into knots in response to the face that materialized in my mind. I shook my head. I didn't want to think about his face, let alone describe it.

"Okay." He sighed and took a moment to consider a different question. "How tall is he?"

I drew in a breath to answer but then realized I didn't know. If he were standing next to me, I might be able to make an educated guess, but the man in my memory felt so much larger than he probably was. Terrifying things had a way of doing that. "I don't know. Stanley said the killer is six four. I know he's not six four."

"Stanley was drunk. He probably thought the fire hydrant was a poodle. Just give me an estimate. Under or over six feet?"

I shrugged helplessly. "He's bigger than me."

He pressed his lips together. "Ninety-nine percent of the male population, includin' teenagers, are bigger than you, Holly. That doesn't exactly narrow it down."

"Why do you want him to be the killer so badly?"

"What are the chances you have two men stalkin' you? The man you're hidin' from has a habit of followin' you, does he not?" He took my silence as confirmation. "You lived in the same foster home, and you've received two messages tellin' you to come home. The simplest answer is usually the correct one."

I didn't notice the folder in his hand until he tapped it against his palm. "What's that?"

"I got a warrant for your foster history."

Dread pooled in my stomach. I knew he would dig when he started asking questions, but I'd hoped he wouldn't find much.

He looked almost apologetic as he dropped the folder in the center of the bed. "Your former caseworker faxed it over last night. It took them a few days to pull the information together."

I dragged the folder toward me with icy fingers and opened it. Every family I had ever stayed with was listed on that sheet of paper, including phone numbers and addresses.

"Twelve foster homes in five years, Holly. Why?"

Ten of those placements were in the first three years. I stared down at the long list of families who had opened their homes to me and closed their doors just as quickly. Some of them could've been a home, but no one wanted the child with an unknown history. I was a risk that no one wanted to take for long.

It was an old wound—not being wanted—and it was difficult to hide that pain from my voice. "Because no one wanted to keep me."

"I don't believe that," Marx replied gently. And I could see the doubt in his eyes. It wasn't that he didn't believe *me*, but that he had a hard time believing all those families had rejected me.

I had tried to be the perfect child: courteous, helpful, friendly, and happy. But it was never enough.

My voice was barely a whisper. "You had no right to do this."

"I had to do that."

"You put my name on a warrant. You . . . you compiled a bullet-point list of my history."

"Because gettin' information from you is like pullin' teeth. You didn't leave me much choice."

I closed the folder and tossed it back toward him. I was so frustrated I could cry. "I told you he's not your killer. You're wasting time and effort looking for someone you shouldn't be looking for."

"Shouldn't? Holly, two men are dead and your life is in danger. Give me another alternative."

"I can't and you know it."

"Then answer me this: is he capable of murderin' someone?"

I pressed my lips together and glared at him. The answer to that question was a resounding yes. I had no doubt that if he hadn't taken a life yet, he would soon. I'd seen that eerie craving in his eyes.

"Did he try?" He must have read the answer in my face, because he asked, "What stopped him?"

I drew my feet in closer to my body. The scars on my feet were my reward for interfering with his plans. I had tried to stop him from killing someone, and he'd made sure doing so would be excruciating. "I did," I murmured.

Marx hesitated. "Was it you he tried to kill?"

That would depend on a person's definition of "tried to kill," because he'd certainly tried to shatter me into a thousand irreparable pieces on more than one occasion. "I'm not answering any more of your questions."

"If you won't tell me what I need to know, I have to work my way through every person on this list. But I will find him."

My name and information were in the local police database, and he'd just had my county compile a digital list of my information. It was only a matter of time. "You don't have to find him; he's gonna find me. Now please move," I said wearily as I slid off the bed.

Marx hesitated for just a moment, probably worried I was going to run, and then backed toward the wall by the couch to give me space. I stormed out of the apartment. I heard him start to call my name, but the slam of the front door overshadowed his voice.

I didn't run. As much as every instinct in my body begged me to run and never look back, I sat down against the front door and dropped my head into my hands.

"Hey! I was just coming to see you!" Jace said excitedly.

I looked up to see her wheeling down the sidewalk toward me. She stopped at the edge of the steps and looked around curiously. "Where's . . . ?" Her face twisted as she strained to remember the name of the officer who should have been standing guard in my front yard right now.

"Jacob?"

"Yes, that one."

"No Jacob. Marx gave him the day off."

All lightness drained from her face. "There's no one here? But what if . . . ?"

"Marx is here."

"Oh!" She brightened. She ran her fingers quickly through her wild, blue-tinged hair and smoothed out her shirt. "Is he inside?"

"Yep," I said through clenched teeth.

She narrowed her eyes. "Is he in the metaphorical dog house?"

"Yep."

"What did he do?"

"My job," I heard him declare grumpily through the door.

I spoke to Jace, but loudly enough that he could hear every word. "He's putting his nose where it shouldn't go."

"He's a detective, Holly. That's what they do. They snoop."

I sighed in exasperation and dropped my head back against the door. Being a detective didn't give him the right to tear apart my life in search of something that wasn't any of his business. I didn't know how to make him listen to me, to convince him that he was doing more damage than good.

I flinched when a massive pink box came flying toward me. Jace's sharp "Catch!" came too late to be helpful, and I barely caught it before it could smack me in the face.

"Have I insulted in you in some way that you feel the need to throw things at me?" I turned the box over curiously and shook it. Something heavy shifted around inside.

"It's a box, Holly, not a bomb. Just open it."

"Well, remind me when Christmas rolls around and I'll chuck your gift at your head. It'll be a new tradition." The box opened like a boot box, and I moved aside the tissue paper. I blinked at the pair of three-inch lime-green stiletto heels. I lifted one out of the box and examined it. "So . . . if I wanna kill myself but I want it to look like an accident, I wear these?"

Jace scowled at me. "Those are nice shoes."

"I think we define shoe differently." I placed it carefully back in the box.

"You could use a little height."

"You're four feet tall," I reminded her.

"Sitting. You're five two standing. You're stumpy."

"Hey!"

"A little more height makes you look intimidating. You could stand to be a little intimidating."

Unbelievable. "If I wear these in public, people are gonna offer to pay me for indecent services."

"They also double as a weapon," she said quickly. "You could totally stab somebody in the eye with that heel."

"Ew, why would I do that?"

"Well, if it comes down to you or his eye, I pick his eye."

I sighed and set the box of frightening shoes aside. "Jace, I appreciate that you care, but a pair of shoes is not gonna scare this guy away."

"I know." Her voice became soft, as it usually did when she was wrestling with emotions too heavy to put into words. "I just . . . I don't know how to help. I want you to be safe, and I just . . . I guess it was a dumb idea."

I would take ugly shoes over her tears and fear any day. "It was a . . . creative idea."

"They're really nice shoes."

I nodded and said, "They'll look really nice under my bed."

She laughed and some of the sadness and worry evaporated from her features. "I also wanted to see if you could come to basketball tonight."

"I don't know, Jace." I could probably convince Jacob to take me. Sam was a little bit more strict, but Marx would probably barricade the door with me inside if I so much as suggested going out in public. Then again, he couldn't really stop me. "Gimme a second."

I pushed myself to my feet and grabbed my box of shoes before opening the door. The moment I stepped inside, Marx said, "It's not a good idea, Holly."

I slid the box onto the counter and replied irritably, "And hiding is better?"

"If it keeps you safe, yes."

"I can't stay here until you catch him. I need to do something. Something that doesn't revolve around stalkers and death and . . . creepy stuffed animals."

He heaved an aggravated breath. "If you do this, I can't protect you. I will try, but there are too many things that can go wrong."

I stepped toward him. "It's a basketball game full of people in *wheelchairs*. I'm pretty sure a six-foot-four lunatic will stand out."

"You're not goin'."

"What are you gonna do to stop me? Handcuff me to the radiator?"

For a moment it looked as if he might actually consider it, and I took a wary step back. "Fine," he gritted out. "But if you ride in the car with her, you're puttin' her at risk."

"Then I'll ride with you," I replied with equal irritation.

14

I sat uncomfortably in the passenger seat of Marx's car, my body angled away from him as I gazed out the window. Red, yellow, and green lights streaked by in the darkness as we drove.

I couldn't help but wonder if my stalker was out there, still watching somehow. I shook that thought away before it could ruin my evening.

"Are you warm enough?" Marx asked. He reached across the car, and I stiffened before realizing he was just reaching for the heater dial. This arrangement made my personal bubble impossible. He caught the subtle shift in my posture and returned both hands to the wheel.

I slouched in my seat, torn between guilt and relief that he'd withdrawn his hand. "Sorry," I muttered.

"You have nothin' to be sorry for, Holly. I asked you for the chance to earn your trust. It's only been ten days. I don't expect miracles."

I was genuinely trying to trust him, but I wasn't there yet. I knew he would go to great lengths to keep me safe from the man stalking me, but I didn't trust him with my secrets, and I was *pretty* sure he would never hurt me. But people rarely showed you their true identity—just some socially acceptable version of it—and ten days wasn't long enough to know what actually lay beneath the shiny surface.

I snuck a glance at Marx. "Why are you doing this?"

"Why am I doin' what?"

"Protecting me."

A crease formed between his eyebrows, and he chanced a quick look in my direction. "It's my job."

"No, it's not. You're a detective. Your job is to investigate crimes. Your job description doesn't include bodyguard duty."

The corner of his mouth quirked up in a slight smile, but he didn't say anything. I sat up a little straighter and said, "None of you have to do this. Guarding me is putting you in danger."

"Holly, we're cops. We live and breathe danger. Every time we set foot on the street, every time we track down a suspect, we're at risk."

I considered that before asking, "Then why do it?"

He looked pensive for a moment, and then lifted a finger off the wheel to point at the car ahead of us: Jace's car. "If you knew somebody was tryin' to hurt your friend, would you step in to help her?"

"Yes."

He glanced at me. "No hesitation?"

"No." I would protect Jace with everything I had, which wasn't much. But I would try.

"That's why. An innate desire to protect those weaker or less able to protect themselves."

"I'm gonna tell Jace you think she needs protecting because she's in a wheelchair," I teased.

Marx smiled. "Of that I have no doubt."

There was a minute of silence as he concentrated on the road, and I thought about his answer. I wasn't sure I liked it. "So . . . you took my case because you think I'm weak?"

Marx shook his head with a smile. "How did I know that question was bouncin' around in that little head of yours?"

"My head is not little," I objected. "It's perfectly proportional to my body."

"Yes, yes, it is." He tapped his fingers on the wheel. "I took your case because it was assigned to me. And I knew from the start that somethin' wasn't right with it. Do I think you're weak?" He took another moment to carefully consider his answer. "The harsh truth is that men are physically stronger. Unless a woman is trained to defend herself, there's just no comparison. I wouldn't call you weak,

Holly, but you're certainly less able to protect yourself than some. And in this case, you're far outside your weight class."

I frowned as I tried to work through his answer. Outside my weight class. "Are you saying I'm fat?"

He laughed—actually laughed—and it made me smile despite the fact that I was pretty sure he'd just, in a roundabout way, called me chunky. "No," he said once his laughter faded. "Weight class is a boxin' and wrestlin' term. I mean you're outmatched."

Hmm. I wasn't so sure that was what he meant. I crossed my arms over the seat belt and looked out the front window at Jace's taillights. "So you, Jacob, and Sam volunteered to protect me around the clock because you don't think I can protect myself." Not that I had proved I could.

"I've worked a few minor stalkin' cases before. The stalker always escalates, and in some cases, we weren't called in until he'd already attacked the victim. Nobody died, but the resolutions weren't ideal. The man stalkin' you has already killed two people." He pulled his eyes from the road to look at me. "I didn't wanna find your body, Holly."

I swallowed uneasily. I shrank back down in my seat and let the matter drop. I didn't want to think about what he'd said. Jace pulled into the parking lot of the activity center, and we followed.

"Holly," Marx said quietly after we parked. "I have no doubt that he'll be in there somewhere. If he can, he'll take advantage of the fact that you're out in public just like he did at the hospital. Under no circumstances do you wander off. Are we clear?"

"I will stick to you like rubber cement." At his puzzled expression, I clarified, "It's . . . really cool . . . sticky stuff." I took a deep breath to calm my nerves and replied more sensibly, "No wandering. Promise."

"All right then."

We got out of the car and followed Jace into the building. She was vibrating with excitement. She was competitive by nature, though having an older brother so close in age had probably contributed to her love of sports and compulsive need to pulverize her opponent into dust.

The gymnasium was enormous, and there were three courts sectioned off by heavy black nets so more than one sport could be played simultaneously. The first court was abuzz with men, women, and children in wheelchairs. Jace wheeled into the fray with an overly cheerful, "Hey guys!"

Marx surveyed the room for danger as he followed me to the bleachers. I sat down on the lowest bench and bounced my legs as I waited for the game to start. I wasn't a fan of sports, but wheelchair basketball never failed to be entertaining.

"How exactly does this work?" Marx asked quietly as he found a comfortable spot to stand.

"They bounce a ball and then throw it in the hoop." He gave me a look, and I shrugged. "I don't do sports."

"Then why are we here?"

"Because Jace does sports."

I braced myself for some awkward social interaction when one of the guys spotted us and headed our way. He was a little older than me, with dark hair and moss-green eyes that occasionally faded to blue. I tried desperately to scrounge up his name before he reached us, but the unfortunate thing about wheels is their tendency to move quickly

He glided to a stop in front of me. "Hey, Holly." He grinned warmly.

"Hey . . . Craig," I said.

His grin widened. "Warren."

Right. One of these days I would remember that. I noticed that the red T-shirt he was wearing had my favorite Bible verse on it: Philippians 4:13—"I can do all things through Christ who strengthens me."

"You weren't here to see me crush Jace last week. I made a three-pointer to win the game."

"Did she throw a tantrum?"

He gave a noncommittal grunt. "She talks a lot of trash, but people who always lose tend to do that." He had raised his voice just a little so Jace could hear him as she came up behind him.

She took the comment in good humor, as it was intended. "This guy cheats," she declared, throwing a thumb in his direction.

"You're confusing cheating with skill," he threw back.

Jace rolled her eyes as she turned back toward the court. "Are you ready yet?"

"I've been ready. I was waiting on you."

"I'm gonna wipe the floor with you," she taunted.

"You gotta catch me first." He wheeled ahead of her with a burst of speed, and her skinny arms pumped frantically as she tried to catch up with him.

Marx stood in contemplative silence for a moment before asking, "Are they . . . together?"

"Nope. He's married. Happily."

The game started slowly, and then the ball blurred as it zipped back and forth between players, disappeared behind wheels, and occasionally flew in the complete wrong direction. Not all the players had the same physical capabilities as Jace and Warren. Despite their battle against each other on the court, they made every effort to pass the ball and include everyone.

Like traditional basketball, it had its moments of disaster. Some of the players collided head on, someone was accidentally elbowed in the head, and Jace flew forward out of her wheelchair and face-planted on the floor. I hissed through my teeth in sympathy.

"Should we help her?" Marx asked with a concerned look on his face.

"She's good."

Jace pushed herself up and, with more strength than anyone would know she had, climbed back into her wheelchair. The spill didn't even slow her down.

"That happens at least once a month," I told him. She occasionally got a little overexcited.

The remainder of the game played out without incident, and Jace and Warren parted ways with laughter and a few taunts about who would win the next game.

I waved good-bye to Jace from across the court as Marx ushered me toward the door. I knew she would want to mingle for a bit before heading home; she was a social butterfly, and she thrived in the type of social setting that made me want to slink away and hide.

Although we'd only been at the activity center for an hour and a half, the normalcy of it tempered some of the stress and fear that had been growing inside me for the past ten days. It was nice to feel normal again, if only for a little while.

Jacob was waiting outside the apartment when we arrived. I barely had my seat belt unsnapped before Marx opened my door. I climbed out and walked toward my apartment. Jacob smiled as I passed him.

I paused with my key in the door and turned around. "Marx." He was halfway into his car when I called him, and he stood up so I could see him. "Thank you. For tonight."

"You're quite welcome, Holly." He got back into his car and disappeared down the quiet street.

I looked at Jacob. "Where's Sam? I thought he usually covered the night shift."

"Usually, but his sister's having a rough night, so we traded shifts so he could take care of her." He gave me his boyish grin. "So you're stuck with me for the night and probably most of the morning."

"I guess I can live with that," I said with a small smile. "Goodnight, Jacob." I stepped inside and closed the door.

Despite the relaxing evening, I couldn't sleep. When I found myself staring at my ceiling at two a.m., I knew it was hopeless. I had tried everything from deep breathing to counting fluffy sheep, but nothing seemed to push me over the edge of tiredness into sleep.

I dragged myself out of bed and walked into the kitchen. Maybe something warm would help soothe me to sleep. I made a mug of hot chocolate with marshmallows for myself and made a second one for Jacob. I knew I wasn't the easiest person to protect, and I was starting to feel a little guilty for all the cold days and nights he and Sam had to spend on the lawn.

"Jacob, I'm coming out."

I opened the door and leaped back with a startled scream when something fell through the doorway. It landed on my kitchen floor with a muffled thump.

The mugs of hot chocolate shattered across the cement. I stared down at the body sprawled between the patio and my kitchen floor in momentary shock.

"Jacob?"

15

Jacob lay sprawled on his back on the floor, and there was a ribbon of blood across his throat. Shock froze me where I stood, and I could feel that familiar panic raking its claws against my insides.

And then his brown eyes blinked once. He was still alive. I dropped to my knees beside him and pressed my fingers to his wrist, just to be certain I hadn't imagined it. A quiet, irregular rhythm met my fingers, and I released the breath I hadn't known I was holding. He was alive.

He needed an ambulance. I glanced at the radio on his belt and then thought better of it. They used some sort of code or something.

I looked past him through the doorway at the wall of eerie blackness. The full moon was hidden behind a sheet of clouds, and all I could see were pockets of orange street lights.

"Hold on, Jacob."

I scrambled back to my side table and grabbed my phone. I dialed 9-1-1 as I sprinted back to the front door. I grabbed a towel off the counter and draped it over Jacob's throat. I pressed my hand down on the towel, hoping to slow the bleeding without cutting off his airway.

Please, God, don't let me kill him.

The dispatcher answered. "9-1-1 What is your emergency?"

"I have an officer . . . um . . . down. Jacob. He was guarding my door. He's bleeding."

Jacob blinked at the ceiling, but there was no sign of awareness in his eyes. I leaned over him. "Jacob." He gave no indication he heard me. "Jacob, help is coming."

When the towel beneath my hand was saturated, I threw it aside to grab another. My gaze caught my bloody hand, and I hesitated as memories pressed in on me. *Focus.* I forced my mind out of that dark room and away from the lump on the floor that could only be a body, and grabbed the fresh towel. I pressed it to Jacob's throat.

"Your name?" the dispatcher asked, and judging by her tone, it wasn't the first time she'd asked for my name.

"Holly," I answered after a brief hesitation. "Smith. Please call Detective Richard Marx. He knows . . ."

My voice trailed off when something shifted in the darkness outside. I saw it out of the corner of my eye, and I sat up straight. I stared into the dense blackness, but it gave nothing away.

"Holly," a deep, haunting voice called.

That voice . . . it sent a chill of recognition skittering down my spine. A figure moved by the main entrance to the apartment building, and I saw the street lamp glint off something metal in his hand.

The man started toward the open doorway, and terror made me drop the phone. It wasn't of any more use anyway. I looked down at Jacob. His body was blocking the doorway, and I couldn't close the door.

The man stalked closer, unhurriedly, like a predator who knew his prey had nowhere to go. The sound of his feet stepping carefully through the dead leaves raised the hairs on the back of my neck.

The sight of him drawing nearer made me want to run and hide, but that wasn't an option. There was no climbing out a window or hiding under the bed from this man.

"You can't run from me, Holly," the man taunted, as if he knew the desperate thoughts tumbling through my head.

A fragment of memory slid into place: I was running through the woods at night, desperate to find a place to hide, when those words, in that voice, echoed through the trees around me.

It did nothing to help me survive now, so I blocked out the memory and tried to think. I looked at the knife drawer as I weighed my options. The killer had a knife, and he'd slit Jacob's throat with it. I could barely cut a tomato without taking off my own finger.

I didn't like my chances.

I had nothing else to defend us with. Our only hope of survival was the door that was standing wide open. I locked my fingers around Jacob's wrists and heaved.

He was somewhere around 170 pounds, and I felt like my head would burst from the pressure as I tried to move an immovable object. My feet slipped in the spilled hot chocolate, and my legs nearly went out from under me.

The man who walked toward my apartment was dressed entirely in black, making him seem like little more than an apparition in the night. But the blade gleamed in his hand. I remembered Cambel's tortured body, the words carved into him, and wondered if that was the knife.

This man wasn't just a stalker; he was a killer.

Desperate, I pulled harder, and Jacob slid an inch at a time across the floor. Why did he have to be so heavy? I gritted my teeth and pulled for both our lives. His boots snagged on the threshold.

Come on, come on, come on . . . stupid shoes!

The killer reached the top of the steps, and I knew we weren't going to make it. I dropped Jacob's arms and pulled the gun from his holster. I didn't know how to use one of these things.

It was heavier than it looked.

There was usually a magic button somewhere—a switch to make it work, a safety thing—but I had no idea what I was looking for. I could only hope it would work if I needed it to. I lifted the gun in both shaking hands and aimed it at the killer.

He hesitated on the steps.

He was at least as big as Cambel, and he was fifteen feet away. I couldn't let him come any closer. If he made it through the doorway, Jacob and I were both dead. I rested my finger on the trigger. If I fired, I was bound to hit him somewhere . . .

"You won't shoot me, Holly," the man said. I hated the way he said my name, as if he liked the taste of it on his tongue. But he wasn't as certain as he pretended to be. He'd hesitated.

"I'll try," I promised. I didn't want to shoot him, but I would. I needed to get the door closed. I trusted the metal door; I didn't trust this weapon in my hands. Help needed to come before I accidentally killed us all or some poor pedestrian.

I stepped forward slowly and kept the gun trained on the killer as I tried to nudge Jacob's legs aside with my feet. He would wind up twisted like a pretzel on my kitchen floor, but that was infinitely better than dead.

"You always were the brave sister," the man said.

I recognized this man's voice, but it didn't belong to my foster brother. It was older and deeper. Marx was very wrong. There *were* two of them, but convincing him of that would be nearly impossible.

"I don't have a sister."

"Not anymore."

For some reason, his response was like a punch to the gut. It made me feel like I'd lost something precious I didn't even remember having.

He took another slow step forward. "Stop," I demanded. My voice shook as much as my hands.

"You value life too much to take it, Holly. You were the one who cried when you saw the kitten dying on the front porch. Someone had slit the poor thing's throat. What was its name? Buttercup?"

His soft-spoken words struck a nerve in my memories. I didn't remember the kitten, but the grief of a child who'd lost her pet seeped through me.

"You're starting to remember," he said, and there was a hint of pleasure in his voice. "I can see it in your beautiful brown eyes. The fear, the confusion . . ."

The man twisted the knife in his hand as he took another step forward. He wasn't going to listen to me. He was going to force me either to pull the trigger or to back down, and I suspected he thought I would back down.

The pressure of the leg against my ankle reminded me that, no matter how much I didn't want to pull this trigger, it wasn't just my life on the line. Jacob was dying on my floor.

"Please stop," I begged.

He took another measured step forward.

I kept my eyes open, but I didn't remember anything but a blinding sound after I squeezed the trigger. The bang that reverberated around my apartment was petrifying, and I found myself crouched by the open doorway a moment later with my hands over my ears. The gun was still in my right hand.

Good grief, I was going to accidentally shoot myself in the head. Before I could drop the gun, I saw movement on the steps out of the corner of my vision. I scrambled over Jacob's legs for the door.

Jacob was just far enough out of the way that I was able to slam it shut. The killer turned the knob and pushed before I could bolt it, and I let out a yelp of terror as my feet slid backwards. I pushed, but I had no traction. He forced me back with ridiculous ease until my feet connected with Jacob's side.

My arms were exhausted and trembling from dragging Jacob, and if the killer wanted in badly enough, he could probably just blow on the door and knock me over. I felt him lean his weight against it, and I whimpered from the added stress.

And then suddenly the resistance was gone and I fell into the door, knocking it shut. I bolted it with practiced quickness and hunkered down with the gun gripped tightly between my knees. I was afraid to put it down; what if he came through a window? They were narrow, but if he was a contortionist, he might manage it.

"You're mine, Holly," the man whispered through the door, and I shuddered.

I braced myself for violent slamming on the door or shouts of rage, but there was only the distant wail of sirens. I closed my eyes as relief washed over me. Help was coming.

I wondered if the police had scared the killer off or if this visit had only been intended to terrify me. If terror was his goal, he deserved a gold sticker. I was still shaking when heavy pounding erupted on the door minutes before the sirens arrived.

"Holly," Marx called. I could hear the fear in his voice. The dispatcher had called him, and the news she would've relayed wouldn't have sounded promising. Of course he would be the first to arrive.

I stood slowly and opened the door. Marx looked rumpled from a night of interrupted sleep, but his eyes were alert. I caught the subtle stiffening of his shoulders as he looked me over. "Holly," he said carefully, "Give me the gun."

I looked down at the gun in my right hand. My finger was still poised over the trigger. Oh . . . I'd forgotten I was still holding that. I removed my finger and placed the weapon carefully into Marx's palm with a shaky hand. I was happy to be rid of it.

Marx's shoulders relaxed a fraction as he breathed, "Thank you" and handed the weapon to someone behind him. His hand came back to grip his own gun, which he angled toward the ground. "Where is he? Where did he go?"

It took a moment for my brain to catch up. He was looking for the killer. Everything had happened so quickly that I couldn't remember. "I don't know."

I saw uniformed officers spreading out behind him, searching the property for the killer. I couldn't even give them a direction.

"I . . . shot at him," I said numbly. "He didn't think I would do it."

"I imagine he was unpleasantly surprised," he grumbled. He shifted his weight so I could see past him to the bullet that had been mangled by the cement steps. "Unfortunately, you missed. And you're lucky it didn't ricochet back. Do you even know how to use a gun?"

I stared at the bullet as I muttered, "I just took a crash course." There was a pained expression on his face that I expected all members of law enforcement got when they found out a clueless person had just fired a gun. "I didn't have a choice. Jacob . . ."

113

I opened the door so he could see the body sprawled out across my kitchen floor.

"Was the killer in here?" he asked from the threshold.

"No."

He slid his gun back in its holster before stepping inside. He knelt on one knee beside Jacob and checked for a pulse at his wrist. "Paramedics!" he shouted over his shoulder, and then looked at me. "What happened?"

"I opened the door to give him a hot chocolate and he was against the door. He just . . . fell. But his throat—"

Two paramedics hurried through the doorway, and Marx moved out of their way. He caught my arm lightly and guided me into the living room. I stumbled as my eyes lingered on Jacob.

"Is he . . . ?"

"They're gonna do everythin' they can." He tried to sound reassuring, but I could hear the fear in his voice. He cared a great deal about Jacob.

I melted onto the edge of the couch as I watched the paramedics work on the young officer. His color was fading.

"Holly," Marx said, drawing me back to the moment. "Did he hurt you?"

I shook my head.

"Did he say anythin'?"

I shivered again as I remembered his last words to me. "He said 'You're mine, Holly'." I couldn't mask my fear when I looked at him.

His expression was carefully neutral, but his voice was soothing as he said, "It's gonna be okay. Did he say anythin' else?"

"When I pointed the gun at him, he said I was always the brave sister."

Marx frowned. "I thought you didn't have a family."

"I don't. I have . . . a dozen foster sisters, but . . . I don't think that's what he meant. When I told him I didn't have a sister, he said 'not anymore'."

"Detective," a female officer said as she strode across the apartment to meet us at the couch. There was a small, plain box in her gloved hand. "This was left on the patio."

She removed the lid and tilted the box so we could see the contents. There was a small, stained collar that probably would've fit around the neck of a kitten. She removed the photo beneath it with gentle, gloved fingers and held it up for us to see.

A small, red-haired girl sat on the steps of a porch, cradling a white kitten in her lap. She stared at the photographer with bright honey-brown eyes and an impish smile.

The collar in the box was the same band that was around the kitten's neck. And there was something silvery on the girl's left wrist—a piece of jewelry. I lifted my arm and rubbed the old, worn bracelet on my wrist.

"This looks an awful lot like you," Marx pointed out.

"That's because it is me." I had no doubt about that, but I couldn't remember a single detail about that moment. The killer knew things about my past that I didn't even know, which tipped the odds even more in his favor. We weren't getting any closer to finding him because we had none of the information. I realized in that moment: in order to survive this . . . I needed to find a way to unlock my memories.

16

I scrubbed at the dark stain on my kitchen floor, but it refused to come clean. This was the fifth time I had returned to it—after cleaning my bathroom and my refrigerator and even attacking the dust bunnies under the bed—but it wouldn't disappear.

A stranger walking through my door wouldn't see blood, but I would never be able to look at it without seeing it. Jacob's blood had become a permanent focal point of my home.

Surrendering, I pushed myself to my feet and grabbed the rug Jace hated. I arranged it over the stain and then stepped over it. It would have to do for now. I walked to the door and tapped quietly with my knuckles.

Sam released a patient sigh on the other side. "You're like clockwork. That's the second time this hour. You know you don't have to keep checking on me, Holly."

I did, though. The killer had snuck up on Jacob and attacked him without anyone hearing a sound. I didn't want the same to happen to Sam.

"I prefer you breathing," I told him through the door.

"Stop worrying about me."

I unlocked the door and cracked it so I could see him through the narrow opening. Apart from looking exhausted, he was alive and well. "Are you gonna stop worrying about me?"

His lips curved into a thin smile. "No."

"Then we've reached a stalemate."

I closed the door on his quiet grunt of amusement and returned to scrubbing the walls and baseboards. There had to be a speck of dust somewhere, and I was going find it.

A car door slamming broke the monotony of my cleaning almost an hour later, and my attention shifted to the door; I hadn't locked it after I checked on Sam. The flutter of anxiety in my chest calmed when I heard Sam say, "Marx."

"I need to talk to Holly," Marx replied, but his tone sounded more tense than usual.

I heard Sam shift away from the door to let him pass, but there was a hint of uncertainty in his voice as he said, "I'm not sure that's the best idea."

Marx came through my door a second later and slammed it behind him. His eyes were puffy and bloodshot, and his face was a tempest of barely controlled emotion.

The anger in his movements brought me to my feet. Staying on the floor made me feel too vulnerable. He threw the folder that contained the list of my foster homes onto the table and flipped it open.

"I want answers, Holly, and I want them now." His voice was so tight it was on the verge of snapping.

"I don't have any answers for you."

He squeezed his eyes shut in an obvious effort to control his emotions. "No more secrets. Stop protectin' him."

"I'm not protecting him. I don't —"

He slammed his hands on the table, and I flinched. "Stop, Holly!"

Marx never yelled or slammed things, and I wasn't sure what to make of it. The eyes that held me smoldered with anger and grief, and while I didn't want to believe he would hurt me, my instincts urged me to back away.

I bumped into the wall behind me. "Is Jacob —"

"Jacob's dead."

His declaration startled me more than the low vibration of anger in his voice. I struggled to digest the news that Jacob had died. It was hard to reconcile it with the memory of the young man with the boyish smile and big brown eyes.

I didn't know him well enough to cry for him, but the tightening in my chest told me I wouldn't escape the guilt and temporary grief that his death would leave behind.

"This man slit his throat and left him on your doorsteps like a gift for you to find." Marx's voice was quiet with pain. "He was twenty-six years old, Holly. An only child. What am I supposed to tell his family when their flight arrives?"

An only child . . .

Jacob had been a casualty of this lunatic's desire to taunt me. Guilt made my voice waver. "I'm sorry about Jacob."

Marx sighed heavily. "I don't blame you for that. But I need you to help me before this man kills somebody else. I need you to tell me the truth, Holly, who he is, how I can find him, and what he wants from you."

"I told you the truth," I said quietly. I recognized the man's voice, but I didn't know his name. I wasn't sure I had ever known his name.

"No, you haven't. You have more secrets than the president. You dodge my questions every chance you get."

"Maybe you're asking the wrong questions," I challenged. His hands fisted on the table, and I took another cautious step back along the wall. *Or maybe I should keep my mouth shut.*

"I want his name."

"I don't have his name."

"A cop is dead!" he shouted, and I cringed at the dangerous volume of his voice. It could've been the emptiness of my apartment that exaggerated its booming quality, but that didn't make it any less frightening.

He's not gonna hurt me. He's just upset, I told myself. But in my experience, this kind of anger was often a stepping stone to violence. I tried to take slow, steady breaths through my nose to stay calm, but I was pretty sure I was panting like a racehorse.

"This isn't just about you anymore," he continued. "He crossed a line when he killed Jacob, when he killed a cop. The NYPD will not let this stand. They will tear this case apart, and you had better not be standin' in their way when they do, Holly."

I wrapped my arms around myself as the true meaning of his statement hit me. He wasn't just talking about the NYPD; he was talking about himself. He cared about Jacob, and in his eyes I was standing between him and the identity of the man who killed him.

"No more games, Holly. No more twenty questions," he said, and I could see the effort it took for him to keep his voice level. He rested his hand on the list of foster homes and said with strained patience, "Who is he?"

I swallowed the same old argument that sprang up in my throat—there were only so many times I could tell him he had the wrong person—but my silence only seemed to enrage him further. I cringed into the wall behind me when he slammed his hands on the table hard enough to hurt and shouted, "What. Is. His. Name!"

"Marx," Sam said with enviable calm. He had opened the door and stepped inside.

"What, Sam?" Marx ground through his teeth.

"You're angry and you're grieving. I don't think this is the best time to have this conversation."

Marx shot Sam an impatient look. "This man killed Jacob. There is no better time."

"You're scaring her."

His words dropped into the silence like a bomb, and I saw Marx draw back with a startled blink before turning his gaze on me.

I stayed pressed against the wall as I watched him warily, wondering what he would do next. If he lost it again, I was ducking for cover.

"Holly . . . ," he began.

I slid toward the bathroom when he stepped forward. He stilled, visually tracking my movement towards the small room where I'd hidden from him the last time he'd made me "uncomfortable." He swore quietly under his breath, grabbed the file off the table, and walked out of my apartment.

I released a shaking breath before sliding down the wall to the floor. I dropped my head into my hands and ran my fingers through my hair.

"I know he can seem pretty intense when he loses his temper, but he would never hurt you."

I glanced at Sam, who hovered awkwardly by the open front door. He looked ready to make a quick exit if I burst into tears, but I had no intention of crying.

I wished I could be as certain as he was about Marx. But we hadn't known each other long enough for me to be completely sure he wouldn't hurt me, and it was that shadow of doubt that kept me from shouting back.

Sam sighed when I didn't say anything. "He doesn't have any kids; his ex-wife didn't want any, and Jacob was . . . as close as he was ever gonna get to a son."

He was grieving.

"He's hurt and angry right now, and the only way he knows how to deal with it is to find the person who killed Jacob. He'll settle down, and then he'll regret this conversation," he explained.

I regretted that conversation.

"Why does he think you know the killer's name?"

I puffed out a breath and tucked my hair behind my ears. "He's convinced the killer is someone I grew up with, but he's wrong. And I've told him so, but he won't listen."

"How do you know he's wrong?"

"Because if the killer was someone I grew up with, we would've been children together. Children's voices change as they grow older." I met his eyes, desperate for him to understand what I was saying. "But Sam, I recognize this man's voice, because when I heard it eighteen years ago, it was exactly the same."

I wasn't sure why, but I knew—all the way to my bones— that the man who had killed Jacob was a part of the reason I couldn't remember the first ten years of my life.

17

I sat on a blanket against the inside of my front door with my sketchbook, charcoal, and a bowl of miniature marshmallows. I popped one of the marshmallows into my mouth.

The more people who passed through my apartment, the less secure it felt. I didn't intend to let anyone else in for a while, even if they pried the keys away from my landlord.

There was a quiet double tap on the outside of the door, and I glanced at the clock on the microwave. Sam. I couldn't let go of my fear that he would wind up dead just like Jacob. We had settled on an hourly check-in during the day. I tapped back. He was safe. I was safe. We could both breathe a little easier.

I was finishing up the last few details of what should've been a sketch of a butterfly when Sam said, a little more loudly than necessary, "Marx."

He was giving me a heads up.

"I'm on my best behavior, Sam. I just wanna talk to her," Marx said in his normal relaxed drawl.

I hadn't seen Marx since yesterday morning when he stormed out of my apartment. I stopped drawing and sat up a little straighter.

"I'll give you two some privacy," Sam said.

"Holly," Marx called quietly through the door. His voice was as smooth as honey. He was trying very hard not to sound threatening.

"I don't really wanna talk to you." I propped my knees up and continued shading in the image with the small piece of charcoal.

"May I come in?"

My fingers stilled at his request. The last time he'd been in my home, it had left me rattled. "No."

"Then will you come out?"

"Nope."

I'd hoped my refusal to let him in would send him on his way, but I heard him sit down on the other side of the door with a regretful sigh.

"That's okay. I can wait until you're ready," he said.

I set down the piece of charcoal with delicate care despite my frustration. "What do you want from me, *Detective?*"

He was quiet for a moment. "I owe you an apology for yesterday. I had just come from the hospital, and I was . . . not myself."

I could hear the pain in his voice. Losing Jacob had hurt him deeply, and even now he was struggling with it. "I'm sorry for what happened to Jacob."

Marx made a quiet noise in the back of his throat that sounded like pain. "It's not your fault, Holly, but knowin' you, I expect you think it is."

"He was out there to keep me safe."

"He volunteered."

I blinked back the tears that burned my eyes and released a shuddering breath. "That doesn't make it better."

"I know."

He fell silent, and I returned my attention to the sketch in my lap, trying to focus all the pain and confusion into the image I was creating.

"Holly, I'm sorry," Marx said, and I could hear the genuine regret in his voice. "I asked you to give me a chance to earn your trust, and then I came into your home and scared you. I had no right to do that. I expect you've had enough scare in your life without me bein' a part of it."

Trust was a fragile thing—easily shattered and difficult to repair—and I wasn't sure how I felt about him now.

"But it's important to me that you know—no matter how angry I get, no matter what I say or do in that anger—I will *never* put my hands on you. I was so wrapped up in my own anger and pain that I didn't recognize my own stupidity until Sam pointed it out. And I'm sorry for that."

Despite being overwhelmed by anger and grief yesterday, he had still respected my physical boundaries by staying behind the table and away from the door.

"My tenth foster father had a temper," I said. "It usually kicked in around his fourth beer. We tried to hide them from him once, but that didn't work out so well. There were three of us, and we learned to scatter pretty quickly."

I wasn't sure why I felt compelled to share that with him. Maybe to convince myself he never would've crossed that line, or maybe I just needed him to know I understood the difference between his emotional outburst and the actual threat of violence. He'd caught me off guard yesterday, but I recognized the difference.

"What happened?" he asked.

I rubbed my fingers across the white edges of my drawing, leaving charcoal smudges as I recalled the events that had brought an end to my stay in my tenth foster home. "We had a class project, a simulated volcano, and my foster brother and I worked together on it. We named it Mount Nicolas, after our foster father."

"Because he erupted?"

"Yep."

"Fittin'."

"I thought so," I said. "We even put a little moat of beer around it."

He chuckled on the other side of the door. "Why do I get the feelin' that was your idea?"

"Yeah," I said as I remembered the maelstrom of consequences that followed that project. When it came to light that we had free access to alcohol in our foster home, someone was sent to investigate.

If I'd known then what waited for me in my next foster home, I would never have made that volcano. At least my drunken foster father had somewhat prepared me for what would come next.

"What happened then?"

"We were removed, separated, and sent to different homes."

"That happened a lot for you, didn't it?"

"Only like . . . ten or twelve times," I replied, trying to keep my tone light. I had run away from some of my placements, including my tenth one, but the police had tracked me down and taken me back.

"That must have been difficult."

"Yeah, well, nobody's childhood is perfect."

I puffed out a heavy breath and pushed myself to my feet. I gathered up my blankets and notebook and set them on the table. I knew I couldn't hide behind this door forever, not if I wanted this madness to end, and I needed to find a way to put Marx on the right track.

I steeled myself before unlocking the door and pulling it inward a fraction. It would be fine . . .

Marx climbed to his feet on the patio, looking just as tired and threadbare as he had yesterday, but I saw only guilt and sadness in his eyes.

I kept one hand on the door as I silently debated whether or not to let him in, and he waited patiently for an invitation. "Don't *ever* yell at me again," I warned him.

"If I do, you're welcome to smack me."

I narrowed my eyes at him. "Why, so you can arrest me for assaulting a police officer?"

His eyebrows drew together. "Holly, if I arrested a woman your size for smackin' me, I would be the laughin' stock of the department."

I rolled my eyes and stepped aside to let him in. He walked into my kitchen and stood by the table, giving me the space he knew I wanted.

I closed the door and turned to find him studying my sketch with wrinkles of confusion across his forehead. "Is this a flyin' sausage?"

I gritted my teeth. "It's a butterfly."

"Why does it look like it went through a blender?"

Really? A blender? I snatched my notebook off the table and flipped it shut before he could offer up any more insults. "I assume you came here for some reason other than insulting my artwork."

"I just wanted to make sure you were all right."

Oh. That was . . . thoughtful. I tucked my hands into the back pockets of my jeans and tried not to look awkward. "I'm fine."

He caught sight of the bowl of marshmallows on the counter and smiled. "You have a thing for marshmallows."

I grabbed my bowl of marshmallows protectively. "It's practically a food group. Marshmallows, chocolate, and then everything else."

He arched an eyebrow. "I'm not sure marshmallows are even in the food pyramid."

"Maybe not yours." I popped a marshmallow into my mouth. "Are you hungry? Do you . . . want some food? I have Swiss rolls somewhere." Actually, I was pretty sure I'd stashed those in my feminine hygiene box under the bathroom sink. "Or Nacho Doritos." Those were safely in the cupboard.

One habit I learned in foster care that had stuck with me was to hide my food if I wanted to keep it. In foster homes it had a tendency to vanish into thin air, and shockingly, no one ever saw a thing. Not even the kid still licking the powdered cheese from his fingers while hiding your chip bag behind his back.

"I'm not particularly hungry."

"I have chocolate milk."

"No," he said quickly, and at my puzzled frown he added, "But thank you." He glanced around the apartment, probably noticing that it reeked of bleach and ammonia. I had scrubbed everything until my hands hurt. "Your wall isn't finished."

"Yeah, I'm not tall enough," I said as I glared at the three inches of zigzagging yellow paint between the ceiling and the fresh coat of purple.

"Even with the chair?"

I released an exasperated breath. "Even with the chair."

Marx stripped off his jacket and laid it over the blanket on the table. When he unbuttoned his sleeves and started to roll them up, I gave him a wary look. "Whaaat are you doing?"

"Finishin' your wall."

"You don't have to do —"

"Where's the paint?" he asked, ignoring my protest. He looked at me expectantly until I folded and grabbed it from under the kitchen sink. I gathered the roller and paint tray as well, and he took them into the living room. "So purple is your favorite color, huh?"

"Not this purple."

"What kind of purple?" He shifted the couch aside with embarrassing ease. That had taken me a lot longer to move.

"Eggplant purple."

He grunted. "Eggplant. That is not one of God's finer vegetables. Ranks right up there with Brussels sprouts and spaghetti squash. That is not spaghetti." He picked up the folding chair and set it down in front of the wall. When he climbed up with the roller, his head was less than a foot from my ceiling.

A small flicker of jealousy passed through me.

I stood uselessly off to the side as he filled in the unpainted portions of the wall. It may not have been my favorite purple, but it was worlds better than pee yellow.

"You missed a spot," I teased.

He gave me a flat, unamused look. "I did *not* miss a spot."

As he added a second coat of paint to the entire wall, I pondered how to approach our miscommunication problem. I needed him to believe my foster brother wasn't the killer. If he continued working under the assumption that he was, then he wasn't trying to find the man who was actually responsible for the pictures . . . and the bodies.

My fear was that the only way Marx would believe me was if he saw the truth for himself. That meant I had to give him a name. I didn't want to open that door, because there was no closing it.

But Jacob . . .

This man had murdered him and left him on my doorstep. Someone needed to find him and put an end to this before anyone else got hurt. All things considered, the decision was obvious, but that didn't make it any easier to accept.

I stared at the finished wall as I considered my words carefully. "I think . . ." My voice trailed off as I struggled to find the courage to continue. "I think I'm ready."

"Ready for what?" Marx asked as he climbed down from the chair and laid the roller back into the tray of paint.

"To tell you the name of the man responsible for the extra dead bolts on my door." A small tremor started in my voice, and I couldn't seem to will it away.

Marx's expression turned carefully neutral. "Okay."

"He's not the man who killed Jacob, and the only way you're gonna believe that is to see it for yourself. So I'll tell you his name under three conditions."

He didn't look thrilled that we were negotiating information again, but after his outburst yesterday, I didn't expect he would put up much of a fight. He rolled down his shirt sleeves and buttoned them as he sat down on the furthest arm of the couch. "I'm listenin'."

"I'll tell you what you need to know about him, but after that, no more digging. You don't ask me any more questions about him or . . . or about anything he did to me."

He studied me for a long moment before saying, "Okay. If he's not our guy and he's not an immediate threat, I promise I won't ask anythin' else."

That wasn't exactly the answer I was looking for, but it was probably the best I would get from a detective. They were addicted to unraveling mysteries, and my past was certainly a mystery.

"Fine," I agreed. "He grew up in Maine. I don't know where he is now. But I'm sure you'll find him. When you do, you can't give any indication that you know me."

He frowned. "Why not?"

Fear made my voice sharp. "You just can't."

"All right," Marx said with deliberate calm. "What's your third condition?"

"You can't talk to him."

"Holly, I have to —"

"You *cannot* talk to him!"

A muscle flexed in Marx's jaw as he clenched his teeth. "You do understand that as a cop, a part of my job is interrogatin' suspects, which does in fact require me to talk to them."

This wasn't an issue I was willing to budge on. "Then I can't give you his name."

He shifted on the arm of the couch, visibly frustrated, and pressed his hands together in front of his mouth as if he were going to pray. He sat that way for a moment as he tried to make sense of my conditions. "*Why* can't I talk to him?"

"Because he'll figure it out."

"Figure what out?"

"This," I said, gesturing to everything around me: my home, my few belongings, the woman upstairs who meant more to me than anyone else on this earth. "I told you he found me before. He's found me three times in the past ten years. Sometimes I see him coming, but last time . . ." My throat tightened against the words.

Marx's lips thinned.

"I was so careful not to leave a trail, but when he wants to find me, he always finds a way. With my information in your database and the fact that you had information about my foster homes sent to you, I know I don't have much time. But I want that time. Every second of it."

Marx didn't speak right away. "For the sake of argument, this man is not our killer, and you're afraid that if he finds out I'm in some way connected to you, he'll follow me here," he summarized. "And he'll do what?"

I hugged myself. That was one of those things I wasn't sure I would ever be able to talk about. "If he finds me and I don't see him coming, then . . . I hope you get assigned my case."

Marx blinked as he absorbed the implications of my answer, and then something icy slid beneath his careful expression. "Give me his name."

I drew in an unsteady breath and gave him the name I hadn't spoken to anyone in almost twelve years. "Collin Wells."

18

I brushed aside the sheer curtains over my kitchen sink and squinted into the darkness at the uniformed officer standing like a statue in my front yard. Sam had introduced us the other night. He was Jacob's replacement.

I was pretty sure his name was something vaguely feminine like Marilyn or Meredith. I decided that if I ever spoke to him, I would just call him "Officer." Then I would get it right either way.

His face was hard to forget. It looked like someone had taken a strip of leather and stretched it over a skeleton. There was no softness to him.

"That guy creeps me out," Jace announced from my living room. She was running a thoughtful finger above the playing cards lying face down on my floor.

I gave her a chiding look as I walked back into the living room. "He's trying to help protect me, so don't be so mean."

She rolled her eyes at me and returned her attention to the cards. "Red two, red two . . . where are you . . ." She held the red two of diamonds in her hand, and was trying to match it with the two of hearts. She loved memory games.

I slid my hands into the back pockets of my jeans and watched silently as she tried to puzzle it out. She hesitated over every card and then moved on. She hated to lose, even to herself apparently.

I was going to turn eighty-five before she picked a card. "Middle row, second from the left."

She flipped it over and scowled at the two of hearts. "How . . . ?"

I grinned. "It has a little Cheetos smudge on the corner from the last time we played."

Jace laughed. "You're such a cheater." She pulled the pair out of the playing field and set them aside. She flipped over an eight of spades, and the hunt began for its mate. "So what do you think of Sam?"

I gave her a puzzled look. "Serious, focused, no-nonsense kind of guy . . . but he's also very competent and I think he cares." Though it was sometimes hard to tell. "Why?"

She grinned sheepishly. "No reason."

Ha! She had a crush on my bodyguard. "What happened with Gale?"

She had tried at least twice to have a date with him since all this began, and I felt like such a selfish person for forgetting to ask long before now how it had gone.

"Eh," she said, giving me a so-so gesture with her hand. "He wanted to touch my feet."

"Excuse me?"

She huffed and set the card down as she looked up at me. "He has an amazing accent. I could listen to him talk all day long, but the man has serious foot issues. I can't feel my feet, which I mentioned when he asked, and he wanted to know if he could touch them right there in the restaurant. He actually asked if he could remove my shoe for me."

I covered my mouth as I tried not to burst out laughing, but her appalled expression did me in and I laughed until I couldn't breathe. "In the restaurant?"

"He asked if I would enjoy having my toenails painted. A pale peach color, because he was *quite fond* of peaches." She rolled her eyes. "He probably cancelled the first date so he could give his mother a foot massage," she grumbled. "Seriously . . . that's the kind of guy you find sniffing your shoes when you walk in the room. That is just . . . too much for me."

She tried to be bitter about it, but the absurdity of it was just too much to ignore, and we spiraled into an uncontrollable laughing fit. After everything that had happened, it felt refreshing just to laugh.

131

"Feet," I gasped as the moment faded and I wiped the tears from my cheeks. I couldn't remember the last time joy had brought me to tears. I dropped to my knees on the floor next to Jace as she dried her own face. "Do you think he goes to shoe stores in his spare time and fondles the shoes?" I asked.

Another laugh bubbled out of Jace, and she struggled to control it. "Stop, just stop," she pleaded. "My sides hurt." She picked up her eight of spades and tried to find the mate through tear-glazed eyes. I gave her a moment to look and then pointed to the correct card. She flipped it to find the eight of clubs. "Stop doing that," she protested, but she was laughing when she said it.

"You're terrible at this game. Maybe you should quit while you're ahead."

She stuck her nose in the air and adopted an atrocious English accent as she declared, "I *eschew* that kind of talk." A quiet squeak of amusement escaped me at her "shoe" pun.

A loud knock at the door drew our laughter to an abrupt close. The heavy weight of reality settled over the room as I gathered my legs beneath me and walked into the kitchen.

"Oh, could you toss me my root beer?"

I grabbed the nearly empty bottle off the table and tossed it to her before climbing back on my chair to see who was at the door. Officer Meredith stood outside on the patio, his expression pinched.

We'd disturbed him with our laughter.

I opened the door and his beady eyes swept over the apartment suspiciously. He looked down at me and asked, "I heard a lot of noise. Is everything okay in here?"

I tried to stop myself, but I just couldn't help it. I had to say it. "No worries, Officer. Nothing is *afoot*."

Jace choked and spewed her root beer all over the floor behind me. I bit down on my lips to contain the laugh tickling the back of my throat.

Officer Meredith's beady eyes narrowed as the joke breezed past him. "Okay. I'll be right out front if you need me."

I closed the door, locked it, and dropped back against it with a quiet laugh.

"I can't believe you pulled out the word *afoot*," Jace said.

I pushed away from the door and walked back into the living room. "At least I didn't say *eschew*. Who says that?" I sat back down on the floor with her and crossed my legs, eyeing the spread of cards as she tried to line up her next pair. "So . . . Sam, huh?"

She blushed. "I don't know. He's cute, but you're right about the no-nonsense thing. I wonder if he even understands jokes." She pulled up the edge of a card and peeked at it before setting it back down with a frown. "And then there's the fact that he's a cop, which is a major drawback."

Jace didn't share my dislike of law enforcement, so I wasn't sure I understood her meaning.

She sighed and there was a seriousness to her face that hadn't been there a moment ago. "I know he's not interested in me. But what if I let myself like him and he . . . ends up like Jacob?"

My insides twisted with regret. "I worry about that too."

"They're supposed to worry about you, not the other way around."

I shrugged and tapped a card. She flipped it over and gave me a flat look. She picked it up and set it aside with the matching card before drawing another.

"I don't really understand how you're holding it together," she said. "You're always protected, but he seems to be able to get to you anyway. Doesn't that scare you?"

It terrified me. "A little."

"So what do we do?"

"I have to remember," I told her as I drew my knees to my chest and wrapped my arms around them. "He's in there somewhere."

"He who?"

"The man who's doing all this."

"Have you told Marx about your memory problems?"

I returned the flat stare she'd given me earlier. "Why would I do that?"

"Because if the killer is from that forgotten part of your life, he needs to know. Your lack of memory is a huge curveball for his investigation. You should tell him."

I had already given Marx Collin's name. How many more secrets would I have to share before this was all over?

"I know how hard it is for you to share private things, but I think Marx is trustworthy. I don't think he'll judge you or broadcast your secrets to the world. He's just trying to help you."

"Maybe," I conceded.

There was another knock at the door, but it was quieter than before, as if the person on the other side of the door was making an effort not to startle me. I only knew two people who would take that much care.

"Holly, it's Marx."

Fear fluttered through my stomach. He shouldn't have been back this soon. He'd only left a week ago to track down Collin. Something must have happened.

I walked to the door slowly and unbolted it. I peered at Marx through the crack. "Why are you back so soon?"

"May we come in?"

I glanced beyond his shoulder to see Sam. Sam wasn't on duty for a few more hours, and it was strange to see him in street clothes.

I stepped back to let them in. Their grim expressions made me wonder if someone else had died. I leaned to see past them into the yard. Nope, Officer Statue was still present and accounted for.

"Ms. Walker," Marx greeted.

Jace froze for just an instant when she saw Sam come through the door in his street clothes. He looked entirely different in a sweater and jeans.

The expression on Jace's face told me Sam had just moved up the rank from cute to something more in her mind. Great. Now I would worry even more about him dying. Because I needed that pressure . . .

"Holly." Sam greeted me with a nod.

"Sam," I replied, trying to mimic his flat, deep voice.

A ghost of a smile crossed his lips.

"I need a word with Holly alone," Marx said.

Jace glanced at me with uncertainty. She didn't want to leave me alone with what was apparently going to be bad news. "It's fine," I said after a moment of hesitation. If we were going to discuss Collin, I didn't want her here.

"I'll make sure she gets home safely," Sam announced.

Jace looked at me again, her eyes a little wider this time. I gestured for her to be on her way with the cute but perpetually grumpy officer. To my surprise, she let him help her up the ramp.

Before Sam pulled the door shut, I saw Jace mouth the words, "Tell him."

I watched Marx with apprehension as he dropped a folder onto the table and stripped out of his coat. He hung it on the back of the metal chair. He was moving with purposeful slowness, and I recognized the tactic. He was either avoiding an uncomfortable subject or delaying in order to give himself time to think.

I slid my hands into my back pockets and searched his face for the information he was stalling to give me. "Well?"

He opened the folder and slid a picture toward me. Fear squeezed my lungs as I stared down at the close-up shot of a man seated at a café table.

Collin looked exactly as I remembered him: pale features, black hair, and eyes as hollow as chips of ice. That was the face that haunted my dreams.

I hastily flipped the picture facedown on the table and took a few steps back. I knew his evil couldn't seep through the photograph into the room, but I still didn't want to be anywhere near it.

"Where . . . where did you find him?" My voice quivered, and it took me a moment to realize it wasn't just my voice; my entire body was shaking.

Marx's eyes softened with sympathy. "He's in New York."

19

The shock of that news knocked the breath out of me. New York. Collin was closer than I thought. Even with the information floating around in the police database, I'd expected it to take him longer to find me.

"I'm sorry, Holly. There was no easy way to break that news to you," Marx said. "It looks like he's been in New York for less than two weeks."

I stared at him, feeling a bit dazed. "How f-far away is he?"

He hesitated. "About two hours from here."

"Two . . ." Fear choked my voice. I pressed my hands to my abdomen and tried not to sink into the panic pooling in my stomach. *Breathe. Breathe, breathe, breathe, breathe, breathe . . .*

Memories of the last time he caught me flooded through me, and I felt suddenly sick to my stomach. I fought back the urge to vomit all over the floor. I knew what would happen if he found me again. Even if my mind tried to forget, my body always remembered.

"I-I have to go."

I rushed to the bed and fished my travel bag out from under it. I started stuffing clothes into it with practiced quickness. This process had become so familiar to me that it was almost comforting, and I could probably do it in my sleep.

I wouldn't get far on foot, but I could at least put enough distance between me and this place that I would be okay for the night.

"Go where?" Marx asked.

"I don't know. Somewhere . . ." I might have said safe, but there was no such place. "Somewhere he can't find me." I wasn't sure that place existed either.

"You don't have to run."

"You don't understand."

"Then help me to. Holly . . ." I heard his heavy sigh of frustration as I went into the bathroom to grab my brush and toiletries. "If you walk out that door, you're not just abandonin' your friend, you're forfeitin' your life. There's a killer out there huntin' you. You're not gonna get very far."

I stilled at the mention of my friend Jace. She meant the world to me, and it would break her heart if I left. She wouldn't understand. I had never intended to befriend her because I knew, inevitably, this moment would come, and now I was reluctant to give her up.

But this was how I survived. It was how I had always survived. My head and my body knew what to do in this situation, but my heart was struggling to accept it.

I sank onto the edge of the tub and stared at the items in my hands with indecision. What was I supposed to do?

God, I don't know what to do. Please tell me what to do.

I looked up when Marx appeared in the doorway. I just stared at him, too lost to figure out what to say or do. He crouched down so we were at eye level. "It's gonna be all right, Holly."

I tried to hold back the tears as I admitted hopelessly, "I'm scared."

"I know," he said in an exceedingly gentle voice. "And I know that when you're scared you run. You've been runnin' all your life—from one foster home to another, from one state to the next to avoid this man. You deserve a better life than that."

The tears spilled down my cheeks against my will as I choked out, "If I stay, he'll hurt Jace. He'll hurt her to make me suffer."

"We won't let that happen."

"You can't stop it from happening."

"Watch me," he said with intense determination. "If or when he comes for you, Sam and I will be here to give him a very warm welcome." His eyes implored me to trust him, and I wanted to.

I didn't want to run anymore. My spirit was so weary from moving from place to place and always looking over my shoulder. I was pretty sure the only glue holding me together was God. Without Him, I would've given up and fallen to pieces long ago.

"I made you a promise, Holly, that I would keep you safe to the best of my ability, and I intend to keep it. That doesn't involve you runnin' off." He held out his hands to me. "Please at least give me a chance to keep you safe."

I looked down at the bottle of shampoo and the hairbrush in my hands as I wrestled with whether to trust him or to trust the path I knew. He was asking me to take a huge leap of faith, to put not only my life in his hands but also Jace's.

I forced out a slow, quivering breath and then reluctantly placed the items into Marx's waiting hands. His lips twitched with a barely restrained smile, and I realized he'd intended for me to put my hands in his, not the shampoo and hairbrush.

"Good enough," he said as he stood and set them back on the sink.

A quiet knock on the door startled me.

"It's just Sam," he informed me as he strode out of the bathroom. "I told him we would need ten minutes or so. I knew it wasn't gonna be an easy conversation. I also wanted your permission before I fill him in." When I drew in a breath to argue, he clarified, "No personal information. But you and Jace will be a lot safer if he at least knows the basics."

Sam didn't strike me as the kind of man who passed along information lightly, but telling another person about Collin still made me nervous. "Okay."

"Come in, Sam!"

The front door opened slowly and Sam stepped partway through the doorway. He glanced around cautiously, and his eyes snagged on me with a glimmer of concern.

I had wiped away the sheen of tears before coming out of the bathroom, but my eyes were probably still puffy, and the tip of my nose had the irritating habit of turning as pink as a radish when I cried.

That wasn't embarrassing at all . . .

"Everything okay?" Sam asked.

Marx nodded. "Shut the door."

Sam obeyed and then walked to the kitchen table. I stayed by the wall near my bed, craving the comfort and security of space.

Marx pulled two wallet-sized photos out of the folder on the table and handed them to Sam. "This is the man I went to investigate in connection with this case."

"Did you find any evidence that he's our killer?"

Marx sighed. "At most he's five eleven. Our killer has a significant size advantage. I did notice him dinin' in a restaurant . . . with a redhead," he added with a glance at me. I stiffened. "Holly is his type, but he wasn't in New York at the time she found the note card taped to her door, or durin' the assault in the park when Jimmy was murdered."

"So he's not our guy."

"In this instance, no."

Sam stared intently at the picture of Collin. "In this instance," he repeated, picking up on Marx's careful wording. "In what instance *is* he our guy?"

"His name is Collin Wells," Marx explained. "He's in no way connected to this case, but he's very much a physical threat. It's only a matter of time before he makes his way here, and if he so much as breathes in Holly's direction, arrest him. We'll work out the details later."

Sam's black eyebrows knitted together, and he turned his attention to me. He studied me as if he were trying to figure out just how the man was a threat to me.

"Okay," he finally said, returning his attention to Marx. "I'll make sure Mer gets one of these." He slid the pictures into the back pocket of his jeans. "So what do we know about the killer then?"

Marx rubbed the back of his neck in frustration. "I just cleared our only suspect. None of her clients or their significant others are involved. We're back to square one."

Jace was right. I needed to tell them about my memory, because the answer might be in there somewhere. I didn't want to part with that secret, because I was almost positive they would think I was crazy.

"You said he has a significant size advantage. How significant?" Sam asked.

"The Crime Scene Unit lifted a boot print from outside Holly's window: a size thirteen carpenter boot. Given the depth of the print and the soil saturation, they estimated the man's weight at about two-fifteen to two-thirty, and we know he's approximately six four."

Sam let out a low whistle. "So not a lightweight then."

"No."

Sam stepped closer to Marx and leaned in to whisper, "What are your thoughts on training Holly how to use a gun?"

"That there isn't enough time to teach her to be comfortable with it, and it's more likely to be used against her," Marx answered without hesitation. "Why?"

Sam glanced discreetly over his shoulder at me and then said in a voice so quiet I wasn't meant to hear, "I wouldn't bet on either of us in an unarmed fight with this guy. If he gets his hands on her and she doesn't have a weapon, there's no way she doesn't end up dead."

I flinched at the unmistakable certainty in his voice.

"We're not talkin' about this in front of her," Marx said, and there was a distinctly angry edge to his voice. "Holly, we'll be right back." He pushed away from the table, and Sam followed him out the front door, closing it behind him.

I puffed out a breath and walked over to my bed. I began pulling the packed items back out of the bag and putting them back where they belonged.

I considered how I might approach the topic of my memory loss. I didn't want to just walk outside and shout, "I have no memories!" But subtlety wasn't exactly my forte.

I knew no matter how rational the speech sounded in my head, I was going to sound like a lunatic when I put it into words. I just needed to get it over with.

I put the last of my things away and walked back into the kitchen, pausing by the front door when I heard the two men talking.

"Because she knows more than she's saying," Sam said, and his frustration added just a pinch of inflection to his normally monotone voice.

"I realize she's not forthcomin' about everythin', but she has her reasons," Marx replied.

There was a moment of silence before Sam sighed, "Look, I like Holly. She's one of those irrationally caring people . . . and she's also a little frustrating. I understand that you wanna protect her. So do I. But she's endangering everyone, including herself, by withholding information."

I cracked the door open and peered at them. Both men went completely silent at the top of the steps. I wasn't sure what expression was on my face, but Marx narrowed his eyes at me.

"Were you listenin' to our conversation through the door?"

"You whisper like you're trying to be heard over the roar of a jet engine," I informed him.

Sam closed his eyes and let out a pained breath.

"Don't worry, Sam, I think you're frustrating too." I stepped out onto the patio. "I need to tell you both something."

They both shifted until they were facing me, which only added to the intense pressure building inside me. "I can't . . ." I twirled my hands slowly, but for some reason that didn't make the right words magically appear in my brain. I exhaled in surrender and said, "I have no memories."

142

20

"You remember trippin' over a body," Marx said, testing my memory. He rested his hand on the table, his pen poised over a page in his notebook.

He'd taken the news of my amnesia better than expected; I was both surprised and touched that he hadn't thought I was crazy.

He'd simply believed me.

Then he'd sat down on the steps beside me and asked me to tell him what I did remember.

Sam had a more difficult time accepting my condition. His logic just wasn't that flexible.

"Do you remember why you tripped?" he asked.

I rubbed my hands together anxiously as I paced around the table, searching the black void of my memory for details that just weren't there. I kept coming back to the same few images. "I slipped in blood."

"Describe the blood," Marx said. "Was it in front of the body, behind the body . . . just around the head?"

I closed my eyes and tried to envision the scene. I remembered the moonlight illuminating the room. "It was all around the body. It was like . . . tiny fissures had burst all over her body."

Marx sat up a little straighter, and there was a focused gleam in his eyes. "A girl or a woman?"

I stopped by the refrigerator and looked at him in confusion. "What?"

"You said 'her body'."

I frowned as I thought back on the memory. I could scarcely see clearly enough to identify the mass on the floor as a body, let alone decipher whether it was male or female. "I don't . . ."

"You do remember, or you wouldn't have said it."

I strained my brain to figure where that thought had come from. "When I was at the café, after Cambel died, I remembered tripping over the body, and I just had a feeling it was a woman. I can't explain it. I didn't see it. It was just a passing thought."

"That doesn't mean your memory wasn't tryin' to find its way back. What happened when you fell over the body?"

"I dropped my stuffed rabbit."

"Why didn't you pick it up?" He gazed at me expectantly, and I was starting to feel flustered.

I couldn't summon the memories at will. The only thing that had triggered them to date was fear—and morbid little reminders that the killer left for me to find.

I sighed. "I don't know."

"It's okay, Holly. Don't get frustrated."

Why hadn't I picked it up? I couldn't remember. *Remember. Broken brain, remember.* Whatever had happened next made the rabbit unimportant; it slipped away from my attention as something more frightening took its place. "The moon came out and I saw what was on my hands."

"Did you scream? Cry?"

"No," I said with absolute certainty. With that memory came the full cinematic experience, and I had been lucky to be able to breathe past the knot of terror in my throat, let alone scream. I hadn't uttered a sound.

"Why not?"

"I was too scared."

"Why?"

My heart rate picked up as I remembered a small detail that had escaped my attention before. Something so faint it should hardly have mattered. The floorboards behind me had creaked. "Someone was in the house."

"The person who chased you through the woods?"

"The man."

"This memory came to you the night in the park when those men were chasin' you." He tapped his pen on the notepad with a stony expression. "I think we can both agree what their intentions were for you that evenin'. I'm wonderin' if that might be what triggered the memory."

At my bewildered look, he sighed. "Some men's desires are driven more toward children. Did you have any sense that the man chasin' you that night . . ."

"No," I said a little more forcefully than I'd intended. The suggestion sent pinpricks of revulsion across my skin. "No, I . . . I don't think so."

"So probably not a child predator, but we can't rule it out. What do you think brought on the memory? Was it the surroundin's? In your memory you said you were runnin' through the woods."

"I don't know."

"Tell me about the woods."

I sighed in frustration. I felt like we were getting nowhere. The memories made no more sense to me now than they had before. But Marx continued to take notes. "Big. I couldn't see the end in any direction. Cold. My toes were numb."

"You were barefoot?" At my nod, he frowned. "Forest floors are covered in nuts, twigs, roots, debris from litterers . . . and you were barefoot?"

"And in my nightgown."

"Was there snow on the ground?"

I thought about it for a moment and then shook my head. "Crunching leaves. I could hear his boots stomping through the dry leaves. The tree branches were bare . . ."

Marx leaned forward in his chair. "It was fall. Probably mid to late fall. It's mid fall now, and you were runnin' through the trees in the park from the sound of men's footsteps in the dry leaves. Your mind might have repressed your memory of that night in the woods, but there were too many similarities in the park for it to stay buried."

I heaved a tired breath and dropped into the opposite chair. "That doesn't help us find him." I played with the cup of hot chocolate he'd brought me when he arrived. He'd brought himself a coffee, and the terrible smell of it clouded the apartment.

"No, it helps us find you, which will help us find him."

I wasn't sure I quite followed that bouncing ball. "How exactly does that work?"

Marx leaned back in his chair. "Well, we know that a red-haired girl named Holly went missin' in the fall approximately eighteen years ago, which would've made her ten years old. She fled the scene of a crime where at least one person died, likely a woman, and she ran through the woods, which suggests a rural area, and disappeared." He set his pen down and closed the notebook. "It's not a lot, but it's more than we had yesterday, and it gives us a time line to work with. "

Relief made me slump in my chair. I had done something to help. That was a first. Usually I just screwed things up.

Marx got up from the table and took his notebook with him as he pulled out his cell phone. "Sully, I need you to look into a missin' child for me," he said, stepping onto the patio. "I don't have a city to narrow it down with, so search countrywide." He paused. "Yes, I know that's a lot of missin' children to go through."

He pulled the door shut.

I tugged off my slippers and pulled on a pair of gray flats. Slippers were far more comfortable, but apparently wearing them outside of the house wasn't socially acceptable.

I grabbed my jacket off the back of the door and slipped out into the cool afternoon. I hopped up the steps and started toward the main apartment building when Marx snapped, "Holly."

I came to an abrupt halt and turned back. "What?"

He covered the mouthpiece of his cell phone. "Where are you goin'?"

"To visit Jace."

His gaze flicked to the building behind me, and he shook his head. "Not by yourself, you're not."

"But . . ." I looked back at the building. "It's twenty feet away."

146

He gestured toward Officer Meredith, who was so silent and stiff that he might have been a standing corpse on the lawn. I crinkled my nose. Marx's eyebrows lifted, revealing that he wasn't moved by my expression of displeasure.

I sighed and walked over to Officer Meredith. He rotated his head slowly, like an owl, and looked at me with a face completely devoid of emotion.

Yeah, that's not creepy.

"Hi," I greeted a little uneasily. "Would you, um . . . mind coming with me?"

He stared at me, blinked, and then started toward the apartment building without a word. *I'll take that as a yes.* I turned on my heel and scampered to catch up with him.

I walked stiffly up two flights of stairs with Officer Meredith at my back, and paused just outside the doorway to the second-floor hallway. An unpleasant smell seeped through the door into the stairwell, and I pressed the back of my hand against my nostrils to try to block it.

"That smells awful," I muttered before continuing up the steps toward the tenth floor.

Officer Meredith lingered by the door for another moment and then turned to follow me. He lifted his radio, and the words he said nearly made me trip up the steps.

"Detective, I think we may have a body on the second floor."

"What?" I gasped.

"Keep walking," he instructed, and he marched me up the remaining flights of stairs without answering any of the dozen questions I peppered him with. I could only guess it had been the smell that made him think someone had died, but he wouldn't confirm that either.

I barely had a chance to knock on Jace's door before it flung inward with startling quickness. For a moment she just blinked, and then she exhaled, "Oh, you're not Chinese."

"Nope, just a lowly Caucasian."

She snorted. "I meant Chinese food, smart aleck." She moved back to let me inside and then eyed Officer Meredith. He made no move to come in, and Jace happily closed the door. I found it interesting that when Sam arrived for the changing of the guard, she invited him in.

He hovered quietly and unobtrusively by the door as we watched movies and nibbled on food. I picked through the bowl of popcorn in my lap as I sat curled into the corner of Jace's plush couch amidst a mound of pillows and blankets.

Jace sat on the other end of the couch, her blue eyes glazed as she stared at the TV screen. It was late, and we were watching some movie about elves and hobbits. I couldn't really follow the plot.

Jace yawned and I tossed a piece of popcorn at her face. I almost made it into her mouth, but it went a little high and bounced off the tip of her nose. She snapped her mouth shut with a click and shot me a mock glare.

"You should cover your mouth," I teased.

"You should learn to aim." She flicked a piece of popcorn back at me, and I tried to dodge it, but it snagged in my hair. I tried to untangle it without breaking it into a thousand tiny pieces.

Jace chuckled tiredly.

My attention shifted to Sam when I noticed him checking his cell phone. He typed a lightning-fast response and then tucked it back into one of his pockets.

"Was that Marx?" I asked.

His warm black eyes shifted to me. "Yes, why?"

"Did he say anything about . . ." I glanced at Jace and, not wanting to frighten her, phrased my question carefully. "The smell on the second floor?"

Sam's eyes considered Jace as well, and then he said vaguely, "Yes, he did, and yes, Mer was right."

I swallowed. Mr. Stanley lived on the second floor. He'd been rushed to the hospital once before when he consumed a toxic level of alcohol and passed out in the hallway. I couldn't ask Sam if it was him without alarming Jace, so I decided to keep that question to myself for now.

"You know," Jace began, her blue eyes fixing on Sam like a hawk zeroing in on prey. "I've been meaning to talk to you about something. And since you're here . . ."

Uh-oh. I sensed trouble.

"I hear you didn't believe Holly when she told you about her memory," she said, and the sharpness of her voice made Sam hesitate for a beat.

"It's an unusual problem to have."

"So you automatically assumed she was lying?"

Sam's expression turned flat, and he shifted his gaze to me. "Thank you for throwing me under the bus."

"I was not involved with this bus." I raised my hands innocently.

"I heard you," Jace explained. "My window was cracked open. It also sounded like you pretty much think all of this is her fault because she's withholding information? Maybe she was withholding information because she knew you wouldn't believe her."

Sam looked like a deer in headlights, and for a moment I thought he might duck out the door into the hallway. She would only follow him. "I didn't say that."

Oh boy. I pushed aside my blanket gently and slid off the couch. "I'm just gonna . . . go . . . pee for like . . . the next twenty minutes or so," I mumbled. I grabbed my bowl of popcorn and carried it with me as I tiptoed into the bathroom at the other end of the apartment.

I closed the door and turned on the sink faucet to drown out their voices. They deserved a private moment to work out their misunderstanding. It might be about me, but I had no intention of getting involved.

I put the toilet lid down and sat on the puffy blue covering as I nibbled on my popcorn. Why did I have a habit of eating in the bathroom? That wasn't weird at all. I hummed a tune to myself as

149

the minutes crept slowly by. I wished I could remember the words. Something about balloons . . . ninety . . . or nine hundred . . . well, anyway, there were balloons.

I paused when I saw something move outside. I squinted, making out a figure sprinting across the lawn with his gun drawn.

Ummm . . .

I stood up and turned off the faucet. When I opened the bathroom door, Jace was sitting there with her hand poised to knock. Her blue eyes were rounded with fear.

"What's wrong?" I asked.

"There's a man outside," she said in a frightened whisper.

"What? Outside where? The hallway?"

She shook her head. "*Outside,* outside. Sam didn't say who exactly, but I kinda got the feeling he meant your stalker guy."

I stiffened and looked into the living room. "Where's Sam?"

"Marx sent him a message. He said the man was outside, and he needed backup immediately. He left." Her eyes glistened with fear. "He drew his gun, told me to lock the door, and then he just . . . left."

That didn't sound right.

I ran back into the bathroom and looked out the window. The figure I had seen sprinting across the lawn with a gun must have been Sam. He was gone. This didn't make sense. If the killer was outside, Marx would've called for backup; he would never have told Sam to leave us.

I fished my cell phone out of my jeans pocket with shaky fingers and punched in Marx's number. I held my breath as I waited for him to pick up, but the number returned as busy.

I hung up and tried again.

Pick up, pick up, pick up . . . please pick up.

Jace parked her wheelchair in the doorway to the bathroom as she watched me frantically try to call Marx. Dread unfurled in my stomach when the line rang busy a second time and switched over to voice mail. I closed the phone with icy fingers and stared at her.

Something was wrong. I could feel it.

The knob on the front door rattled. I walked to the doorway beside Jace and watched the knob twitch back and forth. Someone was trying to get in, and it wasn't Sam. He would've announced himself. Something heavy hit the outside of the door and it bowed.

Fear gripped me.

"Inside. Now," I whispered, half pulling Jace's wheelchair into the bathroom with me. She was frozen. I shoved her into the walk-in shower and turned her around so she wasn't facing the wall.

I closed the bathroom door quietly and locked it. Neither the flimsy door nor the cheap button lock would offer much resistance for a six-foot-four man who wanted inside. He would just break through it. I turned in a frantic circle in search of anything we could use to barricade the door.

There was nothing. Everything in the small bathroom was a permanent fixture. I rifled through the cabinet drawers for a weapon. I pulled out a pair of scissors.

"Holly." Jace's voice trembled. "What's happening?"

"It's gonna be okay," I told her, even though I doubted it would be.

I heard the outer door burst under the weight of the intruder, and there was the quiet patter of wood shards littering the floor. He was inside.

I grabbed a can of hair spray from the counter and climbed into the shower with Jace. I hunkered down beside her and forced the can of hair spray into her shaking fingers. I had a far better chance of stabbing someone because I could at least maneuver in this small space. I laced my fingers through hers, and she squeezed them painfully.

I looked up at her and saw the stiff expression of terror on her face. In that way we differed. She froze in the face of fear, and I froze in the face of memories.

We listened to the sound of the floorboards as they creaked beneath the weight of slow, heavy footsteps. The sound stirred memories in the void of my mind, but I clamped down on them and shoved them aside. What good would remembering do if we died in the next five minutes?

The footsteps drew closer, and I could see the light shifting under the door. Jace gripped my fingers tighter, and I had to clench my teeth to keep from crying out. An obscene amount of strength was hidden in her slender arms and fingers. I blamed the wheelchair.

I tried to pry my fingers from hers to call Marx again, but she wouldn't let go. I set the scissors on the shower floor quietly and hit redial on my phone. When the call went to voice mail, I could've cried.

I remembered Sam's words—the ones he'd whispered that I was never meant to hear: "If he gets his hands on her and she doesn't have a weapon, there's no way she doesn't end up dead." I set the useless phone down and picked up the scissors. I had a weapon—a meager one—but at least this one I knew how to use.

The killer twisted the doorknob both directions, but the lock held. Neither of us breathed as we waited to see what he would do next. A heavy force hit the outside of the door, and the wood split from the top of the door to the lock. Jace screamed.

He hit the door again, and a chunk of wood splintered from the frame and fell on the floor. If he hit the door again, it would give. *God, please . . . help us.* He slammed into the door again, but it didn't break under his weight.

"You can't hide forever, Holly," the man on the other side of the door said. His voice sent a chill twisting down my spine.

Sam. I had tried to call Marx, but I hadn't tried calling Sam. I scrambled out of the shower and over to the window, nearly pulling Jace with me when she refused to relinquish her grip on my hand. I unlocked the window with clumsy fingers and shoved it up.

I had done this before . . .

I fumbled the old lock open with slick fingers and grunted as I pushed up the heavy window. A rush of cold, autumn scented air swirled around me, and I shivered in my Hello Kitty nightgown.

152

"Go, baby, run," a man's quiet voice urged. There was love and despair and desperation all rolled up in that voice.

The creak of floorboards echoed in the hallway, and I froze in terror as I gripped the edge of the window. I looked back at the bedroom door, expecting to see the monster, but no one stood there.

"Run, Holly," the man urged again. "Don't stop running until you get to his house, do you hear me?" I glanced at the patch of darkness where the voice came from, and nodded numbly.

The sound of a girl crying in the hallway made me hesitate. I didn't want to leave her, but he'd told me to go. The sound of heavy footsteps sent me scrambling out the window. He was coming back. My feet landed on the cold tiles of the porch roof, and I shuffled quickly to the edge where the flower trellis was bolted to the side. I climbed down as I had done so many times before, but my fingers were wet. I slipped and fell the last three feet to the ground.

I landed hard on my back and coughed as I tried to recapture my breath. I froze when I heard a strange man's voice in the bedroom upstairs: "Where's the other one? Where's Holly?"

My heart pounded through my chest, and I climbed to my feet. I caught a glimpse of a dark figure leaning out of the second-story window as I darted through the dew-dampened grass toward the trees.

"Holly!" Jace's frantic voice ripped me out of the terrifying memory, and I glanced back at the bathroom door. It was falling to pieces, and it was all that stood between us and a killer.

I leaned out the window and looked down—ten dizzying stories to the ground. Even if there had been a trellis, Jace would never be able to climb down it, and I wouldn't leave her. Neither of us would survive the drop to the ground.

"Sam!" I screamed, and my voice pierced the quiet night like a knife. I hoped he could hear me wherever he'd gone.

A figure sprinted around the outside of the building, gun still drawn, and hesitated for the briefest moment as he looked up at me. Something hit the door again, and I ducked reflexively as Jace let out another petrified scream.

Sam tore across the grass and back into the building. I turned my back to the window and gripped the scissors tightly in front of me. The tip of a knife was lodged in the bathroom door. I kept my eyes on the door as I backed into the shower and angled myself in front of Jace, desperate to keep her safe.

We listened with bated breath for the next blow that would level the door. The minutes seemed like hours as we shivered in the shower, waiting.

We both let out a shriek of terror when something smacked the outside of the door. "Holly, Jace?" a familiar voice called.

"Ssssam." Jace gasped through chattering teeth.

"Are you both okay?" he asked. He sounded as rattled as we felt.

I stepped out of the shower on shaking legs and unlocked the door. More splinters of wood rained down on the floor as I pulled it open. Sam stood just outside the door, one hand bracing the door frame and the other holding his gun.

There was a light sheen of sweat on his skin from sprinting up so many flights of steps. His dark eyes scanned me for injuries and then moved over my shoulder to Jace, who was still hiding in the shower with her can of hair spray. I dropped the scissors on the floor in relief and sagged back against the bathroom counter.

Sam pushed the bathroom door the rest of the way inward and looked at the knife embedded in the wood. My gaze lifted to the picture the killer had pinned to the door with a knife: it was a profile shot taken last night when I was sitting on the steps next to Marx, and the blade was pierced through his head. Written in blood-red marker across the bottom was a message: *See you soon, Holly*.

21

I sat on Jace's couch with a blanket wrapped snugly around my shoulders and stared at the broken front door. It was fractured into kindling.

Jace's hand slid slowly under the edge of the blanket and came to rest on my socked foot. She was leaning forward in her wheelchair to touch me, reminding herself we were both all right, and her right hand was holding a mug of lavender tea in a white-knuckled grip.

I shifted so I could touch her hand, and her wide, shimmering blue eyes lifted from the mug of tea to my face.

"I'm sorry," I whispered, guilt stripping all strength from my voice. "I'm sorry I brought him here."

Jace turned her hand so that she could squeeze my fingers. "You didn't bring him here," she said with equal softness. "He came to hurt us. That's not your fault."

Marx's furious voice drew our attention to the hallway. "I didn't send you this text! Why is my name on it?"

Although I hadn't been able to figure out what happened at the time, I knew Marx would never leave us unprotected.

"I don't know," Sam offered meekly. "I got the text, I told the girls to lock the door, and I came to help. I thought if he was outside and you had eyes on him, they would be fine. I didn't know it was . . . I didn't know."

"It's called SMS spoofing." To my surprise, it was Jace who offered that tidbit of information.

She dragged her eyes from the depths of her tea to the fuming detective who stepped into the doorway. Sam lingered behind his shoulder with an unhappy look on his face.

"It's called what?" Marx asked tightly.

"SMS spoofing," Jace repeated, a little more firmly this time. "There's an app that allows you to disguise your number as someone else's, and you can send a text without the recipient knowing you're someone other than who they think you are. The . . ." Jace hesitated as a small spark of fear flashed in her eyes.

"Killer," Sam offered after a moment.

Jace squeezed my fingers for strength. "The killer disguised his number as yours because he wanted Sam to believe you sent him the text so he would . . . leave us." There was a world of questions in those last two words as she looked past Marx at Sam. She had never expected him to just disappear and leave us on our own.

He dropped his eyes.

Marx blinked as he tried to absorb what she was saying. His face darkened with anger and frustration, and I leaned a little closer to Jace, bracing for the explosion. She looked a little worried too.

Marx sucked in a deep breath and checked himself before he started shouting. He slammed the phone back into Sam's hand and said, "No more texts. If you don't hear my voice, it's not me."

He disappeared from view, and we could hear him swearing and grumbling up and down the hall. He was livid. I was amazed he didn't rip Sam to pieces.

Sam looked at the broken door with a mixture of guilt and confusion. I knew exactly how he felt. I had brought the monster to the door, and he'd left it unguarded.

His eyes moved to us, and he said softly, "I'm sorry."

"Sorry?" Jace repeated bitterly.

"Jace . . ." I began.

"No," she snapped. "He left us. Marx didn't answer his phone." That fact hurt me too. He'd promised he would do everything in his power to keep me safe, but he hadn't answered his phone when I desperately needed him. If it had just been my life on the line, I might not have been angry at all, but Jace had needed him too. "Now my front door is firewood, my bathroom door, what's left of it, has been shish-kebabbed with a knife and a creepy stalker picture. There was a killer in my apartment, and I had to hide in my shower with a can of hair spray. And all this with your promises of protection. What good are you people?"

She slammed her mug of tea on the coffee table and wheeled into her bedroom. The door closed hard enough to make the wall vibrate. I cringed as a picture fell to the floor and shattered.

"She's right," Sam conceded as he leaned against the door frame. "That's twice this guy has gotten close to you on my watch: once outside your window, and now this. What's gonna happen next time?"

I shrugged with a nonchalance I didn't feel. "Maybe next time he'll succeed and you won't have to spend all your free time guarding me anymore."

Sam's expression hardened. "That's not funny, Holly."

I wasn't sure I meant it to be funny. I really didn't know how I felt at the moment, but funny wasn't anywhere in there.

"Why do it?" Sam asked, his expression sour. "Why even take the risk of coming here when he could've just left the picture on your apartment door?"

"You're asking this about a man who plastered pictures on my window while you were standing there, a man who killed a cop and then hung around to toy with me while reinforcements were on the way," I reminded him.

"Right. So he either has no sense of self-preservation or he's very brave."

"He's cocky," Marx corrected. He squeezed past Sam into the apartment, stepping carefully over the debris. "There's a difference. Bravery implies he might fail but he's willin' to put forth the effort anyway. Cocky means he honestly doesn't believe there's any chance we can stop him, which means it's no longer a risk." He sounded more annoyed than angry now, but maybe he was just trying to conceal it for my benefit.

"So he thinks we're idiots," Sam summarized.

"We haven't done much to disabuse him of that notion." Marx pulled on a pair of latex gloves and walked past me to the bathroom door. He pinched the blade of the knife carefully and wrenched it out of the door. The picture dropped into his other hand.

He carried the knife back to Sam, who silently offered an open evidence bag, and slid the knife carefully inside.

Sam caught a glimpse of the picture. "I don't think he likes you very much."

"I gathered that, what with the knife through my forehead," Marx grumbled. He sat down on the edge of the chair across from me and studied the picture. There were a number of places the killer could have put the knife to secure the picture to the door; there was something about Marx that bothered him.

"Sir," a woman said as she appeared in the doorway beside Sam.

"Let me guess," Marx sighed as he looked in her direction. "You've got nothin'."

"Yes, sir. I mean . . . no, sir. We checked everywhere, stairwells, elevator. We even knocked on doors. He's not in the building, and we couldn't find any trace of him on the grounds. We swept the area around Ms. Smith's place, but if he's hiding somewhere nearby, we can't find him."

Marx rubbed the back of his neck wearily and said, "Thank you. Let me know if anythin' turns up." He turned his attention back to the photograph.

A quiet, choked sound drew my attention to Jace's bedroom. I slid off the couch and padded softly across the room to press my ear against the door. Muffled sobs came from inside the room and my heart twisted. She was crying.

Was I supposed to go in and hug her? Was I supposed to think up witty jokes that would turn her tears into laughter? Maybe I was just supposed to give her space. I needed a manual for this.

"Holly," Marx said, and I glanced at him over my shoulder. "Give her some time. It's been a stressful day for everybody." I rested my hand on the door for an indecisive moment and then let it fall back to my side.

I glanced at Sam, who was staring at Jace's door with an unreadable expression. I didn't really understand relationships. My only boyfriend had been a classmate when I was thirteen, and it had been brief. If I wasn't mistaken, though, there was interest there.

He caught me watching him, and his lips curled into a ghost of a smile before he disappeared into the hall.

Hmm.

"You haven't said much, Holly," Marx observed.

"There's nothing to say." I crouched down and started picking up the larger pieces of glass from the broken picture frame

"Why do I get the feelin' you're angry with me?"

I grunted softly. "There's that cop intuition again."

"Holly."

Emotion tightened my throat, and I tried to keep my voice quiet so I didn't upset Jace any more than she already was. "You didn't answer."

I carried the glass shards to the garbage and grabbed a trash bag from under the sink. I sat down on the floor to collect the chunks of wood from the front door. "I called you three times. He was breaking down the bathroom door and you didn't answer."

He crouched down beside me. "I'm sorry. I knew Sam was here with you. You should've been safe, and I was on another call. I . . ." Whatever he saw in my face when he looked at me made the rest of his excuse die in his throat, and he closed his eyes. "I'm sorry, Holly."

I stared at him. "My friend is crying because a psychopath broke into her apartment tonight, and we had scissors and hair spray to defend ourselves. I don't know what to do with that. I don't know how to make it better. But it can't ever happen again."

"I promise you, I'll answer next time," he said.

I nodded, but I wasn't certain I believed him. If my life relied on him answering his phone sometime in the near future, I wasn't sure I would bother calling.

"Jace means a lot to you, doesn't she?"

159

"You have no idea." I picked up a few more pieces of wood and deposited them into the bag. "Why did he leave that picture?"

"I expect its meanin' is three-fold," he answered as he handed me a piece of wood that had landed behind him. "The clear message at the bottom: 'See you soon.' And obviously he wanted to illustrate his dislike of me by puttin' a knife through my face, but I think the more important message he was tryin' to convey is the subject we were discussin' when this picture was taken."

"When I told you about my memories? Why is he interested in those?"

"Because he's in them." At my blank expression, he clarified, "I think he's actually offended you don't remember him."

I made a small noise of uncertainty as I tried to work my mind around that logic. It didn't make sense that he would want me to remember something that could ultimately lead to his capture or death.

"You're thinkin' of him as a common criminal. A burglar or an alleyway mugger doesn't wanna be remembered. But a stalker is a whole different breed of monster. He studies every nuance of his target's daily life, and he sees himself as an important part of it. It's a relationship. Granted it's often alarmin'ly twisted and impossible for the healthy human mind to comprehend, but it's a relationship to him nonetheless. He wants to feel important, recognized, remembered. He wants you to remember him, Holly. The gifts from your past, the little comments he makes—he's tryin' to trigger your memories."

He offered me the picture and I took it, gazing at the snapshot of our conversation. This man wanted me to remember him so he could finish what he started eighteen years ago. "If he was listening to our conversation when he took this picture, then he knows I've started to remember."

"But not enough. He wants more. That's why he said, 'See you soon.' He's not happy with your progress."

If the killer had known about the memory that seeped through the cracks of my mental wall tonight, would he have broken through the bathroom door and taken me with him? That door did not withstand his efforts—not a man of his size and determination; the only reason it was still on its hinges was because he let it remain that way.

I set the picture on the floor and pushed it away from me. "What if I just don't remember? What if I . . . refuse?"

"He intends to finish what he started no matter what, and judgin' by this 'soon,'"—he tapped the word on the picture—"we don't have much time. We have until you remember, or he loses patience, and I suspect . . ." He trailed off as he glanced at the remnants of the two doors. "That time is rapidly approachin'."

"We just had the conversation about my lost memories yesterday. How could he possibly have known before that?"

"Who else knows?"

I sifted through my daily life and my past, trying to create a mental list of who might have known about my memory loss. The list was a lot longer than I had ever really considered, and he could've learned about it from anyone. "All my former case managers know, my childhood therapists, doctors who checked for brain trauma, every foster home I ever stayed in. Jace knows, you know, my . . ." I trailed off as my brain threatened to trespass into forbidden territory.

"Your what?"

Crap, I didn't want to talk about them. I stood up and walked to the hall closet to grab the broom and dust pan. I started sweeping up the remaining glass from the floor.

"Holly, your what?" Marx insisted.

I let out a flustered breath and leaned on the broom. "My . . . second family. I don't know what to call them."

"Your foster family."

I hesitated before saying slowly, "Not . . . exactly. You know how I was a little vague on my first memories?"

"Mmm hmm."

I puffed out a breath and forged ahead. "I sort of came to in a cabin in Maine . . . with . . . strangers. They um . . . they didn't exactly have legal custody of me."

He blinked. "Are you tellin' me you were abducted?"

I sighed and rested my forehead on the broom. "I knew you were gonna take it there."

"Well, where else should I take it?"

For all I knew they had rescued me, but that didn't make my relationship with them any less strained. "They were good to me. So can we just set aside the kidnapping conspiracy for the moment?"

Marx's expression became unreadable, but he still sounded irritated. "Fine. By all means, continue."

"They knew about my memory, and I know it's probably nothing, but whenever I was scared—really about anything—Izzy would remind me that . . . the bad man couldn't hurt me again."

"The bad man," he said carefully. "They saw this bad man?"

I shrugged. "I didn't remember him, so I never said anything. They seemed to think he was the reason I was always afraid of the dark, the trees . . . pumpkins."

"You're afraid of pumpkins?"

"Just the ones with faces."

"What happened with this family?"

I chewed anxiously on my bottom lip before saying, "They were arrested for drug trafficking . . . in Maine."

"Dru —" He bit off his words and stared at me. "You lived with drug traffickers?"

I smiled at the look on his face. "Don't worry, I didn't pick up any nasty habits."

He rubbed his forehead and glanced down at the picture again. He knew as well as I that if we were ever going to get ahead of the man who intended to kill me, we had to find a way to identify him first. The only hope of that was fingerprints or DNA on the evidence, which I doubted he was clueless enough to leave behind, and whatever details lay in my past.

I'd given him everything I had with exception of the latest memory, so the only thing left to do was speak to the people who may have taken me out from under the killer.

"We need to go visit your *second family*," he decided, spitting the phrase with distaste.

"I was really hoping we could just call."

He shook his head. "It's only an eight-hour drive. We'll set up an appointment and talk to them in person. We're likely to get more information that way."

I really didn't want to see them again.

"We can't just . . . ," I started to protest. "I won't abandon Jace while this lunatic is still around."

I couldn't begin to understand the mind of the man stalking me, but I hoped he would recognize that he already had my attention and there was no reason to hurt her.

"He won't come back. He came here for you, not for her. But just to be on the safe side, Sam will stay here with her."

My gaze shifted to the officer who reappeared in the doorway. "I swear, Sam, if you leave her for any reason and she gets hurt, I will . . ."

"I won't leave her."

"Sam will do what he needs to do, Holly. You don't need to threaten him," Marx said. "Besides, it wouldn't be a fair fight."

I looked at Sam, who probably outweighed me by fifty pounds and was at least six inches taller, and then at Marx. "Because he has a gun?"

"No, because he knows if he so much as lays a finger on you, I'll make him cry."

"Why?"

Sam tried to suppress a smile as he looked at the floor. "Because his Southern mama raised him to always be respectful of women, even if they're screaming in your face or throwing punches. Which means, if you decide to swing a skillet at my head, he just expects me to dodge. And if you manage to hit me, it'll teach me to get out of the way faster next time."

I slid a curious look at Marx. What kind of family did he come from where they swung skillets at each other?

"In other words," Marx said. "It's not a fair fight, because you'll always win."

Interesting. I would have to keep that in mind. I looked around the apartment. "We can't just leave things like this."

"We'll look into doors first thing in the morning," Sam said.

"Maybe something blue. She likes blue."

"Holly," Sam said a little impatiently. "I'll take care of it."

"It's almost three in the mornin', Holly. We should get some sleep. We have a long drive tomorrow," Marx reminded me.

I rubbed my hands on my jeans to wick away the nervous sweat that this entire situation was causing. Leaving Jace, being stuck in a car with Marx for eight hours, the uncertain sleeping arrangements, and seeing the woman I had promised myself I would never see again . . .

I was going to be a wreck tomorrow.

22

I watched the raindrops trickle down the glass as I stared out the passenger window of the car. I huddled as close to the door as possible, craving space.

I couldn't recall the last time I had been in a car for such a long stretch of time. I could grit my teeth and endure a ten-minute trip across the city, but our time in this coffin on wheels was approaching three hours.

I was about ready to crawl out the window and take my chances on the highway. I pressed the lock button on the door and watched the lock pop up and down repeatedly. I flinched when Marx's voice broke the silence.

"Holly, you're gonna break my lock."

I pressed it one more time to make sure it was unlocked, and then lifted my finger off the button. "Sorry." I gave him a small, tense smile.

He chanced a look in my direction, and I could see the gears churning in his head. He was trying to figure out just what exactly was twisting me into a bundle of nerves.

Tapping an anxious rhythm on my thighs, I glanced at his hands on the wheel. *Ooo, a distraction.* "Why do you still wear your wedding ring if you're divorced?"

He blinked in surprise at the sudden question. "How do you know I'm divorced?"

"The first time we met you mentioned your ex-wife thinks your handwriting looks like chicken scratch." I thought she was being generous. "Do you wear it because you miss her?"

His lips flattened into a reluctant line. "That's a very personal question, Holly."

"You ask me personal questions all the time."

"Pertainin' to the case."

165

"Not always." I looked back out the window, following the sparse trees that whipped by. The scenery made me long for my camera.

Marx drummed his fingers on the steering wheel in agitation. "Because I still love her," he finally admitted. "And I hope we'll be able to work it out eventually."

His answer surprised me. I had expected him to just brush off the question because it was personal. "She left because she didn't want kids?" *Wow, did I just blurt that out?*

Marx's brow furrowed, but he didn't look at me. He was trying to figure out how I knew that. "Yes, that's part of it. She also didn't like my job. It got in the way of a lot of things."

I could only imagine. If he spent half as much time on other cases as he did mine, his wife would've been a very lonely woman.

"How about you?" Marx asked after a quiet, thoughtful moment. "Has there ever been anyone special in your life? Aside from your friend."

Given everything he knew and probably suspected about my history, I would've thought the answer to that question would be obvious. "No. This . . ."—I gestured to the two of us—"is the most in-depth relationship I've managed with . . ."

"A man?" he finished. There was a hint of sadness in his voice.

I wasn't sad about it; I was quite proud of this relationship. If someone had told me a month ago that I would willingly sit in a car next to a man and do something other than claw my way through the upholstery to escape, I would've thought they were insane.

"No pressure, Detective," I said, adopting a teasing tone. "You're just the first stable male relationship I've ever had. Don't screw it up."

He laughed and some of the uncomfortable tension in the car broke. "I'll do my best."

I rolled down the passenger window to extend the claustrophobic space, and damp icy air swirled through the warm

166

car. I rested my chin and arms on the door and closed my eyes, savoring the open air as it wrapped around me. It was refreshing, but it wasn't enough to soothe the growing anxiety in my chest.

I jumped when Marx honked the horn. "What are you doin'?" he demanded. "That's not a lane!"

I relaxed slightly when I realized he wasn't yelling at me. The highway was clogged with traffic, probably due to an accident, and a man in a blue sports car was trying to weave his way between the crowded lanes.

Marx grumbled angrily at the driver, and I felt obliged to point out the obvious. "You know he can't hear you, right?"

"Thank you, Holly, I figured that much out for myself," he replied irritably. "He'll hear me if I roll the window down." He slammed his hand on the horn again, but the man paid him no mind.

I rubbed my ears to alleviate the ringing. "You're one of those angry drivers, aren't you?"

"I am not angry," he said carefully as he rested his right wrist over the steering wheel. "I just hate people who don't know how to drive."

I gave him a funny look, and it took him a moment to recognize his mistake. "I hate people *with licenses* who don't know how to drive," he amended with a glance my way. "You don't count."

"You've only been in the car with me for three hours," I said. "We'll see how you feel in three more."

"I don't think there's anythin' you could do to make me hate you, Holly. Unless you get your license and drive like this . . ." The person in front of us honked, drowning out Marx's voice, but I saw his mouth shape an inappropriate word.

"I don't foresee that happening," I sighed. I had long ago accepted the fact that my life would never be "normal": worrying about yoga classes and hair appointments, having a driver's license and a debit card with an account that actually had money in it. Those were luxuries meant for people who weren't hiding from psychotic foster siblings.

Of course, Collin already had all the information he needed to find me. That thought fed my already expanding anxiety.

"You're not gonna have to hide from him forever," Marx said.

"If that day comes, I'm not sure I'll know what to do," I admitted honestly. I had never even considered it, because it seemed like little more than a desperate fantasy.

"Whatever you want."

I'll settle for not being afraid anymore.

The compassion in his green eyes when he glanced at me made me think he'd read that thought loud and clear on my face. I released a frustrated breath and turned my attention back to the window.

I tapped a rapid staccato rhythm on the passenger door with my fingers; there was no chance I could endure five—possibly six—more hours of this. I despised small spaces and the way they seemed to suck all the air out of my lungs and slowly fold in around me.

I could feel Marx watching me as we crawled down the highway. "Is my company just that bad or are you claustrophobic?"

"Both?" I offered, trying to keep my voice light.

He peeled the car out of the line of traffic and onto the shoulder. The moment the car rolled to a stop, I whipped off my seat belt, flung open the door, and hopped out of the car. It probably looked like I was trying to escape a madman.

Oh, blessed freedom.

I pressed my hands to my stomach and took a few deep breaths of the open air, letting the space and freedom wash over me.

"You should've told me you're claustrophobic, Holly." Marx crossed his arms over his chest and leaned back against the passenger door.

I hadn't known what to expect when I got in his car. Apart from my bathroom, I hadn't been in a confined space for that long in years. "I'm sorry." I seemed to be causing him no end of trouble.

"Is this a childhood anxiety or a recent development?"

"Childhood."

He fell silent for a long, thoughtful moment as he watched me pace. "People aren't usually claustrophobic for no reason. Is this because of him? Somethin' he did to you?"

I cringed at the memory of being locked inside a box so small that it had been difficult to breathe, and I gave Marx an icy look.

He pressed his lips together. "Right, I said I wouldn't ask." He glanced at his watch. "Our appointment isn't until tomorrow mornin', so we can take as many breaks as you need. Is there anythin' else I should know for this trip?"

"I can't share a room."

"I figured as much, but my room is adjoinin' so I'm right there if you need me. Anythin' else?"

I thought about it, but if we had separate rooms, I didn't see an issue. "I prefer a king-size bed with chocolates on my pillows."

"Now you're just pushin' it," he said with a suppressed smile.

He waited for me to completely unwind before we got back in the car, and by that time the traffic had thinned. The rest of the road trip became routine: we pulled over every two hours, and Marx leaned against the car as he waited silently and patiently for me to wear myself out and climb back in. It was dark by the time we reached Maine.

23

I stood on the patio outside the single-story hotel with my bag and surveyed the row of numbered bright-red doors as Marx unlocked the door to my room.

I hadn't been in a hotel since I was twelve. My foster family had taken a trip for a funeral, and my foster sister Sarah and I had shared the second bed. It had been my first time in a hotel, and I'd been thrilled.

Now, as I looked at the doors, I longed to be home. Living on the run had stripped away any thrill about staying in some random place for the night.

Marx pushed the door inward and waited for me to enter. I stepped into the room cautiously. It didn't smell musty like my home, and I missed the comfort of that smell.

Marx flipped the light switch on the wall and closed the door behind us. I took in the bland, functional space and the queen-size bed. Wow . . . a queen-size bed all to myself.

There was something resting on the pillows. I stepped tentatively toward the bed and looked at the item: a packet of hot chocolate with tiny marshmallows. I drew in a breath and looked at Marx.

"How did you . . . ?"

"I called the hotel while you were takin' a break," he replied. Was that what we were calling it then—taking a break? "I thought it would help make you feel more comfortable. Oddly enough, most people don't just have bags of marshmallows lyin' about."

It was such a small gesture, but it meant so much more to me than what it had cost him. "Thank you."

Marx stood by the wall as I inspected the room, memories of the last time I was in a hotel drifting to the forefront of my thoughts. Sarah and I had bounced on the beds and pummeled each other with pillows. The memory brought a smile to my lips. We'd grown quite close in the six months we spent together. We had opened every drawer and every little complimentary item in the hotel room. We'd washed each other's hair with tiny shampoo, and even tried the coffee, which was awful.

I opened one of the tiny shampoos in the bathroom and smelled it: a similarly vague scent.

"How long's it been since you were in a hotel?" Marx asked, watching my behavior with interest.

I rubbed a dot of lightly scented lotion into the back of my hand as I walked out of the bathroom. "Sixteen years."

He did the math. "You were with your first foster family or your second?"

"First. We were here for a funeral. I loved it."

"Yes, funerals are a real riot," he said dryly.

I smiled. "Not the funeral. The hotel. My foster sister Sarah and I had a lot of fun."

"You were happy with that family," he observed.

"I was. But . . . they only wanted one child, and they fell in love with Sarah." It hurt when I learned they'd only taken both of us so they could decide which one they wanted to keep. Sarah had been sweet and bright, and I couldn't blame them for choosing her over the girl with the unknown history and defective memory.

"I'm sorry, Holly."

I shrugged off his sympathy. "Sarah deserved a good home."

"And you didn't?"

I stared at the flowered wallpaper above the bed. There were a lot of good kids in the system who were shuffled from one placement to the next with no hope of finding a home. I hadn't been the only one. "You said that when I don't have to hide anymore, I can do anything I want."

"You can."

"I don't wanna move anymore. Ever." I didn't even want to travel.

"You don't have to move," he assured me. "You're not alone anymore. There are people in your life who will look out for you. I can't speak for Sam, but I'm only ever a phone call away."

I sank onto the edge of the bed and regarded him thoughtfully. I had never expected to be more to him than an inconvenience he felt obligated to protect—the unfortunate case that had dropped into his already busy lap. But the past few weeks had left me feeling uncertain. "Would you really show up?" I asked, my voice tinged with doubt. "If the case was over and you and Sam went back to your daily lives, would you really come if I needed you?"

He looked a little startled by the question. "Of course I would come. Why would you even doubt that?"

"You're a cop."

"I did notice that when I got dressed this mornin'."

"Cops step in and out of people's lives on a daily basis," I said, trying not to let my deep dislike of law enforcement infect my voice. "They don't get attached to the people they help or hurt. They resolve the issue one way or another and they move on."

"I'm not just a cop, Holly, and you're not just some case to be solved." He studied me from across the room as if he were trying to read my thoughts, and I made a valiant effort to keep my face blank. "What's this about?"

"We were talking about cops," I said slowly, as if he'd forgotten. "It was a pretty brief conversation and we're done with it now." I hopped off the queen-size bed and walked to the window.

"I'm pretty sure we were discussin' somethin' else."

"Nope." I didn't want him to know how insecure I felt. I'd learned a long time ago that I wasn't worth caring about—it had pretty much been pounded into my head—and I didn't see the point in hoping it would change now. Jace was the only one who apparently hadn't gotten the memo, and I loved her for that.

"What are you thinkin' about?"

I stared at my ghostly reflection in the glass. Sometimes I felt like that—a ghost of a person drifting aimlessly through life with no true identity or history. "Can I see your wallet?"

Marx gave me a puzzled look, but pulled the wallet from his back pocket and crossed the room to hand it to me. Wow, he must really trust me. I could just take his money and credit cards and bolt. It wasn't like he was willing to shoot me to get them back.

I pulled out his small, shiny driver's license and studied it. "Why do you look so angry in this picture? Did someone cut you off when you were pulling into the parking lot?"

He grunted in amusement. "No. You're not supposed to smile."

"Oh, well . . . someone needs to teach those people how to properly take a photo. It looks like a mug shot." I ran my thumb over the smooth surface of the card. Looking at his name and picture on the colorful card reminded me just how much I wanted one. Proof of existence. "I want this," I declared, showing him the card. "Someday when we find out my name, and I don't have to hide anymore, I want one of these with my name and picture on it."

Marx frowned. "You've never had any form of identification? Even before Collin?"

"Just this." I held up my wrist to show him my bracelet. "Nothing I could hold in my hands. Nothing with my picture on it."

"When you're ready, I'll teach you how to drive if you want. And we'll get you an ID."

"Will you teach me how to yell at people through the windshield too?"

He snorted. "You don't need me to teach you that. The first night I met you, I thought you looked fragile sittin' on that curb wrapped in a blanket. Then you told me you'd had worse days, shoved the blanket in my face, and yelled at me for accusin' your friend of murder."

I smiled a little at the memory. "Well, you did overstep."

"I did not overstep. It was a good theory, and I wasn't exactly wrong. You do know the killer; you just don't remember him."

I slid the card back inside the sleeve and handed the wallet back to him. "I suppose that's true. But you *were* pushy."

"That's part of my job." He walked to the corner and grabbed the flimsy wooden chair with an upholstered seat. He tipped it backwards and wedged it beneath the door handle so no one could enter my hotel room even if they had a key. "I assume it goes without sayin', but don't open the door for anybody."

I snapped my fingers in mock disappointment. "And I was gonna throw a wild party and invite the neighborhood."

"Cute," he said, unamused. "And don't stand by the window."

"Why?"

"Just don't," he repeated without any additional explanation, which was infuriating. He gestured for me to leave the area.

"But I like the window."

"No," he said flatly. I frowned and took three small steps toward the bed. He frowned back, and I lifted my chin. I didn't appreciate being told what to do, and I wasn't willing to concede any more than that. He grumbled under his breath as he yanked the papery white curtain shut. "Stay away from the window, and if you hear a knock at either door, come get me. I'm gonna take a quick shower."

"Okay."

"You gonna be okay over here?"

I glanced at the red door with its single lock and the chair tucked under the handle and nodded without meaning it. It didn't strike me as secure. "I'll be fine. Thanks for the hot chocolate."

"You're welcome."

He unlocked the doors that divided our rooms, and then disappeared to take a shower.

The delicious aroma of chocolate and sugary marshmallows spread through the room as I prepared my hot chocolate. I walked back toward the bed and set it on the nightstand. I slid onto the mattress and stared at the red door. I wasn't really sure what to do now. What did people do in hotels other than sleep?

"Hey! You! Yeah, you!" a disembodied voice shouted.

I jumped so abruptly that I fell off the edge of the bed and landed on the floor. It took me far too long to realize the voice shouting at me was coming from my bag. I stared at it, too stunned to move, as it continued to scream at me. "You have a phone call! Answer already!"

I picked myself up off the floor—suddenly grateful no one was around to see my amazing leap of terror—and crawled back onto the bed. I stuck my hand into my bag and pulled out the hysterical phone.

Jace's name flashed across the display screen. I flipped it open and the screaming ceased. Oh, thank God. I didn't think it would ever end.

I pressed the phone to my ear and demanded, "What did you do to my phone? It's possessed." I had asked her to change my ringtone because I couldn't figure it out, and the whistling tune wasn't exactly a pleasant reminder after the incident in the park.

"I gave it a personality," Jace replied.

"Well . . . it doesn't need a personality. It's a phone. How do I exorcise it?"

She laughed. "Fine, sorry. I guess I should've chosen something less startling. I can try to talk you through it, or Mr. Southern can probably figure it out."

I sighed and folded my legs beneath me on the bed. I certainly wasn't going to let *her* change it again. "So did you pick out a new door?"

"Yep, it's blue . . . like sapphire blue. Sam actually tracked it down. I don't remember mentioning I like blue."

I smiled to myself. And he said he had it handled without my input. "Your couch is blue. Maybe he picked the door to match your couch?"

There was a long pause. "You told him, didn't you?"

175

"What's that saying . . . I can neither confirm nor deny . . . something, something . . . it's not my fault?"

Jace laughed again. "Nice. Wrong, but nice. He put it up for me and everything, which was unexpected."

"Shouldn't Stanley have put it up?"

"Yeah, about Stanley . . ." There was a beat of silence. "He . . . um . . . well, it looks like he sort of died from alcohol poisoning."

"Sort of? How does someone sort of die?"

"Sort of as in . . . he did. And . . . oh, hey, I have to go. We ordered pizza. Be safe, okay? And call me tomorrow after your meeting."

"K bye." I hung up and gave the possessed phone one last unhappy glare before tossing it aside. That ringtone had to be changed as soon as humanly possible. I spared a moment of regret for Stanley before dragging my notebook out of the bag and scooting back against the headboard to write my thank-you note to God.

I bounced the pen off the page and tried to mentally collect the things I was grateful for today. My eyes strayed to the window when I saw something shift behind the thin white curtain.

Alarm skittered through me. I knew it was foolish: it was a hotel and people would have to walk by the windows to reach their rooms. He couldn't have followed us, not this far.

I forced my attention back to my notebook and started writing.

Dear Jesus,

I'm sorry I didn't write last night. My brain fell asleep after all the chaos. I'm thankful that, despite the circumstances, nobody was hurt. I'm thankful for Sam, who's keeping Jace safe, and for Marx. He's sort of rugged and funny, and I want to trust him.

I paused with my pen on the page and then added, *Is he safe?*

I closed the notebook with a sigh, that last thought lingering. I was sharing an adjoining hotel room with a man I barely knew, and I needed him to be safe.

I stiffened when something tapped against the window. What was going on out there? I stared at the curtains uneasily, and when the tapping sound came again, fear congealed in my stomach like a ball of ice.

I slid off the bed and walked cautiously to the window a few feet away. I hooked a finger around the edge of the curtain and peeled it aside slowly. I yelped and dropped the curtain when something black thumped up against the glass.

I stood there for a moment, trying to scrounge up the nerve to take another look. I crept forward and drew the curtain aside. A black cat stood on the sill, rubbing his head against the glass. I could've melted to the floor in relief. I had almost expected to see a face.

I tapped the glass with my fingernail—I was so grateful to have those back—and the cat looked at me with bright golden eyes. He tried to rub his cheek against my finger and smacked face-first into the glass. Oh, maybe tapping to get his attention wasn't the best idea.

He made me miss my own cat. I hoped my fuzzy baby would be okay for two days without supervision. He had plenty of food and water.

I peered at the parking lot to see if anyone was out there, and the brief idea to open the door and let the cat inside skittered through my brain before I squashed it. I wasn't that stupid.

"Sorry you're stuck out there," I muttered apologetically.

The curious tapping resumed, and I stilled. I had thought it was just the cat, but he was casually licking his paws. I scanned the parking lot and sidewalk, but there was nothing but dark cars.

"Holly," Marx said sternly, and I jumped again. At least I was getting my aerobics in for the day. I hadn't even heard the shower shut off. "Did I not tell you to stay away from the window?"

I let the curtain drift back into place as I folded my arms and turned to look at him. "I heard something."

He tossed aside the towel he'd been using to dry his hair and walked to the window. He opened the curtain and searched the darkness. "What did you hear?"

"Tapping."

His brows drew together. "Like that night at your apartment?"

I nodded, and the carefully calm expression on his face confirmed my earlier fear. "He followed us, didn't he?"

Marx closed the curtain. "I figured he would. After all the trouble he's gone to, he's not just gonna let you slip away. This trip isn't a part of his plans, and stalkers have no reservations about crossin' state lines."

He drew his gun, and a fresh wave of fear shot through me. "You're going out there? But what if . . . what if he's outside the door?"

He gave me a patient look. "Then I'm gonna shoot him."

I followed him back into his room. He peered through the peephole in his door as he said, "I'm leavin' my key inside. If by chance he surprises me, I don't want him to be able to let himself in. If I'm not back in five minutes, call the police and barricade yourself in the bathroom. Understood?"

Images of Jacob dying on my floor flashed through my mind, and I didn't want him to go outside. "Please don't go."

"Holly," he said gently. "I'm gonna be fine." He opened the door and stepped outside. I locked it behind him and ran back to my room to grab my phone. I counted the seconds as I waited anxiously in front of the door.

God, please don't let him end up like Jacob.

I stared at the unmoving door expectantly as the time hit the five-minute mark, but no one knocked. I didn't even hear anyone outside. I decided to wait another minute and give him more time.

Six minutes passed. *Crap*. I dialed the police with shaky fingers. I didn't have the best history with the local police, and I didn't trust them to help us, but there really was no other option.

"9-1-1, what is your emergency?" the operator said.

I described the situation to the best of my knowledge: Marx had gone into the night armed because I'd heard a strange tapping sound. The man on the other end of the line probably thought I was drunk.

"There's a man with a gun?" the operator asked.

"He's a New York City detective. His name is Richard Marx."

Eight minutes.

"We're dispatching a unit to your location now," the man informed me. "Please stay on the line."

I hung up. I wasn't going to answer any more of his questions, and staying on the line wouldn't bring help any faster. I walked to the window and peeked outside. The night was perfectly still, but it shouldn't be. If everything was fine, Marx would be back by now.

Ten minutes.

My eyes traveled to the bathroom door where he'd told me to hide, and then back to the window. If he was hurt, I didn't want to just hide in the bathroom like a coward.

I wrestled with whether or not to go outside and look for him. I knew he would be angry with me if I left the hotel room.

If he's still alive.

That thought cemented my decision: I wasn't hiding in the bathroom. I ran to fetch the kitchen knife from my bag and then returned. I peered through the peephole and, seeing no one on the other side, opened the door.

I clung to the door frame with one hand as I stood in the doorway, afraid to leave the relative safety of the room for the unknown darkness outside.

I glanced at my phone. Fifteen minutes.

I sucked in a breath to call out to him and then thought better of it. If the killer was out here, then he would follow my voice right to where I stood. I stepped forward, and my fingers dropped from the door frame. This was stupid. I knew it was stupid.

But Marx was important to me, even if I didn't fully understand why. I crept into the parking lot with my knife gripped sideways in my fist.

My hands trembled as I walked between two cars. I couldn't see anything or anyone. I didn't even realize I was passing Marx's car until something shiny caught the light of the moon. I stepped back and leaned over the hood of the car to see the object on the windshield.

A Polaroid picture was taped to the front window. I squinted to make out the image. It was of Marx and me on one of my "breaks" during the road trip. I was crouched down with my eyes shut as I tried to relax, and Marx was watching me as he leaned against the side of the car. There was a red X through his head, and written in capital letters beneath it were the words "She's mine."

"Holly," a voice hissed from behind me.

I squeaked in fright and nearly leaped onto the hood of the car. I slashed blindly at the person behind me, but they caught my wrist and pulled me forward when I tried to scramble back.

"Stop it," the man growled in a low whisper. He held my wrist immobile, and the knife was useless. I tried to kick him and pull away at the same time, which really wasn't very effective. "Holly, stop flailin'."

I stopped when a hint of his Southern accent bled through into the hoarse whisper. I gasped for breath as I twisted around to look into Marx's shadowed face.

"What are you doin' out here?" he demanded as he plucked the knife from my hand.

My voice carried a nervous tremor as I said, "You didn't come back."

"Because I'm lookin' for him."

"You said five minutes."

"I said call the police in five minutes if I wasn't back," he snapped. "Not wander around a dark parkin' lot with a knife."

"I was worried."

He sighed angrily through gritted teeth. "Back to the room. Now."

A scraping sound pierced the quiet night—like boots on pavement—and Marx jerked me to the ground by my arm. I crouched beside him between the two cars, trying to breathe silently. I noticed that the front tire of his car was flat, then glanced over my shoulder at the rear tire. It was flat too. The killer had slashed them.

"Don't move," Marx whispered, his tone leaving no room for argument. I nodded, and he shook his head in exasperation, as if he expected me to do exactly the opposite. He crept around the car in a crouch and peered through the parking lot.

Another quiet scrape of footsteps emanated from somewhere nearby. I remembered that sound from the first night I'd been followed back to my apartment. He'd probably wanted me to know I was being followed, just like he wanted us to know he was hunting us now. Marx looked back over his shoulder at me and motioned to the car. I blinked in confusion.

"Under the car," he whispered.

I shook my head. I didn't want to go under the car. Marx came back and crouched beside me. "I know you're afraid of small spaces, but he's in this parkin' lot somewhere. He's here for two reasons: to kill me and to take you back, but I expect he'll be plenty satisfied if he just gets you. So get under the car." I shook my head again. "Holly, don't fight me on this. If I'm worried about you bein' exposed out here, it makes it harder for me to protect myself."

I glanced at the car next to his. It was slightly higher off the ground, and if the killer looked under cars to find me, he would look under Marx's car first. I sank to my stomach reluctantly and wiggled under the car. It was such a tight space, and I could feel the familiar anxiety blossoming in my chest, but I couldn't crawl back out. I squeezed my eyes shut. A song I'd heard years ago popped into my mind, and if I weren't so anxious I would've laughed at how appropriate it was.

They paved paradise and put up a parking lot. With a pink hotel, a . . . a . . . something and a swinging hot spot . . . Something like that. I retraced the lyrics in my mind, trying to remember how the song went. As I concentrated, some of the anxiety ebbed. *Trees in a tree museum.*

The sound of approaching sirens shattered my concentration, and I opened my eyes to see flashing lights igniting the darkness in the distance.

24

The officer, whom I thankfully didn't know, finished scribbling down Marx's statement and then closed his little black notebook. "I'll forward this information to one of the local detectives, and I'll see that they get your card in case they have any more questions or anything comes up." He stashed his notepad and pen in a pocket on his uniform and extended his hand. "Pleasure to meet you, Detective."

Marx shook his hand.

"Ma'am." He tipped his hat politely in my direction before exiting the hotel room.

Marx closed and locked the door and then dropped onto the edge of his bed with a tired sigh. He rubbed his hands over his face.

"He's angry with you for bringing me here," I said softly.

Marx nodded as he pulled his hands down his face and dropped them into his lap. "I noticed that. He threw a temper tantrum like a five-year-old. If he was thinkin' clearly, he never would've slashed my tires, 'cause now we're stuck exactly where he doesn't want us to be."

He picked my knife up off the bed where he'd dropped it and turned it over in his hands. I saw the unspoken questions wrinkle his forehead. "I'm curious why you brought a kitchen knife on our road trip, but I have a feelin' it's one of those things I shouldn't ask about."

I gave him a tight smile, and he held the knife out to me. I took it. "I'm gonna take a shower. I'll see you in the morning." I walked out of the room, gathered my things, and went to clean up.

After my shower, I stretched out beneath the strange blankets in the uncomfortably hard bed and closed my eyes. I tried to sleep, but my body refused to relax.

When I glanced at the clock on the side table, it was almost four a.m., and I was no closer to sleep now than when I'd crawled beneath the blankets two hours ago.

I stared at the doors standing open between the adjoining rooms; they allowed too many dark memories to slink into bed with me. I flung off the blankets and slipped out of the bed.

I tiptoed across the room to the doors and peered through the doorway into the dark room. I could hear the quiet rhythm of Marx's breathing. I knew he would probably be angry with me for closing the door, especially after the killer had paid us a visit, but if I didn't, I would never be able to sleep.

The door clicked quietly as I pushed it shut, and my fingers hesitated briefly on the dead bolt before I flipped it. Some of the tension immediately drained from my body. I grabbed the knife back out of my bag on the floor and curled up beneath the blankets. It wasn't long before I drifted to sleep.

25

We arrived at the prison thirty minutes late because I overslept. Marx hadn't said a word to me about the fact that I had locked the door between our rooms, but I knew he'd noticed, because he woke me up by knocking on it.

He was getting better about not asking uncomfortable questions.

I hesitated in the doorway of the prison visiting room when I saw the woman I had once thought was my mother. She sat at a round metal table in the middle of the room. Her blond hair had thinned, and it hung over her shoulders in wisps of blond and silvery streaks.

Isabel Lane. She was the only mother I could ever remember having. She and her husband had cared for me for two years, and I thought they were my family. That was, until they were arrested for drug trafficking and I was tossed into the foster care system. No one really knew how I came to be in their care.

Her blue eyes flitted around the room in search of her visitor. I almost turned around and walked out the door I'd entered through, but Marx was standing behind me.

"Are you sure you wanna do this?" he asked quietly.

"No," I admitted pathetically.

I couldn't quite untangle my feelings for her. She and her husband had found me or taken me from somewhere and pretended to be my family, and that made me want to hate her. But they had never hurt me, and they had provided for me as if I were theirs. And no matter what crimes they had committed, or lies they had told, they were the first people I remembered and I had loved them with the unconditional devotion of a child.

"There's somethin' you should know, Holly. I meant to tell you last night, but . . ." He sighed.

"What?" I asked warily.

"Isabel's not just in here for drug traffickin'. I had Sully look into her for me before we left New York." He hesitated. "She and her husband murdered somebody—a rival drug dealer."

I wished I could say I was surprised.

I remembered Izzy whisking me away when a confrontation broke out on a dark sidewalk between Paul and another man. Paul had come back to the camper later that night agitated and covered in blood. In hindsight, I didn't think all the blood on his clothes had been his.

Now I couldn't help but wonder if Paul had killed that man. But Izzy had been with me that night; she hadn't murdered anyone. Unless . . . that man wasn't the drug dealer they were accused of killing. I tried to push aside the awful possibilities. I didn't really want to know.

"None of that changes the fact that we still need answers," I said. I drew in a deep breath and then forced myself to walk toward Izzy's table.

Her eyes skipped over me and then snapped back with a spark of recognition. She straightened, and an expression of affection and astonishment brightened her haggard face. "Holly?"

Her emphatic greeting almost made me miss a step. I forced a reply from my tense throat as I stopped in front of her table. "Hello, Izzy." It came out a little more hollow than I had intended.

Her gaze swept over me, comparing the woman before her with the child she remembered. A lot had changed in sixteen years, but enough had stayed the same that she recognized me. "You were such a pretty girl. I knew you would grow up to be beautiful."

Her praise made me self-conscious. I sat down on the metal bench as if it were a bomb and I might need to run for my life at any moment. Izzy reached across the table in the hopes that I would take her hands, and I forgot to be civil as I snapped mine away from her. She had no business touching me.

The initial shock of my rejection played across her face before hurt took its place. She drew her empty hands back and gripped the edge of the table.

"I'm . . . sorry," I said after a moment. I hadn't come here to hurt her. "I don't like to be touched."

She tilted her head as she regarded me quizzically. "That never used to bother you. You were a very cuddly child."

A memory of her tucking the blankets in around my body, cocooning me in safety, as she gently rubbed my head until I fell asleep floated to the front of my mind. I cleared my throat. "Well, things change."

"That must make relationships difficult," she said.

Twist that knife in my heart a little more, Izzy, thanks. I glanced subtly at Marx, who lingered several feet to my left. She was so enthralled by my presence that she hadn't noticed him yet. I wasn't sure how she would react when she did. "I manage," was all I told her.

"I tried to write you," she said. "But no one would tell me where you were."

"I moved around a lot." I hoped she wouldn't ask too many questions. I hadn't come here to give her a summary of my messed-up childhood.

"Oh," she said, her face clouding with sadness. "I always hoped you would find a good home. You were such a sweet girl."

Anger and hurt crowded my chest, and I glanced away so she couldn't see them on my face. "If you really believed that, Izzy, you would've made more of an effort to keep me."

She flinched. I knew it wasn't a kind thing to say, and it was off topic, but I couldn't seem to stop the words from escaping.

"I . . . I wanted to keep you. I would have, but . . ."

I bit down on my lips as she stammered meaningless excuses. I needed to get this conversation back on track before she crumbled into tears or I got up and left. "Do you remember the night you found me?"

She stopped stammering and nodded. "Of course I do. That was the best day of our lives. I always wanted a little girl, and you just . . . dropped right into our laps like it was meant to be." Her blue eyes grew distant with memory.

I saw the disapproving clench of Marx's jaw out of the corner of my vision. I had no doubt he would describe me "dropping into their laps" as kidnapping.

I tried to ignore him as I pushed forward. "You never really told me about that day."

Her pale skin took on an ashen hue, and she looked down at the table as she shook her head. "There's nothing to tell, really." But her body language belied her words. She was hiding something, and that secret frightened her. "Tell me about you. Do you have a boyfriend?"

Wow, she was definitely avoiding my question. If she expected to distract me with small talk, she was going to be very disappointed. I didn't do small talk—at least not without butchering it to pieces.

"A pretty girl like you must have boys falling at your feet," she said.

Most men didn't bother with me. I assumed it was because they either didn't find me attractive or because I gave off a touch-me-and-I'll-stab-you vibe that sent them fleeing in the other direction. "No, no boyfriend."

"A husband? You're not wearing a ring, but I hear that's the thing these days for independent young women."

Marx tried not to smile when she described me as independent. I shot him a glare out of the corner of my eye. She didn't even know me.

"Izzy, I'm not here to talk about my personal life."

Her attention shifted to Marx when she suddenly noticed him hovering *oh so covertly* a few feet to my left, and she squinted at him suspiciously. She sat back a little stiffly, and her blue eyes took on a frosty sharpness I'd never seen before. "You look like a cop."

Marx arched an eyebrow at her. Well, there was no dancing around his presence now. Izzy had scented him out like a bloodhound, and now her guard was up.

"It's the cop face," I told him. I waved my hand in front of my face for emphasis. "You get this look."

"What exactly does my cop face look like?" he asked.

"Um . . . I-wanna-slam-your-head-off-the-hood-of-my-car-and-handcuff-you-because-I-think-you're-the-scum-of-the-earth," I tried to explain. It's not like it was an easy thing to describe.

"I have never slammed anybody's head off the hood of my car. That would dent my car," he said with complete seriousness. "The pavement, though . . . that's a whole 'nother matter."

Izzy's eyes bulged with disbelief as she looked between us. "You can't be serious. You two are . . . you're too old for her."

"Izzy, I'm twenty-eight," I pointed out.

"And when you were ten, he was what . . . thirty?" she asked in obvious disgust. "You shouldn't be touching her at all, you pig," she spat, turning her venomous glare back on Marx. "She deserves better than the likes of you."

Marx's expression remained neutral, as if her words bounced right off him. I, however, was a little disturbed by the image she was painting, and wanted to scrub the inside of my head out with a Brillo Pad.

"We're not *together*," I explained.

"Then why did you bring him?" she demanded.

"He's a friend."

She gave me a pitying look as she explained in a voice that was disturbingly motherly, "Cops are not friends, Holly. You can't trust them." . . . *says the lying drug dealer* . . .

"He's trying to help me."

"Into a jail cell or into his bed? Because that's the only way they work." She sneered at Marx, and he gave her a flat look that conveyed just how little he thought of her opinion.

I stared at her in silent disbelief. I had my reasons for disliking the police, but my hatred of them paled in comparison to hers. If she could've set Marx on fire with her eyes, she would've kicked back and watched him burn with a smile on her face. What could possibly have made her despise anyone with a badge so completely?

Marx crossed his arms over his chest and looked appropriately intimidating as he grumbled, "Hate me all you like, Ms. Lane, but if you care about Holly at all, you'll answer her questions."

Izzy drew herself up like an angry cat. "I *love* Holly. Don't try to manipulate . . ."

"Stop it, Izzy!" I shouted, smacking the table with my hands as I stood up. She blinked in surprise and snapped her mouth shut. I had learned that tactic from Marx firsthand, and it worked like a charm. "He didn't put you here. You did."

She folded her arms and gave him one last hateful glare before returning her attention to me. "Whether it was him or some other cop who put me here, it doesn't matter. They're all the same."

Hearing her bitter words was like looking into a mirror a month ago, and I didn't like what I saw. I had believed that same thing, but I couldn't anymore. Jacob hadn't been cruel—he'd been innocent; Sam wasn't indifferent—he was loyal; and Marx broke just about every mold I expected cops to fit into.

"You chose this life when you chose to break the law for a living," I told her, my voice quiet but taut with anger. "You . . . killed someone, Izzy. You trafficked drugs."

She lifted her chin proudly. "I provided for my family."

"Illegally."

She scoffed. "You sound like a cop. Is that what you are now?"

The coldness in her voice stung, and I sat back down on the bench slowly. "I'm a photographer. I take pictures of landscapes and people." Why did it matter to me what she thought? I didn't need her approval or her acceptance.

She searched my face to see if I was telling the truth. "You always did love nature . . . except for the woods. You would never go near the woods." Her stiff posture relaxed, and she rested her hands back on the table as she leaned forward. "I know most people don't approve of what I chose to do for a living. But it put food on the table and clothes on your back. We had a home. We were a family, Holly, and we were happy. That's all that mattered."

I closed my eyes briefly and shook my head. She'd convinced herself that the ends justified the means, but they hadn't. The means destroyed everything she had tried to build. "You should've gotten a job to support the family. Paul should've gotten a job. But you chose drugs over me. Do you know what that cost me?" Emotion made my voice higher than usual even as I tried to whisper. "Do you have any idea what your *illegal support* put me through?"

"Holly," Marx said in warning. We had discussed this conversation on the trip over, and I knew I was steering it from information gathering headlong into painful personal history, but I couldn't stop myself. Her selfish, warped perspective was too much for me to swallow.

"Twelve foster homes, Izzy," I told her. "You have no idea what that did to me. What *they* did to me."

She struggled to find a response. "We were just doing what we always did."

"You should've stopped." Hot tears blurred my vision. "When you decided to include me in your family, you should've stopped selling drugs. You *should've* chosen me."

She drew back as if I had slapped her. "Holly, I . . ."

"You didn't choose me," I whispered with more pain and sadness than I ever realized I'd buried. I could've been happy with them as my family. My life could've been so very different.

"Maybe that's enough for now," Marx suggested.

"No!" Izzy shouted, pounding the table with her fist hard enough to startle the entire room full of visitors. She leveled an icy glare at him. "You are not taking her. I've waited sixteen years for this day."

"I don't think you deserve this day," he replied evenly.

I got up from the table and walked to the other side of the room despite her pleas for me to stay. I couldn't stand to sit at the same table with her anymore. I needed a minute to pull myself back together before there was any hope of finishing the interrogation.

191

"Holly, baby, please . . . I'm so sorry. I'm so sorry we didn't make better choices. What can I do? How can I make it right?" She pleaded from across the room. I could hear the tears in her voice, but I turned my back to her and rested my forehead against the wall.

"You can't make it right," Marx told her, and there was no sympathy in his voice as she sobbed at the table in front of him. Her cries grew muffled as she covered her face with her hands. "If I were her, I would never forgive you."

Izzy drew in a long, shuddering breath and snarled, "I don't care what you think. You don't know her. She was mine for two years. *Two* years."

"She wasn't yours," he snapped. "You took her. There's a difference."

"She was mine! I took her in. I cared for her. I tucked that little girl in every night, and I've thought about her every day since. I love her."

"Then prove it."

Izzy hiccupped a breath and asked, "How do you expect me to do that?"

"Tell me what happened the night you found her," he said.

"Why?" she hissed suspiciously. "So you can add more years to my sentence?"

"I couldn't care less about your sentence, Ms. Lane," he growled under his breath. "You can rot in here for all I care. What matters to me is that young lady over there, whose life is in danger. If you *love* her as much as you say you do, then help me keep her safe."

"I don't talk to cops," she said coldly. "But I'll tell Holly whatever she wants to know. Convince her to talk to me again."

Marx sighed. "I won't do that."

I exhaled slowly and cleared my expression before I pushed away from the wall. I had come here for a purpose, and I needed to finish what I'd started. I didn't spend eight torturous hours in a car so we could leave with nothing because I couldn't control my emotions.

I walked back to the table, and Izzy looked up at me with unguarded hope and desperation in her face. Marx was leaning on the table across from her so that he was at her eye level, and he straightened at my approach.

"You don't have to talk to her, Holly."

"I do." I gave him a small, tight smile to let him know this was my choice and nothing he could say would change my mind. "I'll stay as long as she answers our questions."

I sat back down on the bench and Izzy stretched her hands across the table to touch me. Marx gave her a sharp look, and she jerked them back with surprising quickness and stuffed them under the table.

"Tell us about the night you *found* Holly," he demanded.

I felt the warmth of his body as he leaned on the table beside me, staring down my former mother with frightening intensity. I could see the internal struggle reflected on Izzy's face. In order to tell us the story, she would have to admit to a crime she didn't want anyone to know about.

She hissed in a breath, and her voice quivered with emotion as she began to speak. "We didn't kidnap you, Holly. It wasn't kidnapping. We rescued you from him." Her eyes pleaded with me to understand. "We were traveling. Moving . . . product. We were headed back here to Maine, where we lived, and we passed through a small town in Kansas."

The word Kansas sent a jolt through me, and I looked at Marx. He made the connection too. The note card had been sent to me from Kansas. We had both wondered if it was sent to lure me to the killer's "home" or my own.

"We were on a back road, and the next thing we knew, this little girl—this beautiful little girl—ran out of the woods covered in blood. She ran straight in front of the car. Paul tried to stop, but we hit her." I caught a glimpse of the pain and guilt that secret had burdened her with before she looked down at the table. "She was just lying there on the road, and we thought . . . we thought she was dead. But then she mumbled something. A man came running out of

193

the woods after her. He was a big man, and there was no good reason he should've been chasing that little girl through the woods. He had a knife, and it was covered in blood. Paul pulled out his gun and shot him. We picked up the little girl, put her in the back of the camper, and drove as fast and as far as we could."

Marx's fingertips curled in anger on the tabletop. "You didn't think to take her to a hospital?"

"She was fine."

"You hit her with your car," he bit out.

"What were we supposed to do? A hospital would ask questions, and we couldn't exactly tell the police, now could we?"

Not with a bunch of drug paraphernalia in the back of the car.

"Maybe she had a family," he pointed out.

"Officer," Izzy said with a patronizing lilt to her voice. "If she had a family, they were dead. The blood on that knife, and all over her clothes, it wasn't hers. He killed *someone* with that knife."

Marx's eyes slid to me, but I was too shocked to do anything but stare at Izzy. She'd known all this time and had never uttered a helpful word of it to anyone.

"Where did your husband shoot him?" Marx demanded.

Izzy shrugged. "Somewhere in the torso. He dropped like a rock, and we just assumed he was dead." Her eyes widened with sudden comprehension, and I saw a spark of fear in their depths. "He's not dead, is he?" Her gaze darted to me and then back to Marx. "That's why you're here." She wrung her hands anxiously. "No, you have to do something. He was gonna hurt Holly. What if he comes after her?"

She was begging a police officer for help on my behalf. That had to taste bitter on her tongue.

"He already has. He came for her last night, and not for the first time," he explained. "I need to know everythin' you can tell me about him so I can stop him from hurtin' her."

Izzy was so pale I thought she might faint. "He's here? In Maine?" She grappled with that concept for a second and then seemed to pull herself back together. "Okay. What can I tell you?"

"Where in Kansas did this shootin' take place?" Marx asked.

"Stony Brooke. It was a back road between the trees. I don't remember the name of it. We tried never to travel on main roads." She glanced at me with worry. "If it helps, he was well over six feet with dark hair. And he was young, probably in his twenties. And his nose looked . . . crooked, but it could've been the shadows. It was too dark to see much else."

"It helps. Can you remember anythin' else?"

Izzy strained to remember anything else that might have stood out, and then shook her head in frustration. "Just that he wore black."

"Do you think you can work with a sketch artist?"

Izzy shook her head. "I'm not good with faces. I can't remember enough. Oh! One more thing. It was the night before Halloween."

Marx sighed and stood up. "Thank you for your time, Ms. Lane." He offered me a hand, which I blatantly ignored as usual. He would get used to it eventually.

I rose from the table and looked at the woman I'd once thought was my mother. She did care about me in her own way, and after all the rejection I had experienced in my life, it mattered to me that she cared. But I wasn't sure I wanted her to be a part of my life.

"Will you come back?" she asked hopefully. "You're all I have. Paul . . . Paul passed away in prison."

Paul died in prison? I stared at her, unsure what I was supposed to feel. I had only known Paul for two years, and I hadn't been nearly as close with him as I had been with Izzy. She'd cared for me. But if she was to be believed, Paul had saved my life eighteen years ago. Surely that counted for something.

I knew how it felt to drift through life alone and disconnected, and that wasn't a life I would wish on anyone. "I'll write." It was the most I could offer her. Izzy looked a little crestfallen as we left her sitting alone at the table, but we left the prison a few details richer.

26

The road trip back to New York was even worse than the trip to Maine. The few breaks we took were nerve-racking, because we both knew the killer was lurking somewhere in the background, taking pictures and planning his next attack.

Relief swelled through me when Marx pulled his car up to the curb outside my apartment. I was finally home. Before I could open the door and hop out, he said, "Holly, there's somethin' I wanna talk to you about."

The gravity in his voice made my fingers freeze on the door handle. The last time he took that voice, it was to tell me that Izzy was a murderer. "Okay . . ."

He looked as though he was still working through his thoughts when he started to speak. "God forbid it ever happens again, but . . . if the killer manages to get you alone, I need you to pretend you don't remember any more about him than you did when we left New York."

Unease crawled through. He was usually careful not to alarm me unnecessarily, which meant he thought this scenario was a very real possibility, and it worried him.

"You want me to lie."

"I want you to give him reason to doubt that it's the right time to take you," he said, with a quick look my way. "Give us a chance to get to you. He might take you anyway; there's no tellin' with his state of mind."

"You've given this a lot of thought."

"After last night, yes, I have," he said, and I could hear the tension in his voice. "I just want you to be prepared."

I inhaled a shaky breath and looked out the window. The killer had bided his time for who knew how long, and now he was running out of patience. "Okay," I agreed. I wasn't the most convincing liar, but if my life depended on it, I would try.

I climbed out of the car and into the fading light of evening with my bag, and started toward my apartment. The door swung inward with a familiar squeak of metal, and I welcomed the scent of must and lilac air freshener as I stepped inside. I dropped my bag on the counter and took a moment to just breathe in the comforting smells of home.

Jordan trotted across the room with a chirp of delight, and I crouched down to meet him. "Hi, fatty." I smiled and scooped him into my arms with a grunt of effort. I really had to revisit that diet idea. I rubbed between his ears as I turned in the doorway to see Marx still standing by his car. He was on his phone.

A man jogged by on the sidewalk, and it took too long for his face to register. I tried to duck out of view, but judging by his breathy exhalation of my name, he'd spotted me.

Wonderful. I'd been home for all of thirty seconds.

I gritted my teeth and stepped into the doorway to see the man striding down the sidewalk toward me with his hands on his hips. He was panting heavily from exertion, and his gray T-shirt stuck to him in damp patches of sweat.

"I didn't know you lived here," he said.

I stared at his face as I strained to remember his name: *Lance, Luther, Lucky . . . Luke!* He was the man I usually crossed paths with while jogging, and the same man I had politely refused to have drinks with at the café.

I gave him a tense, unwelcoming smile. "Yep."

I saw Marx straighten and murmur a parting comment into his phone before snapping it shut. He looked at me with a silent question in his eyes: do you need help? I gave him a subtle shake of my head. I was pretty sure this situation wouldn't require police involvement.

Luke descended the few steps to the patio, and I stiffened when he stopped less than two feet from me. If backing up wouldn't communicate that I was inviting him inside, I would've taken three

197

giant steps back to give myself some breathing room. I set Jordan on the floor and folded my arms instead to express that I didn't want him coming any closer.

"How are you?" he asked. He looked me over, his visual inspection more clinical than intimate. "I heard what happened at the café that day: a guy died, and when I looked up an article on it, I saw your picture online. You were covered in blood."

My throat constricted. Online?

"I was worried something happened to you, and I felt really bad for leaving when I did. If I'd stayed a few more minutes, maybe I could've done something."

"I'm fine. And there really wasn't much to do. He died quickly."

"I'd like to think I could've done something. I am an EMT."

Well, that was interesting. I would've never pegged him as an EMT; something more like a businessman or an office worker.

"I jog by here sometimes, and I've noticed there's almost always a police officer standing out front. Are you in some sort of witness protection program?"

"Something like that."

Marx cleared his throat just loudly enough to draw Luke's attention. He gave the man a friendly smile, but Luke seemed to understand that it was time for him to leave.

"Well, I just wanted to check in with you and make sure you were okay." I got the impression it wasn't what he'd originally intended to say. "I hope to see you jogging sometime." He hopped up the steps and then paused at the top. He gave me an oddly sweet smile as he said, "Have a good night, Holly."

Marx watched him jog away down the sidewalk before returning his gaze to me. "Well, he seems normal." At my noncommittal shrug, he said, "I take it he's not your type."

I blinked at him, unsure what I was supposed to say to that. I knew most people had types. Jace preferred men with accents. I preferred men fifteen feet away, but I didn't think that qualified as a type.

I could appreciate a man's handsome features like I could appreciate a beautifully taken photograph, but whatever was supposed to trigger an attraction between two people . . . was broken.

Somehow that made me feel even more defective.

"He has a nice smile," I offered before Marx could notice my hesitation. His dark green eyes were speculative as he walked down the sidewalk. My answer hadn't come quickly enough.

I sighed and walked away from the door, leaving it open so he could come in when he was ready. I opened my refrigerator and pulled out a bottle of fruit punch. I gripped the cap and twisted, but it didn't budge.

I only had this problem with screw caps. I cursed the person who invented them. For the life of me, if I managed to get them off without a wrench, I could never get them back on straight.

Marx stepped inside and closed the door. With a frown, he asked, "Would you like a hand with that?"

"No," I grumbled. I grabbed a towel off the counter and wrapped it over the lid, but the lid was stuck to the bottle as if someone had melted them together. The towel slid uselessly around the cap along with my fingers.

"All right then," Marx said. He sat down at the table and watched my struggle with a vaguely amused smile.

I flung the towel aside and banged the lid off the edge of the counter, trying to break the impenetrable seal. Jordan ducked for cover when the violent banging erupted. I made one last valiant effort to twist off the dented cap, and then admitted defeat. I slammed it on the countertop with a hateful glare.

Marx hunched over the table and buried his face in his hand. It took me a moment to realize his shoulders were shaking in silent laughter.

"Stop laughing at me," I demanded as I reached into the refrigerator and grabbed another bottle of fruit punch. The cap popped right off. Apparently, the first one was the devil.

He dropped his hand on the table, but his face was still flushed with laughter. "I'm sorry," he said after a moment. He cleared his throat. "I've never seen quite a display of . . . determination."

I scowled at him as I took a sip of my drink. "Well, you're welcome to have it since I'll apparently never get it open." I tossed the first bottle to him.

He caught it and twisted the cap off with embarrassing ease. His lips twitched as he tried not to laugh at my frustrated expression. "This is one of Sam's favorites."

"I didn't know that."

"He's a pretty private person. Not unlike yourself."

He took a swig of the red liquid and made such a face of disgust that I nearly choked on my own fruit punch. "That bad?"

He forced himself to swallow and screwed the cap back on. "I think I'll stick to coffee." He slid the bottle back across the table.

I grabbed a glass from the corner of the counter, checked it for cat food, and filled it with water before setting it on the table in front of him. "Thank you," he mumbled before he took a gulp. He swished it around in his mouth to erase the flavor of the punch and then swallowed.

"So what happens now?" I asked. There had to be somewhere we could go with the information we'd gathered. I couldn't stand to just wait for the killer to make his next move.

"I received a call from the crime lab while we were on our last break, but I wanted to wait until we got back to discuss it," he said.

If he'd wanted to wait, it probably wasn't good news. I gripped my punch with both hands and leaned back against the counter for support. "Okay. Let's hear it."

"There were no suspicious fingerprints on any of the items, not even the pictures. Probably because he wears gloves."

Matte black leather gloves that absorbed the light rather than reflected it, helping him to melt into the darkness.

"The blood on the cat collar appears to be feline," he continued. "The name on the collar says Buttercup, and there was a small fingerprint on the heart-shaped name tag—probably a child's."

The photograph the killer had left for me the night Jacob died materialized in my mind: a younger version of myself cradling a kitten with a silver heart name tag dangling beneath its chin. "The fingerprint is probably mine."

"That was my thought as well." He pulled out his phone and pressed a few buttons, scrolling through something I couldn't see. "The knife that killed Jimmy, Cambel, and Jacob . . ."—he hesitated for just an instant on the last name— "were the same knife. There were no stab wounds to get a good mold of the blade, just slices. Take a look at these and see if any of these knives look familiar."

I accepted his phone and scrolled through the pictures slowly. I shook my head and handed it back. "None of these are right."

"What do you mean they're not right?"

The knife I'd seen in the killer's hand looked far more frightening than any of those, but it could've just been the fear that shaped my perception of it.

I grabbed my notebook and pen from my bag and sketched a quick, rough image of the knife I remembered. The blade wasn't that long, maybe three or four inches, and the top of it wasn't perfectly straight; it curved upward to a frighteningly fine point.

I stared at the completed image to make sure it was somewhat accurate—I wasn't the best artist after all—and then handed it to Marx. The grimace on his face made me wonder if I'd done something wrong.

"Holly, this is a skinnin' knife." At my blank expression, he clarified, "For flayin' the skin off animals, usually fish. This is what he was carryin' the night he came here?"

I really didn't like where this was headed. I rubbed my arms, trying to dispel the chill that came over me as I nodded. I liked my skin very much attached to my body.

Marx's expression darkened and he glanced back at the picture. I had no doubt his mind had just traveled to the same terrifying place mine had: did the killer intend to skin me like an animal?

After a moment's pause, he said, "This knife can also make very quick, shallow cuts." As if that would somehow make either of us feel better. "If he was skinnin' people, the press would know about it by now. That isn't the kind of story that stays quiet."

That was true. Stabbings and shootings were too mundane to attract much attention in the media, but if a person had been skinned, it would be in every newspaper and on every news channel by the following morning. So at least I only had to worry about being stabbed to death. That was an improvement.

"I'll have Sully look into possibilities. Maybe he bought it from a special store or website and we can use it to help track him down," Marx said. He tore the page out and handed the notebook back to me.

"What about the rabbit?" I asked.

"The blood on the rabbit is human. There was a DNA match in the system to an open homicide case in Stony Brooke, Kansas, from October 30, 1998."

I sank slowly into the chair across from him and stared numbly at the bottle gripped too tightly in my hands. I had appeared on the road the day before Halloween, Izzy had said, and I'd been fleeing from a man who had already murdered someone that night.

"Who?" I asked reluctantly.

"The DNA matches a woman named Emily Cross."

I didn't remember her, but her name unleashed a torrent of conflicting emotions inside me: love, hatred, safety, terror . . . longing. My voice came out hoarse with emotion. "Who was she?"

"I don't know." He sighed as he watched my face. "I don't have many details yet. Apparently, the locals prefer hard copy files to an electronic database. I reached out to the local police department, but they weren't involved with the case. They referred me to the sheriff's department, and I'm waitin' to hear back."

I closed my eyes and squeezed the bottle in my hands. I'd known deep down that the body I tripped over had belonged to a woman or a girl. Now I knew her name, and I knew that she'd meant something to me.

27

"Add one cup of chocolate chips," Jace said in a monotone voice as she squinted to read a nearly illegible recipe. All I saw was "one c-smudge of smudge-ate chips." Someone apparently hated this recipe, because they'd cried all over it, making the ink bleed.

Jace handed me a measuring cup. "Be precise," she instructed.

I looked at the measuring cup in my hand and then at the bag of chocolate chips. Pfft. I ripped open the bag and emptied every last chocolate chip into the bowl.

"Holly, that's too much!" she shouted.

"You said be precise. I poured the entire bag in with expert precision. Didn't drop a single one."

She groaned and plopped her face into her hands. "These are gonna be disgusting."

"At least I can differentiate between a tablespoon and a teaspoon." She clearly couldn't, evidenced by the heaping mountain of baking soda she'd added to the mix.

She scowled at me.

I mixed the cookie dough batter with a wooden spoon until it was thick enough to make my arm ache. I was pretty sure it had transformed into leather somewhere along the way. I grabbed a spoon and popped a glob of batter into my mouth.

"Don't eat it! It has raw eggs in it!"

I gave her a befuddled look as I finished chewing the tasty leather, and then licked the spoon clean. There was a psycho trying to kill me . . . like I was worried about salmonella. "Raw eggs. Really?"

She rolled her eyes and opened her mouth to scold me when her phone rang. She tugged it out of her pocket, glanced at the display, and groaned loudly. "My mom. I need to go pretend I'm listening for twenty minutes." She wheeled out of the kitchen, and I heard her shout, "Don't eat the cookie dough, Holly!"

I ate another glob of cookie dough. Sugary sweetness—with a hint of salty bitterness from too much baking soda—melted over my tongue.

I plopped some golf ball–sized cookies onto a baking sheet with a fresh spoon and glanced at the recipe card: "Bake at 350 degrees for smudge-minutes." Right . . . so, thirty minutes?

I popped them into the oven and set the timer.

Being alone in the kitchen as I watched the timer gave me too much time to think. I was trying to avoid that. I had too many questions and too few answers.

My mind kept drifting back to the woman whose body I'd tripped over all those years ago. Emily Cross. I couldn't remember her face or why her name filled me with so much longing.

I couldn't help but wonder if she'd been my mother. Had I ever stood in the kitchen and baked cookies with the woman I couldn't remember? Would she have let me eat the raw cookie batter or lick the bowl clean?

Then there had been the man who called me "baby" and urged me to safety. I didn't want them to be my family; the thought was too disheartening. I wanted them to be strangers I had just happened to find myself in a bad situation with.

I sighed and crouched down in front of the oven. Wondering would get me nowhere; Marx would have answers for me soon enough. I peered through the glass panel of the oven door at the cookies bubbling on the sheet. I really wanted them to be done so I could eat one. I tapped the glass with my fingernail impatiently.

"They're not lizards in an aquarium, Holly," Marx commented from across the room. "You can't make them go faster by tappin' the glass."

I grinned and dropped my hand back to my lap. If only. I sat cross-legged on the floor against the wall to watch them bake. I could hear Jace's muffled voice through the wall. She was arguing with her mother again.

I glanced over at the two men leaning against the wall by the door when I heard Sam say quietly, "What if I insist on staying inside? It would be safer for her that way."

"I think she'll slam the door in your face," Marx replied in an equally hushed tone.

I was pretty sure they were talking about me, because I would definitely do that. I had considered doing it to Marx the first time he came to my apartment.

"She doesn't trust me enough to let me inside," Sam said, managing to sound a little hurt. "What do I need to do in order for her to trust me?"

"Get rid of that permanently angry fixture on your face."

"I'm not angry. That's just my face."

I opened the oven and was bombarded by the sweet smell of chocolate chip cookies. The timer hadn't gone off, but they looked done-ish. I scooped three of the hot cookies onto a plate and carried them over to the officers, who promptly fell silent. Sam tried very hard to arrange his expression into something that didn't look angry, but he was right: it was just his face.

Marx offered me a warm smile. "Never figured you for a baker."

I shrugged. "I usually avoid the kitchen, but there are few problems a tasty cookie can't solve." I held out the plate of cookies to Sam. "Have some cookies."

He took the plate cautiously and muttered, "Thanks." He glanced at Marx, who gave him a look that clearly communicated, *Eat at your own risk.*

I tucked my fingers into the back pockets of my jeans and waited for Sam to try one. He gazed at me with uncertainty before he realized why I was still standing there.

"Oh, you meant right now." He eyed the cookies like they were made of dirt rather than chocolate chips and flour. "You didn't scoop these with the same spoon you were licking, did you?"

I scrunched my nose indignantly.

"Right," he muttered. He picked up a cookie carefully and blew on it before taking a small bite. "It's actually not bad. A little salty, but not bad." He ate a second one and offered the remaining cookie to Marx.

"I'm fine, thank you," he refused politely. I was a little offended; he was assuming that just because I had a part in making them, they must be awful. "Don't give me that face, Holly."

I wasn't aware I'd been giving him a face.

He sighed. "Give me the cookie."

Sam smiled faintly as he held out the plate.

Marx eyed the misshapen blob suspiciously. "What's in it?"

"Everything," I said.

"That's helpful, thank you." He took a tentative bite and chewed slowly. He seemed to have a bit of difficulty swallowing it. "That was far more edible than I thought it would be."

I rolled my eyes and took the plate back. If nobody else liked the cookies, I would eat them all myself. I loved cookies.

"I think you offended her," Sam whispered.

Marx whispered back, "That was the worst cookie I've ever tasted." And then in a voice I was meant to hear, he said, "Holly I'm gonna head home. Try not to burn the apartment buildin' down."

"No promises!" I waved good night with the cookie spoon before he left the apartment. I worked my way through the bowl of batter, alternating spoonfuls into my mouth and spoonfuls onto the baking sheets.

I jumped and nearly dropped the tray of cookies I was sliding into the oven when a door banged open. Jace rolled out of her bedroom in a cloud of fury. Her face was still splotchy from the stress of the conversation with her mother. "My mother's coming," she gritted out.

"What? When?"

She folded her arms and huffed. "Now. She's in the neighborhood."

"Um . . . your mother's allergic to this neighborhood. Was she dragged here by wild dogs?"

"I guess we'll find out."

If her mother was coming, that was my cue to leave. She wasn't fond of me.

"I'm gonna go." I walked to the couch to fetch my jacket. "Don't forget about the cookies in the oven."

Sam walked me home in his usual state of silence. After hearing his hushed conversation with Marx across the room, I felt guilty for leaving him standing on the patio when I opened my front door. To his credit, he didn't ask to come in or even make a move toward the opening.

I paused in the doorway. "Sam . . ."

"Holly . . ."

I wanted to be able to invite him to stand guard inside—for his safety and mine—but I just couldn't do it. I held up a finger before walking to the refrigerator and grabbing one of the fruit punches. I brought it back and held it out to him. "Peace offering?"

He took it hesitantly. "I didn't realize we were at war."

"You want inside; I want you outside."

He sighed. "You overheard our conversation."

"Like I said before, the two of you whisper like you're trying to be heard over the roar of a jet engine." I shrugged a little uncomfortably. "I'm sorry I can't invite you in."

He rested his shoulder against the brick siding of the building. His eyes met mine. "You don't have to apologize. I know you care, so there must be a good reason you won't let any of us inside. Marx knows you better than I do, and I trust the line he's drawn."

I bounced a little awkwardly on my toes as I said, "Thanks."

Sam held up the punch and said, "Thanks for this. It's my favorite."

"Oh," I said, remembering I needed his help with something. I pulled my phone from my pocket and shoved it at him. "Would you mind fixing this?"

He took it and turned it over in his hands, looking for visible damage. "What's wrong with it other than the fact that it's ancient?"

"It screams at me."

"The ringtone?" he asked. At my nod, he opened the phone, and I watched as he pressed a series of buttons. I couldn't follow it. The phone made a cute little water drop sound, and he snapped it shut before handing it back. "Done."

"Thanks," I said with a small smile. "Good night."

"Night."

I closed the door and locked it, leaving him out in the cold. Before heading for the shower, I grabbed my own fruit punch from the refrigerator. It opened easily, thank goodness, and I set it on the bathroom sink before I climbed in. I dressed for bed in the bathroom after my shower; it had become a habit after finding the film strip of pictures across my rear windows.

I took a few sips of my punch as I combed my fingers through my hair, and then slid my bare feet into my green slippers before opening the door. A wave of dizziness washed over me as I walked out of the bathroom, and I put a hand against the wall to brace myself. The room tilted dangerously around me.

That was unnerving.

I blinked at the swirl of colors and lights outside my front window, trying to solidify the image. It snapped into focus for just an instant, and I saw a warped face lit from within: uneven eyes, slashes for a nose, and a cavernous mouth with a row of crooked, disproportionate teeth. It was a jack-o'-lantern. Recognition stirred through me as I stared into the face pressed flush against the outside of my window.

"How does mine look, Daddy?" I asked as I grinned up at him from the front steps of the house.

My arm was stained to the elbow with pumpkin guts, and I held a small sharp knife in my right hand as I sawed through the last bit of skin that held the pumpkin's eye in place. I poked it out and leaned back to stare at my masterpiece. His eyes were crooked, as if they were melting down his face, and his teeth were reminiscent of a beaver in need of braces.

I knew without a doubt that the jack-o-lantern in the front window was mine, but there was no way it had survived for so many years. The memory faded, and the pumpkin on the window sill blurred into disorganized shapes and colors.

I'd only ever felt like this once before, and it had been after I swallowed a bottle of pills in the bathroom at the Wells' family home. After every other attempt to free myself from that house had failed, that bottle of pills had been my last hope.

Pills. I looked down at the bottle of fruit punch in my hand and dread flooded through me. It was the only thing I'd consumed that could've been tainted . . . but he would've had to get inside to drug it.

I sucked in a terrified breath. Stanley's keys . . .

I dropped the bottle as if it had burned me, and it spilled across the cement floor of the living room. I stared at the growing pool of red as I hugged the wall, trying to breathe.

This couldn't be happening.

I stumbled slowly along the wall to the kitchen and fumbled to grab the salt bottle. I knocked over glasses in my clumsy haste, and they shattered across the floor. I grabbed the salt and poured it into a glass with shaking fingers, filled it with water, and chugged.

The salt water hit bottom, and my stomach heaved to push it back out. I vomited red fluid into the sink and prayed that enough of the drug went with it to keep me conscious.

"Sam," I called. I banged a hand on the window desperately, but my strength was already waning, and it sounded like little more than a quiet tapping. "Sam," I tried again.

I gripped the counter tightly to keep the world around me from spinning as I looked at the front door. It was still bolted from the inside. If the killer had Stanley's keys, the dead bolts wouldn't keep him out, but they would keep Sam out.

I wasn't sure I had the ability to make it to the door and unlock it. I took one step forward, and the room bent around me, nearly sending me to the floor. I pulled my foot back and huddled in the crook of the cabinets. I needed to get to Sam.

I spotted my phone on the edge of the counter and reached for it. I barely managed to grab it before my legs gave out beneath me and my body melted into a puddle on the floor. Whatever was in the punch was moving too quickly. I didn't have enough time to react.

My fingers trembled as I flipped open my phone. I blinked at the dial pad, trying to pin down the shifting numbers with my eyes, but they wouldn't stop moving.

If I could manage to dial 9-1-1, they would ask for my address, and I didn't have one. I wasn't even sure I had enough strength to explain the situation. It was taking all my effort just to breathe and hold my phone.

I had the strangest sense of being outside myself, a bystander watching as I stupidly stared at the numbers on the phone. I needed to make a decision before I lost that ability too. What was wrong with me?

I hit redial and the phone automatically called the last number I had dialed. *Please answer, please answer the phone this time.*

Marx's groggy voice came on the line, "Holly."

Thank the Lord he answered. Now I just had to force words from my throat. "Help," I rasped into the phone.

All traces of tiredness fled his voice and he sounded alert. "What's wrong?"

A shadow shifted across the room near my bed, and my breath caught in my lungs. He was already inside, concealed behind the edge of the drapes that cordoned off my bedroom.

"He's . . . here," I forced out.

"I'm on my way, Holly. Can you hide?" I heard a car door slam in the background a second before an engine roared to life.

I couldn't hide; I couldn't even pull myself up against the cupboards. I was slumped against them like a puppet whose strings had been cut, and I had no control over my body. I could barely hold the phone to my ear.

"He's inside," I tried to tell him, but I wasn't sure the fleeting whisper traveled across the line.

I heard the rattle of hangers over my bed as he rifled through my wardrobe. I couldn't imagine what he wanted with my clothes.

My heart nearly stopped when he appeared beside the foot of my bed. He wore the same ensemble he'd worn the night he killed Jacob, except for one glove. I could see the skin of his hand as he gripped the tank top I'd worn yesterday and pressed it to his face, drawing in the smell.

It sent a shiver of revulsion through me. He rubbed the soft material between his fingers before setting it gently aside. He ran his bare hand over the soft throw blanket draped over the end of my bed.

He moved with luxurious slowness, absorbing everything around him as if he were trying to memorize it. He even ran the back of his hand along the wall, careful not to leave fingerprints. I knew the drug was trying to pull me under, because one moment he stood by the bed and the next he was in front of the couch.

"Holly," Marx called through the phone. "Talk to me, Holly."

I watched the killer as he picked up the two flat pillows on the couch and smelled each one of them before returning them to their proper place. I blinked and then he was walking toward me. Every slow step sent another jolt of fear through me.

He was too close. Too close . . .

He crouched down in front of me, and I wanted more than anything to pull myself away from him. I pressed my palms to the floor and tried, but someone had filled my body with lead, and it was too heavy for me to move.

I remained slumped against the cupboards, panting from the exertion of trying to move. My heart felt like it was trying to outpace death, and it made it hard to breathe.

God, please help me . . .

The killer lifted his ungloved hand and brushed the back of his knuckles down my cheek in a gentle caress. His touch sent goose bumps cascading across my skin. "You grew up nicely, Holly," he said, his voice a pleased purr.

His fingers were light as they moved over my jaw and down my neck. I cringed inwardly at the feel of his hand near my neck—remembering the feeling of someone else's hand there—and he let his fingertips trail all the way to the hollow of my throat. "Such beautiful skin."

I tried not to tremble under his inspection. I felt so exposed in my tank top; there was too much skin left vulnerable to his touch, and I desperately wanted him to stop. "Stop . . . touching me."

His hand followed the curve of my shoulder and down my right arm, pausing at the thin strip of visible skin on my stomach. I let out a choked whimper. He leaned into me, and I felt his breath rustle through my hair as he said, "Sh, there will be time for crying later."

His fingers glided torturously slow across my bare skin, sending a shudder through me, and then moved down my other arm. I didn't even realize I'd dropped my phone until his hand came to rest on mine, and I saw it lying on the floor beside me. He leaned over and picked it up with his gloved hand.

He made a thoughtful noise as he pressed it to his ear. "Detective Marx, I had hoped we might have a chance to talk." His voice was quietly taunting. I could hear Marx's measured voice on the other end of the line. "Oh, I intend to do much more than touch her, Detective."

I saw the skinning knife as he drew it from a small black sheath in his pocket. It was just as terrifyingly sharp as I remembered. I closed my eyes and prayed he wouldn't skin me alive.

"She's so lovely and vulnerable." I felt the tip of the knife as it danced playfully across the skin of my forearm. "Such perfect, pale skin that it practically glows in the moonlight. So unfortunate for her that you're still at least ten minutes away."

He chuckled softly at whatever Marx said on the other end of the line. "Come now, Detective, we both know it's pointless to lie. I know where you live, what kind of car you drive. I know how

213

long your commute is during traffic and when the roads are clear. Even if you speed . . ."

I blinked and time shifted forward again. There was a thin trickle of red running down my arm, but I hadn't felt the knife bite into my skin. There was an odd numbness creeping along my nerve endings, and I stared at the bleeding wound, my foggy mind trapped somewhere between horror and fascination.

"Good-bye, Detective," the killer said, and he snapped the phone shut. He tossed it behind him, and it slid under the table, well beyond my reach. "He's fond of you." He petted my hair slowly, letting his fingers linger in the strands as he pressed his face close enough to mine that I should've been able to feel his breath on my skin. It smelled like mint and moisture. "But you're already taken. It's time to go home."

No. I couldn't let him take me. Marx would be here soon, and I needed to give him time to get to me. As tired as I was, I couldn't let the drug take me under. I tried to remember Marx's advice. I knew it was locked in my muddled brain somewhere, and I searched for it frantically.

Give him reason to doubt that it's the right time to take you.

It was difficult to form a coherent thought, let alone put it into words. "I don't . . . go . . . home with . . . strangers." The effort of speech was draining.

"We're not strangers, you and I," he replied gently, still stroking my hair. I wished I could bite him. If I could just fall over onto his arm with my mouth open, and somehow find the strength to clamp my teeth, I would be all set. "We've just been apart for a very long time."

"I don't . . . know you."

I caught the slight stiffening of his shoulders as his hand dropped away from my hair. "You remember me."

"Sent . . . me . . . a . . . stuffed r-r-rabbit."

"Yes, I did," he said, sounding pleased.

"Your . . . gifts . . . suck," I spat. His hands clenched into fists, and I hesitated to continue. I didn't want him to hurt me; I just

214

wanted to make him doubt that I remembered who he was. "You . . . chased me . . ." I paused to gather my breath. "Through . . . the . . . woods. Were you . . . some kind . . . of . . . child . . . p-pervert?" I knew why he'd chased me; he had intended to kill me along with anyone else in that house, except I escaped. But he didn't need to know that.

If I'd hoped to make him angry, I succeeded. He hit me. I didn't feel the pain that should've come with it, but it sent the room spinning again. When it finally stilled, I was lying on my back on the cold floor, staring up at the ceiling.

"Don't insult me," he growled. "You remember who I am."

I opened my mouth to argue, and I tasted something coppery on my lips. It trickled down the back of my throat. "Don't . . . even know . . . who . . . I am." Unbidden tears glazed my vision, and the figure leaning over me blurred into a fuzzy mass.

He went very still, and I was afraid he would kill me right then and there. "You're lying," he said, but he didn't sound certain this time. Maybe it was the tears that lent credibility to my story. "You remember that night."

"Woods . . . rabbit . . . running . . . a v-voice. Only . . . f-fragments."

"Why can't you remember?" he demanded angrily, slamming a fist on the cement beside my head.

"Trying . . ." I didn't have the strength to continue speaking, and my voice fell away. Either he would believe I didn't remember either of us at this point or he wouldn't. But he needed to make his decision. Marx would be here soon.

He grabbed the sides of my face and pressed his forehead to mine. He looked directly into my eyes, but I couldn't see anything. "You will remember me. I will make you remember." I felt a tug on my hair before he pulled back, and the last thing I saw before my eyes drifted shut was him holding a clump of my red hair under his nose as he inhaled slowly.

28

A distant voice broke through the fog that clung to my mind; it sounded familiar and worried. I fought my way toward it, but tendrils of blackness tried to drag me back down.

"Holly," a silky Southern voice called. "Come on, sweetheart, open your eyes. Look at me." The drawl made me think of fried green tomatoes dipped in ketchup and sweet tea made with heaping spoonfuls of sugar. *Sugar. Mmm.*

My eyelids fluttered open, and I glimpsed a blurry figure kneeling over me before they slipped shut again. The floor beneath my back was cold and hard, and I couldn't remember how I got there.

"Did he drug you? Look at me, Holly," the voice insisted. I could feel the warmth of someone's hands on my cheeks, a man's hands.

No. I needed to get away from him, I needed to fight back. I tried to move, but I felt vaguely detached from the rest of my body. I was pretty sure it was still there somewhere below my neck—my head couldn't be rolling around on the floor by itself—but I felt anchored down.

I tried to tell the man to stop touching me, but my voice sounded like a garbled whimper.

"You're safe, Holly," the gentle sugary voice assured me. "It's gonna be all right; you're gonna be fine." Something about his voice soothed me, and I stopped trying to fight my way free of the invisible weight crushing me to the floor.

Calm slowly washed over me, and my mind began to drift: *The grass was cool and soft beneath my feet, and I dug my toes into the damp dirt. I bounced eagerly and held my hands out in front of me. "Come on, Jordan, throw the ball already!" I demanded in the small voice of a girl no more than ten.*

The boy standing in the yard across from me smirked, and his sapphire-blue eyes glinted with amusement. "You're standing like a girl."

"I am a girl. How am I supposed to stand?"

He rolled his eyes and bent his knees, hunching a little with his chest forward. "Like this." He stood up and tossed the football back and forth in his hands as he waited for me to adopt the proper stance.

I tried it, but it made me feel like an awkward pigeon, and I almost fell forward. "I can't. Just throw the ball," I pleaded as I stood up and bounced on my toes.

Jordan drew his arm back with the ball and laughed. "Stop bouncing, Holly. You're never gonna catch it." He flung the Styrofoam football, and I resisted the urge to duck and squeal like a girl.

I caught the ball and hugged it to my chest. "Ha!" I grinned. "I caught it!" And then I promptly dropped it when I clumsily lost my balance. "That doesn't count!"

Another voice spoke from somewhere nearby. It wrenched me from the yard, even though I wanted to stay, and back to a cold cement floor. "What happened?" he demanded.

"I think she may have been drugged," the Southern voice explained softly. He was seated on the floor by my head, and I could feel the warmth of his hand as he gently smoothed the hair away from my face.

A blinding light shined into my right eye, and I flinched away from it. It flickered to my other eye immediately afterward, and pain lanced through my eye sockets and into my brain. "Her pupils are the size of saucers. She's been given something. Holly, it's Luke, can you hear me?"

His voice was too loud; it rolled around inside of my skull like a bowling ball, crashing into things, and I winced.

"She may have a concussion," he shouted. Why was he shouting? Didn't he realize I had a headache? "It looks like she took a blow to the head. Was it some sort of domestic dispute?"

"Home invasion."

"Sexual assault?" he asked in what was clearly his *outside* voice.

The answer came slowly. "I don't know. He was alone with her for maybe fifteen minutes, and part of the time I was on the phone with him." At least *he* wasn't shouting. His name floated up from the depths of my mind, and I clutched at it before it could slip back beneath the murky surface of my thoughts: Detective. Detective . . . Sugar.

The room descended into a moment of blissful silence, and all I could hear was the echo of thunder between my ears.

"Holly," Luke called again, and his voice triggered another earthquake of pain inside my head. I was pretty sure all the neural pathways in my brain had just caved in under the violent quaking. I was officially brain-dead. "Can you hear me?"

"I hate your voice," I forced through my sticky lips. My words came out hoarse and oddly slurred. My throat felt like sandpaper.

"Hey," he said quietly. "How are you feeling?"

My head hurt, and there was an uncomfortable prickle in my extremities—like thousands of tiny hot needles trying to pierce through my skin. Beyond that I couldn't feel much of anything. I peeled my eyelids open to see a pale smudge of a person above me. I blinked to try to clear his features, and two faces came into a hazy focus. "That's . . . a stupid question. Which one of you asked it?" I looked between the two identical men in confusion.

The men held up fingers in front of my face and asked, "How many fingers am I holding up, Holly?"

I squinted and tried to count them, but they kept moving. "Stop moving them. You're cheating." Both of the men frowned—it was really weird how their brains and faces seemed to be connected. "Sssix."

They dropped their hands into their laps and announced, "She's seeing double."

I tried to wiggle my fingers in front of my face, but I couldn't find them. I stared down at my body, perplexed. "Where did *my* fingers go? Did you take them?" Maybe I was lying on them, but surely I would feel that. Maybe they fell off . . . down the drain. That could happen.

"Nobody took your fingers," the silky Southern voice said from somewhere behind my head. I tilted my head to look up at him. The sight of him soothed away the last of my anxiety, and a little happy laugh bubbled out of me.

"Hi, Sugar."

He blinked. "Hi."

"You're sweet . . . like sugar. Even though . . . you're a cop . . . and sometimes you're a man . . . I don't hate you at all."

He stared at me for a moment, then looked up at the other two men and asked with a hint of worry in his voice. "What's wrong with her?"

"Could be the concussion," one of the other men offered. "Or a side effect of the drug. I can't be sure, but she's obviously disoriented."

"I know exactly where I am," I said. I looked around at my blurry surroundings, trying to find something familiar, but all I could see was the ceiling. "I'm on the floor."

"Yes, Holly, you're on the floor," the sugary voice said patiently.

I flicked my eyes toward the man behind my head and giggled, "You sound funny when you talk. So . . . Sssouthern. Southern sweet tea. Can I have sweet tea? I like sweet tea."

"Nothing to drink until we get you checked out," one of the other men said. He was wrapping something white around the wound on my arm.

"Am I a present? Are you wrapping me? Can I open it?" I tried to lift my head to see if he was going to put a bow on it; he didn't. "No bow?" I pouted.

"We'll draw a bow on it later," the sugary voice promised.

I smiled dreamily and then blinked in confusion when I looked down my body. "Who stole my toes?" I couldn't feel them, and they were nowhere in sight. I tried to twitch them, but nothing happened. They'd vanished!

One of the identical twins in the blue uniform plucked something fuzzy and green off the bottom of my leg that looked like a moss-covered rock and said, "Your toes are right here." Both of the men frowned, and then plucked a green, moss-covered rock off my other leg. "Detective."

The man behind my head shifted and moved down by my legs. There were suddenly two of him. Whoa. That was a neat trick. "Two cubes of Sugar," I said, giggling.

"Holly, what happened to your feet?" the two cubes of sugar asked.

"I don't know. Are they missing too? Maybe they went to the market with my toes." I giggled until tears spilled out of my eyes.

"We won't know what she was given and what kind of effect it will have on her until we get her to the hospital," the identical twins pointed out. "Help me get her on the gurney."

"I'm not going anywhere with you . . . either of you," I said, frowning at the two identical men in blue uniform. "I'm in a relationship. In fact, I'm in two relationships, so you're both out of luck." I tilted my head to the side to look up at the Southern man who bent down beside me. "Isn't that right, Sugar?"

He exhaled with a pained expression. "Holly, you gotta stop callin' me Sugar." He moved behind me. "Let's get you on your feet."

"But I can't feel my feet," I explained, and then giggled. Jace couldn't feel her feet either. "Sugar . . . go steal Jace's wheelchair so I can go for a ride. She won't mind."

"The only place you're ridin' to is the hospital." He scooped me up seemingly effortlessly and cradled me against his chest.

I closed my eyes with a contented sigh, enjoying the sensation of flying. In my mind, I landed on one of the fluffy clouds and sank into the softness. It was peaceful.

I opened my eyes to find myself lying on a mattress. "Let's do that again," I suggested. I tried to climb off the floating bed, but I could barely move. I managed to get one leg over the edge before someone straightened me out. Fine, I would climb off the other side.

"No, Holly," Detective Sugar said as he maneuvered me back into the center of the floating bed. He gripped the bed on either side of my waist to keep me from moving while someone else pulled a belt over me and snapped it in place.

"But flying is fun."

"You're already flyin' pretty high," he stated evenly. "It's time to come back down to earth."

"Earth is boring." I sighed. The fog crept along the back of my mind, trying to lure me back, and I smiled as I melted into the mattress. I blinked groggily at the comforting face above me and murmured, "You came."

"Of course I came."

"Nobody ever comes."

He frowned as he stroked my hair. "Nobody ever comes when?"

"When Collin hurts me."

"Who's Collin?" Luke asked.

"My foster brother. But he's not *really* my brother."

"What do you mean he hurts you? Hurts you how?"

I parted my lips to answer, but Sugar put a finger against my lips and said sharply to one of the other men, "You start askin' her personal questions when she has no inhibitions, and you and I are gonna have a problem."

Protective, Detective Sugar.

"If someone's hurting her . . ."

"Then I'll take care of it. Do your job, not mine." He sounded angry, and it made his voice sound more like vinegar than sugar.

"Because you've done such a great job so far? She was just drugged and assaulted on your watch."

"Don't push me, Luke. I am not in the mood . . ."

"Am I dead?" I asked as I stared at the bright light above me. Was this heaven? Heaven was chilly . . .

"No, you're not dead," he replied, the vinegar disappearing from his voice and leaving only sweetness. "He just put somethin' in your drink to make you sick."

I licked my parched lips. "He was scary. I was scared."

He closed his eyes and exhaled a quiet breath. "I know. I'm sorry it took me so long."

"I did what you said." He stepped aside briefly as one of the other men threw a blanket over me and tucked it in to keep me warm against the chilly air. "I'm a terrible liar 'cause I don't like liars, but I lied 'cause you told me to."

"Good."

"He was really angry."

His jaw tightened. "I see that."

I let out a musical sigh and closed my eyes. "I'm tired."

"We need her to stay awake. She has a concussion," Luke explained.

"Holly, you have to stay awake."

"Mmm hmm," I moaned, snuggling deeper into the blanket. I heard his soft Southern voice calling my name in the distance as it faded away behind the heavy fog that drifted over my mind.

29

A violent throbbing in my head woke me, and I stifled a moan as I dragged a hand from under the covers and rubbed my forehead. It felt as if someone had hit me with a two-by-four. I cracked my eyes open and immediately regretted it as light sent fire sizzling down my optic nerves and into my brain.

I squeezed my eyes shut and curled into a ball beneath the blankets. It didn't feel like my bed. The blanket was knitted, and the pillows were too fluffy. Ambient sounds came into focus, and I heard the familiar beeping of machines and the distant sound of coughing and crying.

I was in a hospital.

There was a reason I avoided hospitals, and it wasn't because I was afraid of needles. It was too easy for Collin to find me in a hospital. I may as well hang up a flashing neon sign with my name and room number on it.

I opened my eyes slowly, bracing for the pain, and blinked at the dim glow of light that filtered into the dark room through the open doorway and around the drapes that covered the windows.

I lifted my arm and looked at the white bandage on my forearm. I grazed it thoughtfully with my fingertips, and the memories from last night came trickling back: the light pressure of the knife against my arm, the sickening feeling of his skin against mine.

I touched my bottom lip with my tongue and hissed in a quiet breath of pain. I hadn't felt it when the killer hit me in the kitchen—thanks to whatever he'd slipped into my drink—but I felt it now. The entire left side of my face hurt, especially my mouth.

I didn't notice the figure sitting in a chair in the corner with his elbows on his knees and his face in his hands until he stirred at my sharp intake of breath. He lifted his head and looked at me from

223

across the room.

"Hi," I said. My voice sounded raspy.

Marx sat up straight and released a breath of relief. "Hey, sweetheart, how you feelin'?"

I tried to swallow, but my throat was dry. "Thirsty." I looked around the room for something to drink, but by the time I spotted it, Marx was already there with the pitcher of water in his hand.

Either he was really fast or someone had removed my brain while I was sleeping and replaced it with a cotton ball, because I couldn't seem to focus. I hadn't even seen him move.

He poured water into a small plastic cup. "You had me worried there for a while. Sam woke up three hours ago." He set the pitcher down and approached the bed. His expression was pained as he regarded me. "How's your head?"

I pushed myself up in the bed slowly, pausing halfway when my head began to pound violently. "There are tiny percussionists inside my skull making a racket," I mumbled as I very carefully propped myself up against the pillows. I accepted the cup of water he held out to me.

I ignored the burning in my lip as I took a small sip. I felt dehydrated. I wanted to gulp it down, but I forced myself to sip it slowly. "How's Sam?" My own voice was absurdly loud inside my head.

"Cranky, but fine."

Relief washed over me. I'd been so worried he was dead. I had left him completely vulnerable when I gave him that bottle of poisoned punch. "Was he hurt?"

"Only his pride."

I finished the water and set the empty cup on the side table. The tape on my skin snagged on the blanket, and I traced the needle in my arm back to an IV bag hanging from a hook above the bed.

The bag blurred in the darkness, and I pressed a hand to my forehead in the hopes that it might bring the world back into focus.

"Dizzy?" Marx asked worriedly. I groaned in confirmation. "It's probably the concussion."

I vaguely recalled someone shouting that I may have a concussion. That man had no volume control and should consider a vow of silence. I rested my aching head back against the pillows and pressed the heels of my palms against my eyes. I could swear I felt my heartbeat inside my eyeballs. "Is this what a hangover feels like?"

Marx grunted in mild amusement. "I take it you've never drunk before. And by drunk I mean anythin' more intense than chocolate milk with marshmallows."

I smiled a little. "I tried coffee once. I'm pretty sure dirt tastes better."

"I'll take your word for it. I can call the nurse and she can give you somethin' for the pain."

"No," I said quickly. I finally had control over my body again; I wasn't lost in a state of disconnected numbness or mental fog, and I had no intention of taking anything that would dull any of my senses. "No drugs," I told him. "I just need a few minutes to get used to it."

It was just physical pain. I could push through it. I rubbed my eyes and blinked at Marx until his fuzzy image sharpened.

He stood a few feet from the bed with his arms crossed over his chest and a grim expression on his face. It was the first time I'd ever seen him without his suit jacket.

He wore jeans and a black short-sleeve T-shirt, and if it weren't for the gun on his hip, I would never have guessed he was a cop. He looked remarkably average. Except for the intense green eyes that missed nothing.

I looked from him to the beeping monitor beside him. My heartbeat made consistent little zigzags on the screen next to my blood pressure. "I wish you hadn't brought me here," I told him quietly. "I can't be here."

"I didn't have a choice, Holly," he said, and he sounded weary, as if we'd had this argument a dozen times before. I was pretty sure my concussion wasn't bad enough to make me forget that much. "I knew the risk, but if Collin decides to pay you a hospital visit, he's gonna get a face full of tile before I arrest him."

The thought of seeing him again made my heart rate pick up, and Marx glanced at the monitor. The last time I had dared to step into a hospital for treatment, Collin had tracked me down, and I had barely gotten away.

Even though I'd checked myself in as a Jane Doe, he knew exactly what injuries I needed treatment for, because he'd given them to me. It wasn't exactly difficult to narrow it down from there.

"I would've been fine," I tried to argue. "I don't need to be here."

"The killer drugged you, and none of us had any idea what he gave you or what it was gonna do to you. Not to mention the fact that you were bleedin' on the floor."

I cringed at the memory.

There was something humiliating about being found completely vulnerable. I had never had to worry about it before, because no one had ever been there when I had to pick myself up off the floor, and no one had ever cared enough to step in on my behalf. I hated that Marx had found me that way.

"You should've asked me," I said. I wasn't sure if it was fear or embarrassment that made my voice curt; maybe it was both. I scraped at the edges of the tape on my skin, trying to peel it away so I could pull the needle out of my arm.

I was not staying here.

Marx released a patient breath. "He hit you hard enough to give you a concussion. And you were high as a kite. You weren't exactly in a position to make an informed decision. I did what needed to be done, and there's no point in arguin' about it now."

I ripped off the tape with a hiss of pain and glanced at the door. I didn't want to be here; I wanted to leave, but I wasn't sure I could even stand without the room tilting around me.

"You're perfectly safe here, Holly." Marx punctuated his words to make sure I understood. "Mer's in the lobby, Sam's down the hall, and I'm stayin' right here. Even if he does track you down, he's not gettin' within fifteen feet of you."

There was a promise in his eyes, and I wanted to believe him, but promises of safety hadn't been working out so well for me lately. I was beginning to think safety was nothing but an illusion.

But even Collin wouldn't be stupid enough to come after me when there were three police officers in the hall. He was arrogant but he wasn't reckless. I paused with my fingers on the IV as I considered whether or not to stay.

Where would I even go if I left? I couldn't go home. Not yet. And there was no safe place within walking distance. I would have to take a cab, which I couldn't pay for, or hitchhike, which was only ever a last resort. Crap. I was stuck here.

I released the IV reluctantly and hoped I wouldn't regret it. "I guess I can stay for a few minutes." I reclined back into the pillows. If God didn't forbid stealing, I would take one of these criminally fat pillows with me when I left.

Marx relaxed a little. I knew he wanted me to stay in the hospital, but I doubted he would've forced me back into the bed if I had tried to get up.

"Is there sick-people room service? Can I have pistachio pudding?"

Marx smiled a little. "Pistachio? Really?" He grabbed one of the chairs from along the wall and set it down beside the bed. He tried to be quiet, but the sound of the chair legs hitting the floor ricocheted around inside my skull. "We might be able to scrounge up some chocolate or vanilla. But we need to talk first."

Was he seriously holding the pudding for information ransom?

He sat down in the chair and leaned forward, resting his interlocked fingers on his knees. The position brought him entirely too close. I drew my knees into my chest and curled my toes into the mattress in a subtle attempt to put some more space between us. I had no doubt he noticed—he was perceptive that way—but he didn't comment.

"I'm sure you're gonna fight me on this, but I need you to tell me what happened last night," he said.

I stared into his dark green eyes briefly before dropping my gaze to the blanket. I picked at the fuzzy pills of fabric on the threadbare blanket with my fingernails as he studied me quietly. "I don't really wanna talk about it."

"I figured as much. But it needs to be done." He tilted his head in an effort to see my face, but I deliberately kept it averted. I didn't want him to be able to read my thoughts. "You're avoidin' my gaze again," he said, sounding thoughtful.

"Maybe the blanket is just more interesting than your face," I replied with a small shrug. I knew he was going to ask me for every detail about last night, and I didn't want to revisit those memories just yet.

"I know this is gonna be an uncomfortable conversation— for both of us—but we don't have the luxury of secrets this time."

I looked up at him, puzzled by his choice of words.

"Yes, I said both of us," he said when he read my expression. "Most of my victims are dead, Holly." I resisted the urge to flinch at the word victim. I didn't want him to think of me that way. "Occasionally, I have a live victim, but my interaction is minimal. A few interviews at most. I've never tried to protect somebody before."

That surprised me.

"When you called me last night, I wasn't sure I was gonna get to you in time, and I wasn't sure what I was gonna find when I got there," he said. I could hear the pain in his voice. His knuckles turned white as his fingers tightened around each other. "I knew by the sound of your voice that somethin' was wrong with you. When you stopped talkin' to me, I was worried I was already too late. Then I heard the two of you in the background. I knew he was hurtin' you in some way, but I couldn't drive any faster."

There hadn't been a lot of conversation to overhear, but there had been enough. And he'd probably heard every pathetic whimper I made while the killer was memorizing my skin. The thought made me want to crawl under the bed and hide.

"What did he do, Holly?" Marx asked quietly.

I twisted the blanket into tiny knots to help keep my

228

emotions under control. "If you heard everything on the phone, then there's nothing more to say."

"I wanna hear it from your perspective."

My vision had been warped and my perception of events had been distorted by whatever drug the killer had graciously dumped into my drink. I hadn't been able to focus on most of the details, and I had faded in and out of consciousness more than once, so I didn't feel the least bit guilty for answering, "Blurry."

Marx frowned. "You're avoidin' my question."

"Well, maybe you should stop asking it then," I offered helpfully. Maybe if I stalled long enough, he would get frustrated and leave the room, and I wouldn't have to discuss it.

"I can't do that, Holly. I need to know what happened last night." Well, so much for getting frustrated and leaving the room . . .

I lifted my gaze to his briefly. "Are you gonna arrest me if I refuse to give you the details?"

He gave me a flat, unamused look. "You know very well that I won't, so it's pointless to even bluff."

"Then I have nothing to say." I didn't want to talk about it, and he wasn't willing to do the one thing that would force me to.

He hung his head between his shoulders and sighed. "Don't do this, Holly." When he looked at me again, his eyes were beseeching. "After everythin' we've been through, after everythin' that's happened, please don't shut me out."

The raw emotion in his voice made me hesitate to say the snippy retort that sprang to my tongue. I didn't want to hurt him. "Why do you always have to push? Why can't you just . . ."

"Pretend it didn't happen?" he asked when I trailed off. "I know there are things in your past that you would rather forget, and you try never to think about them. But I'm a cop. I don't have the option of pretendin' a crime didn't happen just because it makes me uncomfortable. This man killed one of my friends, and he broke into the home of a girl under my protection and attacked her. I cannot let that stand. He doesn't get a free pass."

My home—the only place I had managed to feel safe since I

was twelve—had been violated. That wound was far more painful than the throbbing in my head or the cut on my forearm. He'd taken something precious from me that I had strived my entire life to find.

How was I ever supposed to walk through that door without thinking about what happened there? How was I ever supposed to feel safe inside those walls again? Tears burned across my vision, deepening the ache behind my eyes, and I tried to blink them away.

"Please tell me what happened."

Apparently, I wasn't escaping this conversation no matter how much I wanted to avoid it. I pulled the blanket tighter around me and tried to keep my voice even. "He was already inside when I came out of the bathroom after my shower."

"How'd he get inside?"

"Stanley's keys."

"Stanley's keys are in evidence. I put them there when I processed his apartment with the Crime Scene Unit."

"Then he made copies," I replied a little impatiently. "I locked the door before I got in the shower, and he was already inside when I came out. There's no way he fit through a window." The windows were barely large enough for me to squeeze through.

Marx closed his eyes and swore under his breath. "The killer didn't send Stanley to your apartment that night to scare you. There were probably fifty or sixty keys on that ring, and he wanted to know which ones were yours. He probably made copies the night he killed him."

"Stanley was murdered?"

"There was a very high concentration of alcohol in his blood stream, accompanied by trace amounts of ketamine," he explained. "It's what the killer laced your drinks with. It's most commonly used as an animal tranquilizer, but it's developed several recreational uses on the street. A low dose can give the user a sense of euphoria. And in a high enough dose, it induces a nearly paralytic state so the victim can't fight back. If you remember . . ."

"I couldn't move." I remembered all too well. No matter how hard I had tried to make my body move, it refused to obey me.

The memory of the killer's hands caressing my bare skin as I sat there, unable to do anything except endure, sent a shiver down my spine. I steered my mind away from those frightening memories. "Why kill him? Why not just make copies of the keys while Stanley was sleeping?"

"No one knows for sure whether or not the killer intended for him to die. But mixin' ketamine with any other form of depressant is very easily lethal. Stanley's heart stopped."

I closed my eyes in regret. Stanley had been murdered so the killer could make copies of my keys. What a pointless reason to take a person's life.

"It's likely he made copies of other select keys as well. That would explain how he seemed to vanish into thin air the night he broke into Jace's apartment. He never left. The officers knocked on doors, but not everybody answered," Marx continued.

"Why didn't he make a copy of Jace's key?" I asked.

"It's possible he did. But if he'd used the key to open the door instead of kickin' it down, we would've figured it out sooner. And then we would've had your locks changed."

Fear tightened my chest. We needed to change Jace's locks before the killer decided to use her against me. "Jace . . ."

"She'll be fine. She's in the waitin' room with Mer until I decide she's calm enough to come in. She can be a bit . . ."

"Intimidating?" I offered.

He smiled and clarified, "Overwhelmin' and impulsive. She actually threatened to take out my ankles if I didn't let her through the door."

That didn't surprise me. Jace could be as protective of me at times as I could be of her.

Marx continued summarizing the events of last night as if we'd never veered off topic. "We found Sam unconscious around the back of the buildin'. Apparently, he chugged the entire bottle of punch, and it knocked him out cold. It's probably the only reason the killer left him alone. The killer then let himself into your home while you were in the shower and waited for the drug to take effect."

"Why even bother drugging me?" I asked bitterly. It was obvious he didn't need me paralyzed in order to subdue me. My aching head was a testament to that.

"Because he wanted you docile. He might be bigger, but if he had any intention of takin' you with him, he probably realized how difficult it would be to shove a flailin', screamin' woman into the trunk of his car without anybody noticin'."

He *had* intended to take me with him. I had been so certain I'd failed to change his mind before I slipped under, but something had changed his mind. He'd left me lying on the floor, unconscious, for Marx to find.

"So, after you realized you were drugged, you tried to throw it up in the sink. Then what happened?"

"I called you."

"And then?" His voice softened when I stared intently at the blanket and said nothing. "You have nothin' to be embarrassed about, Holly."

I looked into his warm green eyes and I *was* embarrassed. I didn't want him to know how weak I was, how incapable I'd been. I didn't want him to describe me as one of those "victims." I drew my legs tighter against my body and tried to keep my spine straight. "Promise you won't think I'm weak?"

"You are not weak, Holly. You were drugged. Nobody in your situation could've done anythin' more than you did. The fact that you had the presence of mind to throw up as much of the drug as possible so you could fight back just shows how capable you are."

I wasn't sure why his opinion of me mattered so much, but it did. "Okay," I agreed reluctantly. I described the events for him as thoroughly as I could. There were a few gaps in my memory, and I was a little fuzzy on some of the details, but he listened quietly, only interrupting with a follow-up question here and there.

He didn't say anything when I finished; he just sat in the chair with his elbows on his knees and his hands interlocked under his chin. He looked pensive as he stared at the floor.

"Holly," he began, but he paused, seeming to choose his

words very carefully. When he looked up at me, there was worry in his eyes. "You weren't . . . examined when we brought you in. You were unconscious and unable to give consent."

It took me a moment to understand the point he was dancing around, and then every muscle in my body tensed. "I don't need an exam."

"You were unconscious when I found you, and you were alone with him for ten minutes. Given his possessiveness and the way he had his hands on you . . ."

"No," I choked out, stopping him before he could say anything more. This conversation dredged up too many painful memories, and if we didn't change the subject, I was going to throw up all over him.

"I realize it's an uncomfortable process, but it's . . ."

"No one is touching me, and I'm not . . ." I struggled to push the words past the nauseating lump in my throat. "I'm not talking about this. I can't talk about this."

Marx let the matter drop, but there was a question burning in his eyes as he studied me, one he couldn't give voice to because he'd sworn he wouldn't ask.

I dropped my eyes and shifted my gaze to the covered window before he could pull the unwilling answer from me. The room descended into silence, and I listened to the distant murmur of voices and whirring of machines. The rhythm of the hospital was surprisingly soothing.

A quiet knock echoed from the doorway, and I looked up to see Sam standing there. He was wearing sweatpants and a hoodie; it was a step up from the hospital gown someone had dressed me in, but it was the most relaxed attire I'd ever seen him wearing.

"It isn't a good time, Sam," Marx said.

Sam stepped into the dark room anyway, but even in the low light I could see the shadows under his eyes. He'd had a much larger dose of the ketamine than I had, and I was surprised to see him on his feet. I caught the slight flinch as his eyes landed on me.

Apparently, I looked worse than I thought. Awesome. I

shifted self-consciously and tucked my hair behind my ears.

"I'm sorry I roofied you," I said to break the awkward silence in the room. "And I'm glad you're okay."

It took him a moment to find his voice. "Yeah . . . I'm fine." He shot Marx a questioning glance, and a silent conversation I couldn't follow passed between them.

Marx stood up and said, "I'll be right back, Holly," before walking out of the room with Sam on his heels.

They barely made it through the doorway before Sam demanded in a hoarse whisper, "What happened? You said she was okay. That isn't my definition of okay."

"I said she was fine; I didn't say she was uninjured," Marx replied quietly.

Their conversation faded as they continued down the corridor until the only voice I could hear was Sam's, and even then I could only hear fragments.

". . . supposed to keep her safe. That was my only job . . . let him waltz right through the front door . . . supposed to be guarding."

I tried to hear the remainder of the conversation, but their voices dropped too low for me to hear anything more than agitated whispers.

I snuggled back down beneath the covers and stretched out. It was nice to be able to feel my body again. I turned my hands over in front of my face as I studied my fingers and tested their flexibility. Normal.

I rotated my ankles and wiggled my toes beneath the blanket experimentally. Normal too. I did a methodical inventory of my entire body. All of my feeling and control had returned, and I was in pretty good shape, considering.

"You'll be happy to know all ten of your toes have been found and safely returned," Marx commented from the doorway. I wasn't sure when he'd returned or even how long he'd been gone. My perception of time was a little off.

He leaned against the door frame with a slight smile on his

lips and a plastic cup of brown liquid in his hand.

I vaguely recalled wondering if my feet and toes had wandered off to the market together. "Where did Sam go?" I asked as I drew myself back up against the pillows.

"Bed." He pushed away from the doorway and strode into the room.

"Is he angry with me?" He had a right to be angry with me; I could've gotten him killed.

Marx frowned as he sat back down in his chair. "No. Nobody is angry with you. He's been worried about you since he woke up." At my skeptical expression, he said patiently. "You matter to people, Holly. Get used to them carin'."

I didn't understand why he cared so much. I had done nothing to earn his trust or his affection, and I kept waiting for the other shoe to drop. When it finally did drop, I would probably trip over it for good measure.

"There wasn't any pistachio puddin', but I brought you somethin' better." He held out the cup of brown liquid with a straw in it. "A sweet tea, since you were so insistent last night."

I smirked and accepted the drink. I played with the straw as I asked a little reluctantly, "Did I say anything else embarrassing?"

"You mean aside from callin' me Sugar?"

My cheeks heated and I dropped my face into my hand. "I can't believe I said that," I mumbled into my palm.

"Neither can I," he said, holding back a laugh. "I'm fairly certain Luke got the wrong impression after you told him you were in a relationship, then looked up at me and called me Sugar."

I pressed my covered face into my knees and groaned, mortified. "I'm so sorry."

I could hear the smile in his voice as he said, "You were by far the most adorable high individual I have ever seen. If you'd been able to walk, I expect you would've been chasin' invisible butterflies on a cloud of cotton candy."

I blamed him for that. Even drugged, I would never have been able to relax into that euphoria without someone I trusted beside me.

"I can't believe I lost my mind like that," I admitted. "I'm sorry if I embarrassed you."

"You didn't. But please . . . don't ever call me Sugar again. It's . . . unnervin'."

I started to laugh and then stopped short when the gash on my lip threatened to split open again. I pressed my fingertips to it to make sure it wasn't bleeding. "No promises," I replied. I took a small sip from the straw. Mmm, that was good. Heaven in a cup.

A muffled ringing came from inside Marx's jacket draped over one of the far chairs. He stood up and crossed the room to answer it. His expression shifted into neutral when he looked at the caller ID on the phone's display screen.

"I need to take this. It's the Stony Brooke Sheriff's Department. I'll be right outside the room." He stepped out into the hallway, and I heard his formal greeting, "Detective Marx," before he moved too far down the hall for his words to carry.

I thought about slipping out of bed and creeping over to the door to slake my curiosity, but I was pretty sure I would trip and fall over my own feet if I tried it; I felt more uncoordinated than usual. I sank back into my pillows instead and sipped my sweet tea. It was a nice treat.

It felt like ages before Marx stepped back into the room. Anxiety fluttered through me at the sight of the manila folder he carried. The last time he'd come into the room with one of those, it hadn't contained anything good. He didn't look angry this time, but something was responsible for the dark cloud hanging around him.

He stopped beside the bed and tapped the folder against his palm as he worked up the nerve to give voice to whatever was troubling him. "Holly . . ." He cleared his throat. "We need to talk. About your family."

30

"The sheriff's department faxed over some information for me." Marx sat down in the chair beside my hospital bed. He wore the expression a doctor might wear when he had to tell his patient he was dying of cancer.

"I take it it's not good news," I said, regarding him cautiously. I gripped the cup of tea with both hands as I braced myself.

"A bit of a mixture, I suppose." He pulled a crisp sheet of paper from inside the folder without opening it, paused as if to reconsider, and then offered it to me.

I accepted it cautiously and turned it right side up. I squinted at it, but the letters blurred together in the darkness, and the only word that stood out boldly enough for me to read was at the top of the page: MISSING.

There was a grainy picture beneath it, but I couldn't pick out any of the details. It looked like one of those missing child posters plastered on the back of milk cartons or stapled to telephone poles in the city. "I can't read this in the dark."

"Do you think you could handle the lights?"

I glanced at the open doorway and had to look away when the light from the corridor made my eyes throb. "No, sorry." I shook my head and offered the page back to him.

He took it and slipped it back into the folder. "That's all right. I read it before I came in." He leaned forward, resting his elbows on his thighs and interlocking all but his index fingers. "We've been workin' under the assumption that you disappeared when you were ten years old. You didn't. You were nine."

I blinked at him. "But that would mean . . ."

"You're twenty-seven years old. Not twenty-eight."

I released a stunned breath. No one had ever truly known how old I was because no one knew when I was born; it had been an estimate. I just seemed to pop into existence around the age of ten. "The state picked an arbitrary date for my birthday so they would have something to put in the file. June thirtieth. When . . ."

"January eighteenth, 1989." He didn't even have to check the sheet.

I didn't know whether to smile or cry. I had a birthday. For the first time in my life, I knew when I was born. It wasn't some meaningless date picked for convenience or record keeping by the state.

"You'll be twenty-eight in fifty-eight days," he said. I counted the days on my fingers because I was awful at mental calculations—fifty-eight days and I would be twenty-eight . . . again. Marx smiled a little. "Didn't trust my math?"

"I've never had a birthday to look forward to," I admitted.

His eyebrows knitted together, and for a moment I thought I had somehow managed to make him sad. "You didn't celebrate the day the state designated as your birthday?"

"Sometimes my caseworker sent me a birthday card around that time, but I moved placements so quickly . . ."

No one really bothered to acknowledge, let alone celebrate, my birthday. And I knew the date was no more real than my last name. So what was the point?

"You've never had a cake? Presents? Balloons?"

I thought back and settled on a moment in time when I'd blown out a candle and sliced into a long cake with a frightening-looking serrated knife while someone gripped my hands so I didn't cut myself. "Izzy made me a cake."

"Drug dealers baked you a cake," he said dryly. "Okay then." He shook his head as if he couldn't wrap his mind around that idea.

"They didn't put any *extra* ingredients in it if that's what you're wondering," I assured him with a wry grin.

Izzy and Paul might have dabbled in illegal substances, but they had been very careful to keep that life separate from me. There had been times when they needed to travel to "deliver packages"—as if they were nothing more than postal workers—and they decided it was safer to leave me at home. I imagined not all of their associates would have appreciated a nine-year-old witness to their criminal activities.

The longest they left me on my own was a week, and Izzy had frantically stocked the cabin with sweets, drinks, coloring books, and anything else she could think of to keep me occupied. In hindsight, I think she was afraid I would wander off and disappear. She'd even bought me a can of pepper spray and explained how to use it in case someone tried to break into the cabin.

I accidentally sprayed the cat.

He didn't like me much after that.

"That's good to know," Marx grumbled, more to himself than to me. "I really don't need any more reason to dislike that woman."

So I probably shouldn't tell him about the time Izzy took me out for ice cream and we ran into one of her and Paul's competitors on the sidewalk.

"And we finally have your real name."

I sat up a little straighter against the pillows. "What is it?"

"Holly Marie Cross."

It took a moment for his words to settle. *Holly Marie Cross.* I turned it over in my mind as I tried to absorb the name that had been lost to me nearly eighteen years ago. "Are you sure?"

"I'm sure."

I mumbled the name aloud, tasting it on my tongue. There was a tingle of familiarity, as if I'd spoken it before, but it could've been the name of an acquaintance for all the attachment I felt to it.

"The Stony Brooke Sheriff's Department has been lookin' for you for a very long time," Marx explained. "They faxed over an old Missin' Child flyer with your information on it. There's no doubt it's you."

It surprised me that anyone had searched for me. But I hadn't been a transient who melted in and out of people's lives without notice then; I had been a nine-year-old girl with a family.

"Did you tell them I'm alive?"

"I didn't have to. Apparently, they never stopped believin' you were alive."

I looked up at him in surprise. Who in their right mind would believe a missing child was still alive after eighteen years? I had vanished into thin air with no trail to follow.

"I wasn't able to reach the sheriff who originally worked your case, but I spoke to his son, Jordan Radcliffe, who seemed awfully familiar with the details of a case he's far too young to have worked. He firmly believes you're still alive."

Jordan. The name sounded familiar, and it took a moment for my mind to offer up the memory of the little boy with the football. I remembered his charming grin and his crystalline-blue eyes that twinkled with amusement as he told me to stop bouncing.

"He was very interested to know why I was askin' about the case," Marx continued. "I thought it best not to mention you until we decide how to proceed."

I frowned in confusion. If Marx hadn't contacted them about me specifically, then why would they send him a flyer concerning my disappearance? I doubted it was the sheriff's department's policy to attach MISSING posters to every fax they sent out. Although that probably was an efficient way to find missing children.

My mind resisted when I tried to find the connection: Cross.

The woman whose body I had tripped and fallen over the night I fled from the house had been named Cross. I had dropped my stuffed rabbit into her blood, and Marx had said it flagged an open homicide case from Stony Brooke. Any hope that she'd been a stranger trapped in a nightmare with me died instantly. "Emily . . ."

Marx spoke carefully, as if afraid I might dissolve into tears. "She was your mother."

My heart twisted painfully in my chest. A part of me had already known she was my mother, but it still hurt to hear it. Marx pulled another sheet of paper from the folder and handed it to me. I was about to remind him that I couldn't see it in the dark when he pulled his phone from his pocket and flipped it open, careful to keep the light angled away from my face.

A dim glow spilled across the image in my hand. A beautiful woman with fiery red hair and honey-brown eyes stared back at me from the picture. Her skin was as pale as porcelain, and she had a light dusting of freckles across her nose. Everything about her face exuded warmth and love. I touched the picture with my fingertips as if I might be able to feel it through the paper.

"She was beautiful."

"Yes, she was," he agreed. "It explains where *you* came from."

I smiled a little as tears gathered in the corners of my vision. There was no denying that I had her hair and her eyes, and even the pale color of her skin, but I wasn't beautiful or warm; on my best day I could manage put-together and not completely frigid. No one would ever describe me as warm.

It was strange learning about a mother I couldn't remember *after* learning she was murdered. There was a slight tremor in my voice as I asked, "What did he do to her?"

Marx released a slow, measured breath before saying, "You don't need to know the details."

I knew what that meant. Whatever the killer had done to my mother was too horrible for Marx to put into words. He didn't want me to know.

"Did she suffer?"

I lifted my gaze to his when he didn't answer, and the hard set of his jaw delivered the answer more powerfully than words. Yes, she had suffered.

A part of me grieved for Emily because she was my mother, and the other part of me grieved for the fact that I would never have a chance to know her. She was a stranger who shared the color of my hair and the shape of my eyes.

I wished I could remember something about her: the way she smelled, the sound of her laughter, the tone of her voice when she reprimanded me for doing something I shouldn't . . . which was probably often.

I cleared my throat, trying to dislodge the thick layer of emotion that threatened to strangle my voice. "What about my father?"

Marx's face was drawn with sadness. "He didn't make it."

I sucked in a slow, shallow breath and released it with equal slowness, trying to control the burn of grief in my chest. I couldn't remember my mother, but I remembered a moment with my father. And in that moment I had loved him and trusted him implicitly. "My father was still alive when I left."

"How do you know that?"

"He told me to climb out the window."

Marx sat up straight in his chair and gave me an interested look. "You didn't tell me that. When did you remember?"

I tapped my fingers on the cup of tea in my lap as I looked down at the blanket. "The night the killer broke into Jace's apartment. I don't know if it was the sound of his boots on the wooden floor or the moment when I opened the window." Maybe it had been a combination of the two.

"What happened in your memory?"

"My father was in the room where my mother died. I couldn't see him, but I could hear him. He told me to climb out the window and run until I reached 'his' house. I could hear the killer coming back down the hall that night. Heavy boots, and I panicked. I just . . . climbed out the window. He brought someone else into the room. I could hear her crying before I ran."

When I glanced at Marx, he was quiet and his head was bowed. He could've been praying, but I could see the flutter of his eyelashes as he blinked. His words came slowly. "That was your sister."

"I have a sister?" I asked with a glimmer of hope.

"*Had* a sister," he whispered, and his voice was tight with sympathy.

The memory of my brief conversation with the killer as he stood on my front patio floated to the surface of my mind: I'd told him I didn't have a sister, and he'd said, "Not anymore."

"He killed her too?" Marx's face blurred behind a veil of tears as I looked at him. I had always wanted a sister, and now I knew why. I might not remember my family, but my heart still longed for what had been taken from me.

He lifted his eyes to mine and said with difficulty, "You were . . . the only survivor."

Somehow I managed to hold onto my breath as that news hit me somewhere between the ribs. For once I was grateful I couldn't remember them, because I didn't think I would be able to hold myself together in the face of those memories. I wiped away the few hot tears that burned down my cheeks. "What were their names?"

"Your father's name was Cristopher Anthony Cross, and your sister was Ginevieve Eliza Cross. Accordin' to a friend of the family, she had a bracelet like yours with three letters etched into it: Gin."

Gin. I closed my eyes and tried to envision her face, but the mental barrier gave me nothing. The sound of her name made me think "gentle," and I wondered if she'd been the grace to my mischief.

"I'm sorry, Holly."

I released a shuddering breath and nodded. It was heartbreaking to finally learn that I had a family only to realize they were all gone and I would never know them.

31

I tried to find a way to breathe in the spandex pants that Jace had lent me for the trip home from the hospital. They were like a second layer of skin—an absurdly long second layer of skin.

"Are you dressed yet?" Jace's muffled voice called impatiently through the hospital door.

Apparently, there was some girlfriend code I had violated by asking her to leave the room while I changed, because she'd given me an affronted look when I told her I wanted some privacy.

"Yeah," I grumbled as I pressed a hand to my head and breathed through the wave of dizziness. Leaning forward to roll up my pant legs was obviously a bad idea with a concussion.

"I'll get them," Jace said as she wheeled into the room. "Before your dizziness makes you face-plant and you get an even worse head injury." She leaned forward and rolled the extra three inches of pants up to my ankles. "You're like a dwarf."

"You're like a popsicle stick," I retorted. "How do you wear these things?" I slid a thumb beneath the waistband and tried to loosen them.

"Don't stretch them out," Jace scolded. "It's really hard to find extra-smalls for someone my height. And they're supposed to be formfitting. I think you look cute."

"That's not really what I'm going for," I mumbled. Not that I could manage it with a bruise the size of Africa on my face and a split lip.

The resultant headache had faded to a dull, consistent hum between my ears, and I didn't flinch at a pinprick of light, but I had the balance of a drunken pelican—and they weren't terribly coordinated to begin with.

She pulled back and looked me over with a critical eye. I was wearing her spandex pants and one of her pink hoodies that read, *I put the hot in hot-wheels.* It honestly made me a little uncomfortable wearing that logo . . . not that I had wheels.

"You look . . . almost normal," she said with a brittle smile. A fine mist clouded her blue eyes as she stared up at my face. Crap. She was going to cry. I wouldn't know what to do if she cried.

"Yep, all I need are my green streetwalker heels to go with these skintight pants, and I'm in business," I said.

She hiccupped a laugh and wiped her eyes. "Don't be ridiculous. Those shoes would look absurd with your pant legs rolled up." She sniffled and blinked away the remainder of her tears.

I thought about telling her they were just cuts and bruises and they would fade within a week or two, but I was afraid even mentioning them would tip her over the edge. I could only imagine how she reacted when someone called to tell her I was in the hospital.

"Who told you I was in the hospital?"

She blushed.

Ah, Sam. He'd gotten in touch with her. Probably the moment he figured out what was going on. "So . . . you two exchanged numbers?"

The crimson in her cheeks deepened. "I was in the city with Mom, and I sent you a text about how overbearing she was being. When you didn't answer, I got worried. So I sent Sam a text. He didn't get back to me for almost two hours, and then he told me where you were."

"So are you two—"

"I just have his number because . . . he was watching over my best friend," she interrupted.

I tilted my head thoughtfully. "So you have Marx's number too? And Officer Meredith's?"

"No." She froze like a deer in the headlights when she realized she'd just undermined her own excuse for having his number. "Fine. Yes. Sam gave me his number, but he doesn't want anyone to know. Not until this is all over."

"Why?"

"Because he's worried that if Mr. Southern thinks his focus is split, he'll pull him off protective detail, and he really does care about your safety," she explained.

Someone knocked lightly. "Everybody decent?" Marx called out.

Jace's eyes widened, and we exchanged a slightly concerned look. If he'd been out there for longer than ten seconds, he would've heard what she said about Sam.

"Yep," I answered. "You can come in."

Marx strolled into the room and paused at the foot of the bed. His gaze flickered over me from head to toe, and he frowned. "Where do you think you're goin'?"

Jace cleared her throat. "I'm gonna grab a drink. I'll be back in a while." She slipped out of the room.

I fortified myself with a breath. I had come to a decision I knew he wouldn't approve of, but it was my decision to make. "I'm going to Kansas."

I had waited my entire life for a family. I knew now that they were dead, and all I had left of them were memories trapped somewhere in the back of my mind. I wanted every single one of those memories back, and if I had to go to Kansas to get them, I would.

32

The room was startlingly quiet after my declaration, and for a moment I thought I hadn't spoke loudly enough. Marx leaned forward and rested his hands on the footboard of the bed. "Run that by me again."

Of course he thought he'd misheard. It was an outrageous idea, and one that I never thought I would entertain given everything that had happened. "I'm . . . going to Kansas."

"Absolutely not," he said. The finality in his tone made me bristle.

I folded my arms and lifted my chin defiantly. "It's not your decision to make."

He stared at me, his jaw set in a hard line. I had a feeling he wanted to shout, but he'd learned that particular tactic didn't work so well with me.

Sam, who had materialized silently in the doorway, glanced back and forth between us. "Holly, that's exactly where the killer wants you to go."

"I'm aware of that, Sam. But it also happens to be where I wanna go."

It really didn't matter if I stayed here; the killer would only keep coming until I chose to go to Kansas—where he wanted me to be—or until he was able to abduct me and take me there himself. Personally, I thought the road trip would be better if I wasn't drugged and stuffed into a trunk for the duration.

"Why?" Marx asked in a measured voice.

"Because I wanna remember my family. Everything is in there somewhere. *He's* in there somewhere. And maybe going back will help me remember."

"You really wanna walk into the lion's den?"

God was in the lion's den with Daniel. He was also with me. I was absolutely terrified of the idea of going to Kansas and finding the killer there amidst my memories, but I knew I could do this. I pushed determination into my voice. "Yes."

"You're not goin'."

Anger ignited in my chest. "You can't stop me."

Marx lifted his hands an inch off the footboard, and I braced myself for him to slam them back down in the anger I could feel building around him, but he caught himself and returned them to the footboard with deliberate slowness. "Do you have any idea what this man intends to do to you?"

I swallowed the knot of fear that lodged in my throat. I didn't know the details, but I knew what he'd done to my family was too awful to put into words.

"What he did Sunday night . . . druggin' you and puttin' his hands on you . . . doesn't even compare, Holly. This isn't a fun road trip down memory lane. He has no intention of lettin' you leave that town alive," he explained.

"And if I stay, is he just gonna leave me alone?" I asked. The answer was as clear as glass in their grim expressions. "Our only hope of learning who he is and how to find him is if I remember him. Tell me I'm wrong. Tell me we have some evidence that will do that for us."

Marx pursed his lips. "Please. Do. Not. Do this."

The desperation in his voice gave me pause. "I'm going."

"I can't protect you there, Holly!" I flinched involuntarily at the volume of his voice, and he bit down on his lips and clenched his fingers into fists as he tried to reign in his temper.

"I'm not asking you to come," I said softly.

"This is reckless," he replied in a much quieter voice.

"I've made up my mind."

He closed his eyes and bowed his head. I waited for him to say something, but he didn't. After a long moment of tense silence, he pushed away from the bed and walked out of the room.

I sagged back against the pillows. I had expected him to argue with me, to even be angry, but I hadn't expected him to leave. I wasn't sure why, but it kind of hurt that he just . . . walked out.

"Holly, you can't go by yourself," Sam said, and his voice held only calm reason.

"Yes, I can." I would find a way to get there.

"Okay, you *shouldn't* go by yourself."

I rubbed my face with my hands before looking over at him. "I would rather go alone than put anybody else in danger."

He frowned. "Noble but illogical."

I sighed in frustration. "And why is it illogical?"

"Don't get angry with me for saying this, but of the two of us, I'm bigger, stronger, probably faster, trained to defend myself, and I have a gun. What do you have?"

"Mmm . . . experience?" I couldn't argue against most of his points, but I doubted he was faster than me. I was pretty quick on flat ground.

"In what?"

That was a good question. I had plenty of experience with danger and trying to wiggle my way out of it with as few scrapes and bruises as possible. I also had plenty of experience in running away, staying under the radar, avoiding social interaction. "Rolling with the punches?" I said.

He shot me an irritated look. "That's not funny."

Apparently, he was still sore about the fact that he hadn't been able to protect me. "Sorry."

"My point is, it doesn't make sense to go alone in order to protect a cop when we're better equipped to protect ourselves and you. The logical choice would be to take one of us with you if you insist on going."

"It's gonna be a long trip, and I know that you guys have some sort of jurisdictional stomping ground issue. And Kansas is like . . . way out of your jurisdiction." I didn't really understand how all of that worked.

"True, but if there's a way to make it happen, Marx will find it," Sam assured me. "Besides, if you go alone, how are you gonna get there? You don't drive. You don't even have a car. You won't involve your only friend who has a car because it might put her in the line of fire. You don't have any ID for a flight. That leaves city buses and hitchhiking."

"I've been moving from place to place for ten years, Sam. I'm familiar with the methods of travel," I said hotly.

"So you understand the potential dangers."

I did. But apart from being stared at or hit on by guys who thought the bus was a speed-dating bar, I had rarely encountered a problem on the city buses. I did witness a gang fight that broke out on one of the buses and then trickled out onto the sidewalk, and I was fairly certain someone had gotten stabbed. But other than that . . .

"I'll be fine on my own."

"Maybe," he agreed. "But you don't have an ID for a cross-country bus, so how do you get across state lines? And if you say hitchhike, I will explain in vivid detail all of the awful things that can happen to you if you hitchhike. I've already had this conversation with my sister, so I'm well prepared."

I blinked in surprise.

"Yes," he said unhappily. "The younger sister of a cop hitchhiked. She got lucky."

"Sometimes hitchhiking is the only option."

He sighed as if I had disappointed him, and came to sit in the empty chair near the bed. "You have no idea how vulnerable you are, Holly."

I glared at him.

"I don't mean that in a chauvinistic or insulting way. There are women out there who can take down a full-grown man under the right circumstances or with the proper training. You're just not one of them," he clarified.

"How . . . is that not insulting?"

"It's reality. Hitchhiking is a bad idea for anyone, but especially a woman." His gaze slid over me, considering. "I'll tell you what I see when I visualize you standing on the side of the road, trying to get a ride. You're a young woman traveling alone, which means you probably have no friends or family in the area and no one knows where you are. That means you could likely disappear without drawing too much attention. You have a jitteriness about you, which makes you look even more vulnerable. You're small, so you probably can't put up much of a fight and you're easier to pick up and carry off. And you're . . . well, you're somewhat attractive, which . . . won't do you any favors."

I stared at him, stunned.

"All of that makes you a prime target for a sex offender or murderer looking for a victim."

"Well, I ask them if they intend to murder me *before* I get in the car, just to avoid that uncomfortable confusion later," I replied, keeping my voice serious.

He frowned at me, clearly unamused. "Even if you do manage to make it to Kansas in one piece, the killer will probably grab you at the first opportunity."

"Nobody's ever accused you of being an optimist, have they?" If his intention was to scare me away from ever hitchhiking again, he was heading in the right direction.

"No," he said evenly.

"I'm not stupid, Sam. I don't get in cars with men." I was very careful about whose vehicle I climbed into, and it was always an elderly couple or an older woman driving alone.

"Whether you get in the car or not, standing on the road and waiting for someone to pick you up puts you in a very vulnerable position. It takes less than ninety seconds to abduct a person, especially a woman your size."

I gave him a wary look. "Why do you even know that?"

He offered me a ghost of a smile.

251

Marx stepped back into the room, his expression closed off. He tapped his phone against his palm as his eyes came to rest on me. "You're sure you wanna do this?"

I drew myself up in the bed. "I am." I would figure out the details of the trip after another night of sleep, but I knew without a doubt that I needed to find my way there.

"Sam, what are your thoughts on this?"

"I think she's gonna go one way or another, and if we don't want her taking a bus or worse, we should probably find a way to make it happen."

"My thoughts as well," Marx agreed. "I spoke to the captain and informed him that I believe you will go with or without protection. I'll have no more authority in Kansas than I had in Maine, but since you're the only witness to the murder of an NYPD officer, he wants you protected so that you can testify when we catch this guy." I would never testify and he knew it. "He's not happy with your decision. Neither am I. But since we have no grounds to keep you from leavin', this seems to be our best option."

"You're coming with me?"

"I am."

"And here she was ready to hitchhike and get herself abducted," Sam muttered under his breath with a note of amusement.

I scowled at him. "I think I liked you better when you didn't talk so much."

"We'll leave tomorrow. You're stayin' in this hospital for one more night under observation," Marx explained. When I opened my mouth to object, he interrupted, "There's no room for argument. Unless you're refusin' my help on this reckless and ill-advised trip to Kansas, then you're stayin' put. You need to give your head a little time to balance itself out before you're stuck in a car for two days."

I pinched my lips together without speaking. It would take us more than two days to get there because he would have to sleep, and I couldn't manage more than a few hours at a time in a car.

"Now try to get some more sleep," he suggested. He shooed Sam out of the chair and settled into it.

I slumped down in the bed and tried not to pout at being told to take a nap. Sleep was out of the question despite how exhausted I felt. I hadn't been able to sleep last night either—despite Marx's efforts to make me feel safe by camping out in the hospital room—and I had passed the time trying to remember all the books of the Bible . . . in order. I got stuck on the fifth one: Genesis, Exodus, Leviticus, Numbers, Du . . . dude-autonomy. It was close, but not quite right.

God, I sent silently toward Heaven. *You would tell me if it was a bad idea to go to Kansas, wouldn't You?* If I expected His voice to spill from the walls of the hospital room, I was disappointed. *And even if it is, You're gonna be with me every step of the way. Right?*

I glanced at Marx, who was sound asleep in the chair against the wall. God might not come down in person, but He wouldn't let me go alone.

God had only been a vague idea to me before I overdosed on pills at fifteen—a name I heard whispered in conversation and saw written on cardboard signs next to crosses. But when I was lying on that bathroom floor, dying, He was there with me.

I felt Him pouring over me like sunshine—so warm it was almost overwhelming, and yet somehow soothing. He was like the wind whispering through the trees, brushing across my skin and raising the hairs on my arms. His love wrapped around me so tightly that night that I forgot about the cold, hard tile beneath my body. I tasted His presence with every breath, and I heard Him in the beating of a heart that should've stopped.

That was the night I connected with God.

Of course, my first act as a Christian had been to steal a Bible from the hospital chapel. Later, I realized theft was one of those things God frowned upon. I asked for forgiveness, but it wasn't like I was going to give the book back. I needed it. Besides, someone had just left it there on a bench. Finders keepers.

I smiled at the memory as I stretched out beneath the blankets in the hospital bed. No, Marx and I wouldn't be going to Kansas alone. God would be accompanying us, and so would my stolen Bible.

Jace came by the next morning to "prepare" me before the road trip. Apparently, preparations included face paste to hide my bruise and multiple attempts to stab me in the eye with a brown pencil and a black goo–coated wire brush.

Marx insisted on wheeling me out of the hospital in a wheelchair, despite my objections. "I can walk, you know."

"You can barely think in a straight line right now, let alone walk in one, and I don't relish the thought of pickin' you up off the pavement."

"Because I'm too heavy?" I teased. "I mean, you did call me fat that one time in your car."

He laughed. "I did not call you fat. I said you were out of your weight class. That has nothin' to do with bein' fat. And no, for the record, you're not too heavy." He wheeled me toward the familiar maroon car parked in the closest spot.

I pushed myself out of the wheelchair when we reached the passenger's side.

"Holly," he said worriedly, stretching out a hand to brace me when I swayed suddenly.

I moved my arm out of his reach and planted my hand on the roof of the car, balancing myself until the wave of dizziness passed. "I'm fine." But man did transitioning from sitting to standing give me a head rush.

He opened the passenger door of the car for me, and I gave him a funny look. "What is it with you and doors?" I had never really noticed it until we traveled to Maine together, but he had a habit of opening doors: car doors, hotel room doors, restaurant doors. On the rare occasion, I made it to the door first, but more often than not, he arrived and held the door open for me.

His brow furrowed. "What do you mean?"

"I can open my own door."

"It's called bein' polite. Gentlemen open a lady's door when they're able to. They also usually offer them a hand to their feet, but some women are too—"

"Don't say it," I interrupted as I climbed into the car, and he smiled as he bit back the word *independent*. "And I don't think I like this whole door thing."

He squinted his eyes as he tried to reason out why I didn't like it. "It's not meant to imply you're incapable of openin' your own door or standin' under your own power, Holly. It's a sign of respect."

"I respect you. So should I offer you a hand up the next time you can't get off the floor?" I asked teasingly.

He grimaced. "Just how old do you think I am that I can't get up off the floor?" At my small smirk, he said quickly, "Don't answer that."

He closed my door and walked around the car to slide in the driver' side. It wasn't long before we pulled up to the curb outside my apartment. Being home should've filled me with a sense of comfort, but the sight of the yellow front door sent anxiety coursing through me.

Marx pulled a ring of keys from the inside pocket of his suit jacket and dropped them into my hand.

"I had your locks changed as soon as CSU was finished collectin' evidence," he explained. "There are duplicates on here if there's anyone you want to have spares in case of an emergency. But as of the moment, you're the only one with keys."

"Thanks."

The air of safety my home had once held was gone, and I felt lost when we walked into my apartment. I gathered my things as quickly as I could and locked up before it brought me to tears. I climbed back into the car with Marx, and we started our long road trip to Kansas.

33

Thick trees blurred by in a kaleidoscope of colors as we drove down a back road. We were nearing the end of the second half of our trip, and my anxiety of small spaces melded with my anxiety about coming back to a town I didn't remember.

"Get your tiny shoes off my dashboard," Marx scolded lightly.

I was hunkered down in my seat with my feet on the dashboard, bouncing on my toes. I shifted upright in my seat and dropped my feet to the floor. "Sorry."

"Do you need a break?"

I shook my head. "Not here." As beautiful as the fall colors were as they streaked by, thick patches of trees made me nervous. At least now I knew why. Apparently, when a psycho killer chases you through the woods, it leaves you with a slight anxiety problem down the road.

"They know we're coming, right?" I asked.

"Yes. I spoke with Jordan over the phone and let him know we would be there sometime after dark."

"Does he know I don't remember him?" The last thing I wanted to deal with was having to explain that, while we might have been childhood friends, I had no idea who he was. There was no way someone wouldn't get hurt during that conversation.

"I told him. He's aware of the situation. But I expect it will still surprise him that you don't remember him." Marx glanced at me. "That's a difficult thing for a person to wrap their mind around."

"You believed me."

He smiled warmly. "Yes, I did."

I leaned forward and dug through my bag in the floorboard until I found a package of Swiss rolls. I gripped the plastic with shaky fingers and tried to pull it open.

"You're gonna eat sugar?"

My fingers froze on the package, and I glanced at him. "Yeah," I said slowly. Did he have some kind of weird sugar ban in his car?

"You're already bouncin' off the roof," he observed, and I followed his gaze to my leg bouncing up and down at a rapid pace.

"But . . . I like Swiss rolls."

"Lord help us," he muttered, shaking his head.

I grinned and finally succeeded in ripping open the package. I peeled one of cakes off the cardboard and took a small bite. Sugary sweetness melted over my tongue. Mmm.

I looked at the second roll, considering, and then glanced at Marx. I offered it to him. "Want one?" Ordinarily, I was very protective of my food, but I could share with a friend.

"I don't know. That's the first thing I've seen you willin'ly eat in days. I'm afraid if I eat it you'll starve to death."

"Trust me, I have more."

He accepted the treat. I continued nibbling mine down to a nub as I peered out the window. Although the trees were scary, they were strikingly beautiful at the same time.

"How long until we get there?"

"About an hour. I know you're not terribly fond of the trees, but if you're gonna need a break anytime soon, I'd rather stop before it gets dark," he replied.

I dragged my eyes away from the trees to look at the horizon. The sun was dropping quickly, and it would be dark in the next ten minutes or so. "I think I can make it."

I was both relieved and rattled when our headlights glinted off a worn wooden sign hanging on a post alongside the road that read, "WELCOME TO STONY BROOKE. Population 1,492."

Well, they were precise. What would happen if a resident died tomorrow? Would someone drive all the way out here to repaint the population number?

Marx popped open the console between the seats and pulled out a small purple box with a sparkly ribbon on it. He held it out to me on the palm of his hand. "I got you a little somethin'."

I gazed at the pretty gift box on his palm with uncertainty. Hot chocolate and iced tea were innocuous and thoughtful, but a gift made me a little wary. "Why?" Was I supposed to give him something back? I didn't have anything I was willing to give.

His brow furrowed. "Because I wanted to. I don't expect anythin' in return." He looked more concerned than offended by my wariness. "If it makes you feel better, you gave me cake. So we're even."

I plucked it gently from his palm and turned it over in my hands. It was so pretty and delicate looking that I didn't want to ruin it by opening it. "What's in it?"

"I don't think you understand the concept of a gift, Holly. You're supposed to unwrap it."

I turned it upside down and shook it lightly. "Is it breakable?"

He smiled. "Well after that let's hope not."

I observed the perfect bow. "Did you wrap it?"

"Accordin' to my mother, I tie bows like I tie my shoes, which for some reason seems to be a problem. So no, I had someone else tie it. A bow is a bow in my opinion."

I couldn't help it: I glanced at his shoes, taking note of the haphazardly tied laces, and then tapped the box with a finger. "Your mom's right. This one's nicer."

"It wouldn't be if you would just open it."

I nestled it on my lap and slowly untied the pretty ribbon. Sparkles peppered the seat cushion and floorboard. "Um . . . I think we just emasculated your car."

"It'll recover."

I opened the box and parted the purple and pink tissue paper. In the center of the gift box was a sleek purple canister on a lanyard. I lifted the canister out of the box and examined it. It was a slightly different design, but I had held one of these before. "Pepper spray?"

"If for any reason we get separated in this town, I wanted

you to have somethin' to protect yourself with."

"It's purple." My favorite color. That probably hadn't been easy to find.

"It comes with a lanyard, but don't wear it around your neck. It's too obvious that way, and it also makes it easier for an attacker to strangle you. Please keep it in your pocket."

Good to know.

"There's a lever on the back. You have to move it to the left to unlock it before you press it down. It's a safety feature."

I knew how to use pepper spray, but I let him explain because I knew he wanted to. He enjoyed making people feel safe.

"Thank you," I said with a grateful smile. I tucked it into my coat pocket.

"Let's just hope you never need to use it," he said, and I could hear the worry in his voice.

It was dark when we finally arrived at the sheriff's department in Stony Brooke, and I surveyed the autumn trees and Halloween decorations warily as I stepped out of the car.

The sheriff's department resembled an old library from the outside—quaint and outdated—and someone had plastered colored leaves across the inside of the windows.

Marx closed his car door and kept one hand on his gun as he turned in a slow circle. "Festive people," he remarked absently, but I knew he was searching the darkness for danger.

I didn't remember this place, and he was out of his element. The killer had sent me a note card from this town's address with the very obvious message of "come home," which meant he wanted me here. Neither of us had any doubt he was watching from somewhere in the shadows.

Marx walked around the car to my side and put himself between me and the ominous parking lot. A few cars were scattered throughout the lot beneath dim security lights, but overall the parking lot had a very dark, eerie feel to it.

"You ready?" he asked.

I clung to the door, a little reluctant to let go and step back into a world I couldn't remember.

"You don't have to do this, Holly," he reminded me. "You have nothin' to prove. We can find another way to help you remember that doesn't involve puttin' you in harm's way."

"He's gonna be wherever I am, which means whether I'm here or whether I'm in New York, I'm always in harm's way." I closed the car door and tucked my cold hands into the pockets of my jacket. My fingers wrapped around the small container of pepper spray Marx had given me, and I steeled myself as I started toward the building.

Something stirred in the brush beyond the parking lot, and my footsteps faltered. Marx paused beside me and surveyed the darkness. There wasn't a lot of ambient light in the country—no orange glow cast off by nearby factories or neon street signs. It was just . . . dark.

"It's probably just an animal," he said, but his eyes remained fixed in the direction of the sound. He nudged me forward with a gentle touch on my arm. "Keep walkin'."

I started up the sidewalk with him by my side, but came up short when a figure stepped out of the doorway less than six feet ahead of us. Marx drew his weapon on instinct as he stepped between me and the unexpected man, but he kept it angled toward the ground.

A bulb over the door illuminated the man in a pool of yellow light. He was around six feet with blond hair and a lithe frame that reminded me of Jacob, but his eyes were too shadowed to be visible. He wasn't wearing a uniform, but his right hand was clearly resting on a gun attached to his belt.

"Detective Marx?" the man asked, and his voice was low and smooth.

"Jordan?"

"Yes, sir," the man replied. He moved his jacket aside, and a badge gleamed in the lamplight.

Jordan. I knew that name. My stomach tightened at the memory of the little boy with the football. He wasn't so little anymore. The sight of him made my nerves flutter.

His attention moved from Marx to me, and there was a subtle shift in his posture when he noticed me. There wasn't much to see in the darkness, but he tried.

"Hello, Holly," Jordan finally said, and his smooth voice was suddenly tense with restrained emotion. "It's good to see you."

"Hi," was all I managed to say.

Marx glanced down at me as he holstered his gun. "I'd like to get her inside quickly."

His voice seemed to snap Jordan's focus back to the matter at hand. "Of course." He stepped aside and held the door open.

"After you, Holly," Marx prompted, urging me forward, and I gripped the canister in my pocket a little tighter as I walked stiffly up the sidewalk. I hugged the wall to put as much space as possible between me and Jordan as I slipped through the doorway.

"We weren't expecting you for another two hours," Jordan said as he followed Marx through the doorway. "We intended to meet you in the parking lot."

"We made good time," Marx explained vaguely.

Jordan locked the door and dropped the blinds after we were all inside.

"What's with the glass door? It's not gonna keep very many people out," I whispered to Marx.

His lips twitched in amusement, and he whispered back, "Believe it or not, there aren't that many people who try to break *into* a sheriff's department."

"Right," I muttered, feeling dense.

Jordan turned around, and I caught a glimpse of the sparkling blue eyes from my memory. I got the sense that I had trusted the boy with those eyes implicitly, but I didn't know the man.

"Marx, it's good to meet you," he said as he offered his hand.

Marx shook it briskly. "Same to you. Is your father here?"

"No, he actually retired. He's almost seventy. But he stops by from time to time. I run the department."

Marx looked him over. "Awfully young, aren't you?"

261

Jordan gave him a tight but unoffended smile. Apparently, it wasn't the first time his abilities had been called into question due to his age. "I'm twenty-eight, Detective, not twelve. I do know how to handle a crime."

His gaze shifted to me, and he took a small step forward—whether to hug me or shake my hand, I wasn't sure—but I took an equally small step closer to Marx that stopped him in his tracks.

Jordan cleared his throat and looked a little uncomfortable as he moved back to where he'd been standing. "Sorry. This is . . . kind of an unusual situation for me."

I had no doubt about that. He'd been looking for me for a very long time, only to realize that I didn't remember him. His blue eyes roved over me under the new lighting in a polite but interested way. I tried not to squirm self-consciously.

"What happened?" he asked, tapping his lip.

I tucked my lips between my teeth and tried to think of an explanation. "I . . . walked into a . . . door." *Yeah, like he's gonna believe that . . .*

Jordan frowned and slid a look to my right that fell somewhere between questioning and accusing.

Marx crossed his arms indignantly. "It wasn't me." I had never meant to suggest that it was, but somehow we'd gotten there, and I wished we could *un*-go there. "I believe I mentioned she was in the hospital earlier this week."

Jordan's face lit with understanding. "From when the killer broke into her apartment." Technically he hadn't broken in; he had keys.

"I'm fine," I said quickly before Jordan could form the question he'd no doubt opened his mouth to ask. "Could we get started? I'm kind of tired and I don't really wanna be here all night."

He grinned, and it was a full, warm smile with a hint of mischief that revealed dimples in his cheeks. "Staying the night isn't so bad. I've done it a time or two. The chairs are almost comfortable and there's always burnt coffee and day-old doughnuts to look forward to in the morning. And if it's too quiet for you, you can always prop open the basement door and listen to the drunk prisoners serenade you with unintelligible ballads."

"Temptin'," Marx grumbled unenthusiastically.

Jordan nodded down the hall. "I have a room set aside if you two wanna follow me." He looked at Marx and then back at me before heading down the hallway.

Marx fell in step beside me as we followed Jordan. "A door, Holly?" he asked quietly. "You do realize that's code for *the man standin' next to me hit me and I can't tell you.*"

"I . . ." No, I hadn't even considered that. I just hadn't been able to think of anything more creative than a cliché in the moment. "Sorry?" I offered, looking up at him sheepishly.

He chuckled softly at my pained, apologetic expression. "It's fine. I couldn't care less about his opinion of me."

"Do you actually care what anyone thinks of you?"

"A few people, yes." The look he gave me made me wonder if I was one of those few people.

I looked around the new environment as we exited the hallway into a large room. We passed a few empty offices and occupied desks. A female deputy was escorting a handcuffed man out of the room as he pleaded, "Come on, Belle, I was just using the cans for target practice."

"Beer cans," the female deputy pointed out matter-of-factly as she dragged him through a doorway into a stairwell. "That you chugged dry before lining them up on the gazebo in town square and shooting them with a handgun." The door closed, cutting off their voices.

Jordan pulled open the glass door to a small office, and Marx ushered me through the doorway ahead of him.

Jordan perched on the edge of the conference table. "Before we get started, there's probably a few things I should mention. One, this town has less than fifteen hundred people, which means the two of you are not gonna go unnoticed for more than thirty seconds. You're new, which makes you automatically interesting. Detective, you might be able to slide under the radar for a while because you have a wedding ring, but Holly . . ." He glanced at me. "Most of the guys in this town rarely see a woman they didn't grow up with. And they haven't dated a woman their first and second cousins haven't dated first. I would expect some extra attention."

I stiffened. I didn't want extra attention, especially that kind.

"What's the second thing we should know?" Marx asked.

"We don't get a lot of crime here—the occasional bar fight or domestic dispute, but never murder. What happened to Holly's family turned this town upside down. News travels fast in a small town. If a single person figures out who she is, it'll be all over town within the hour," he explained. "People will bombard her with questions, try to take her picture. The local newspaper will probably try to interview her for an article. People will follow her around hoping for a crumb of information they can gossip about."

Anxiety crawled through me. I had no desire to be a small-town celebrity with my personal life in the spotlight. "Marx," I said worriedly as I looked up at him.

"What can we do to prevent that?" Marx asked.

"It's the natural order of things in a small town. You and I can try to deflect attention from her, but that's the best we can do. If all else fails, we can keep her here at the department."

I fidgeted uneasily. There had to be a third option. I didn't want to hide in this building the entire time I was here—that would defeat the purpose of coming—but I also didn't want to become a headline in the local newspaper.

Marx looked at me. "We can still leave, Holly. I'll take you back right now if you want." I knew he would. Even as tired as he must be after that long drive, he would slide right back behind the wheel and take me home if I asked him to.

But we had come here for answers and we needed them.

I slid my hands into the back pockets of my jeans and puffed out a breath of courage. "I can do this."

"Okay." He pulled a chair away from the table and gestured for me to take a seat.

I gave him a strange look. "Is this another one of your

perplexing male Southernisms? Because I can pull out my own chair. It has wheels."

Jordan choked off a laugh as he took a seat at the far end of the table beside a pile of manila folders, some of them so thick they looked ready to burst.

Marx heaved an exaggerated breath. "You remember our conversation about the doors?"

"That I'm incapable of opening my own?"

"That is *not* what I said."

I pulled out a second chair, patted the back of it and declared, "This one's for you." I walked around him and took the chair he offered, just to be nice.

He grumbled something about stubborn women under his breath and then sat down in the chair I had pulled out for him. He interlocked his fingers on the table and gave me a small, disapproving frown.

I smirked.

"I apologize for the hard copy files. I realize it's a bit outdated and probably a pain, but like I said, we don't have a lot of crime around here." Jordan slid an overstuffed manila folder across the table to Marx. "So we can't really justify upgrading."

Marx slapped a hand on it before it could slide off the end of the table. There was a file label on the edge of it that read, "Cross," and a red stamp across the front that boldly stated, "HOMICIDE."

"I faxed you the bare bones of the case already, but this is a bit more in depth. It includes all evidence as well as the autopsy results for . . . each member of the family." He shot me a troubled glance before adding, "There are also crime scene photos. I know I sent you a few close-ups of those already, but these lay out the entire scene."

Marx tilted the folder at an angle so I couldn't see the contents as he flipped through the pages. His thoughts and feelings vanished from his face. Yep, it was bad.

Jordan pushed his chair back from the table and stood up. I

265

tried to appear completely calm as he covered the distance between us in three short strides. "I thought we might start you off with something a bit lighter," he began. He set a thin folder on the table and slid it toward me with two fingers. "Pictures of the family, the house. Maybe something will jog your memory."

I shifted uncomfortably at his nearness, and took the folder. "I'll . . . take a look," I said, my throat tight.

He lingered for a beat too long, and I didn't realize I was holding my breath as I waited for him to leave until my lungs started to burn. Marx cleared his throat, and Jordan looked over my head at him. There was a moment of silence as they stared at each other.

"Let me know if you have any questions," Jordan said in a gentle voice that didn't match the irritated expression on his face. He walked back to his chair. I released the breath I'd been holding and sucked in another, trying to find my balance.

Jordan was pretty for a man, but much like paintings, I appreciated him more from a distance. I stole a quick glance as he sat down, and then turned my attention back to the matter at hand.

I opened my folder and looked at the picture of a house: two stories with evening-blue siding, a wraparound porch, and a barn-red door. The sight of it filled my mind with echoes of laughter and joy, swiftly followed by cries of fear and shadows of terrifying memories that I couldn't quite grasp.

Home.

I moved the picture to the back of the stack and stared at the portrait of a family. I recognized my mother instantly from the other picture I'd seen. There was a man with his arm around her and then two children. I blinked a few times to be certain I wasn't imagining things.

I sat in front of our mother, but the girl sitting next to me with little white flowers in her hair and a frilly dress was a mirror image of me, except . . . she looked serene and sweet, while I looked like I might shave someone's eyebrow off while they slept.

"Gin was my twin." I lifted my eyes to Jordan.

"Yeah. She was the innocent, bubbly one. You were . . . kind

266

of a tornado," he said with a crooked smile.

"Somehow that doesn't surprise me," Marx mumbled with amusement under his breath as he continued reading through the file.

I knew it was probably a silly question where twins were concerned, but I wanted to know. "Who was born first?"

"You were. Gin was, I guess you could say, a bit reluctant to come into this world. She was a little . . . slow," he said carefully, as if trying not to offend me. "Oxygen deprivation during birth."

The memory slipped through me as if it had always been there:

We sat side by side on the grass in the backyard. Gin wore a white dress with bright red strawberries embroidered all over it—so delicate—while I looked like I'd been rolling around in the dirt and grass in my striped leggings.

Gin lifted up the hem of her dress and smiled. "I feel pretty today."

"You're pretty every day, Gin-Gin," I told her.

She leaned forward as if to share a secret and whispered, "It's because I look like Holly."

"No, it's because you look like Gin," I said, poking the tip of her nose for emphasis. She broke into quiet giggles.

"Can I play catch with you today?" she asked, and her brown eyes were so wide with hope and excitement. Gin couldn't catch a ball if her life depended on it, but I couldn't shatter that hope.

"Not in that dress. Mom wouldn't be happy if you got grass stains on it."

"I'll wear my green one. You can't see the grass," she whispered.

I smirked. Mom might not be able to see the grass, but Gin would tell her without hesitation that there were invisible grass stains on her dress, but since they were invisible it was okay.

"Okay. But don't tell Mom," I warned her.

She bounded to her feet in excitement. "I won't. I promise. Unless she asks." She dashed up the steps and into the house to change.

"Oh Gin," I murmured despairingly as I looked at her sweet smile. Why would anybody ever hurt her? She was as innocent as innocent could be. "What did he do to her?" I forced myself to ask. I looked up when no one spoke. Marx and Jordan exchanged an uncertain glance, and it irritated me. "I'm not a child," I reminded them.

"We know you're not a child, Holly," Marx said softly. "But you don't need to know all the details."

"You of all people know it's too late to shield me from the harsh realities of the world. I can handle the details."

Marx pinched his lips together unhappily. "That doesn't mean you should have to."

"Jordan," I said, looking at him expectantly.

His eyes held mine. He looked as reluctant as Marx to share the details with me. But then his gaze wavered, falling to the table, and he said, almost too softly for me to hear, "Her, uh . . . her throat was cut."

The breath rushed out of me, and I dropped my eyes back to the picture. Little Gin with her strawberry dress and gentle nature, my baby sister . . . my imagination failed me when it came to her death, and for that I was grateful.

"Did he . . ."—the words clung to my throat as I tried to push them out—"hurt her in any other way?" If he'd hurt my mother in such a way that Marx refused to describe it to me, what had he done to the rest of my family?

"No," Jordan said. "She didn't suffer. Evidence suggests he dragged her out of bed at the last minute and took her into the master bedroom. She was still in her nightgown, and it didn't look like she was bound at all, so she probably slept through most of it."

That was a small comfort.

I drew in a breath of courage. "Okay, what about the rest of my family?"

Jordan cleared his throat, and I realized for the first time that this must be difficult for him too. He'd known my family. "Your father was found bound to a chair, beaten, with his throat cut."

I hadn't been able to see my father that night, but I had assumed he was bound in some way. I should've taken the time to untie him, and maybe then he would've had a fighting chance. Maybe he could've saved Gin . . .

I had left both of them there unable to defend themselves because I'd been scared. That knowledge made my heart ache.

"Your mother . . ." Jordan kept his eyes on the table as he spoke. "She was . . ."

"Jordan," Marx said sharply.

Jordan glared across the table at him. He didn't bow down to Marx's experience or authority; it only seemed to strengthen his resolve. "She has a right to know, whether either of us wanna tell her or not." He shifted his attention to me and asked with some difficulty, "Have you ever heard of . . . death by a thousand cuts?"

I stared at him blankly for a moment, and then my hand went to the cut on my forearm as the reality of what he was saying finally sank in. The killer had taken that terrifying knife and done this to my mother over and over again until she eventually died.

He'd . . . tortured her to death.

God, why?

The thought turned my stomach. I needed some fresh air. I pushed away from the table and ran out of the room with the men's protests echoing in my ears.

I weaved through the office, trying to ignore the stares of the deputies seated at the desks, and found my way back to the front door. My shaking fingers fumbled with the lock. I flung the door open and stepped out onto the dimly lit sidewalk. I took in a few gulps of refreshing cold night air.

Marx pushed the door open a second later and stepped outside with me. "You shouldn't be out here, Holly. It isn't safe."

"I know," I said. I leaned back against the side of the building and shoved my hands into my jacket pockets to keep warm. I stared at the stretch of darkness ahead that was probably a field. "I just need some air."

Marx sighed. "Just for a minute and then we're goin' back in."

I tipped my head back and gazed up at the night sky. It was like glittering black velvet; there was no orange city haze to mute the glow of the stars. It was amazing. If ever there was a moment I questioned God's existence, this was proof enough that He existed.

"About your family . . . " Marx began.

"I like the sky better here," I interrupted. "It's so much clearer. It smells different out here too. Like . . . grass and hay."

"And cows," he added dryly.

"Don't like cows?" I asked.

"I like my cows medium rare and smothered in onions."

I smiled. "I like mine with a mountain of French Fries and another mountain of ketchup. Really, the steak is just there for decoration."

He laughed. "So you just want the fries?"

"Yep. Lots and lots of fries. And maybe a chocolate milk shake."

He opened his mouth to say something else, but his phone rang. He pulled it out of his pocket and frowned at the caller ID. "Holly, would you mind givin' me a minute? I need to take this in private."

I peered at the caller ID curiously: Sully. That was the man he'd called after I told him about my memories. He'd asked him to look into a few things, which probably meant he was one of those computer wizards.

"Um . . ." I didn't really want to go back inside, but he wouldn't step inside and leave me out here alone. "Sure." He answered the call as I retreated into the building.

"Sully," he said by way of greeting. "What do you mean hacked? I don't . . ." He trailed off as he listened. "What files did he access?" Another beat of silence as he listened. "Just hers?" He closed his eyes. "Is there a way to trace it back to him?" He listened and then swore under his breath.

34

Marx hung up and looked as though he was ready to throw his phone into the weeds. He squeezed it in his hand and grumbled under his breath.

"Everything okay?"

I jumped at the sudden voice behind me, and my concern about Marx's phone call gave way to irritation. People needed to stop doing that. I turned and glared at the person who had spoken.

Jordan.

A small, apologetic smile played across his lips. "Sorry. I didn't mean to startle you." He leaned back against the wall and folded his arms as he looked past me at Marx on the patio.

I followed his gaze. "Yeah, everything's fine. It's just been an intense couple of months." I knew this case was wearing on Marx, and the complications of my past were only adding to the crushing weight of it.

"Have you two known each other long?"

I tilted my head in thought as I tried to mentally calculate the exact number of weeks we'd known each other. It felt a lot longer than it had actually been. "About two months, I guess. He was assigned my case." I wondered if he ever regretted it; I couldn't blame him if he did.

"The men in the park—the ones who tried to hurt you. That case?"

I hadn't realized he was aware of that incident. "Marx told you?"

"Just the highlights." There was a grim set to his mouth that looked out of place on his face. "I'm glad you made it out okay."

"Yeah." I glanced at Marx through the door. He was on his phone again, and he looked distinctly unhappy.

"He's very protective of you."

His comment caught me off guard. "Marx?"

"He gave me an earful about remembering my place and respecting boundaries." He smiled at me so I would know he hadn't taken offense at Marx's warnings.

Somehow it didn't surprise me that he'd given Jordan a lecture about boundaries. It also wouldn't surprise me if he'd threatened him with bodily harm if he violated them. "He didn't threaten to make you cry, did he?"

"No." He laughed. "But out of curiosity, what are the boundaries? I'd like to know so I don't get shot."

I smirked and slid my hands into the back pockets of my jeans. "Five feet."

He glanced between himself and me. "Oh, so I'm trespassing." He slid along the wall another foot and then gauged the distance again. "How's this?"

"Mmm, better."

"Am I on the border?"

"Yep."

"Good. What are the rest of the boundaries? Can I ask you intensely personal questions like coffee or hot chocolate? Or is that crossing a line?"

I smiled. "Hot chocolate. Coffee smells terrible."

His blond eyebrows crept up a fraction. "Clearly you've never had burnt coffee. Because if you had, unburnt coffee would smell amazing by comparison."

"That's not exactly a selling point."

He smiled and it brought out the dimples in his cheeks. I remembered those dimples from when we played catch in the yard. "We have packets of hot chocolate in the back. You want a cup?"

"Um . . ." I glanced back out of the glass door at Marx, who was still engaged in a whispered, heated conversation on the phone. I wondered what had upset him so much. "I'm not sure if . . ."

If it was wise to wander off alone with Jordan. He might know me to some degree, but as far as I was concerned, we'd just met for the first time a little less than an hour ago.

As I considered it, I gnawed on the half of my bottom lip that wasn't in the process of healing. If I based every decision I made on whether or not it could be dangerous or uncomfortable, I would never leave my house.

"Sure," I finally decided. Jordan maintained a comfortable distance from me as we walked. "So why don't you have a uniform?"

He was wearing a pair of dark jeans, a blue T-shirt, and a dark-brown jacket that brought out the gold in his blond hair. "I do. Today's my day off, and I probably won't wear my uniform while I show you around town either. If I dress in plain clothes, it'll look less like official business and more like a friendly reunion. Hopefully it'll draw less attention."

I looked down at his shoes: they were bright-blue Converse sneakers with green laces. "Interesting shoes."

His eyes skimmed over my outfit and landed on my feet. "Says the girl wearing red slippers in Kansas."

Ha! A Wizard of Oz joke. I suppose I should've seen that coming. "They're flats. Not slippers."

"If you say so."

Jordan walked into a side room where there was a small kitchenette, a miniature refrigerator, and a corner table with two chairs. He walked to a coffee pot full of charred black sludge and poured some of it into a mug.

Ew. I crinkled my nose in disgust.

He grabbed a second mug, and I smelled the powdered chocolate the moment he ripped open the package of hot chocolate. He prepared it and popped it into the microwave.

He turned around to face me and seemed surprised to find me still lingering in the doorway. "I know it's a small room, but I promise to stay on the five-feet perimeter," he said as he leaned back against the counter and sipped his coffee.

I forced a thin smile. "I'm good here."

His blue eyes regarded me with quiet speculation. "I know you've had a really difficult few months and I feel like a stranger to you, but I promise I'm not dangerous."

I had no intention of explaining that he made me nervous or that the small space that was barely larger than my bathroom made me feel claustrophobic. "So . . . the gun on your belt is just a toy?"

He grinned. "Okay, I'm a little dangerous, but only to people who break the law. You strike me as pretty law-abiding."

"Eh . . . a little jaywalking here, nose breaking there . . ." I shrugged.

"I've had my nose broken before," he admitted. He set his coffee on the counter when the microwave beeped. "By a red-haired girl who took offense when I made fun of her pigtails. She whacked me in the face with a tree limb. Broke my nose and blacked both of my eyes."

Astonished, I asked, "Was I the redhead?"

"Yep, and man did you have a mean swing for a six-year-old girl. I was almost afraid to talk to you after that for fear you'd hit me with a brick next. But we worked it out, and you decided I wasn't so bad." He removed the mug of steaming hot chocolate from the microwave and carried it over. He paused at the invisible five-feet boundary he'd promised to respect and requested playfully, "Permission to cross over?"

"I'll grant you a temporary visa of five seconds, and then I'm deporting you."

"*Five seconds.* You have very strict border laws, my lady." He approached me slowly and gripped the rim of the hot cup with tentative fingers as he held it out to me. I slipped my fingers through the handle. "May I ask why they're so strict?"

My fingers tightened on the mug, and I dropped my eyes, watching the tiny marshmallows dissolve into frothy rings. I didn't know Jordan well enough to share the details of my past.

I heard him release a slow breath as he leaned back against the counter. "Sorry, I didn't realize that question would make you uncomfortable."

"I'm not uncomfortable," I said, drawing myself up against the door frame and meeting his eyes.

He smiled, but it was a pale imitation of the warm, easy smile he'd flashed a few minutes ago. "You're about as good at lying now as you were when you were nine, which is to say, not at all."

"I guess I'll have to practice."

He lifted the coffee cup to his curved lips. "If you haven't figured out how to lie convincingly in twenty-seven years, there really isn't much hope for you on that front." He took a swig of coffee and added, "Which isn't a bad thing. Honesty is a dying trait . . . right up there with integrity and loyalty."

Truth be told, I never put much effort into learning how to lie well. I had watched Collin spin easy webs of lies to explain away injuries my foster siblings had mysteriously sustained, and it wasn't a quality I held in high regard.

"I guess I just value the truth too much to be any good at lying." But I could avoid the truth like it was a dangerous flesh-eating bacteria if necessary, and I often did.

"Okay," he said, looking contemplative. "Truth or dare."

I frowned, not entirely certain I understood what he meant by that, but then I realized he was referring to the childhood game. "I'm not really a fan of that game."

"It's a good icebreaker. I'll go first. Truth. Ask me anything."

He was serious. I had so many questions about my past and my family that I didn't really know where to begin. "Tell me something about my mother."

He tilted his face toward the ceiling as he thought. "She was kind of like a second mom to me. She was kind, but never afraid to put me in my place, which happened often because you were always getting us in trouble."

I smiled a little at that.

"She was busy a lot of the time because of her job, but when she was around, she was a great mom. She adored you and Gin, and she spent as much time with you as she could. Now it's your turn. Truth or dare?"

I shifted uneasily. "Dare?" If he asked me to hop on one foot or do cartwheels across the room, I was leaving.

He grinned at my hesitation. "I dare you to take a drink of your hot chocolate, which you've been avoiding."

I peered down into the mug of hot chocolate I had yet to touch. I loved marshmallow hot chocolate, but this was the first drink I'd accepted from a stranger since discovering my fruit punch wasn't as safe to drink as I had believed it to be. It left me irrationally uneasy at the thought of drinking it.

"It's not drugged, Holly."

His comment startled me. "I never said—"

"Marx told me the killer slipped something into your drink earlier this week when he intended to take you. It's only natural for you to be cautious, especially since I seem like a stranger. I probably should've let you prepare it yourself. There's more packets here if you want to make your own. I promise I won't be offended."

He might not be offended, but I would feel ridiculous. I lifted the mug to my lips and took a cautious sip. I was not going to be paranoid.

Wow. It was the temperature of molten lava, and I was pretty sure my tongue had just melted off.

Jordan watched quietly as I swallowed, and then asked with a wry smile, "Well?"

I licked the chocolate from my lips. "Well, the room isn't spinning and I don't feel faint, so I guess Marx doesn't have to shoot you."

"Oh good, I was worried about that," he said with teasing sarcasm. "Truth." Apparently, he had no secrets he was afraid I might ask him to reveal.

"Did my family get along? I mean . . . were we happy?"

"Yeah, I mean every family has its problems. Gin struggled socially, but we always included her. Your mom was busy all the time since she was the town veterinarian. Sometimes she had to leave unexpectedly because there was an emergency. But other than that, you guys were happy."

It was so strange having to learn about my family from someone else. I should've known my mother was a veterinarian, but

I hadn't figured out how to unlock any of those memories. I sighed and my breath rippled across the top of the hot chocolate.

"Truth or dare?" Jordan prompted again.

"Dare."

"You know most people choose truth because they would rather answer questions than risk doing something embarrassing."

"I don't really *do* questions," I admitted as I took another tentative sip of hot chocolate.

He gazed at me thoughtfully. Marx could look at my face and unravel my thoughts like a ball of string, and while Jordan struck me as intelligent, he didn't have that same insightful gleam in his eyes. I was pretty sure my thoughts were safe.

"Why is that?" he finally asked. "Why don't you do questions? Even the most private people I know answer some questions about themselves. Their favorite color, favorite food . . ."

"I chose dare," I reminded him.

"Then I dare you to answer my question."

I narrowed my eyes at him. "That's cheating."

"Yes, it is." He grinned. "But it's cheating for a good cause. I'm interested to know why you won't answer any personal questions, and how I can bribe you to do so."

"I'm not bribable."

He sighed and tapped his thumbs on the handle of his mug as he tried to figure me out. He'd known me for all of sixty minutes, so his chances weren't good. I leaned silently against the door frame, offering him nothing.

"You're not gonna make this easy, are you?" he asked. At my questioning look, he set his coffee cup down and gripped the edge of the counter. All the amusement and lightheartedness evaporated from his voice, leaving behind traces of sadness and longing. "Holly, I have a lot of questions, and you're the only one who can answer them."

I realized an interrogation was coming, and my defenses slammed into place. I straightened in the doorway and tried to make my voice firm. "I don't have any answers to give you."

277

"When I was ten years old, one of my friends died, her entire family was brutally murdered, and my *best* friend vanished off the face of the planet for eighteen years." I met his eyes and saw the pain that those losses had caused him. "I need to know what happened."

I understood that he needed closure after all the years of wondering, but I couldn't offer him that. "I don't remember what happened. That's why I'm here."

"I don't mean the crime. I've pretty much pieced that together myself," he replied as he pushed away from the counter and crossed the room, apparently forgetting the invisible boundary between us. "I mean you, Holly."

"I don't understand."

"What happened to you that night? How did you just vanish? Where have you been all this time?"

I tried to stand my ground and not back away from him, but when he came close enough that I could see the gold flecks in his blue eyes, my palms began to sweat and my heart rate picked up. A familiar spark of panic in my stomach drove me back a step, and I bumped into a plastic plant beside the doorway.

"I don't . . . wanna talk about it." I stumbled around the plant, desperate to put a physical barrier between us.

Jordan paused, suddenly seeming to realize there was far less than five feet between us. There was maybe a foot and some change, and half a plant. I was fighting the instinct to bolt.

"Jordan," Marx called out from the hallway; there was a low note of warning in his voice. "A word." I hadn't heard him come back inside.

Jordan clenched his jaw and rubbed a hand over his short blond hair before gritting out, "Sure." He cast me an apologetic glance before walking away to speak with Marx.

My spine relaxed one vertebra at a time, and I gripped the mug of hot chocolate with both shaking hands, hoping it would somehow bring a sense of steadiness. It didn't. I wished I could get a grip. Jordan had in no way threatened me, but at the same time, his proximity had very much felt like a threat.

I retreated into the conference room. I didn't want to hear their hushed, angry argument. I set my mug on the table and looked at the stack of folders in front of Jordan's empty chair. I knew I probably shouldn't snoop, and I tried not to—I did—but I was already picking my way through the pile before I thought better of it.

I turned them as I read the labels. I came across one labeled "SUSPECT," and I opened it cautiously. There was a copy of a hand-drawn sketch portraying a man's face, and I turned the page as I studied it. There was something familiar about it. There were two more copies attached to it by a paper clip.

I slid the tiny bundle of pictures aside, and my heart fluttered at the next picture. Somewhere in the back of my mind, I recognized those bottomless dark eyes. I wasn't sure how I knew, but the rest of the picture was wrong. I pulled out one of the copies and set it aside before moving on.

The third picture in the pile depicted a grisly looking man with eyebrows as thick as caterpillars, but it was the crooked nose that caught my attention. Izzy had said the man who chased me out of the woods had a crooked nose, and this one felt familiar. I set a copy with my other picture.

I worked my way through the folder. All the pictures were different, some of them shockingly so, but some of them contained bits and pieces of a puzzle my broken memory was trying to rebuild. I had to have seen him at some point, and the fear of that moment had seared his image into my memory . . . somewhere.

I spread out my selected pictures and stared at them. Matching. I just had to match the pieces to the face in my mind— the one I couldn't consciously remember. Ugh. I grabbed a pair of scissors from the cup in the center of the table and cut out the familiar parts of the faces before arranging them into some semblance of a head.

I fitted the last piece into the collage: a mouth that resembled a bow, arched on the top and flat on the bottom, like it was perpetually contorted in a grimace. I drew in a shaky breath and took a step back from the table as I gazed into the face of the man who had murdered my family.

I saw him in my mind as he leaned out the window, his face caught in the pale blue glow of the security lights on the house. He'd seen me, and I had seen him before scrambling to my feet and darting into the trees. I had seen him more than once, I realized, as another memory of him lurking in the backyard at the crack of dawn materialized in my mind. It had only been a flicker before he realized I was watching and melted into the trees like a ghost.

The door to the conference room opened slowly, and I lifted my eyes from my grisly collage to see Jordan and Marx coming into the room.

"Holly, what are you doin'?" Marx asked as his attention lingered on the picture in the center of the table.

"Building a puzzle," I said evenly. I couldn't draw a face to save my life—at least not one that remotely resembled a human being—but I excelled at matching things I'd seen before. "The shape of the face isn't quite right. His jaw is . . . like one of those G.I. Joe dolls, not this rounded."

Marx picked up one of the original sketches and looked at it. "Where did these come from?"

"Witnesses around town after the family was murdered," Jordan answered, and he was looking at me in an odd way. "Strangers don't go unnoticed in a small town, but none of the sketches produced any results. They were all so different that we couldn't be sure which one, if any, were accurate."

Marx dropped the original sketch back on the table and looked at the one I had assembled. "This is the man you remember?"

"Yep." The mere sight of the image gave me goose bumps. "When I climbed out the window to escape, he leaned out of it and I saw him. I also saw him sometime before that . . . in the backyard."

Jordan looked completely stunned. "You never told me that."

"So he watched the house," Marx said, as if to himself. "Specifically, the girls' windows or the house in general?"

Jordan cleared his throat and pulled his eyes away from me. "I would guess he watches the entire family, but he seems to fixate on the wife. Holly's mother reported feeling like she was being followed frequently in public. She left the veterinary clinic one Saturday and found a note on the door describing how nice she smelled."

The killer had an odd fixation with the way people smelled and how their skin felt, and it seemed to carry over from people into the things they wore and touched. My stomach turned at the memory of him smelling my hair.

"It looks like he stalks the families for four to six months before making his move, which is why we have so many witness sketches of him. He didn't exactly blend in, but he didn't stick around either. My dad looked into him, but if he was staying somewhere in town, he couldn't find him. He moved completely under the radar."

I stiffened when he said families. Had it been a slip of the tongue or did he mean to imply the killer had done this more than once?

"He's done this before," Marx said, giving voice to my question.

"He's done this since," Jordan corrected. "In all my digging, I couldn't find any homicides before the Cross family that completely match up. A few similarities. But after . . ." He trailed off for a moment. "We'll talk about that in a minute. Let me call Angie, the art teacher who did the original sketches for us, and see if she can smooth this into a single image for us. Then we'll run it and see what we come up with." He carefully slid it into a folder, trying not to disturb the placement of the pieces, and closed it.

I was relieved not to have the creepy Frankenstein monster face staring back at me from the table anymore. He took it out of the room with him to one of the desks and made a call.

Marx watched me as I started collecting the scraps of paper off the floor and table and balling them up in my hands. "How are you doin' with all this?"

I paused at his question. My insides felt like they were twisted into an ever-tightening knot. "I'm fine."

He gave me an incredulous look.

I was at a loss to understand what I was supposed to feel or do. I was completely off balance with Jordan, this place, this new information, and my feelings were in a constant state of flux. "I'm *fine*," I insisted. I walked over to the trash can and tossed the ball of paper scraps away.

"Holly, you stormed out of the buildin' not twenty minutes ago when Jordan told you about your mother." I tried not to think too hard about what had been done to my mother; I may not remember her, but no one deserved to die like that. "So don't give me 'I'm fine.'"

I gave a slow shrug, trying for indifference. "Bad things happen to people all the time."

"And if we were talkin' about some random person off the street, you wouldn't be afraid to admit that it was sad or scary. But we're talkin' about your family. And that closed-off expression on your face is the one you wear when you're tryin' to hide from what you feel."

I narrowed my eyes at him. "If we're discussing how things make us feel, I bet you a chocolate bar that you won't tell me what that phone call was about or how it made *you* feel."

He grimaced. "What kind of chocolate bar do you want?"

Figures.

Jordan opened the door to come back in and paused at the palpable tension in the room. "Am I interrupting something?"

Marx sighed, "No, I think we're done for now. Let's get started."

I plopped down in my chair. I gripped the lukewarm mug of hot chocolate with both hands as I tried to mentally prepare myself for the uncomfortable conversation we were about to continue.

Jordan cleared his throat and sat down at the head of the table behind his pile of folders. "I'll try to keep this brief since we're all tired. I've reached out and, unofficially, compiled a list of homicides that resemble the Cross family murders."

He slid another folder across the table to Marx, and I waited expectantly for mine. He gently slid a copy toward me, but he didn't appear happy about it.

I sucked in a sharp breath of shock as I looked at the list. "There are . . ."—I recounted just to be sure—"sixteen families on this list." Not including mine.

"And they're all over the country," Marx pointed out grimly. "How sure are you about this list?"

"Very. I've been putting the pieces together for seven years now."

"Then why didn't you tell somebody?"

Jordan gave him a flat look. "You honestly think I didn't? I'm a twenty-eight-year-old sheriff from a town no one has ever heard of, suggesting there's a serial killer working his way across the countryside. On top of that, when they find out I was friends with the victims, they just assume I'm blindly jumping to conclusions because I'm desperate for answers. Would you have believed it before you met Holly?"

Marx took a moment to consider that. "If I hadn't met Holly and seen the killer's handiwork myself, or if I hadn't spoken to him on the phone, then no, I probably wouldn't. You don't have enough experience or education to convince me you discovered a serial killer."

Wow, he didn't sugarcoat that at all.

Jordan glared at him from across the table. "Then you see my point. And for your information, Detective, I did connect the dots and assemble this list on my own."

"My concern isn't about how many names you pulled together on this list, but how many of them are accurate. Have you spoken to any of the detectives who worked these cases?"

"A few. Not all of them were willing to speak to me. Either

because they were too busy working on other cases or because they weren't interested in sharing information."

"How many is a few?"

Jordan looked as if he'd bitten into a particularly sour lemon. "Seven."

Marx tapped his fingertips on the open file in front of him. "So you've verified information for less than half of the homicides you've compiled on this list."

"I read the reports and reviewed the available evidence summaries. I don't need a detective to help me interpret that information."

"Did you at least confer with the medical examiners who worked the cases?"

"For some of the cases, yes. In others I had to consult our local coroner to get his opinion on the evidence and the state of the bodies. He was able to confirm that the manner of death for these victims is too similar to that of the Cross family to be ignored."

"Did you get access to witness statements?" Marx pressed.

"Some. Enough to make the connection."

"Enough in your mind, you mean. It seems to me the reason no one has bothered to follow up on your theories is because you have too many holes that need filled. There's no way what you have would stand up in a court of law."

"This isn't New York City, Detective. I don't have the world at my fingertips; information is a bit harder to come by, and I worked hard for every piece of it."

"You're not a profiler, Jordan. You're a small-town sheriff. You can't even tell me with 100 percent certainty that all of these cases are connected because you don't have all the facts."

"You're here as a courtesy, Detective. I don't need your help with this case," Jordan shot back.

"Seriously?" I asked, drawing their attention. They both seemed to have forgotten I was sitting there while they debated who was the better law enforcement agent. "You two bicker worse than teenage girls. When you're done pulling each other's hair, can we move on?"

Marx's mouth quivered as he tried to contain a smile. Apparently, he found me amusing, and I glared at him. "Okay fine," he said, keeping his voice civil. "What makes these victims targets of the same killer? How are they connected?" He leaned back in his chair and folded his arms, waiting to be impressed.

"Victimology: all the victims were heterosexual married couples in their late twenties to early thirties. All Caucasian. The male victims were all physically fit, successful, driven. The female victims were physically fit and attractive. The only variable was the children. Only six of the couples on the list had children, and given how little time the killer spent with them, his interest was not in the kids."

"Okay, how were the bodies found?" Marx asked.

"From what I could gather, all the male victims were found tied to a chair, beaten, with their throats cut," Jordan explained with a careful glance my way. "Each of the female victims was found in the same room as her husband. Unbound."

"That's because he's big enough to physically restrain the women," Marx commented absently as he flipped through the file. "He's six four and around two hundred twenty pounds. He knows he can control her while he hurts her. He also carries a knife, which is probably incentive enough not to resist. What about the children?"

"It looks like he brings the children in last and just . . ."— Jordan hesitated and I saw pain in his eyes—"disposes of them in front of the father."

I cringed as I thought of Gin.

"And the pattern?" Marx continued.

"He stalks the victims and torments them in small ways leading up to the murders. Most of the families reported dead pets, belongings inside and outside of the house being slightly out of place as if someone had gone through them, the feeling of being followed and watched. He studied them, learning their schedules."

The killer had followed me for months, and he'd gone

through all my belongings. He had, thankfully, left my cat alive. My cat . . . Jordan, with . . . the blue eyes.

I glanced at the man at the head of the table with renewed interest. I wondered if a part of my mind had remembered him, and that was why my blue-eyed furry companion was named Jordan. That was a little weird.

"So he stalks the family for months, memorizes their home inside and out while they're away, and then lets himself in one night," Marx summarized.

"Yeah," Jordan agreed. "In the six cases involving children, it looks like he used ketamine to pacify them, but the husband and wife were completely coherent."

I sat up straighter in my chair. "I wasn't drugged that night."

"Neither was Gin," Jordan confirmed.

That didn't make sense. I glanced at Marx, and he looked thoughtful. "My guess would be you were the first child to ever get out of bed and wander off, and he had no intention of lettin' that happen again."

Jordan said the killer had known our schedules; he would've expected me to be asleep, but I had gotten out of bed for a drink of water in the middle of the night and ruined his plans.

"He takes something from each of the victims. With the children it's usually a piece of jewelry or a toy, some small item that reminds him of them. Gin had a bracelet with her name on it that Holly gave her. She wore it every day. It was missing from her body."

A mental image of her bracelet sharpened in my mind and brought a fragment of memory with it:

I clipped the silver bracelet around her wrist and straightened it. I had worked really hard to scratch her name into it so she would feel special too.

Gin lifted her wrist and gazed at the bracelet with wonder-filled eyes. She gasped, "It says Gin, Holly. It says my name!"

The expression of pure joy on her face made me smile. "Yes, it does."

She snatched my arm off my lap and looked at my bracelet, comparing it with hers. Mine was professionally engraved and had been a gift from Jordan, but I hadn't been able to do the same for her. The too-big, misshapen letters didn't seem to bother her, though.

"Now we both have one!" she declared. She threw her arms around me and squeezed me in a hug. "I love you, Holly. You're my best sister!"

I was her only sister, but I was pretty sure she'd meant friend. I hugged her back gently. "I love you too, Gin-Gin."

Jordan was still speaking when my mind snapped out of the memory and back to the present. "With the husband . . . well . . . I'm not sure on that one. Nothing of his ever appears to be missing, but I just assume it's being overlooked somehow."

"He takes his wife and children," Marx said grimly, and I noticed that he was toying absently with the wedding ring on his finger. "What more can you take from a man? That's all the trophy the killer needs. What does he take from the wife?"

"The attack on the wife is . . . obviously intimate in his mind. She's the only one he tortures with the knife, and he always takes a lock of her hair."

I stopped breathing.

"Holly," Marx said, and I must have looked as terrified as I felt when I looked at him, because he asked, "What's the matter?"

I hadn't told him about my hair. I wasn't sure I wanted to. I gathered up my long waves in one shaking hand above my head, and the tuft of hair the killer had severed hung chin length on the right side of my face. He intended to kill me in the same gruesome way he'd killed my mother.

Marx's expression darkened, and he didn't say anything for a long moment. "You didn't tell me he took some of your hair."

"I didn't . . . realize it mattered so much." I let my hair fall loose down my back and wrapped my arms around myself.

The muscles in Marx's jaw flexed, and I knew he was angry.

Jordan turned a shade paler. "I just assumed he would try to do what he originally intended, like with Gin, but . . ."

"She's not a little girl anymore. She's a woman, and he's made it perfectly clear he's attracted to her," Marx explained, and he sounded as if he were on the verge of snapping.

287

"I'm sorry I didn't tell you," I offered, hoping it might cool his temper. I didn't want him to be angry with me for withholding that information.

He sighed. "I'm not angry with you, Holly. I'm angry at this man's sick mind, that he thinks just because he's attracted to a woman, it's okay to do somethin' like that to her. I'm angry that he's even fantasizin' about doin' it to you."

I tightened my arms around my stomach and pulled my feet up onto the edge of the chair. I wished I could go home where I felt safe, but then I remembered that safety was just an illusion.

35

I huddled against the wall in the narrow second-floor hallway of the bed-and-breakfast as an elderly woman showed Marx his room.

I wasn't sure how much more there was to discuss about the ongoing murder investigation, but after I showed the two men my hair, we had collectively decided to take a break for the night.

Jordan had accompanied us to the bed-and-breakfast, but he didn't intend to stay; he didn't live too far down the road. Marx, on the other hand, was hovering like a papa bear. I glanced at him, and he arched an eyebrow at me as if to say, "What did you expect after that revelation?"

The innkeeper pushed open the door to my room next and stepped aside. "There you go, dear," she said in a voice that had grown brittle with age. "Everything you need should be in there, but I'm in that room just down the hall if you need me. You're welcome to help yourselves to anything in the ice box. It's well stocked." She smiled sweetly and dismissed herself.

I had a feeling I should know her . . .

"There's a deputy standin' guard on the front porch and one around back, and I'll be in the next room," Marx explained.

I nodded as I stretched my shirt sleeves over my hands and twisted them anxiously. I stared into the dark, unfamiliar room, and for once I was actually afraid to be alone. Despite the obviously cozy air of the old building, I felt very far from comfortable.

My nerves must have been transparent, because Marx suggested, "Why don't we go down to the kitchen and see just how stocked the refrigerator is."

I wasn't hungry, but it would be better than trying to sleep. "Okay."

He smiled reassuringly and walked ahead of me. I followed slowly behind and studied my environment. It was an old house in a farmer's style with lots of rooms, windows, and plain but efficient features.

I ran my hand down the smooth wooden rail as I silently counted the steps I descended. I peered through the vertical window by the front door at the bottom of the steps to see the deputy Marx had mentioned would be on the porch.

"Either you're easily distracted or your legs are shorter than I thought, because you're awfully far behind," Marx commented as he appeared in a narrow hallway.

"Well, considering you thought I was five feet tall and I'm actually five two, it's probably that I have the wandering attention of a squirrel."

A loud noise nearly made me jump, and Marx's hand flashed to his gun before either of us realized it was just an old pendulum clock chiming the hour. And by chime I mean deep baritone dongs that reverberated through the floorboards.

It was ten o'clock, and I stared at the clock as it continued to shatter the quiet. Six dongs, seven . . . "Can we shoot it?"

"Don't tempt me," he said with a grimace. We were both on edge enough without strange loud noises making us twitchy. He turned around and walked toward the kitchen, and I followed.

I could hear quiet voices coming from the kitchen, and I hesitated. "How many people are staying here?"

"Six, accordin' to the innkeeper, and while two of them are men, neither of them match our killer's description. They're just people visitin' family."

Six strangers in one house. That was unnerving, and I was barricading my door tonight. We walked into the kitchen to find the innkeeper exchanging a few last words with Jordan as she was on her way out. I hadn't even realized Jordan was still here. Conflicting emotions flickered through his eyes when he saw us.

290

"Hey," he greeted with a small, guarded smile. I stopped, unsure if he was going to try to hug me or trespass into my personal space again, but he remained glued to the counter.

I gave him a polite but awkward finger wave from across the kitchen. "Hey."

"I figured you would be settling in to bed by now. The two of you had a long trip." Between the frequent breaks and the nights we spent in hotels, it had taken us nearly four days to get here. It was nice not to be moving anymore.

Marx regarded Jordan with cool civility. "What are you still doin' here?"

Jordan gave him a tight smile. "This is where the cookies are. And I was filling my last deputy in before heading home."

"I didn't realize the eighty-year-old innkeeper was also your deputy," Marx said dryly.

"I guess that makes her an excellent undercover agent then, doesn't it?" Jordan replied with equal dryness. There was an obvious thread of tension between them. "No one suspects the eighty-year-old cookie baker."

"Where does she stash her gun?"

Jordan shrugged. "Best guess? Either in her apron, or in the drawer next to the measuring spoons." He leaned forward and opened one of the drawers near the kitchen sink. Sure enough, there was a sleek silver gun tucked between the utensils. "Measuring spoons," he said as he closed the drawer.

"Is she a retired deputy?" Marx asked.

"No. She just likes to be able to protect her guests."

"Is it loaded?"

"Of course it's loaded."

Marx gave me a stern look as he said, "Don't touch it."

I responded to his stern look with an indignant scowl. Just because I fired a gun once and missed the massive human target standing four feet in front of me, and accidentally pointed a loaded gun at my head when the noise startled me into covering my ears, did not mean I couldn't handle a gun. It just meant it probably wasn't the *best* idea.

"You don't know how to shoot a gun?" Jordan asked.

"I know how to pull a trigger," I replied.

Jordan grinned. "There's a bit more to it than that. But I can teach you."

"If anybody teaches her how to shoot a gun, it's gonna be me. And it's not gonna be right now," Marx declared.

The two men exchanged a tense, unfriendly look.

I thought about just tiptoeing out of the room and letting them resolve whatever this was. But if I just randomly disappeared, that would probably only make things worse. "Do you two need a minute? Because . . . I can go glare at the possessed clock in the foyer if . . ."

Marx released a heavy breath through his nose and pulled his eyes away from Jordan to look at me. "No, we don't need a minute. Let's find you somethin' to eat."

I opened my mouth to tell him I wasn't actually hungry, but thought better of it. At least they weren't arguing or trying to burn holes into each other with their eyeballs. He opened the refrigerator and my jaw dropped. "Whoa." That was a lot of food.

The refrigerator was stuffed with drinks, fruits, meats, cheeses, desserts . . . I was pretty sure the innkeeper had managed to squeeze an entire grocery store inside of it. I really wanted to snoop through it and see what all was hidden in there. This was like Christmas.

"That's what a refrigerator is supposed to look like," Marx pointed out, and I picked up on the note of chastisement in his voice.

"I had things in my refrigerator," I reminded him. "It's not my fault your people took them all."

"They were drugged," he said flatly. "And milk, pickles, and fruit punch do not constitute a stocked refrigerator."

"What's in *your* refrigerator? Leftover Chinese takeout and lunch meat?" I asked.

He frowned at me, which was all the confirmation I needed. "Just eat somethin'. Please."

I grinned and started rummaging through the food for something that might awaken my appetite. Stress tended to rob me of my desire to eat, and I knew I was losing weight, which wasn't something I could afford to do.

I pulled out some trail bologna and cheese cubes. Those would help me gain it back. And maybe a cookie. I glanced at the chocolate chunk cookie in Jordan's hand. Yep, definitely a cookie.

I grabbed a heavy jug of chocolate milk and thumped it on the table. Marx shook his head. "You would find the chocolate milk behind everythin' else." He offered me two glasses.

I took that to mean he wanted some this time. I poured him a glass and handed it back. I glanced at Jordan, who was watching our interaction with quiet interest. "You want some?"

"No thanks. I have enough sugar." He raised the half-eaten cookie and gave me that same guarded smile he'd given me when we walked into the kitchen.

Sugar. I smirked and glanced at Marx.

He narrowed his eyes knowingly and said, "Don't you dare."

I snickered and sat down at the table to work on my food. I nibbled on a cheese cube as I studied Jordan. He hadn't been this guarded when we first arrived, so I must have done something to offend him.

"Where are the cookies?" Marx asked.

Jordan nodded to a stout jar on the counter covertly labeled "COOKIES." Marx slid it to the edge of the counter and plucked off the lid to peer inside. "I take it she likes to bake."

"Oma bakes a fresh batch of cookies daily, and she usually sends some over to the department, because apparently she thinks in order to be sheriffs or deputies we all need to have waistlines that hang over our belts," Jordan explained.

"Oma?" Marx said with a questioning arch of his eyebrow.

"She's my grandma."

"So your grandmother owns the inn, your father is a retired sheriff, you're the current sheriff, what does your mother do?" Marx wondered as he grabbed a cookie.

"She runs the diner. And my father might have retired as a sheriff, but he's on the mayoral council with my grandfather."

"Any part of this town your family doesn't own?"

Jordan thought about it for a moment. "The library. We don't really do books."

I liked books, but I had never collected any because they were too heavy to take with me when I moved. "I wouldn't mind going to the library."

"I think I know a place you'll like better. I'll take you there tomorrow," Jordan offered. I hesitated, barely, at the thought of going anywhere alone with him, but he caught it. "Marx can come with us," he added with a strained smile.

I suddenly realized what the problem was. My reaction to him at the department earlier and my caution around him now bothered him. It wasn't as if I was intentionally keeping him at arm's length. I had tried not to shrink away earlier, but I couldn't help it.

I sighed and dropped my half-nibbled cheese cube on the plate. I rubbed my hands on my jeans as I stood up and announced, "I'm gonna . . . take a walk around the house, just to . . . get my bearings."

I didn't have room in my chest for any more guilt than I was already carrying, and I didn't want to feel guilty for being nervous or afraid.

Marx saw straight through my flimsy excuse to leave the room despite my attempt to keep my expression neutral. "I'll come with you."

"I'd rather be alone." When he drew in a breath to object, I used the argument he had used to convince me I was safe in the hospital. "There's a deputy on the porch, one in the backyard, and two officers in the kitchen. I'm safe as . . ."—I stumbled over the expression—"barns?"

"Houses," Marx corrected with a small smile. "You're safe as houses."

I squinted as I considered the phrase. "Don't houses get broken into a lot? That doesn't sound very safe."

"It's just an expression. Like . . . cute as a button."

"Yeah, that doesn't make any sense either. Who decided buttons are cute?" I shrugged and walked out of the kitchen. As I wandered down the hallway, I studied the pictures that hung on the walls around the bronze sconces.

There were a lot of family portraits with Jordan as a child, the innkeeper, and a couple whom I assumed were his parents.

Jordan's somber voice carried through the quiet house. "You know, I've imagined finding Holly hundreds of times. But I never imagined it would involve her being afraid of me."

I closed my eyes in silent regret. Somehow I always managed to hurt people without intending to.

"I understand you had expectations for this day," Marx replied softly. "And that's fine, so long as you understand that what you want to happen isn't gonna happen. She isn't gonna trust you right away, and your childhood friendship isn't gonna pick up where it left off eighteen years ago."

"That's one of my favorites," an elderly woman's voice stated from somewhere behind me, and I glanced over my shoulder to see the innkeeper. She was smiling affectionately as she gazed up at a picture on the wall: a blue-eyed blond boy sitting between two red-haired girls with an arm around one of them.

"The little girl on the left—that's Ginevieve. Sweetest child I've ever met. A little behind the other children on the intellectual track, but she could find sunshine on a cloudy day. The boy in the middle is my grandson, Jordy. He was always running around with those twins. I never saw him happier. The one on the right is Holly." She paused and gave me a curious look. "How interesting that you have the same name and hair color."

I discreetly tugged my sleeve down over my bracelet, which was clearly visible in the picture. No one was supposed to know I was here. "That is interesting," I offered, putting as much disinterest into my voice as I could manage.

"Hmm," she grunted. "Holly was a little ball of mischief, but she had a big heart. She used to sneak through here and steal my cookies. I thought she was just eating them all, and I was amazed she didn't balloon into a little butterball. I knew something wasn't right, so I followed her one day. There was a little boy in town whose parents was terrible poor. He got free lunches at school, but there was never much food at home. I followed her to his house and watched her crawl through one of those little pet doors and leave a bundle of cookies on their kitchen table with a note that said, 'Love God.'"

I smiled. I couldn't imagine myself doing something that kind, let alone going into another person's home without permission.

"Obviously, I never brought it up. She was free to have as many cookies as she wanted, but I did have to let her parents know she was sneaking into someone's house, because that just wasn't safe."

"What did . . . she do then?" I had almost given myself away by asking what *I* had done. It was strange learning about my younger self from other people.

She grinned. "Left them on the doorstep. She was not to be deterred. She was a determined child." She released a mournful sigh. "Sometimes I miss those girls. Well . . ." She patted my shoulder gently and started down the hall. "I'm off to bed, dear."

"Thank you. For everything," I called after her.

She smiled and there was a knowing glint in her eyes. "Goodnight, sweet Holly. And the cookies are in the kitchen." I had a feeling she knew exactly who I was.

I wandered through the quiet, empty rooms of the house well into the night just to keep myself busy. I heard the resonating dong of the pendulum clock clear across the house as it struck midnight.

I was staring through the glass French doors into the back yard when movement caught my eye. Marx strode into the room behind me, and I watched his reflection in the glass as he folded his arms over the back of an upholstered chair.

"I hurt him, didn't I?" I asked.

Marx drew in a breath and released it slowly. "He doesn't understand why you're so afraid, that's all."

I turned around slowly to face him and leaned back against the doors. "I . . ."

"You don't have to explain it to me."

The compassion in his eyes made my throat tighten. Somehow he already knew. "How do you . . . ?"

He gave me a thin, sad smile. "I'm a detective, Holly; it's what I do. I had it pretty well figured out before we went to Maine. Your reaction at the hospital when I suggested you have an exam done just cemented what I already suspected."

A trembling breath escaped me, and I hugged myself as I turned toward the doors. I stared out into the dark patch of trees.

"I'm pretty sure I know who. I just don't know when or . . . if it happened more than once," he said, but his tone suggested he had his suspicions about that too.

I closed my eyes, but it didn't stop the tears from escaping. "So . . ." I began hesitantly. "Now that you know, does it . . . change the way you think of me?"

"It does," he admitted, and I flinched. It was always the people closest to you who knew just where to slip the knife, and his admission cut straight through me to the ever-present shame and humiliation my foster brother had left me with. I wiped at my wet face and wished suddenly that I could be invisible.

"Oh, Holly, don't cry," he pleaded as he came around the chair to sit down on the coffee table closest to me. I stepped back from him, but he stretched out a hand and caught my wrist with feather-light fingers. "Please, just listen." I stiffened at his touch and considered pulling away, but his grip remained gentle and loose.

He wouldn't hurt me. He'd proven that much.

My nerves trembled as I tried to be still, and hurt slipped into my voice. "Listen to what? You already said—"

297

"When I first met you, I saw a fragile girl on the verge of fallin' to pieces. But I've realized that's not who you are. You're not fallin' apart; you're pullin' yourself together. Knowin' just some of what you've been through . . ." He shook his head, as if it were too difficult to wrap his mind around. "You not only survived, you picked yourself up and started to build a life. That takes a phenomenal amount of strength, and I am . . . amazed and proud of the young woman you've fought so hard to become. And I'm very proud to be a part of your life."

No one—in the eighteen years I could remember—had ever said they were proud of me. I wasn't even sure how to respond.

I slipped my wrist free of his fingers, and he made no effort to hold me against my will. I stepped back from him and regarded him with doubt and fragile hope.

"I mean it, Holly," he said, and his green eyes shone with sincerity. He did mean it. He was proud to be a part of my life, and I . . . I didn't know what to do with that. He knew so much about me—so much I never intended for anyone to know. I had always assumed that if someone learned the truth, they would either look at me with pity or walk away because they didn't want to deal with my issues.

I sank down on the edge of a chair.

"I know you're probably waitin' for the other shoe to drop, but there isn't one," he said.

"There's always another shoe. They come in pairs."

"It's gone." He shrugged. "Lost, chewed up by the dog, had an unfortunate encounter with a lawn mower. There is no other shoe, so you can stop waitin'."

I swiped a tear from my cheek and smiled. "A lawn mower?"

His face squinted as if he'd just eaten something bitter. "I don't know who left it on the lawn. It wasn't me. I was just drivin' the mower. And it was less of a shoe and more of a . . . one of those flipper things that people wear in the summer."

I covered my face and laughed. "A flip-flop. You mowed over a flip-flop?"

"Like I said. It was unfortunate. Especially the mess."

I sniffled and wiped away the rest of the tears from my cheeks as the laughter faded. I appreciated his ability to lighten the mood, but there was one more important thing I needed to discuss with him. I rubbed my hands together anxiously. "I don't want Jordan to know . . . about . . . what Collin's done . . . to me." Jordan and I were already trying to find our balance on very thin ice; I didn't want to make it even thinner.

"It's not my secret to share. And you don't have to tell him; you don't owe him that." He rose from the chair. "Why don't we get some sleep? It's been a long day, and tomorrow's gonna be another long one."

I didn't think I could sleep in a strange place, but I would try. He walked me back to my room in silence, and I was pretty sure he stood guard outside my door long after I finished writing in my journal and closed my eyes to sleep.

36

Crisp leaves stirred around my feet as I stood on the sidewalk beside Jordan and stared up at the old wooden sign that creaked in the bitter breeze. It was late November—the time of year when autumn was still clinging and winter was breathing small snow flurries into the air.

The background of the sign was painted with blue and purple diagonal stripes and the worn black letters read, "Criss Cross Books." Recognition stirred through my memory. I had painted the purple stripes, and Gin had painted the blue: our favorite colors.

"Criss Cross?" I said aloud.

"Cristopher Cross. Your dad," Jordan explained. "He loved books. He opened this store when you and Gin were six. You guys spent a lot of time here."

I looked over the front window that was decorated with colored leaves and cardboard pumpkins. Someone had clearly taken over after my father died. "Who runs it now?"

"Georgetta. She was a friend of the family. She decided to leave the name of the store as it was in memory of them. You wanna go in?"

I looked over my shoulder at Marx, who had decided to keep his distance and allow Jordan and me time to get to know each other. He could've stayed behind and let us explore the town alone, but I didn't think he was any fonder of that idea than I was.

He smiled at me. I occasionally checked over my shoulder just to make sure he was still there. A bell tinkled softly when Jordan opened the door to the store and held it for me. Right. This was the part where I walked through and he followed.

I strode stiffly into the store and paused just inside the doorway as the scent of must and old books swirled around me, settling into my bones with a warm and peaceful sense of home.

Rows of bookshelves lined the room, and little upholstered benches with enormous pillows were scattered around the shop. There was a round fountain in the center of the room encircled by a blue-and-purple bench.

I remembered curling up on that bench with Gin as I read to her. She had struggled with the words, but her favorite book was *The Wizard of Oz*. She'd said it was about home.

"I'll be with you in a moment!" a woman's voice called from the back of the store.

I glanced back at Jordan, who was still leaning against the open door out in the cold. It took me a moment to realize why: he was trying to respect my need for space.

Oops. I took five small steps to my left and smiled, a little embarrassed. "Sorry."

He grinned as he came inside, and the door drifted shut behind him. "I don't mind the cold." His red fingertips said otherwise, and he tucked his hands into his jacket pockets. "Good morning, Georgetta!"

A woman in her fifties emerged from between the bookshelves with a mountain of books in her arms. "I'll be just a minute, Jordan. I need to shelve these. Those Huxley boys sure do make a mess of my books when they come in. You'd think since they can read that they might know the alphabet and put things back where they belong. But no, they leave . . ."

Words seemed to fail her when her eyes fell on me. Her eyes were enormous behind her glasses, and she blinked at me in an apparent state of confusion. "Good heavens." The books tumbled into a disorganized pile at her feet, and her mouth went slack. "Is that . . . who I think it is, or am I seeing things?"

Jordan pursed his lips. "You're not seeing things, and it's not who you think. Let me help you with those books." He bent down and started collecting the books for her.

Georgetta stared at me with such intensity that I squirmed. "But it can't be Emily. Emily died. And . . . she was taller, wasn't she?"

Jordan hefted the stack of books onto one of the benches. "No, it's not Emily, Georgetta." He wrapped an arm around her shoulders and gave her a gentle, steadying squeeze. "This is a friend of mine from New York. Her name is Marie. And I'm just showing her around town while she's visiting."

"Oh. Marie?" she asked, looking up at him. Marie was my middle name, and if she had been a friend of my family, then she probably knew that.

"Yes. Not everyone can have a unique name like yours," Jordan said. "Marie is a very common name. We have, what, three Maries in town?"

Georgetta moaned thoughtfully to herself. "Well, I suppose." She forced a smile that must have felt at home on her face because it warmed and spread into a broad grin. "It's a pleasure to meet you, Marie." She stepped forward and offered her hand.

I hesitated briefly before shaking it. "You too. It's a very nice store." She released my hand, and I noticed Jordan watching with an interested expression again—not me specifically, but the way I interacted with people.

"Thank you. I can't really take credit for it, though. Cristopher Cross pulled it all together. Well, him and those precious girls of his. They used to spend hours here. I helped out with the bookkeeping. But when Cris and his family . . . passed on, I kept the store running." She readjusted her glasses self-consciously. "I do the best I can to uphold his memory for this place."

"I love books. Do you mind if I take a look around?"

"Oh, of course, of course. If you need me, just shout. Loudly, though. I don't have the best hearing, and you're so soft-spoken."

"I'll holler if we need you," Jordan assured her with a charming grin. "There's no way you won't hear me."

Georgetta snorted. "That's because you're like your father and you can bellow like there's a bullhorn attached to your face." Her attention focused on the man walking past the front window of the store, and her eyes widened. "Who is this handsome fellow?"

I looked back to see Marx striding toward the door.

Jordan made a slightly strangled sound when she described Marx as handsome. "That's Marx. He's a friend of Marie's."

Georgetta tucked the flyaway strands of hair behind her ears and smoothed out her rumpled blouse nervously. I suppressed a smile as I started down one of the aisles. Marx was on his own with this one.

I ran my fingers along the spines of the books, enjoying the feel of them. Some of them were old and bound in soft leather, while others were slippery from the colored, decorative sleeves they were wrapped in.

Jordan walked one aisle over from me, and I could see him through the gaps between the books. He leaned on one of the shelves and looked at me. "If you could shelve me as a book, where would you put me?"

I smirked. A charming, handsome sheriff who knew he was charming and handsome. Hmm. "I would put you . . . somewhere between Snow White and the Westerns so you can ask, 'Mirror, mirror on the wall, who's the fairest of them all,' while you shoot the bad guys."

He laughed. "Wow, you think highly of me. I would never shoot someone while gazing at my reflection. It's impossible to aim that way."

We kept walking. "Where would you put *me*?" I asked before thinking better of it. He would probably shelve me in the self-help section next to *Five Steps to Finding Your Mind* or *Sanity is Within Your Grasp*.

His eyes narrowed in thought. "Well, let's see . . ." He raised his fingers so I could see them and began ticking things off. "Funny, curious, cautious, mysterious, beautiful . . ."

Anxiety fluttered through me at the word "beautiful," and I wrapped my arms around myself.

"I would shelve you somewhere between Mystery and Crime Novels near Nancy Drew." He glanced at me, and I tried to smile. "You don't do well with compliments, do you?" he realized.

I shrugged.

Jordan pulled a few books off the shelf and rested his chin in the opening, looking as nonthreatening as he could probably manage with his head sandwiched between two books written by Stephen King. "In my experience, telling a woman she's beautiful doesn't usually drain the color from her face. So let me be clear on something. One, I'm not taking it back, because it's the truth . . ."

I pinched my lips together.

"And two, just because you're beautiful doesn't mean I'm gonna forget my manners. My mother would smack me senseless, Marx would probably shoot me, and I don't wanna scare you off, so . . . you have nothing to worry about. Besides, I'm more interested in being your friend."

The knot of anxiety in my stomach slowly loosened. "Friend?"

"Yep. Commonly defined as people who spend time together, usually because they enjoy doing things with each other like . . . playing catch, going for runs, making ice cream sundaes, evening trips to the movies."

That sounded alarmingly like dating, but considering I'd never actually been on a date before, I couldn't really be sure. Maybe we'd done those things as children, and it just felt different now. "I'll take it under consideration," I said slowly, and gave him a small, uncertain smile.

We continued down the aisles as I studied the books. I loved this place; it felt more like home to me than any place I had ever been.

Memories turned through my mind like the pages of a book, and I absorbed them greedily: Gin sitting cross-legged on the floor with her nose in a picture book, our father pretending he was going to drop books on our heads as he shelved them, Gin and me running back and forth between the shelves while playing peekaboo between the gaps in the books.

I plucked a book from the shelf in the children's section: *The Wizard of Oz*. I smoothed my hand over the familiar cover and flipped it open. Written on the inside cover was a note: "To my baby girls, Gin and Holly. May your imaginations take you on an adventure across the world. Love, Daddy." Written beneath it in big, barely legible letters was, "Propty of Gin and Holly."

I released a breath that was tight with unshed tears as I closed the book. "This was mine and Gin's." I looked up at Jordan as he leaned against the end of the shelf. "I used to read it to her on the round bench by the fountain. We . . . never made it to the end."

I remembered the gentle sound of her giggle as she cupped a hand to her mouth every time I read a line from the Cowardly Lion. He was her favorite character.

Lord, I miss her . . .

I knew He was taking care of her, but my heart longed for her. I had only just remembered that I had a sister, and it didn't seem fair that I didn't have a chance to see her. I wanted to hug her and laugh with her. I wanted to see the person she would've grown up to be.

"It's your book. Take it with you and finish it," Jordan suggested.

"I can't just take it. Georgetta owns the store now."

"No, she doesn't. Your father willed it to you and Gin. Criss Cross Books is yours, and Georgetta loved your family. She would hand over the deed in a heartbeat. And she would probably gladly continue to run the place if you wanted her to."

Wow. I owned a bookstore. How did I go from being a transient woman with no name and no home to being a woman with friends, a bookstore, and an entire town filled with people who knew my name? I could stay here and rebuild my life in this small town.

It was tempting.

But there were people I cared about in New York. Jace and . . . I glanced at Marx, who looked awkwardly uncomfortable as he rebuffed Georgetta's advances.

"Come on. Let's talk to Georgetta," Jordan said with a nod toward the front of the store. I followed him up the aisle, wondering how he intended to convince her to give me the book without revealing my identity.

I got distracted by the fountain bench and stopped as he continued on. I sat down and ran my hand over the cushion, remembering the feel of it and listening to the soothing sound of the water rippling behind me. I could curl up on this bench and sleep; it filled me with a sense of safety I hadn't felt in a long time.

Georgetta shook her head as Jordan spoke with her. "Not for sale," I heard her say. She didn't want to part with the book any more than I did. Jordan whispered something to her, and she hesitated. She studied me out of the corner of her eyes and then reluctantly nodded.

A moment later, Jordan slid his hands into his jacket pocket and walked back to me. "The book is yours, with the promise that I'll explain everything to her later."

I hugged the book to my chest. "Thank you." I was already looking forward to curling up in a sunny spot somewhere and reading it.

"Do you wanna drive by the house?" he asked.

Marx crossed his arms. "I'm not so sure that's a good idea."

"I wasn't actually asking you."

"If you two start arguing again, I'm putting you in separate corners until you calm down," I warned as the two men scowled at each other.

Marx gave me a vaguely amused look. "What makes you think you can put me anywhere I don't wanna go?"

"Easy. If you don't go, I won't listen the next time you tell me to go somewhere for my own protection."

He grimaced. "If you try that, I will pick you up and carry you."

"If you ever try to pick me up and carry me, I will beat you with this book." I wasn't some tiny chess piece that could be moved around.

Jordan laughed. "She always did have an attitude three times her size."

I rolled my eyes and walked toward the exit. The little bell above the door tinkled again as I pushed it open and stepped out onto the sidewalk. The air was shockingly cold as it splashed across my face and neck.

I burrowed deeper into my jacket that was rapidly becoming insufficient for the weather as I moved into the sunlight. I took in the center of town with a sweep of my eyes.

It was one single street of "town" with quaint little shops nestled together on both sides of the street and festive decorations hanging in every window. Even the lamp poles were decorated with leaf garland and orange lights.

I hated this season, and I was ready for all things autumn to fade away under a blanket of white. God's cosmic whiteout.

I heard the tinkling of the bell as Jordan followed me out and leaned against the nearest tree to look up through the leaves at the sky.

"You know, I've never quite liked fall as much as I once did," he admitted. "We used to play in the leaf piles and go trick-or-treating—you, me, and Gin—but it just wasn't the same after that October."

"What happened that year?"

He sighed. "When the town realized you were missing, Trick-or-Treat was cancelled, the kids were all gathered in City Hall, and the adults assembled search parties to comb the woods for you. I was supposed to stay in City Hall with the other kids, but I snuck home, got my flashlight, and went out to look for you myself. You told me once that your father had a plan in case of emergencies. If you couldn't get to a phone, you and Gin were supposed to run through the woods to my house. I was your closest neighbor, but my dad was also the sheriff. So I went to your house and followed the path I thought you would've taken."

My heart ached a little for him. He was ten years old, and he'd just lost both of his friends and two adults that he cared about. And he came back to the scene of the murder and braved the dark woods alone in the desperate hope he would find me.

"I came out on the road, and I walked for probably a mile in both directions," he continued, and his voice sounded haunted. "But I couldn't find any sign of you. If there had been any evidence, the rain that morning probably washed it away."

I exhaled a quiet breath. I had tried to reach his house that night, but I hadn't made it. "I'm sorry. That must have been hard for you."

His smile was tinged with sadness. "I imagine it was harder for you."

I shrugged and turned away from him and the dozens of questions burning in his eyes. I knew he wanted answers, but I just couldn't give them to him.

"Holly needs to eat," Marx announced.

I turned back to see him standing in the doorway of the bookstore and protested, "But we just had breakfast."

"No," he said. "I had breakfast, Jordan had breakfast, you had a starin' contest with your pancakes."

"There's a diner a few buildings that way. They started serving lunch about thirty minutes ago," Jordan explained after a quick glance at his watch.

"I'm not hungry," I objected.

"You've barely eaten since you were hospitalized a week ago and it's startin' to worry me," Marx replied. "Please tell me you don't have some sort of eatin' disorder or some irrational complex where you think you're fat."

"No," I said, crinkling my nose at the suggestion.

"Good. Then let's go put some meat on your bones."

"Don't talk about my bones. My bones are fine."

"I know. I can see them," he said evenly.

I hugged the book tighter to me, abruptly self-conscious. "I'm not that skinny." I glanced at Jordan, who deliberately avoided my gaze as he scratched the back of his head, and Marx just stared at me. I sighed in surrender and started walking toward the diner we'd passed on the way to the bookstore.

I heard Jordan release a puff of breath before asking, "Is she always that difficult?"

Marx grunted. "That didn't even scratch the surface of difficult."

Somehow Jordan made it to the door of the diner before me even though he'd been a few steps behind. How did that always happen? He pulled open the door and gestured with a flourish, "After you, milady."

I stepped inside and froze when the crowded diner descended into complete silence. Marx came to stand beside me, and people twisted in their seats to look at us. Even the waitress stopped scribbling down the order on her notepad to look up at us.

"Well, this isn't unsettlin' at all," Marx mumbled under his breath. Concerned and curious eyes darted to the gun on his hip, and a steady stream of low murmurs began.

I leaned toward him and whispered nervously, "Do you think if we stare back they'll blink first?"

"I think they'll shoot first," he mumbled back. "I'm not sure everybody in this town is entirely stable."

"Because New Yorkers are a picture-perfect example of sanity?"

Jordan squeezed past the two of us to the front and whispered, "Just have a seat. They're not used to new faces. They'll get over the shock of it in a minute." He gestured to an open booth.

I walked stiffly toward the booth, feeling self-conscious under the weight of so many gazes. Marx was only a few steps behind me. I slid into one side of the booth and planted my back against the wall.

Marx sat down on the edge of my bench next to the tips of my toes, which, ordinarily, would make me uncomfortable, but I understood that he was using himself as a barrier between me and the onlookers.

I hated when people stared.

I heard a few of the whispers bouncing around between the tables and booths: they were concerned about the fact that Marx was a stranger in town carrying a gun. The men and some of the older women gaped at him with open suspicion, while some of the younger women studied him with interest.

I tried to look at him objectively. I just saw Marx, but he was tall and fit, and his warm green eyes could be mesmerizing. Georgetta had certainly found him attractive.

"You should probably keep that wedding ring on so you don't get mobbed," I advised.

He gave me an amused look. "I think I can handle a mob of middle-aged women. And this ring." He raised his hand and wiggled his ring finger. "Never leaves this finger." Light glinted off the metal, and I saw disappointment register on a few of the women's faces.

Jordan slid into the opposite side of the booth after speaking to a few of the customers.

"I'll give you two some time to talk," Marx said, and he started to get up from the table. I must have given some sort of sign or sound of distress at the idea of being left alone at the table with Jordan, because he looked back at me and gave me a reassuring smile. "I'll be right over there."

He gestured to a table beside the window, and I forced myself to nod. Jordan didn't comment as Marx left, but his pinched lips told me he hadn't missed my unease.

I was unrolling my silverware when a slight, older woman in a flour-splattered apron appeared at our table. "Hi, baby," she greeted, and Jordan stood back up to hug her.

"Hey, Mom," he replied, leaning down to kiss her cheek. Jordan had said his mother owned the diner. They had the same blue eyes, and I could see the similarities in their smiles as her lips curved warmly when she looked up at him.

"What brings you in today?" she asked as she drew back. "Apple pie and ice cream? I made both fresh this morning."

Jordan returned her smile. "No. I thought I might start with a Jolly sundae and then maybe some lunch."

Something shifted in her expression, and her voice took on the soft and soothing cadence of a mother speaking to a wounded child. "One of those days?"

Jordan shook his head. "Not exactly." He nodded in my direction. His mother's eyes slid my way and she looked me over, seeming to notice me for the first time. Recognition sparked in her eyes. "Don't tell Dad."

Looking mildly affronted, she patted his chest. "Don't worry. I know how your father is. He could be blind and mute on an island by himself and still find a way to tell somebody a secret."

She sat down on the edge of my bench, which caught me by surprise, and just looked at me for a long, silent moment before shaking her head. "It's just so hard to believe." She stretched out a hand toward me, and I tensed as she brushed a strand of hair behind my ear. She bit her bottom lip. "It's so good to see you all grown up. We all thought . . ." Tears gathered in her eyes, and she drew herself up with a sharp breath. "I better get those sundaes." She dashed back into the kitchen without another word, and I watched her go, curious about her abrupt exit.

Jordan was giving me another one of those odd looks as he sat back down. "She cries sometimes when she's happy, and she doesn't like crying in front of people."

That I could understand.

"Nervous habit?" he asked, and I looked at him in confusion. He nodded to my hands, and I realized I was shredding my napkin into confetti.

I forced myself to stop. "Not a fan of crowded spaces." I brushed the small pieces off to the side. "Or people watching me," I added when I felt his attention following my nervous movements.

"Sorry." A moment of silence stretched between us before he said, "I know you don't like questions, but can I ask you something?"

I hesitated. "Um . . . you can ask, but I don't promise an answer."

He considered his question carefully before putting it into words. "I guess I was under the impression that you don't really like to be touched, but you seemed fine shaking Georgetta's hand and letting my mom touch you. And you seem pretty comfortable with Marx."

"That's not a question," I pointed out. "It's an inaccurate observation." None of those actions came naturally to me. My first instinct was always to flinch away, and when someone offered their hand, my mind tripped over my instincts and warnings, and I had to make a conscious effort to stretch out my hand.

He tilted his head curiously. "Inaccurate, huh?"

"Completely." I shot him a narrow-eyed look as I shredded the rest of my napkin, daring him to comment. It was a small outlet for my growing nervous energy, and it was better than bolting out the door.

Speaking of doors . . . I did a quick visual check for exits. Front door, bathroom door—I peered over the back of the booth into the kitchen—rear kitchen door. Windows . . .

"Are you scoping out the exits?" Jordan asked with interest.

"Are you watching me scope out the exits? Because I thought we just discussed that I don't like that."

He grinned. "My bad."

Jordan's mother returned with a tray of food. She set a massive bowl of ice cream in the center of the table, a bottle of chocolate syrup, a bowl of sprinkles, and two small metal bowls of miniature marshmallows. "Enjoy, and try not to hit any of the other patrons."

I looked between the different bowls in confusion, and it took a moment for the memory to find its way to the surface:

Jordan sat on the kitchen stool on the opposite side of the island, watching with wide blue eyes as I squeezed the chocolate syrup from the bottle into the bowl of ice cream. There was more chocolate than ice cream.

"It's gonna overflow!" he shouted.

The bottle made an empty sucking sound, and I tossed it in the trash. I scampered to the far end of the counter with my bowl of miniature marshmallows and smacked the counter. "Go!"

Jordan and I began flicking marshmallows as fast as we could, aiming for the bowl. Tiny white marshmallows plopped into the chocolate river. Gin laughed and chased the ones that overshot the counter and bounced across the floor.

"Don't eat them, Gin!" I shouted. "They're dirty!"

She looked like a chipmunk with her cheeks stuffed full of tiny marshmallows. She mumbled something that sounded like "the bore is queen. Nuns wept."

"The floor is clean, Mom swept?" I asked.

She nodded emphatically and chased a few more that landed on the floor.

"Stop missing so much and she won't eat them!" Jordan announced. He shot his last marshmallow into the bowl and declared with his arms raised, "I'm the winner! I got twenty-five in the bowl!"

I crinkled my nose at him and threw my last handful of marshmallows at his head. He laughed and tried to catch them with his mouth.

"All right, Tinker Bell. Time for fairy dust," I announced.

Gin clapped her hands excitedly as she skipped over and climbed on the stool beside me. She had on her sparkly blue dress and strap-on fairy wings that she'd worn for Halloween last year. I grabbed her legs to balance her when she wobbled.

She dumped a handful of sprinkles into her hand and then dusted the bowl of ice cream. "I love fairy dust!" she declared. "It's so pretty!" She licked the last few sprinkles from her palm and added, "and tasty!"

I took her hand and helped her off the chair. I grabbed three spoons and handed them out. "And go." We shoveled our spoons into the heaping bowl of deliciousness.

"Holly Marie!" Mom's furious voice called from the doorway, freezing everyone mid-bite. "Jordan Bartholomew Radcliffe!" Jordan's eyes widened to the size of saucers, and he almost spit the ice cream all over the counter. I covered my mouth as I giggled around a mouthful of marshmallows and chocolate. "What do you think you're doing?"

313

Jordan turned as red as a tomato as he swallowed and looked up at my mother. "Sorry, Mrs. Cross. We were just . . ."

"Having a snack!" I finished for him. I shoved a spoon at my frowning mother. "Want some?"

The memory faded and I found myself staring down into the small bowl of marshmallows. "This was our sundae."

"Yeah," Jordan grinned. "We made it a few times. Your mom always threatened to stop buying ingredients for it, but she never did, which made me think it didn't bother her as much as she wanted us to believe."

"How did it end up here at the diner?"

"When I was having a particularly hard day after losing you and Gin, I would come here and Mom would make this for me. We called it the Jolly sundae. It wasn't the same without the two of you, but it helped remind me of better days," he explained.

Jolly. Jordan and Holly. He'd named it after the two of us.

"The syrup is all you," he prompted.

I bit the corner of my lip and smiled as I picked up the bottle of chocolate syrup and started squeezing it into the bowl of ice cream. "I still love chocolate and marshmallows," I admitted as I filled the bowl to the rim with chocolate and then set the bottle aside. I dipped one of my marshmallows into the chocolate ocean, popped it into my mouth, and licked the sticky sweetness from my fingers.

Jordan grinned. "Yeah, marshmallow hot chocolate was always one of your favorites. I kept some around in case you ever decided to come back. Do you remember the rules?"

He really had believed I was still alive somewhere in the world for all those years. That took a remarkable amount of faith.

"I think so."

He glanced at my hand. Oh, he wanted me to do the thing...

I hovered one hand close to the table, drawing out the anticipation, and then tapped it lightly. "Um . . . go."

Jordan lined his marshmallows up on the table and flicked them one at a time, sending them soaring into the bowl.

The first marshmallow I tried to flick into the bowl hit him square in the forehead. I covered my mouth to stifle a laugh. "I'm so sorry." The stunned expression on his face was priceless.

He picked up the offending marshmallow and ate it before flicking one at me. I squeaked and ducked, and it bounced harmlessly off the back of the bench. I picked it up and tossed it back at him.

I tried to flick a few marshmallows into the bowl, but I had horrendous aim. I spotted Marx out of the corner of my eye, and a sneaky idea popped into my head.

I squinted and lined up a marshmallow. I flicked it and it flew across the room and bounced across his table. I snapped back into my seat before he could see me, but I was pretty sure he heard the mischievous laugh I tried to muffle with my hand.

"Are you flickin' marshmallows at me?" I heard him ask.

I leaned forward and peered at him with a barely contained smile. I sent another marshmallow across the room, and through no skill of my own, it plopped into his mug of coffee. How did that even happen?

Jordan grinned. "Score."

Marx looked from his coffee to me with a puzzled but amused expression. "How on earth did you make that?" He shook his head and gulped down the coffee, marshmallow and all. "At least it wasn't my chocolate milk."

"Okay, time for the fairy dust," Jordan announced. It seemed wrong to do it without Gin. He scooped up a handful of sprinkles and slid the rest of the bowl to me. "I think we should do it together."

"Okay. To Gin."

"Gin," he repeated solemnly. We coated the top of the sundae in sprinkles.

"Excuse me," a woman said, and I smelled the fresh stench of cigarette smoke on her clothes before I even saw her. Her dark hair was coiled in a bun on top of her head, and she wore an apron

315

over her orange waitress uniform. "I was told to give this to the redhead." She smiled. "You're the only redhead in the room."

She set a glass of red liquid on the table that smelled nauseatingly like fruit punch. My heart thumped a little faster just looking at it sitting on the table in front of me.

"Who . . ." I cleared my throat uneasily and tried again. "Who sent this?" My gaze flitted around the room, taking in the faces. It couldn't be a coincidence, not after my last fruit punch had been drugged.

"He wanted to remain anonymous. But he did tell me it was to remind you that red is a beautiful color for your skin, and asked me to give you this." She held out a folded napkin, and I took it after a second of hesitation.

I unfolded it and choked on the fear that constricted my throat. Written in black capital letters were three terrifying words: WELCOME HOME, HOLLY.

37

I lifted my eyes from the napkin to Marx across the room, and he was out of his chair in an instant. He took the napkin from my frozen, slack fingers and read it.

Anger tightened his features. "Who gave this to you?" he demanded from the waitress, and his tone was sharp enough to make her flinch.

She sputtered nonsensical sounds before managing, "I don't know. A man. Tall. Really tall. Out back while I was smoking."

"How long ago?"

"Um . . ." She glanced at the thin watch on her wrist and shook her head. "I don't know. Five minutes maybe?"

Marx tossed the napkin on the table in front of Jordan, who had risen to his feet at the urgency in Marx's voice. Jordan picked it up and looked it over before glancing at me.

"Stay with Holly," Marx instructed as he drew his gun.

He didn't give me a chance to object before weaving through the kitchen and out the rear door. Jordan pulled out his cell phone and called the sheriff's department for backup. I stared after Marx as frantic thoughts tumbled through my mind.

This man had killed more people than I could count; the list of names Jordan had given us was proof of that, and he'd killed four people in the two months that he'd been haunting my footsteps. One of them a cop.

"How many people has this man killed?" I asked, my voice barely above a whisper. Jordan hesitated to answer, and I snapped impatiently, "How many?"

He pressed a button on the screen of his cell phone and answered grimly, "Including your family, the two men in the park, the officer in New York, and the landlord Marx mentioned: fifty-one, that we know of."

Fifty-one people.

I didn't want Marx to go after this man alone, because I wasn't sure he would come back. "You have to go help him."

Jordan shook his head. "I'm not leaving you alone."

"Then I'll go with you."

"No. That's a really bad idea. Backup is on the way."

On the way wasn't good enough. I sprang off the bench and darted for the back door, pausing just long enough to grab a knife off the counter. I heard Jordan call after me before the door slammed shut.

The rear door spat me out into a parking lot with a large dumpster. I gripped the knife tightly as I crept around the dumpster and peered down the alleyway that bridged the diner with the barbershop next door. Except for a few crushed boxes and crates, it was empty.

I spun in a quick circle as I tried to decide whether to go left or right. *Right.* I sprinted through the connected parking lots, checking the narrow alleyways as I went. There was nothing in them but debris and garbage cans.

"Holly! Stop!" Jordan bellowed from somewhere behind me.

I guess he decided to come after all. But I wasn't stopping so he could force me back inside the diner. Marx couldn't have vanished unless he ran into one of the buildings or into the woods.

The killer was too intelligent to trap himself inside a building; the woods were the most likely option. But if Marx had followed the killer into the trees, we would have a very difficult time finding him.

I came to a stop along the tree line and pulled out my cell phone. No bars. Seriously? What kind of backwater, uncivilized town was this? Jordan had used his cell phone in the diner . . . maybe it was just my phone. I smacked it. It didn't help.

I cast Jordan a wary glance as he plodded to a stop beside me and then looked back at the trees.

"It's not safe for you out here, Holly. We need to get you back inside."

318

"We have to go look for him. He's out there somewhere with a psychotic serial killer, and—"

"No, that's not a good idea."

I narrowed my eyes. "You don't get to tell me no."

If he thought he could prevent me from looking for Marx, he was delusional. I started toward the trees.

"Holly, please don't make me stop you," he pleaded as he kept pace with me. He was clearly wrestling with whether or not to physically restrain me before I got to the woods.

I pointed the knife in his direction, letting the sharp tip communicate the unspoken threat. "Don't touch me."

He clenched his jaw as his eyes flickered to the blade. "He doesn't want you looking for him. He wants you safe inside."

"I make my own decisions."

Something stirred in the woods to our left, and we both stopped. Jordan drew his gun, and I gripped my knife with both hands.

Marx stepped out of the woods with a frustrated expression on his face, which quickly gave way to fury when he saw the two of us standing in the bar parking lot.

I exhaled a breath of relief. He was okay.

Marx's eyes focused on Jordan as he closed the distance between us. "I told you to stay with her, not bring her outside where the killer can get to her."

"It was my choice," I explained.

"Of course it was," he grumbled with a reprimanding glance my way. "And I'm pretty sure we just had this knife conversation." He plucked the knife from my hands, and I stumbled forward a step as I tried to hold onto it.

"It was either that or a spoon," I snapped defensively.

"Or, instead of runnin' around with weapons you don't even know how to hold properly, you stay where I tell you to for once."

Yeah, that was going to happen. "I'm not the one who marched off into the woods by myself after a serial killer who's murdered fifty-one people," I shot back.

"Any luck tracking him?" Jordan asked.

"Trackin' is not my forte. Maybe your men will have better luck."

Jordan holstered his gun and nodded before stepping away to place a call. His phone worked just fine out here, I noticed, as I listened to him direct reinforcements to search the woods.

Marx frowned at me. "What were you thinkin' runnin' after me?" I offered him a stubborn scowl. I hadn't done anything wrong. When Jordan hung up, Marx suggested, "Let's get her back to the department. I want her locked down so there's no chance of him gettin' near her again."

"I don't want—"

"Holly," he said sharply, cutting me off. "This is that moment that if you fight me on matters of your safety, I will pick you up and carry you."

I stiffened. "You wouldn't really—"

"Try me."

I looked at Jordan for help, and he shook his head apologetically. "I'm with him on this one." Great. They were agreeing with each other now, which left me the odd one out. I think I preferred it when they argued.

I sighed. "Fine."

We swung by the diner to pick up my book and a few takeaway containers of food for lunch before returning to the car.

The sheriff's department was a standalone building about a seven-minute drive from town, and it didn't look nearly as eerie as it had when we first arrived last night. We followed Jordan into the quiet building.

"Since we're staying here for the night, we'll need to figure out the sleeping arrangements. There are cots downstairs in the cells and the chairs aren't terribly uncomfortable. I'm sure we can scrounge up a few extra blankets and pillows."

Jail cells or chairs . . . oh the options. I didn't foresee myself getting much sleep tonight. That was okay. I had plenty of reading to do. I clutched my book to my chest as I thought about all the times I had read to Gin.

I walked into the conference room and plunked down in my former chair to read. No one had asked what I wanted to eat, so I opened my mystery takeaway container and was pleasantly surprised by the heaping mound of French Fries and mountain of ketchup packets.

Marx had remembered our conversation in front of the department. He followed me into the room and set a Styrofoam cup in front of me before taking a seat at the table.

I popped the lid and peered inside. Chocolate milk shake. Yum. "Thanks."

"You're welcome."

I glanced through the pane of glass at Jordan, who was sitting on the corner of a desk as he spoke to the remaining deputies. I couldn't hear him, but his hand gestures suggested he was formulating some kind of plan.

I squirted a packet of ketchup into the container and stared at the drop of it on my fingertip as the words the waitress had relayed echoed through my mind: *red is a beautiful color for your skin.*

"You're starin' at that ketchup like it's poison," Marx observed in between bites of his cheeseburger.

I wiped the ketchup off onto a napkin. I had no doubt the "red" the killer had been referring to was the blood on my skin when he sliced open my arm. Given the way he intended to kill me, I could think of no other meaning.

That thought nearly made me shudder.

"You're protected inside this department, Holly," Marx assured me, as if he could sense the uneasy turn of my thoughts. "Jordan is postin' deputies at every entry."

"If we're in here and he's out there, how are we ever gonna catch him? We can't just hide forever." And I was tired of being confined.

"Let me and Jordan worry about that."

"Do you think you'll be able to arrest him?"

He set his burger down and wiped his hands on a napkin. "I promise you that one way or another, we will resolve this."

Jordan came into the room as we quietly picked at our food, and the expression on his face was difficult to interpret. There was another folder in his hand. Folders never boded well; I was beginning to hate the sight of them.

"We have a match for the sketch," he announced. "It just came through the fax." He dropped the folder in front of Marx.

I released the curly fry I'd been dangling in midair into my mouth and licked my fingers clean as I stood to see the folder's contents.

Marx opened the folder, grimaced, and then slapped it shut with a hand when I tried to sneak a peek. "No." When I opened my mouth to argue, he said curtly, "Absolutely not."

"It's not pretty, Holly," Jordan explained.

I sighed and walked to the middle of the room as the two men reviewed the contents of the folder in hushed tones. I was getting pretty tired of other people deciding what I did and didn't deserve to know.

"I have a right to know his name and why he's doing this," I said, agitated. "I'm the one he's trying to murder."

Marx gave me a frustrated look. I understood he wanted to protect me from the harsh details, but he needed to understand that I didn't want to be left in the dark. I held his gaze defiantly, and after a moment, he folded. "His name is Edward Billings."

Wow. I hadn't actually expected him to tell me. I must be getting better at my intimidating stares.

"He's forty years old," he continued. "He was released from prison at the age of twenty-one after he brutally murdered his mother and father at the age of fourteen."

"Fourteen?" I gasped. He'd just been a child when he murdered his family. What inspired a child to do something like that?

Jordan nodded. "There were rumors of severe physical and emotional abuse by the father and neglect by the mother. Despite the fact that he bludgeoned his father and stabbed his mother to death, the court decided not to try him as an adult due to the extremely abusive circumstances and his age. So he was paroled at twenty-one with intensive counseling."

His parents had tormented him, and he'd killed them for it. "I almost feel sorry for him," I muttered. Almost.

"Well, don't. He doesn't deserve it," Marx said harshly. "Your childhood was just as difficult, if not more so, and you cherish human life. There was no excuse for what he did."

A question sparkled in Jordan's eyes. Apart from my family being murdered, he wasn't aware of the *difficulties* I faced growing up. And I wasn't about to enlighten him.

"This says he was last seen in Oklahoma," Marx read aloud. "He didn't show up for his shift at the gas station, and the parole officer lost track of him. That was a year and a half before he murdered Holly's family."

"He had to have experimented in between," Jordan thought aloud.

Marx closed the file and tapped it thoughtfully with his fingers. "It's good to have a name, but the rest of the information is rather moot at this point. We already know he's here; we just have to catch him."

"Well," Jordan sighed with a glance at his watch. "The best thing we can do right now is wait to see if my people find anything in the woods. Why don't we take the downtime to figure out the sleeping arrangements."

I shifted uneasily. "About that . . ."

"I was kidding about the jail, Holly. I would never put you down there. Marx maybe." His eyes grew distant as if he were imagining how that might play out, and Marx grimaced. "But we can toss a few mattresses and blankets on the floor in the conference room. It's the biggest room we have."

I tried not to come across as rude. "Um, I don't really... camp out with other people. Do you have a smaller room I can have to myself?"

323

"We have a few offices but they're all occupied in the morning. We have a storage room. It's five by eight and it doesn't have a window, but we could move the stuff out of it and set up a mattress in there for you."

Five by eight. That was a tiny space, but it was better than the alternative. "That should be okay."

It took the three of us nearly two hours to clear everything out of the storage room. When we were finished, boxes were lined up along the wall in the hallway.

Jordan and Marx brought one of the mattresses up from downstairs with a pillow and a few clean blankets. I turned on a lamp in the corner and settled onto the makeshift bed with my book.

"You look cozy," Marx commented as he appeared in the doorway. "The size doesn't bother you?" He looked around the cramped space.

"It does. But . . ."

"But it feels safer than sharin' a room." He leaned in and examined the doorknob, tapping a finger on the lock. "Jordan *does* have a key, though."

I fidgeted nervously. "I know." I had been trying to figure out how to barricade the door when there wasn't any room to stack anything against it.

"I don't think he would come in without askin'," Marx said reassuringly. "He's tryin' very hard to put you at ease. But if he does suffer a serious lapse in judgment, you still have your pepper spray."

I smiled a little at that.

"Here," he said. He tossed something to me, and I fumbled to catch it. "I owed you a chocolate bar."

It was a bag of M&M's. "Technically this isn't a bar," I teased.

He lifted an eyebrow as he sat down in the doorway and pressed his back against the frame. "Technically it's chocolate, so quit your complainin'."

I smirked. "Thank you."

He draped his arms over his knees and studied me, his green eyes trying to gather information from my expression and body language. It freaked me out that he could do that. "How are you doin'?"

"You keep asking me that."

"And I'm gonna keep askin' until I get an answer that isn't evasive."

I sighed as I ripped open the bag of candy. I didn't have an answer to give him. My thoughts and feelings were so twisted up that I couldn't really put them into words.

"Do you believe in God?"

He smiled. "You do have a knack for askin' uncomfortable questions, don't you?"

I shrugged.

"I suppose you might say I'm on the fence. But my mama is a firm believer." He gazed at the far wall for a long moment, seeming to debate whether or not to share something. "I've seen a lot of bad things with my job. And I've asked God why, if He exists, He allows them to happen. I never get an answer."

"Do you ask Him why He allows the good things to happen?"

A thoughtful line formed between his eyebrows. "Can't say that I have."

"If you're gonna hold God accountable for the bad things, you should hold Him accountable for the good things too. There's a lot more good than bad, but if all you do is pile the bad at His feet, you'll never be able to see past it to the good things."

I didn't blame God for any of the bad things that had happened in my life. He hadn't hurt me; people had hurt me. And out of everyone in my life, He'd been the only one who listened without doubting my words, who loved me despite my many flaws, who was determined to keep me alive when I was lying on that bathroom floor after taking a handful of pills and hoping to die.

"I keep a journal of the things I'm thankful for," I continued. "Because if I don't acknowledge those small lights in my life, the darkness in this world will snuff them out."

"I've never thought about it that way," he admitted. "A journal, huh?"

"Well, with the way you write, you may wanna consider a tape recorder." He probably couldn't even read his own chicken scratch. Maybe that was why he always flipped through his crime scene notes but never seemed to read them.

He smiled. "You think you're funny, don't you?"

"Yep."

"Why did you ask about God?"

"Just pondering the age-old question that plagues us all: why is all this happening?" I poured the candy into my palm and started picking through it "Can I borrow your hand?"

"That depends. What are you gonna do to it?" he asked as he offered his hand. I swiveled my finger in the air, and he flipped his hand over, palm up, with a curious expression on his face. I plucked the brown and yellow M&M's out of my palm and dropped them into his. "What are you doin'?"

"I don't like the brown and yellow ones."

He frowned. "They all taste the same."

"They taste brown and yellow."

"You're imaginin' things." At my shrug, he laughed. "Well, what am I supposed to do with them?"

"Eat them, throw them on the floor, flick them at people's heads." I popped a blue one into my mouth.

"Why do I have a feelin' you've done that last one before?" He opened his mouth and poured all the M&M's in at once.

Oh, I had done it before, and it had been boatloads of fun. I was sucking on my M&M when a question drifted through my mind. I knew my family was dead, but there had to be someone.

"Do I have a grandmother or a grandfather? Aunts, uncles, cousins?"

Sympathy clouded his eyes. "No."

"So it's just . . ."

"It's just you."

I pushed through that disappointment with a bit of difficulty. I had hoped to have at least one person I could call family—even a fourth cousin thrice removed, if such a thing existed.

"What about your family?"

"I have a mother, father, and an older sister. Cresceda. A few cousins somewhere."

"No nieces or nephews?"

"No, unfortunately. Cresceda had cancer, and the doctors told her she could never have children. My wife didn't want children. So it's just the four of us," he explained, and I could hear the note of old, lingering sadness in his voice. "Though, if you ever meet my parents, I expect they will probably try to adopt you."

"Why?"

Marx smiled. "You'd have to meet my mother to understand. If Cresceda or I had had a child, she would be about your age, and the fact that I care about you automatically means my mother would spoil you rotten. She goes a little overboard with the Southern hospitality thing from time to time. She would probably take one look at you and declare that you're too skinny, you're absolutely adorable, and that she intends to keep you. My father was always a bit softer with Cresceda, so I expect he would adore you."

His family sounded blessedly normal and inviting.

"I'm gonna run into town and grab our things from the bed-and-breakfast," he said.

I set my book down. "I'll come with you." I had no desire to be alone here with only Jordan and a few deputies I didn't know. I didn't think Jordan would *do* anything, but I wasn't comfortable being alone with him after knowing him for less than twenty-eight hours.

"No. You're stayin' right here behind locked doors and plenty of armed deputies. It shouldn't take me more than twenty minutes or so. We're not too far outside of town. I'll be back by seven thirty. Do you want me to pick you up anythin'?"

I shook my head. "Just . . . be careful. Apparently, there are desperate women who haven't seen a single man who isn't their cousin in decades."

He smiled. "I'll be extra cautious with the desperate women."

38

I was in the middle of a paragraph about little people on a yellow brick road when I pulled my eyes from the book and looked through the doorway at the clock on the wall in the main room. It was five minutes till eight.

Marx had said he would be back by seven-thirty. I tried not to launch into instant panic mode. He was only twenty-five minutes late. It was possible something had come up. Maybe he'd stopped for dinner or Oma, the innkeeper, had convinced him to stay for coffee and cookies.

I was not going to overreact. I forced my eyes back to the book, but after reading the same line five times without absorbing it, I gave up. I closed the book and glanced at my phone beside me. It couldn't hurt to call and ask, right?

That didn't qualify as panic.

I picked up my phone, pressed the number three, and hesitated for one self-conscious moment with my thumb over the send button before pressing it. After the fourth ring, the small knot of worry in my stomach expanded. The call rolled over to voice mail.

I hung up and stared at my phone. Marx had promised he would always pick up when I called. Maybe he didn't hear it. Maybe he was in the restroom. I would just wait a few minutes and then try again.

I watched the minute hand on the clock drag by with agonizing slowness. Five minutes passed and I tried again. The call went unanswered. He wouldn't ignore me, would he?

No. He wouldn't do that. Not with the killer so close. Not when he knew I never called for frivolous reasons. Now I started to panic.

I scrambled to my feet and sprinted into a small office with a plaque on the door that read "Sheriff Jordan Radcliffe." Jordan was seated behind the desk, filling out paperwork. He looked up when I came in.

"What's the matter?"

"Marx. Something's wrong."

He set down the pen. "What do you mean?"

"He said he would be back by seven thirty. And he's not answering his phone," I explained. And I sounded as insane as Jace did when she said things like "I thought you were abducted" because I was ten minutes later than promised.

Jordan relaxed and said with a patient expression, "He probably stopped for food or got sidetracked by someone in town."

"Why wouldn't he answer his phone?"

"I don't know. Maybe he turned the ringer off or he just didn't hear it. It happens to everyone sometimes."

"No," I disagreed. "He always answers my call. He promised. We have to go look for him."

Jordan rubbed a hand through his hair and sighed. "I'm sure he's fine, Holly. He's a big boy. Besides, I don't have the man power to spare. Everyone who isn't here is resting so they can work the dayshift tomorrow."

"But if we all go . . ."

"You're under my protection. I'm not taking you out after dark to look for Marx, who is probably having dinner or trying to talk his way out of Oma's kitchen."

He wasn't listening to me. Why didn't people listen to me? I knew something was wrong. I could feel it all the way to my bones. "So that's it? We do nothing?"

"It's only been thirty minutes. If he's not back in a couple of hours . . ."

A couple of hours could be too late. Jacob had died in minutes. If Marx was wounded, he might not have hours. I knew he wouldn't stop to have dinner or linger to talk with someone with the killer this close. He would've retrieved our things and returned as soon as possible to help keep me safe. That was just who he was.

"I can't do *nothing*," I said.

330

"I'm sorry. But there's no other choice right now. We . . ."

I grabbed the car keys off the corner of his desk and bolted. I didn't know how to drive, but it couldn't be that hard to figure out. By the time Jordan shouted my name and rounded his desk, I was already unlocking the front door.

The deputy posted by the entrance blinked at me with surprise when I flung open the door and ran down the dimly lit ramp to the parking lot. It took me a moment to pick Jordan's car out of the other vehicles in the darkness.

I sprinted through the eerie patches of darkness to the driver's side and fumbled with the keys before realizing there was one of those button things like Marx had for his car. I pressed the left button and the lock clicked up on the driver's side.

"Holly, stop!" Jordan shouted as he came down the ramp. The deputy from the front door followed at his heels. I wrenched open the door, climbed in, and hit the second button a split second before Jordan collided with the side of the car and grabbed for the handle. He pulled, but it was locked.

I panted in the driver's seat as I watched the deputy take up position on the right side of the car. She had her hand on her gun, but she looked uncertain. They were supposed to protect me, not shoot me for stealing a car.

Jordan pressed his hand to the driver's window and said with a calm he was clearly struggling to hold onto, "Open the door, Holly."

"No! I'm going to find him." It took me two tries to fit the key into the ignition. I turned it and the car purred to life. I looked around, trying to figure out what to do next. Was there a manual? A colored pamphlet with three-step directions?

"It's not safe for you to do this. I need you to come back inside," Jordan persisted. He walked around the car, tugging on all the handles. I ignored him as I searched the car for an instruction manual. "Holly, unlock the door."

Driving didn't require a college degree. I had seen people do it. I could figure it out. There were pedals on the floor, and I slouched in the seat to touch my feet to both of them. The engine revved. Okay, that meant I should be going somewhere, right?

Why wasn't I moving?

I glanced at the stick thing in the middle with the letters on it that people usually messed with before driving: P for . . . park. R for . . . rewind. No, reverse. D for . . .

"Do you even know how to drive?" Jordan demanded as he came around the front of the car.

Drive! That was it. I pushed the stick to Drive and sat up in the seat so I could see better. The car started to roll backwards down the sloping parking lot. Okay. That wasn't what I expected. I thought it would go forward. I twisted around in the seat to see another parked car directly behind me.

"The brake, Holly! Hit the brake!" Jordan shouted.

Which one was the brake? I slid back down in the seat and stomped on the right one. I let out a yip of terror when the car lunged forward. Apparently, that wasn't the brake. I stomped on the other one and the car jerked to a stop.

I peered over the dashboard to see Jordan standing in front of the car with his hands on the hood. Good grief. I had nearly run him over.

"Okay!" he said, breathing a little heavier than he had been a moment ago. "I'll drive you. I promise I will drive you wherever you wanna go. Just please don't do that again. Okay?"

"I don't believe you!" I sat up in the seat, and my foot slipped from the pedal. The car immediately started rolling backwards again.

"Park. Park!" Jordan shouted. "Put it in park!"

I winced as the rear end of the car banged into the car behind me and came to a jolting stop. At least it stopped. I pushed the stick back up to the "P" and puffed out a breath. I was going to kill myself if I tried to drive this thing; I couldn't even get it out of the parking lot.

Jordan hung his head between his shoulders as he rested his hands on the hood of the car. I had dented his car. "Please, unlock the door and let me in," he said with strained patience.

I glared warningly at him through the window. "If you're lying about driving me to get me to open the door so you can carry me back inside, I will pepper spray you."

He dropped his head to the hood of the car and groaned quietly. It took him a second to pull himself back together and look at me. "I promise I'm not gonna carry you back inside."

"Or drag me?" Because I certainly wouldn't walk back inside. That didn't leave him many options.

He squinted at me. "I wouldn't do that. I promise I'm not gonna touch you. Now open the door and scoot over."

I hoped he was telling the truth. I unlocked the driver's door and moved into the passenger seat. I sat as close to the door as I could and gripped the canister of pepper spray in my jacket pocket.

Jordan opened the door and slid into the car. His legs fit perfectly into the space that had been too long for me. He didn't have to slouch to touch the pedals. He cast me a look of pure frustration as he closed his door.

"You realize Marx is gonna kill me," he grumbled.

"Tell him I forced you to do it."

One blond eyebrow crept up. "Yeah, he'll believe that." He pulled out of the parking lot with infinite ease—nothing like my jerky driving style. He glanced over at me. "You can be kind of terrifying, you know that?"

"It's a talent."

We drove toward the town in silence. I watched out the side window for any sign of Marx. The road branched into a "Y" as we came closer to town. Jordan started to veer toward the left when I pointed and asked, "What's that way?"

"It leads to the other end of town or out of town. I doubt he would've taken that way."

"Can we take a look anyway?"

He swung the car back and took the right branch. The headlights glinted off something in the trees ahead of us, and fear made me straighten up in my seat. We rolled to a stop along the road, and I peered out through the window. A dark-colored car was stranded in the ditch with the front end folded around a tree.

"Geez," Jordan gasped. "Stay in the car. Lock the doors." I flung my door open and hopped out. "Holly!" He grumbled something beneath his breath as he slammed his door and walked around the car.

The maroon color of the vehicle was muted by the darkness, but I recognized Marx's car. I slid down the slippery bank into the ditch with as much grace as I could manage and stumbled through the weeds. I slipped and fell once, but managed to get my feet beneath me.

"Be careful, Holly."

My heart was pounding too heavily in my head as I rounded the car. I was so afraid I would find Marx inside the car—dead. I didn't think I could handle any more dead bodies. Jacob had been difficult enough to come to terms with, and I hadn't cared for him nearly as much as I cared for Marx.

The passenger door was hanging open, and the glass from the window sparkled across the ground and passenger seat in the headlights of Jordan's car. I grabbed the door frame to steady myself and looked inside the car. I saw Jordan peering in the other side with a flashlight. The beam danced over the empty vehicle, landing on the streak of red that was smeared across both seat cushions.

My throat constricted with dread. The blood stretched across the fabric like drag marks, as if someone had pulled Marx from the car.

"Somebody drove him off the road," Jordan pointed out. "There are white paint marks on the side of the car."

"Could he be in the hospital?" I asked.

Jordan shook his head. "I would've heard it over the radio."

I ran my shaking hands through my hair. As I looked around the interior of the car, my eyes snagged on the shiny silver ring sitting on top of the dashboard. There was no way it had landed there during the crash. I picked it up and turned it over in my hands. Inscribed on the inside of the ring was a small message: *Shannon <3 Richard.*

His wedding ring. He never took this off his finger. None of this had been accident. Someone had purposefully driven him off the road and then dragged him from the car. And they had left his ring as a message for me to find. I suddenly remembered Marx telling me that Cambel had been dumped off at the café by a white vehicle.

The killer had him.

I swayed a little on my feet. The killer *took* him.

Familiar ringing pierced the quiet night, and Jordan and I both looked up. It wasn't either of our phones. Jordan tracked the sound to somewhere on the other side of the road. "Is that Marx's phone?"

"Yeah." But if neither of us were calling it, who was?

"I want you to get back in the car and lock the doors. I'm gonna be less than ten feet away, and backup is coming, but I don't want you standing out here in the dark. There are too many things that could happen, and this wasn't an accident."

"Okay."

He climbed up the embankment as I rounded the car. I paused when I saw something out of place in the woods: a shoe. I glanced at Jordan's receding back as he crossed the street in search of the phone, and then backtracked to the shoe lying on the ground. I slid the wedding ring into the pocket of my jeans as I crouched down. It was one of Marx's haphazardly tied shoes.

The killer had dragged him this way.

I lifted my gaze and stared into the ominous stretch of dark woods. Familiarity trickled through me. I knew these trees. I had passed between them before, but I couldn't remember why or when.

I stood and took a few steps forward. Fear weighted my footsteps, but I pushed forward in the hopes that I would remember why these particular trees called out to me from my memory. I ran my hand over the rough bark of the trees as I ventured deeper. I couldn't see anything more than twisted, gnarled shadows in the moonlight that filtered down through the limbs.

Although my eyes had no idea where I was going, my feet recognized the well-traveled path. Memories came back with every step. I used to walk these woods every day on my way to Jordan's house, and he'd done the same on his way to mine. This was the path I had taken the night the killer hunted me through the woods.

I paused with my hand on the tree that I remembered hiding behind. I had been so terrified I could barely breathe, and I had hunkered down behind this tree to pray, and to try to wipe my mother's blood from my hands.

If I looked back, I wouldn't be able to see the road I'd run across to escape from the killer all those years ago, but I knew Jordan was standing there now. I could hear his distant, worried voice calling out for me.

It wasn't a coincidence that we found Marx's car in the same spot where Izzy and Paul had found me. I'd been taken from the killer that night, so he'd driven Marx off the road and taken him from me.

I was pretty sure I knew where the killer had taken him. If I kept walking, I would find him, but I would also find a monster I wasn't strong enough to fight alone.

I needed to get help.

I turned to go back when a crack of a twig made me freeze. I looked around the dark trees warily as I slid my hand into the pocket of my jacket. My fingers curled nervously around the canister of pepper spray. Maybe it had just been an animal.

I took a step forward and another sharp crack to my right brought me up short. I saw the dark figure lunge an instant too late. He barreled into me, and I flew forward a few steps from the force of the impact, but my scream was cut short when a cloth-covered hand closed over my mouth.

I inhaled a sickeningly sweet chemical smell that made my head spin. *Oh, God please no, not again.* The world faded around me, and the last thing I heard was a man's voice whispering in my ear, "Mine."

39

I became aware of a cold, soft surface beneath me as the heavy fog began to lift. My mind felt lethargic, like I was pulling every thought through a layer of tar.

I shouldn't have been lying down. The last thing I remembered was the scent of old pages, leather bindings, and yellow brick roads.

I cracked open my eyes and tried to focus, but the walls were nothing but a meld of shifting shadows and flickering lights. Nausea swept over me, and I let my eyelids slip shut again.

I lay there on my back on the soft surface as awareness dripped slowly back into my mind and body. My head throbbed painfully with the strangely slow beat of my heart, and I was so cold.

I tried to move my arms, but something metal jingled and my wrists snagged above my head. I peeled my heavy eyelids open, wincing at the overwhelming light and tipped my head back to look up. There was something shiny around my wrists that bound them above my head to a piece of wood. It took my sluggish mind a moment to find the right word: handcuffs.

Panic scorched through me, tightening my airway until I could barely breathe and burning away the disorienting fog. I drew my legs into my body as I struggled into a sitting position and sagged back against the wall.

I pinched my eyes shut as the pounding of my own heartbeat felt like a jackhammer going off inside my skull. This was as bad as the morning I'd woken up in the hospital after being drugged.

Drugged . . .

I'd been searching the woods after Marx went missing, and someone had clamped a sweet-smelling cloth over my mouth and nose. I couldn't help but breathe it in, and it had made the world around me tip and slide into darkness. The last thing I remembered was his voice whispering in my ear, "Mine."

I released a shuddering breath. The killer had found me.

I forced my eyes open and took in my blurry surroundings with little attention to detail: four walls, boarded windows, broken furniture. One open door. No one else in the room with me.

I wasn't in immediate danger.

I took in the smaller details next, hoping to glean something helpful from them. There was a candle burning on the remnants of a dresser in the corner, casting dancing shadows across the walls in the otherwise dark room.

Graffiti and water stains disfigured the lavender walls, and there was a crack stretching from the ceiling to a three-inch hole in the wall. The bed across the room lay in shambles. I knew this room. Even in such a despairing state, I recognized the room I had shared with Gin for nine years. The killer had brought me home.

The bed frame I was handcuffed to was my own. I looked down at myself—something I had been avoiding since I awoke—and realized why I was shivering as I leaned against the wall. It couldn't have been more than thirty degrees in the house and half of my clothes were missing: my socks and shoes, my jacket, and all my layered T-shirts. I was left in my jeans and my thin white tank top.

The fact that I'd been unconscious while the killer stripped away some of my clothes and then handcuffed me to a bed catapulted me to the brink of panic. I twisted violently in the handcuffs, trying to pull free, but only succeeded in slicing open my wrists. The chain clanked against the wood but refused to give.

I choked on a sob and pressed my forehead to the wall. Wrenching and twisting like a snared animal wasn't going to free me. I needed to get myself under control.

Peace I leave with you; my peace I give you. Do not let your hearts be troubled and do not be afraid, I recited silently. "Do not be afraid."

I sucked in a few regulated breaths through my nose and counted to four as I released them.

Breathe . . . just . . . breathe . . .

I focused on counting my breaths until the panic ebbed enough that I was able to think beyond the desperate urge to escape.

I still had some of my clothes on, and there was no pain aside from the throbbing in my head, which I was pretty sure was a side effect of the drug he'd knocked me unconscious with. He hadn't hurt me—yet. If I could just keep my thoughts straight, I might be able to find a way out of this.

Handcuffs. I wondered vaguely if they belonged to Marx; he carried his with him everywhere, just as he did his gun. I looked around the room for any sign that he'd been there. Maybe he was just in a different room. Maybe he wasn't dead.

Lord, please let him be alive.

I was in no way strong enough to break the handcuffs, but if I could slip my hands out of them, I would at least have a fraction of a chance. I gritted my teeth and twisted my wrists slowly, but I couldn't get my thumb joint through the hole.

If I couldn't pull my hands free, then maybe I could loosen the board the handcuffs were looped through. I wrapped my fingers around the edges of the board and tugged on it. It creaked, and I froze, my eyes snapping to the doorway.

I held my breath and listened, but if the killer heard the noise, he wasn't coming. I pulled harder, but the board refused to give. I tried applying my weight to it and pushing on it, but that was even less effective.

"Come on," I whispered. "Of all the cheap pieces of junk furniture in the world, you have to be the durable one." I peered behind the bed and groaned inwardly at the sight of screws. What was I going to do with screws?

I looked at my fingernails. I didn't have anything else. I shifted on the bed and tried to reach the screws with my fingers. My fingertips grazed one of the two screws and I tried to slide my fingernail into the groove. The angle wasn't quite right; it would break my nail.

I picked at the wood around the head of the screw with my fingernails, carving out small gouges in the wood. I created a small furrow around the screw head and then tried to grip the screw with my fingertips and twist. It didn't budge.

A strange sound—like someone punching their fist into their palm—accompanied by a strangled groan came from somewhere down the hall, and I stilled. Someone coughed and wheezed.

"Wake up," an eerie voice demanded.

"Oh, it's just you again," a familiar Southern voice replied, but it sounded breathless and pained. He coughed again. Marx. He was alive. "So what's the plan then? Are you just gonna beat me until I stop breathin'?"

"Tempting, but no," the killer replied in a velvety soft voice. "I'm going to let you watch—helplessly—while I enjoy my time with her. And *then* I'll kill you."

There was a long pause before Marx asked worriedly, "Enjoy your time with whom?" He didn't know I was here. What a way to find out all his efforts at protection had been for nothing.

I could hear the smugness dripping from the killer's voice even from down the hall. "She has an uncanny ability to walk right into harm's way. I found her in the woods looking for you."

"I don't believe you."

"This is hers. Her sister had one just like it. She never takes it off. Very much like your wedding ring," the killer explained.

I looked at my left wrist and realized for the first time that my bracelet was gone. He'd taken it. Why? As a trophy, or so he could taunt Marx with it the way he'd taunted me with his wedding ring? I wanted that back.

"I was planning on just putting you out of my misery, but . . . the two of you have grown so fond of each other. It'll be so much more enjoyable this way," the killer said.

"You leave her alone," Marx growled angrily.

"Mmm, no. I don't think I'll do that. In fact, she's probably waking up now."

My spine went completely rigid when I heard his heavy footsteps coming down the hallway. That same childhood terror flooded through me as I listened to the ominous sound of his impending arrival. I couldn't climb out the window this time. There was no running away.

Come on. Think.

I didn't have time to keep working on the screws. The center of the board was the weakest. I scooted back as far as the chain on the handcuffs would allow and slammed my heel into the center of it. Pain resonated through my entire foot and up into my leg, but the board bowed on impact. I had to kick harder. I kicked it again, but it still wasn't enough force. I needed more room, or steel-toed boots. I kicked it a third time and it cracked, but I was out of time.

The killer—Edward—stepped into the open doorway. His broad shoulders spanned the width of the door frame, and his head was just shy of grazing the top of it. He was . . . enormous.

"Hello, Holly," he said with a small smile.

He wasn't wearing a mask this time. There was no point in hiding his face when he didn't intend for there to be any survivors. It was almost exactly the face I remembered, but older.

I gathered my legs beneath me in a crouch in the corner of the bed and watched him warily. He strode into the room, his dark bottomless eyes slithering over me.

"I realize the handcuffs are unusual. But I couldn't have you wandering out of bed before it was time again," he explained. He paused by the head of the bed and ran his fingers leisurely along the headboard. "You have a habit of disappearing."

His fingers trailed down the slats of the headboard toward me. I tried to jerk away from him, but the handcuffs cut into my wrists and held me in place.

"And you're still trying to disappear." His fingers brushed across the tops of my hands, tracing small circles on my skin, and I clenched my fingers into fists.

"Don't touch me," I said, and wished I didn't sound so afraid.

"Such lovely skin." His gaze followed the lines of my body up to my face. The desire burning in his dark eyes sent my pulse racing. He sat down on the edge of the mattress with more grace than a man his size should be capable of, and I fought a shiver.

I tucked my toes into the mattress and tried to condense myself into as small a space as possible. "Where are the rest of my clothes?"

"I'm afraid I had to remove them. Too many layers interfere." He ran a bare finger down my arm, and I recoiled from him.

I wanted him to stop touching me; I *needed* him to stop before panic overrode my senses. I had to keep my head clear so I could think my way out of this situation; there had to be a way out. I couldn't just curl into a ball and let this happen.

"Where's Marx?" I asked.

"Oh, he's around, but you don't need to worry about him." The tip of his index finger traced the edge of my ear and down the curve of my neck.

"I . . . w-wanna see him."

His fingers froze on my throat and then slowly folded into a fist. Some frightening emotion I couldn't identify lit his eyes, and I braced myself, certain he was going to hit me again. "I decide when that happens. I've been looking forward to this moment for eighteen years and I intend to savor it."

He leaned over me, his body so close to mine I could feel the heat of it on my cold skin. Panic crawled the walls of my stomach and I tried to move away from him, but there was nowhere to go.

He breathed heavily in the crook of my neck, and I felt his fingers twine through my hair. "You smell divine. Like . . . coconuts and fear. Are you afraid, Holly?"

Tears gathered behind my eyes, and I squeezed them shut. He petted my hair like a person might pet a cat, and then his fingers brushed down the length of my arm, sending goose bumps of revulsion across my skin.

The sound of something clicking made my eyes snap open. He was unlocking the handcuffs.

"Let's get started, shall we?" he suggested.

He tossed the handcuffs carelessly over his shoulder, and they landed on the floor. He wrapped his thick hand around my wrist and dragged me across the bed.

I had no idea what he intended to do with me, but now that my wrists were free, I had to take advantage of my opportunity to fight. I twisted my body as I slid across the mattress and kicked him in the stomach. He exhaled a pained breath, and his fingers loosened reflexively. I wrenched my wrist away from him and sprang off the bed. He snatched my upper arm before I could reach the doorway and dragged me back.

"It's pointless to fight, Holly. You can't win."

I grabbed the burning candle and flung hot wax at him. He let out a screech of pain and cupped his face. The room plunged into complete darkness without the candle, and I stumbled blindly toward the doorway.

I slid across the dusty floor in the hallway as I darted toward the staircase. Edward slammed into me from behind and nearly sent both of us bouncing down the steps to the bottom floor. His arms locked around my chest and stomach like iron bars, and my feet left the floor. I screamed and my desperate cry echoed off the walls of the empty, abandoned house.

"I see no one ever taught you your place," he growled.

He tightened his arms around my chest in a vise-like grip, crushing the breath from my lungs. It felt like he was going to break my ribs. I would've cried out in pain, but I couldn't get enough air.

He carried me down the familiar hallway I hadn't seen in years, and I realized he was taking me to my parents' room – the room where every member of my family had died.

Where I would've died if I hadn't snuck downstairs for a glass of water that night. I remembered pausing at the top of the steps on the way back to my bedroom because I heard strange sounds coming from my parents' room.

My father was crying—quiet, wrenching sobs of grief.

Curious, I padded down the hallway in my bare feet with my stuffed bunny—Freckles—to see what was wrong. I didn't see my mother's body until I fell over top of her.

I was too stunned and horrified to scream. I just stared at the dark liquid shimmering on my hands. My father's urgent whisper broke the spell.

He told me not to scream. Just to run. I didn't understand what was happening, but I did as he said. I ran, even as I heard the cries of my sister Gin echoing down the hall as the killer marched her to her death.

I abandoned both of them that night. I left Gin when she needed me the most. She must have been so terrified; she must have wondered where I was and why I wasn't with her.

"No," I wheezed. There were too many dark memories in that room, and I didn't want to go.

"Oh yes," Edward whispered, and he sounded almost giddy. "We're going to have an interesting night where it all began. Just you, me, and the woefully inadequate detective who's incapable of keeping his promises of safety and protection."

Unscented candles were placed around the disheveled room, creating a warm, romantic atmosphere. Nothing remained of the furniture; what hadn't been taken by looters lay in pieces on the floor. The curtains were sheer wisps of fabric that hung over wood-slatted windows.

Edward stepped into a dark stain that expanded across the floorboards. A fresh wave of dizziness swept over me as I stared down at it, realizing this was the very spot where my mother had taken her last breath.

"Holly," Marx called, and his voice was thick with worry. "Are you okay?"

My gaze snapped to him. He'd been stripped of his jacket and gun, and he was missing a shoe. His arms and legs were bound to a chair, and his face looked swollen and red. Edward had tied him up and beaten him.

Something wet stained the right side of his black T-shirt, and I remembered the bloody smears on the car seat. His injuries were far worse than a few blooming bruises.

Edward dropped my feet to the floor, and I tried to squirm away from him and run to Marx, but he pulled me back flush against him and wrapped an arm loosely around my throat.

"I'm afraid we don't have time for tearful reunions," he said.

I felt the edge of a blade press against my stomach, and I stilled. Marx swore under his breath as he pulled at his restraints.

"Let's go over the rules," Edward said as he tapped the blade lightly against my stomach with every musical syllable. "I know you've studied me, Detective, but you don't know me. I like to play fair."

"Fair?" Marx gritted out. "You're about to torture a woman half your size. How is that even remotely fair?"

"It's fair because I say it is. You have a warped view of the world. Let me show both of you how things are supposed to work in this world."

He picked up the nearest candle, and I gasped as he dragged me forward with his arm around my throat. I tried to keep my feet under me, but they slipped and stumbled over the debris on the floor. He turned me so I could see Marx.

"Holly, you burned me . . ." He tipped the candle and poured hot wax onto Marx's forearm. Marx gritted his teeth and his fingers clenched into fists over the arms of the chair. "I burn him."

"Stop," I pleaded. "Please stop."

Edward tipped the candle upright, and the flow of scalding wax slowed to a trickle and dripped down the side of the candle. "Am I clear?"

I nodded. What I did to him, he would do to Marx. If I fought him, he would hurt him.

"Holly," Marx said, and his eyes were pure fury as they slid from Edward to me. "Fight him. Do you understand me?"

I couldn't. There was no way I was going to overpower him, and everyone in this room knew it. Fighting him would only make him hurt Marx more, and he'd already suffered enough.

He must have seen the answer in my eyes because he snapped, "Don't you dare try to protect me, Holly."

He was hoping that if I fought back, the killer would concentrate on hurting him rather than me. I didn't want that.

He'd been trying to protect me for months; maybe now it was my turn to protect him. I couldn't save us, but maybe I could at least save him from any more pain.

Guilt and regret drained the strength from my voice. "I'm so sorry. For all of this. I'm sorry for Jacob."

"None of this is your fault, Holly."

Edward chuckled. "Oh, usually I prefer a husband and wife, but this is an interesting dynamic, even for me. You're more than just a cop to her, and she's more than just another case to you. Is it the face? She does have a very pretty face. Obviously, that's not why she's drawn to you." He dragged the back of his hand lightly down my cheek, and I bit down on my lips to keep from whimpering.

Marx twisted in his chair.

"Does it frustrate you, Detective? That you can't help the damsel in distress." Edward leaned down and drew in the scent of my hair with a moan of pleasure. "And what a lovely damsel she's grown into."

Marx's eyes glittered with hatred as he looked up at the killer. "You're a coward. You drug people, beat them, and then torture them to death."

"Oh, not you, Detective. I'm just going to slit your throat when all is said and done, but Holly and I . . ." He dragged the blade gently across my abdomen in something eerily like a caress, and I shivered. "Oh, we have a long evening planned. Isn't that right, Holly?"

I wasn't prepared as the knife sliced a shallow cut across my ribs, and a small cry of pain escaped my throat. He clamped his bare hand over the wound and pulled me tighter against him as he said, "We're just getting started."

Panic wrapped around my chest, and I could barely breathe. He was going to do to me what he'd done to my mother. I would never survive that much physical pain.

I squeezed my eyes shut and sought the place in my mind where pain was nothing but a distant whisper. My drunken foster father had laid the foundation for that place, and my experiences with Collin had erected the walls, assembled the roof, and attached the door. It was how I had survived his torment for eleven months. I crawled inside the protective walls of that fortress and felt the vise of panic around my lungs loosen.

The blade drew another shallow line across my skin, and I breathed through it. It was a strange sensation; I could feel the pressure of the knife as it bit into my skin, but it was like it was happening to someone else.

"Holly," Marx called. "I need you to open your eyes and look at me."

I didn't want to open my eyes; I wanted to stay in this safe place that blacked out the world around me.

"Please," he said.

Reluctantly, I opened my eyes and saw tears shimmering in his. It was hurting him to sit there helplessly and watch. A small frown line appeared between his eyebrows as he searched my face, and I wondered if my eyes betrayed the fact that I was hiding.

"Stay with me," he said.

I heard the real message behind his words: Don't give up. I wasn't giving up; I was just . . . going away until it was over.

"Focus on me," he insisted. I held his gaze, longing for the promises of safety and hope I saw glistening there. "You're gonna be fine."

"Oh, don't lie to the woman, Detective," Edward said with obvious amusement. "You're supposed to protect her, but you can't. You're tied to a chair like some pathetic kidnap victim awaiting

348

rescue. I can do anything I want with her." He swayed, and my body moved with him in a slow rhythmic dance.

He pulled his hand away from the red stain spreading down my tank top and let out a quiet gasp of pleasure that I tried not to contemplate too deeply.

"When was the last time you went on a date, Holly?" Marx asked too loudly, drawing my attention away from the killer's fingers and back to him. That was an odd question given what he'd recently discovered about my past.

"I've never been on a date," I told him, and my voice sounded hollow.

The tense line between his eyebrows smoothed out, and I realized he must have been trying to get my attention for a while. I hadn't heard him call my name—I'd been distracted by my blood on the killer's fingers—so he'd asked a question he hoped would surprise me.

"What's your favorite color?" he asked.

"Purple."

Edward's knife pressed into my stomach and then hesitated when Marx asked, "Why?"

"Stop talking to her," he growled.

"Because it's the color of lilacs in the spring, and they're my favorite flower. And I think eggplants are . . ." Another shallow slice made my voice hitch as I answered him. "Pretty."

Marx blinked back the tears that threatened to spill down his cheeks, but he didn't close his eyes. He stayed with me as he'd requested I do with him. "You struck me as more of a rose girl."

"It's the red hair," I said without inflection. "Roses remind me of that childhood song, 'Ring around the rosie.' Roses were carried to cover up the scent of death. Creeps me out."

"Be quiet," Edward demanded. He pulled the knife away from my stomach and pointed it at Marx. "You watch. You don't speak."

Marx didn't even spare him a dismissive glance. "My favorite color is blue. Like the ocean."

349

"I've never been to the . . ."—the arm around my neck squeezed, cutting off my voice for an instant—"ocean," I choked out defiantly.

The skin around Marx's eyes tightened. "We'll have to fix that someday."

"I said stop," the killer objected more loudly. I could hear the fury in his normally smooth voice. Marx was ruffling him, though I wasn't sure how.

"Don't interrupt, Eddy," Marx chastised.

"My name is Edward," the killer gritted out.

Marx ignored him as he continued talking to me. "There's nothin' quite like a walk on the beach, though you're more of a runner, if I remember correctly. You should run there sometime. It's just the sound of the waves and the seagulls. No distractions. Peaceful. An escape from the city, the people, the cars . . . which everybody needs from time to time."

If I were in a state of panic, I wouldn't have recognized the message he was trying to communicate, but I heard it clearly. *Run.* Somehow, he intended to provide a distraction, and he wanted me to escape. He expected me to leave him behind, but I didn't think I could do that.

He was strapped to a chair, completely helpless to defend himself, but then . . . I was completely free and I couldn't defend myself either. Edward's rules had made certain of that. I needed to find a weapon—anything—that I could use to keep Edward at bay until help came.

I would *not* let Marx die for me.

"There you are," he sighed, and something in his face relaxed just a little. He'd been worried I was too far gone to understand what he was saying or to even bother trying to survive. His plan forced me to climb out of that safe place and figure out what to do. "What's your favorite food, Holly?"

"Marshmallows," I whispered, and my voice shook. The pain was back; I didn't want it. I wrestled with whether or not to crawl back into my hiding place or to try to fight what felt like a hopeless battle.

My internal struggle must have been visible on my face because Marx pleaded, "Stay with me, sweetheart." Tears burned down my cheeks and I gritted my teeth. *Stay.*

"I said stop talking to her!" Edward bellowed in my ear, and I cringed.

Marx shot him a patronizing look. "We're tryin' to have a conversation here, Edmond. I'll get to you in a minute."

Edward's arm squeezed tighter, and I couldn't breathe. I clawed at his arm, but it was like a metal band locked around my throat.

"You don't decide what happens here. I do!" Edward shouted.

"Use your inside voice, Eddy," Marx suggested calmly. "We don't shout in the house, and we don't interrupt people. Or didn't your father teach you any manners when he was puttin' you in your place? Or was it your mother who was too busy ignorin' you to teach you to be civilized?"

"Holly is mine," Edward declared through clenched teeth.

Marx arched his eyebrows. "I'm pretty sure she's enjoyin' my company more than yours."

He was intentionally provoking him. I gasped for breath as Edward drew his arm up in anger, and everything but the tips of my toes left the floor. *God help me.* He was going to strangle me.

"Maybe you should just accept the fact that you're not good enough to hold her attention. You'll never be good enough," Marx continued.

Edward flung me to the floor as if I weighed nothing, and I landed hard on the scraps of wood and nails. I coughed as my throat spasmed, making it difficult to draw in a breath. I climbed shakily to my hands and knees and looked back to see the killer closing the distance between him and Marx.

No. This was exactly what I didn't want to happen. Marx had drawn his attention away from me, and now Edward was going to kill him. I had to do something.

I stumbled to my feet and looked around the room. I picked up a chunk of wood that looked like a decorative knob for a bed—it felt heavy—and hurled it at the back of Edward's head. I hoped it would be more accurate than the bullet I'd fired at him. It landed with a painful-sounding clunk against the back of his skull, and he whirled around with a snarl just as I scrambled out the door and down the steps.

40

I hopped over the last step and sprinted to the front door. I twisted the knob, but it didn't open. I flipped the dead bolt and pulled, but the door was as immovable as a wall.

I searched the door frantically as I heard his heavy boots thumping down the steps after me. My heart sank when I spotted the nail at the top of the door—pounded in at an angle—and another at the bottom. He'd nailed the door shut.

I ducked sharply out of the way when he came up behind me. He slammed into the door hard enough to make the chandelier above us rattle. I stumbled backwards over the debris, my bare feet barely registering the pain as slivers of wood and glass cut into my skin.

There had to be another way out.

The windows were boarded over with plywood, but maybe one of them was loose enough to pull off. I ran to the nearest window and tugged at the corner of the sheet of wood. It didn't give. I tried the next window.

"You can't escape me, Holly," Edward said in his calm, taunting voice. He straightened by the door and seemed to fold the anger back inside himself before looking at me.

He twisted the knife in his hand as he stalked forward slowly, predatory. I backed away from him, bumping into broken furniture and tripping over old empty beer cans and bottles that someone had left lying on the floor.

The backs of my legs collided with something solid, and I glanced behind me to see the living room couch: old, plaid, and gutted until nothing but the bare bones remained.

Edward covered the distance between us too quickly with his long stride, and I scrambled over the couch. His hand landed where my ankle had been a moment before. He let out a sound of frustration that barely sounded human and shoved the couch aside. I leaped out of the way as it slid across the floor and slammed into the wall, taking a chunk out of the plaster.

He kept coming, and I backed toward the fireplace. There was nowhere to go. "Why are you doing this?" I asked, my voice trembling.

He tilted his head as if the question surprised him. "Because I want to."

"My family never did anything to you."

"Your father was weak."

My father had been a gentle man whose strength had lain in the wisdom of books and the knowledge he shared with his children; it hadn't been a physical strength. "My father wasn't weak," I shot back.

"Your father couldn't even protect his family. He deserved to watch them suffer, to see his weakness play out in front of him before he died. He cried like a child as he watched me with your mother, and when I disposed of that simple creature you called your sister."

I clenched my fingers into fists and wished I could hit him. Gin had been sweet and innocent.

"Do you know what a real man is, Holly? He's strong, in control, dominant." He gestured to himself as an example. "He takes what he wants because he can, he does what he wants because he's strong enough to do so."

My back collided with the wall, and I breathed heavily as I stared at him. He was absolutely out of his mind. There was no rationalizing with someone like him.

I looked around the room, desperate for something to help me, and picked up one of the glass bottles.

"What are you going to do with that?" he asked tauntingly.

"I'm gonna hit you with it, obviously." I knew that my only chance was to throw him off balance and then run and hide. I glanced at the doorway at the far end of the room that led into the dining room and my eyes snagged on a pair of shoes—small red flats—sitting on the floor in the corner.

I blinked, certain I was imagining them.

Next to them was a brown jacket lying on top of a pile of colored T-shirts. My clothes. I hadn't given much thought to where Edward had left my clothes after he stripped me of them. He'd never intended for me to leave my parents' room alive, so he hadn't bothered to hide them; he'd just left them lying on the bottom floor where he never expected me to be.

A plan percolated in my brain.

I might have time to grab one thing and run before he reached me. Shoes or jacket. My feet were bleeding and bruised, and the house was littered with broken glass and splinters of wood. But the jacket . . .

"And let's face it . . ." Edward was still speaking.

I threw the bottle at him, and he dodged it with surprising agility. It shattered against the wall behind him, and I bolted for the far end of the room. I grabbed the jacket off the top of the pile and escaped through the doorway into the dining room.

I slammed the flimsy wooden door behind me and slid the lock into place. My family had shared dinner every evening in this room for as far back as I could remember. Gin and I had gathered the plates from the china hutch, which now lay broken face down on the floor, and placed them around the table with silverware and glasses.

I skirted around the broken china hutch to avoid the glass. Edward shouldered the wooden door, and it split down the middle. He reached his arm through the jagged gap and drew back the lock, flinging the door open. He stormed through the dining room after me with none of the reservations I had about the glass scattered across the floor.

He leaped over the china hutch into my path, and I skidded into him with a terrified shriek. He shoved me back into the wall hard enough that my legs nearly gave out beneath me. I snapped up the small purple canister that had still been nestled in my jacket pocket, turned my face away, and sprayed it into his eyes.

He let out a deep, throaty sound of pain, and his hands flew to his face.

I darted around him to the basement door. I pulled it shut behind me and locked it from the other side. I knew it wouldn't stop him, but I hoped that, between the pepper spray and the lock, it would at least slow him down enough to give me time to hide. I scurried silently down the steps into the darkness.

I groped around for a place to hide. I knew there were windows in the basement, but they must have been boarded over along with the rest of the windows in the house.

Something slammed into the door at the top of the steps, and I jumped. He was coming.

My thumb grazed something that felt like a screwdriver, and I grabbed it. I followed the edge of a desk until I came across the small alcove where the chair was supposed to rest.

I crawled inside and curled up as far from the opening as possible. Pain lanced through the wounds over my ribs with every breath, and the flow of blood hadn't slowed. I wrapped an arm around my stomach to put pressure on the wounds.

I gripped the screwdriver against my chest as I leaned my head back against the desk and closed my eyes to rest. I was exhausted and unbearably cold, and as the moments passed, I started to shiver. I wasn't sure if it was from the cold concrete beneath me or the blood loss.

Another heavy force hit the door at the top of the steps and the door splintered, sending chunks of wood raining down the steps and over the railing to the floor. The staircase creaked beneath Edward's heavy weight.

"That wasn't very smart, Holly," he called out, and his tone was dangerous. The pepper spray had barely slowed him down, but it had made him furious. He was already intending to torture me to death; how much worse could it get if he was angry?

I heard the quiet scrape of his boots landing on the concrete.

I buried my face in my arm to muffle the sound of my rapid breathing. There was no ambient noise like there was in the city. There was pure, absolute silence when he stood still, and I knew he would be able to hear me breathing.

Lord, I'm so afraid. Please be with me.

Slow, quiet footsteps moved through the basement. "You can't hide from me."

A familiar tapping sound joined his voice. He didn't have a window to tap on this time, so I could only imagine he was tapping his fingers on the knife.

"There are only so many places to hide in a basement. I will find you. I found you in New York," he said, his tone inviting me to respond. I said nothing. "I was there for work and I happened to see you out jogging. Your hair, your eyes, your body. You were unmistakable. You can't even imagine how delighted I was to be reunited with you. It was like . . . divine intervention."

God's divinity had nothing to do with his twisted plans. He bumped into something, and I tensed at the sound of boxes crashing to the floor. He kicked them aside.

"I've thought about what I would do to you when I found you so many times," he admitted with a sigh of such primal pleasure that it made my stomach lurch.

His fingers tapped rhythmically on the knife again. "I'm a man who gets what he wants. I wanted your mother from the moment I saw her at the veterinary clinic, so I took her. She was . . . exactly as I expected her to be: gentle, obedient, maybe even a little desperate, and willing to do anything to protect her children. She was what a woman is meant to be. But you, Holly, you seem a little confused."

My pulse pounded loudly in my ears as footsteps brought him closer.

"You seem to be under the impression that you can fight me. You can't fight me. You're small and weak. You seem to think that you can outsmart me, but you're not a thinker. You're just a simple woman who needs to be pointed in the right direction. I followed you for weeks before I sent that note card, and it took a man to figure it out."

I clenched my teeth. I knew I was small, and I wasn't exactly strong, but I wasn't ignorant.

"You're not even capable of saving yourself. What do you think would've happened in the park two months ago if I hadn't been there?"

Did he want a thank-you card for stepping in? We both knew he hadn't killed that man to save me; he'd killed him for even thinking about touching me, because he believed I belonged to him.

"You're pathetically helpless." He drew in a breath to continue his lecture on my shortcomings, when a distant thumping caught his attention. An abrupt silence filled the basement as he stilled, holding his breath along with me, and listened.

Another quiet thump drew my eyes upward. For a moment, I thought it might just be Marx trying to break free of his restraints, but then something thumped again, and it sounded like it was coming from the front of the house.

"Sounds like we have company," Edward said, and I could hear the sound of his shoes scuffing the floor as he turned slowly, listening for the origin of the thumping.

It was moving around the house. I supposed it could be teenagers looking for a place to stir up trouble for the night. Judging by the graffiti on the walls and the discarded pop and alcohol bottles in the living room, it wouldn't be the first time.

A small part of me dared to hope it was someone looking for me or Marx. Maybe they would find a way in to help us. The sound stopped and the silence stretched.

"Now that we've illuminated the fact that you're weak, ignorant, and helpless, why don't you stop hiding and accept that this is inevitable," Edward suggested.

He really did think I was ignorant if he believed I would just give up after that speech and impale myself on his knife.

He walked forward, and I stiffened when the tip of his boot connected with the back of the desk. He tapped his foot against it a second time. Something—probably a hand—slid along the outside of the desk, following the edge of it just the way I had.

I curled into a tighter ball when I heard him step directly in front of the alcove where I was hiding. He was less than a foot away from me. I tried not to breathe.

The thumping erupted again; only this time it was directly outside the basement. It sounded like something heavy repeatedly smashing into wood. Edward backed away from the desk until the sound of his footsteps melted into the darkness with him.

Another thump, and something broke. Moonlight poured into the basement, and I realized someone had just kicked through the board that had been fastened over the window from the inside.

There was a muffled grunt and the quiet slap of shoes hitting the cement as someone climbed through the narrow window and dropped into the basement. I didn't dare crawl out of my hiding place to see who it was.

"Holly," a male voice whispered.

I didn't recognize the hushed voice, but I could think of only one person in this town who might come looking for me: Jordan. He'd probably followed my trail through the woods, and it led him to the house.

A flashlight beam pierced the darkness, and I flinched away from it when it bounced off the floor beside the desk. I watched it with cat-like fascination as it flickered up and down over the walls.

He needed to turn it off. The killer was in the basement with us, and he was broadcasting his location with the beam of the light.

"Holly?" he called again.

I considered coming out of my hiding place, but I dismissed the thought as quickly as it came to me. I didn't know where Edward was hiding, and the last thing I wanted was for him to lunge out of the shadows and grab me.

I barely heard the shuffle of feet before the deafening crack of a gunshot made me cringe and slap my hands over my ears. I heard muffled shouting and the sound of things crashing around the room.

The beam of light flickered wildly across the walls and floor until the flashlight rolled to a stop. It cast shadows onto the wall, and I watched, frozen, as the two male silhouettes wrestled. Edward and Jordan were on the floor somewhere behind me, and the smaller of the two shadows wasn't winning.

I forced myself to crawl out from under the desk.

I gathered my shaking legs beneath me and looked at the two men across the room. Jordan was maybe six feet and 160 pounds. The killer dwarfed him. He was on his back on the floor, gripping Edward's wrist with both hands as the killer tried to plunge the knife into his chest.

"Edward!" I shouted.

The killer jerked and looked at me in surprise, and Jordan punched him in the face.

"Run, Holly!" Jordan commanded as the hit threw Edward off balance. He scrambled out from under him. I darted past the two of them and up the steps. Jordan grabbed the flashlight that lay at the foot of the steps and fled up the steps after me.

I slid to a stop in the dining room and tried to backtrack to avoid the glass. Jordan must have been looking over his shoulder, because he plowed into me and nearly sent me sprawling into the glass. He wrapped an arm around my waist before I could stumble into it and picked me up.

I let out a surprised gasp of pain.

"Yeah, I know, five feet," he said as he carried me over the glass. "I'll apologize later." He mistook my cry of pain as a cry of protest. He dropped me gently in the doorway that bridged the dining room and the living room. "What's wrong with the front door? My key didn't work."

"It's nailed shut," I said as I pressed a hand to my stomach. I slipped my feet into the red shoes along the wall as Jordan swore quietly under his breath.

"Any other way . . . ?" He noticed the blood smeared across his hand and arm and flicked the flashlight in my direction. "Geez,

Holly, what . . ." He took a step closer to me when he saw my tank top.

"I'm fine," I said. "There's no other way out. Where's your gun?"

"In the abyss," he answered as he flicked the light toward the basement. He must have lost it in the fight. He drew in an unsteady breath as Edward squeezed through the doorway at the top of the steps, his face a mask of tempered rage.

I bit back a frightened whimper as my gaze flickered to the knife that was still red with my blood.

"That is a big man," Jordan mumbled a little nervously. He backed me through the doorway into the living room, deliberately keeping himself between me and Edward, as the man stalked slowly toward us. "We need to get you out of the house somehow."

"He has Marx. I'm not leaving him."

Jordan blinked. He'd known Marx was missing, but he must not have connected his disappearance with the killer yet. "Where is he?"

"Upstairs."

He glanced at the staircase and up at the second floor. His fingers twitched a little uneasily on the flashlight as he lowered his gaze back to Edward. "Okay. I'll . . . delay the giant. And pray God drops a slingshot in my lap."

I shoved my screwdriver at him. "It's not a slingshot."

He nodded and puffed out a breath. "It'll have to do."

Edward was nearly on top of him by the time I reached the bottom of the steps, and Jordan gave no indication of backing down. He had to be terrified. He was smaller and armed with nothing but a screwdriver against a giant with a skinning knife.

Edward lunged at him. Jordan ducked, spun out of the way, and kicked the back of the man's knee, sending him stumbling. I had to trust that he would be okay. I ran up the steps on pure adrenaline.

I never used to think the upstairs hallway was so long, but it seemed to take me ages to reach the master bedroom, and I was out of breath by the time I wrapped my fingers around the doorway and pulled myself inside.

Marx paused in his struggles to break free of the ropes that held him to the chair and looked up at me—either because he sensed my presence or because he'd heard me running like an elephant down the hallway.

"Holly, what are you doin' here? You were supposed to run. I told you to . . ." His voice trailed off and some of the color drained from his face. I followed his gaze to my stomach. "How bad is it?"

"I'm okay." I was a little light-headed and I was freezing, but I was still in one piece. Mostly. I picked my way through the debris to him.

"You're not okay," he argued as I sank to my knees beside his chair and started working on the ropes with slippery fingers.

"They're not that deep."

"There's a lot of blood."

"Vomit you can handle, but blood makes you squeamish?" I asked. I tried to keep my voice light and playful, but it came out shaky. He'd held my hair back shortly after we first met, when my memories made me sick to my stomach.

"No, blood does not make me squeamish. You bein' in pain makes me squeamish. You can't be here when he comes back."

A loud crash from downstairs made my heart flutter. I needed to find a way to untie him and get all of us out of here. I couldn't—I wouldn't—leave him behind. I left my family behind and they all died.

"I'm not leaving you." I tried to wiggle my fingers in between the layers of rope to pull it apart, but it was too tightly knotted. "Jordan's downstairs delaying Edward."

"I heard the gunshot."

"He missed." I grabbed a jagged piece of wood from the floor and began sawing at the rope. A few fibers frayed, but not quickly enough.

My hands were slippery with blood, and I kept losing my grip on the piece of wood. I tried prying the rope apart again, but I wasn't strong enough.

Another string of violent thumps came from downstairs. It sounded like they were slamming each other into the walls.

"Holly, if he comes up those steps . . ."

"I said I'm not leaving you and you can't make me," I snapped. "Let it go." I tried the ropes around his right wrist. "Come on," I begged. The ropes on that side of the chair weren't as tight, and I was able to squeeze a finger in between the loops and slowly loosen them.

My fingers were so cold they were numb, and it made them clumsy. I worked at the rope as quickly as I could, and I knew I was making progress, but it wasn't fast enough. Minutes were slipping by.

"Holly," Marx said urgently, and the note of fear in his voice brought my eyes up instantly.

The killer stepped into the room. Crimson dripped from the tip of his knife onto the floorboards, and my gaze flickered to the doorway. Jordan. Edward wiped the knife slowly across his shirt to clean it.

"I told you, Holly. I get what I want, and we're not done," he said.

"Don't you touch her," Marx demanded as he twisted in the chair, trying to pull free of his bonds. I hadn't had enough time to loosen them.

Edward's bottomless eyes shifted from me to Marx, and a chill went through me. There was a glimmer of murderous intent in his eyes, and he twisted the knife in his hand as he stepped forward. "I wanted you to watch, but you're proving to be more trouble than you're worth. I'm just going to kill you now."

I grabbed a chunk of wood the length of a baseball bat and stepped in front of Marx. I hadn't been able to untie him so he could defend himself, and I would not let him die . . . at least not without trying to save him.

"Holly! What are you doin'!" Marx shouted from behind me. "Get out of the way!"

Edward paused and cocked his head thoughtfully, as if my behavior puzzled him. "You can't honestly think you're capable of stopping me."

"Awesome things come in small packages," I told him, and my voice wavered. *Just look at Jesus. He came in a package that probably weighed about seven pounds, six ounces, and He changed the world.* I could at least hit a psychotic, knife-wielding killer with a stick.

We both knew that when he decided to make his move, there was little I could do to stop him. But maybe I could at least delay him until Marx managed to pull free, or help arrived.

I really needed help to arrive.

He took another slow step forward, and I almost fell on top of Marx when instinct drove me back to avoid the approaching threat.

"Holly, please move," Marx pleaded.

Edward advanced another step, and I swung. To both our surprise, I connected with his side, but there wasn't enough force behind it to do more than elicit a grunt of irritation from him. He wrapped his fingers around the end of the chunk of wood and ripped it from my hands. He discarded it over his shoulder.

I ducked when he grabbed for me, but he managed to catch a fistful of my hair. I cried out as he wrenched me back.

"You don't seem to understand how this works, Holly. I'm a man. You're a woman. I can break you easily," he explained.

His grip on my hair tightened, and I hissed in through my teeth. It felt like he was ripping it out by the roots. I drew back my foot and kicked him in the shin as hard as I could.

Anger sharpened his voice. "You want to fight me? Fine!" He locked an arm around my waist, lifting me up to shoulder height with laughable ease, and then spiked me into the floorboards like a football.

Indescribable pain exploded through my entire body, and my vision went white. I coughed as I desperately tried to draw in a breath; breathing sent another wave of pain splintering through my ribs and stomach.

Someone was shouting somewhere, but it sounded like bees buzzing around inside my skull. I drew my limbs slowly into my body as I curled into a fetal position on the floorboards, trying to pull myself together so I could get up. I had to get up.

I blinked at the terrifying face above me through a haze of pain-induced tears. Edward leaned over me as he whispered, "You're mine; you've always been mine, and there's only one way this ends for you."

"No." I dragged myself back from him, scooting through the debris on the floor to get away. He wrapped his fingers around my ankles, and I screamed as he wrenched me back with one quick tug that left me flat on my back.

He crawled on top of me, straddling me, and panic stole any hope of rational thought. "No!" I screamed. I pounded my fists into his chest and pushed at his shoulders in blind desperation. "Get off!"

I tried to squirm out from under him, but he dragged me back. I could hear Marx shouting something in the background, but I couldn't understand what he was saying. My mind was trapped in a place of single-minded focus: *get him off*.

I felt the sharpness of the blade as he pressed it against my abdomen. I clawed at the debris around me for anything I could use as a weapon. I found a sliver of wood and stabbed it into Edward's shoulder. He howled in pain and backhanded me hard enough to leave my ears ringing.

For a moment, I thought I might pass out. I blinked and tried to focus. I had to get away. I tried to drag myself across the shifting floor, but he slammed me onto my back and grabbed for my wrists. He caught my left one easily and pinned it to the floor above my head. I slapped him with my right hand and raked my nails down his face, leaving bloody tracks from his eyebrow down the length of his jaw.

He swore and clutched at his face. When he drew back his arm to hit me a second time, I snapped into a ball with my arms protecting my head. I didn't think I could take another blow to the head from him.

A deafening series of bangs reverberated through the room. I cringed and squeezed my eyes shut. An obscenely heavy weight fell on top of me, and I would've screamed, but it crushed the breath from my lungs.

I cracked open my eyelids and stared into vacant dark eyes. A fresh wave of terror washed through me, and I tried frantically to push Edward's body off me before I suffocated.

I couldn't breathe.

Someone hooked their arms under mine and heaved, pulling me out from under the body inch by agonizingly slow inch. I thrashed once I was clear of the body, trying to escape the person's grip.

Gentle arms folded around me and hugged me. "Sh, sweetheart, you're all right. It's over," a soothing Southern voice assured me. "He's dead. It's all over." He held me against him as we huddled on the floor mere feet from the man who'd tried to murder all of us.

Jordan slumped down against the far wall, looking frighteningly pale. There was a gash just above his eyebrow, and a welt blossoming on his right cheek that promised to be a spectacular bruise. He pressed one hand to the seeping wound on his stomach and gripped his gun with the other.

He would've had to make his way back down into the basement to recover his gun, and then climb two flights of stairs while wounded to get to us. And judging by the wine-colored stain spreading down his T-shirt and over his jeans, it wasn't a glancing wound.

He glared at the dead man as if he wished he could put a few more bullets in him. "Ambulance is on its way. So is backup," he said through a wince of pain. He looked at me and something shifted behind his eyes before he asked Marx, "Is she gonna be okay?"

My panic melted away slowly, replaced by pain and the bone-numbing cold that had seeped into my body an hour ago. I started to shake.

"She will be," Marx said as he rested his head on top of mine—either to hold me closer or to impart some of his warmth—and I didn't fight him. He murmured soothing words to me, and I sagged in his embrace.

And because I didn't have much dignity left after everyone saw me that vulnerable . . . I cried.

Epilogue

Fluffy white snowflakes drifted down outside my kitchen window, and I watched them as I leaned against the counter, sipping my hot chocolate with marshmallows. I had no appreciation for the colder months of the year, but at least the sparkling snowflakes were pretty.

It had been just over a month since Edward Billings, the man who murdered my family eighteen years ago, had tracked me down and attempted to finish the job. If not for Marx and Jordan, he might have succeeded.

None of us had escaped my childhood home unscathed, but considering the three of us had walked away while the killer was rolled out in a body bag, we couldn't complain. Jordan had technically been loaded onto a stretcher and carried out, but the killer had thrown him around like a rag doll and then stabbed him, so he'd earned the right to be carried down the steps.

I didn't really understand why Edward had come after my family, and I doubted I ever would. Maybe if I studied his life and crawled inside his head I could find that answer, but that wasn't a place I ever wanted to go.

Marx continued to dig into Edward's past, searching for details that I was happy to live without. He told me that Edward had gone to college under a false name and had flourished in a career as a pharmaceutical salesman for veterinary clinics. It allowed him to travel the country and gave him access to ketamine, which he'd used to subdue the children of the families he targeted.

He'd met my mother at a veterinary clinic shortly after leaving prison, and I had no doubt he'd chosen that career as some sick reminder of her. She hadn't been his first victim—that had been his own mother—but she'd been *one* of his firsts, and the way he'd spoken about her made me think she held a special place in his icy heart.

I had considered staying in Stony Brooke after everything was resolved. I could have a peaceful life there with my father's bookstore, but I wouldn't be happy. Too many people knew the little girl I used to be, and I wasn't her. I spoke with Georgetta, and she agreed to stay on and tend the store for me. I accepted a small percentage of the income since I didn't technically have a job anymore. I was flat broke and I didn't even have my camera.

The main reason I couldn't bring myself to stay in Stony Brooke were the people I cared about in New York. I loved Jace too much to abandon her, and Marx had grown on me.

I smiled as I sipped my hot chocolate. He was an interesting addition to my life. With his brusque, no-nonsense, cop persona and his fatherly protectiveness, I wasn't really sure where or how he fit into my life now. He just . . . did.

I never thought I would be able to regard him with anything more than strained civility, but now I trusted him with my life. And he didn't seem to mind me either.

It took me a while to understand the reason that God wanted Marx in my life. If I hadn't been assaulted in the park that day, I never would've met him. And if I had never met him, I would've been completely alone when Edward came for me. There would've been no protection detail, no trip to Kansas to meet Jordan, and no one to come to my defense when Edward took me home to finish what he'd started all those years ago. I would've simply . . . disappeared.

The thought chilled me.

God always had a plan, even if I stubbornly fought Him every step of the way. We were always butting heads, but His head was bigger, and He always got His way in the end. Without Him, I wouldn't be alive. I also wouldn't have been reunited with my childhood friend.

Jordan was . . . complicated. I had regained a few of my memories of him: playing ball, tumbling through piles of leaves, creating strange and sometimes inedible things in the kitchen . . . but none of those memories, precious as they were, helped me to know how to deal with the man.

I might not desire anything more than friendship with him, but I could admit that he was handsome . . . in a pretty, charming sort of way. I wasn't entirely certain what he thought of me, but sometimes he looked at me in a way that made my heart flutter in anxious confusion.

We were strangers with a history. We knew absolutely nothing about each other as adults, and I knew our reunion hadn't gone quite the way he'd imagined it would. He was trying very hard to give me space and make me comfortable even though he didn't know why it was necessary.

It helped that he didn't live in New York. For the time being, he'd chosen to remain in Stony Brooke. But he promised to visit.

I lifted my mug to take another drink of hot chocolate when a knock came on my front door. I paused and gave the ghastly yellow door a wary look. I wasn't expecting company. It was eight o'clock in the evening.

Another quiet knock.

"Holly, it's Sam," a baritone voice called through the door.

Odd. He wasn't exactly the visiting type. I set down my drink and tucked my feet into my pair of warm green slippers before opening the front door.

Sam stood on the front patio in jeans and a sweater. He clutched a small box in his hands and was making a valiant effort not to shiver in the cold as snowflakes flurried around him.

"Is everything okay?" I asked. "Is Marx okay?"

"Fine. Everyone's fine. Do you mind if I come in?" I'm not sure what look was on my face—considering his request left me feeling a bit uneasy—but he puffed out a breath. "Right . . . sorry. I guess I didn't really think that one through. I'm good here."

He bounced his legs to keep warm, and guilt gnawed at me. Sam had spent nearly two months out in the cold trying to keep me safe. I leaned out and looked around at the undisturbed powder and eerily quiet night. "So why are you on my porch?"

He opened his mouth to answer and then snapped it shut

again. "Just . . . waiting."

I stared at him intently, waiting for more information. When he didn't volunteer anything, I prompted him, saying, "For . . . ?"

He sighed and just looked at me. Okay, apparently, it was a secret. "It's nothing to worry about. You can close the door. I'll be fine out here. I'm sorry I knocked and bothered you."

I narrowed my eyes at him. "And how long are you planning to wait on my patio?"

"Maybe five minutes."

"Are you waiting for a person? Should I be concerned?" Marx would have called me if there was some sort of problem, and Sam wasn't on duty, so I thought not.

"Yes, I'm waiting for someone. No, you shouldn't be concerned." He looked half-frozen already. The wind chill had plunged the temperature into the negatives.

I sighed and said, "You should consider a coat next time. I'm pretty sure they make them in your size." I opened the door after a beat of reluctance and stepped back. I had never welcomed Sam into my apartment on his own before, and it did make me a little nervous despite the fact that he *seemed* like a good person. I hadn't gotten to know him all that well during those two months. But Jace thought highly of him.

"Are you sure?" he asked.

"I'm gonna be less sure in about ten seconds."

He stomped the snow from his boots before coming inside. He set the small, plain white box on the kitchen counter and then went back outside to throw the wooden plank over the steps, creating a makeshift ramp.

"Jace is coming?" I asked. The two of them had been interested in each other during the case, but Sam had been reluctant to pursue a relationship with her while he was trying to protect me. He didn't want to divide his focus.

"Yeah." He stepped back inside and brushed the snowflakes from his head. "She's getting something from her car."

"You didn't offer to help?"

He gave me a flat look. "And risk bodily harm for daring to suggest she can't do it herself?"

I laughed. "That drives you crazy, doesn't it?"

"Yes, it does," he admitted. He looked me over in that brisk, clinical way he usually did when we saw one another, like he was double-checking that I was still alive and in one piece. "You look better. The bruises are gone."

The last time he'd seen me, I'd looked a little worse for wear after my encounter with the killer in Kansas. Most of my wounds had been hidden beneath my clothes, but I'd had a few bruises on my face and neck. I hadn't looked nearly as rough as Marx, though. Eggplant purple might be my favorite color, but it did *not* look good on people's faces.

"Yep," I said, because I wasn't really sure what else to say. I picked up my mug of hot chocolate and gripped it with both hands. I was going to freeze to death standing by the open front door without something to keep me warm, and I wasn't locking the two of us in here alone together.

"So how are you doing?" he asked.

"Okay. You?"

He gave a stiff shrug. "Fine."

I gnawed on my lower lip. Right. This was why I didn't do small talk. It led to awkwardness. I stared into my mug because the silent eye contact was making me fidget.

We could hear Jace grunting as she hauled something out of the vehicle. She rolled down the sidewalk a moment later with a large box on her lap, and she waved at me with a smile bright enough to light up the night. Another car pulled up to the curb, and I frowned in confusion when Marx got out.

"Am I missing something?" I asked as I looked at Sam. Occasionally, Jace or Marx stopped by, but all three of them on the same night at the same time struck me as suspicious. They didn't exactly run in the same circles.

"It's your birthday," he said with another shrug.

I'd found out recently that my actual birthday was January

18, and I'd been looking forward to it. I had even considered buying myself a cupcake and eating it in a secret celebration. But none of that explained their presence. "And?"

"Traditionally in my family you get presents or a hug on your birthday," he said.

I took a small step back from him and gave him a warning look. "If you try to hug me, I will stab you with a kitchen fork." And I meant it.

He let out a quiet laugh. "That's why I brought a gift."

So the nondescript little box was a gift.

Jace rolled into the apartment with a cheerful "Happy birthday!" and plowed into me with a hug. It knocked me back a step, and Sam caught my hot chocolate before I could drop it on her head. "I'm so happy you actually have a birthday for us to celebrate now," she said as she drew back. "I brought you a present." She set the large box on the counter next to the one Sam had brought.

Sam returned my hot chocolate to me, and I exhaled. "Nice reflexes," I said.

Marx walked down the ramp into the apartment with his arms loaded with boxes. I blinked in astonishment as I closed the door behind him. "Please tell me you brought gifts for everyone." Because those couldn't possibly all be for me.

He slid them onto the kitchen table. "No, I did not bring gifts for everyone," he said. He removed the two wrapped gifts from the pile and set them with the others.

I had expected Jace to bring me a gift because she would be excited to celebrate, but I hadn't expected this from Sam and Marx. "Why . . . ?"

Marx removed his jacket and laid it over one of the chairs before turning to me. "Do we have to have the 'you matter to people' conversation again? Because I was pretty sure we covered that . . . in its entirety."

"But . . ."

He gave me a stern look, and I swallowed my objections. "Sam, grab some plates and silverware please. Does anybody have a

373

lighter?" Sam began rummaging through my cupboards for plates, and Jace pulled a lighter from her pocket and tossed it to Marx.

I folded my arms and lingered by the table, unsure what I was supposed to do. I wasn't used to having this many guests in my apartment. "I can do drinks. I have chocolate milk or water . . ."

"Do you have a knife?" Marx asked.

I walked into the kitchen and came back with the butcher knife. I peered into the box on the table at the chocolate frosted cake with purple flowers and green script that seemed to shout, "Happy Birthday, Holly!!!"

My throat tightened with emotion. He'd brought me a cake. An actual cake. With my name on it. Between the gifts, the cake, and the friends, I was a little overwhelmed. I cleared my throat. "You brought me a cake?"

"It came with the candle," he said teasingly as he pushed a number-twenty-eight candle into the center of the cake. He took the knife from me and gave it a strange look. "Is this . . . ?"

"The knife I almost stabbed you with in Maine? Yep." I had also intended to stab my landlord in the foot with it when I thought he might be the killer breaking into my apartment in the middle of the night. "Did you bake the cake?"

"Of course I didn't bake it. The bakery baked it," he replied with a frown.

"Afraid you would burn it?" I teased.

"That's not a fear, Holly. That's an inevitability."

I smirked and leaned against the table. "I can teach you to bake." At his blank look, I insisted, "I can bake."

"That's debatable," he muttered beneath his breath as he started slicing small squares into the cake.

"The cookies weren't *that* bad." I looked at Sam, who sealed his lips and decided it was better to say nothing than to agree with either of us. He'd eaten two of them, for goodness' sakes.

Another knock on the outside of door—this one more tentative and uncertain—gave me pause. I shot Marx a questioning look. Was he expecting another guest?

He released a breath that sounded vaguely unhappy and then opened my front door with the chocolate-covered knife in his hand. Jordan stood on the front patio. He blinked at the knife for a moment—more thoughtful than alarmed—and then recovered.

"Marx," he greeted evenly.

"Jordan," Marx replied in an equally flat tone. He moved aside and Jordan stepped through the doorway. He stopped just inside the entryway and took in my small, crowded apartment with a brisk visual sweep before looking at me.

"Hey, Holly." He greeted me with a warm, slightly nervous smile. His blue eyes flickered over me from head to fuzzy slippers and then back to my face. "Nice slippers."

I smiled. Fuzzy green slippers weren't exactly the perfect accent to the leggings and skirt I was wearing. "Hi. I thought you were staying in Kansas."

"I'm still evaluating my options, but I wanted to drop in for your birthday." He held up a small gift box tied with a polka-dotted ribbon.

Marx cleared his throat impatiently as he waited for Jordan to step out of the entryway. He was standing in the path of the door, and the bitter winter breeze was blowing snow into the apartment.

"Any chance I can come a little closer than five feet?" Jordan asked hopefully. "Your apartment is a bit on the small side, and if I have to stay on the five-feet perimeter all night, I don't think I can even be in the same room with you. Literally."

It was about four steps from the kitchen into the living room, so he was pretty accurate about not being able to stand in the same room with me. I bit my bottom lip and tried not to smile. "I can work with four."

"Well, that's closer than I was in Kansas." He came into the kitchen and leaned back against the counter in front of the window. He gauged the distance between his feet and mine. "Not quite. Could you maybe just . . . scoot your foot back an inch? I'm trapped by the counter."

I grinned and slid my slippered foot back.

"Perfect," he said. "Four feet."

He was wearing his casual attire: jeans, a nice shirt, and a brown leather jacket that was in no way warm enough for the snowfall outside. He'd left his badge behind, but his gun was attached to his hip. I glanced around and noticed that Sam and Marx also had theirs. God help anyone dumb enough to try to enter my home uninvited tonight. They wouldn't make it very far.

"You look . . ." Jordan hesitated, probably remembering I didn't do well with compliments, and then sighed as he tapped the box lightly against his palm.

"The word is beautiful," Jace whispered hoarsely, dragging out the last word for emphasis, as she leaned forward in her chair. I glanced at her and noticed that she and Sam were holding hands. It was about time.

Jordan grinned. "Yeah, I tried that one. Didn't work out so well."

"I usually just go with nice," Sam said as he extended his hand. Jace gave him a look that had him trying to puzzle out what he'd said wrong. He frowned at her and then returned his attention to Jordan. "I'm Sam."

Jordan shook his hand politely. "*Sam*," he said, pondering the name aloud. "The cop who got roofied?"

Sam grimaced. That was a sore subject for him. "Yeah." He looked Jordan over as if considering whether or not he could take him in a fight. I was beginning to think that was just something men did with each other. "And you're the sheriff who has no chance with Holly."

I stiffened. Where had that come from?

Jordan took the comment in stride and just smiled. "Pleasure to meet you, Sam."

"You too. And thanks," Sam replied. "For watching out for Marx and Holly when I couldn't be there. From what I hear, they wouldn't have made it without your help. It took a lot of courage to go into that house."

"Yes, it did," Marx said quietly. "I don't know if I properly thanked you for that." Jordan and Marx looked at each other, and for once, I saw a glimmer of mutual respect in their eyes rather than friction. "Thank you for savin' Holly."

Jordan nodded once and then glanced at me. "I would do it again in a heartbeat." He could have died trying to save us, and I believed him when he said he wouldn't hesitate to do it again.

"I'm Jace. I'm Holly's best friend," Jace announced as she stuck out her hand. If I wasn't mistaken, she declared herself as my best friend in a very pointed way. I had told her that Jordan was my best friend when we were children, and knowing her, she viewed him as competition.

Jordan shook her hand. "It's nice to meet you."

"All right then, let's get started with gifts," Marx suggested as he closed and locked the door. "There are five of them and I've seen Holly open a gift before, so we're gonna be here for at least a week."

"I'm not that bad."

He arched an eyebrow at me as he handed me a gift wrapped in tissue paper and sealed with a ribbon tied like a shoelace.

"Wrapped it yourself this time, huh?" I grinned.

"Yes I did, and it only took me three tries to get it right." He smiled at me and leaned back against the counter beside the other gifts. "Now open it before it melts."

Melts? I squeezed it with my fingers. Ooh, it was squishy. I pulled off the ribbon and peeled away the layers of tissue paper. A plastic bag of red, orange, green, and blue M&M's sat on my palm. "You took out all the brown and yellow." The colors I hated. I hadn't expected him to remember.

"I saved them in a jar for a rainy day when I develop the urge to flick them at people who irritate me." He tossed me the small box Sam had brought, and I almost dropped it with the candy in my hand.

"Good thing it's not breakable," Sam muttered.

Jordan smiled. "Eighteen years later and you still catch like a girl. All butterfingers."

I gave him a pointed look. "I happen to be a girl, in case you hadn't noticed."

He flashed me a charming grin.

"Oh, he's noticed," Marx grumbled.

Jordan gave him a slightly indignant look as he pointed out, "I'm minding my manners."

I decided it was best to ignore them. I shook the tiny, unwrapped package next to my ear, and something shifted inside. I opened it and tilted my head curiously as I looked at the contents. "Taxi passes?"

"In case you're out late, so you don't have to walk home. And so you don't hitchhike . . . ever again," Sam explained.

"Oh, well, I was thinking about just taking the subway if I'm out till three a.m.," I said, just to see his reaction.

Sam's black eyebrows drew together. "Do you realize how dangerous the subway is? It's like a petri dish for crime. The chances of . . ."

Jace elbowed him in the side, and he swallowed the rest of his lecture. "Stop trying to scare her. She's not serious." She looked at me, suddenly uncertain. "You're not serious, right?"

I laughed. "No, I'm not. Thank you for the passes, Sam." I appreciated that he cared. He gave me a brusque nod and wrapped an arm around Jace's shoulders.

"Mine next!" Jace declared.

Marx took the candy and taxi passes from me and handed me the large package. I tipped it in every direction, trying to figure it out.

"If it's fragile, tell her now," Marx advised. "She has a tendency to toss her gifts around like they're on the spin cycle."

I stifled a laugh. Besides, this gift wasn't fragile. I was pretty sure I knew what it was by the shape of the box. I just hoped I was wrong. I opened the wrapping paper carefully and peered inside one end at the bright shoebox. Good grief.

I pulled the box free and set the paper on the table. I steeled myself as I opened the box, then nearly burst out laughing.

"I saw them and thought of you," Jace admitted with a proud tilt to her chin.

I lifted the shoe from the box to show everyone. It was a bright purple sneaker with a three-inch platform, and it laced all the way up to the knee . . . with hot pink laces. "Because it's purple or because it will make me taller?"

"Both. It will make you look more intimidating, which, in your case, is a necessity."

I tucked the shoe back into the box with a smile. "I have the perfect spot for them . . . right next to the green pair under my bed. They'll add an intimidating element to my apartment from their hiding place." What was she going to get me next? Tweety-Bird-yellow steel-toed boots?

Marx's brow pinched curiously at the shoes as he took them from me and exchanged them for another gift. The wrapping paper was silver with multicolored snowflakes that shimmered in the light. It was beautiful, and the box was decorated with a flowing silver bow.

"This one is fragile," he informed me.

I set the box on the corner of the table and slid the bow off gently. Sparkles littered the floor, and my fat cat, Jordan, watched the sparkles rain down with wide eyes. I unwrapped the gift and opened the box. Nestled in a bed of wrapping paper was my camera.

I gasped.

I hadn't seen it since the night in the park when I broke the lens by swinging it into my attacker's face. The police had confiscated it as evidence.

I picked it up gently and turned it over in my hands. The lens was no longer broken; it didn't even have a scratch on it. It was brand new. I looked up at Marx with wide eyes. "A new lens is several hundred dollars," I said, shocked.

Marx shrugged. "Consider it your Christmas and birthday present, if it makes you feel better."

"It . . . it doesn't," I stammered. "I can't . . . I mean, it's too expensive. I have to pay you back."

He sighed and shook his head with a smile. "It's a *gift*, Holly. You don't owe me anythin'. Just do me a favor and don't stay out too late in the park takin' photos again, all right?"

"If she does, she has taxi passes," Sam pointed out.

"And fiercely intimidating shoes," Jace added.

I struggled to accept the gift even though I wanted it very much. I knew he wouldn't budge on the issue of me paying him back, so I hugged my camera to my chest and forced myself to say, "Okay."

It felt good to hold it again. I draped the strap across my body just to feel the familiar weight of it. It felt right.

Jordan stepped forward and handed me the small gift box. He was very careful not to touch my fingers with his, and then he retreated to his spot in front of the window.

"We found the killer's place of residence. He had a house in Topeka, but he was on the road a lot and he had a mobile home in the woods. There was a collection box, I guess you might call it, in the ice box. We recovered some of the items he took from his victims."

I opened the box and stared down at the silver bracelet. I picked it up delicately, almost afraid it might crumble to pieces after all these years. "Gin" was scratched into the surface of it.

"I had it cleaned. I thought you might like to have it back," he said.

Tears gathered in my eyes, and I closed my fingers over the precious item as I lifted my gaze to Jordan's. "Thank you."

"Yeah." He smiled, and it was edged by sadness. Even after all these years, he missed Gin too. Now I had both of our bracelets back.

"Holly, are you ready for cake?" Marx asked. I nodded, and he lit the candle on the cake before flipping off the overhead light. "Make a wish."

I looked down at the bracelet in my hand, around the tiny bunker I called my home, and at the people in the room with me. I had more than I had ever dared to hope for. "I don't really have anything left to wish for."

"Aww," Jace said sappily. "We love you too."

Sam opened his mouth to clarify something and then clamped it shut, probably deciding it wasn't the best time to be literal about his feelings toward me. I was pretty sure it would involve the adjective *frustrating* or *stubborn*.

My phone started ringing and I frowned at it thoughtfully as I picked it up. Everyone I might expect to call me was in the room with me. It was an unknown number.

"Hello?" I greeted tentatively.

"Are you enjoying your party, Holly?" the silky voice on the other end of the line inquired. "This is the part where you blow out the candle."

My fingers tightened on the phone as I looked at the front window and a chill slithered down my spine. I would recognize that voice anywhere.

Collin.

How to Connect

Facebook: https://www.facebook.com/ccwarrens
Website: https://www.ccwarrensbooks.com/
Email: ccwarrens@yahoo.com

Check out Cross Fire, the next book in the series.

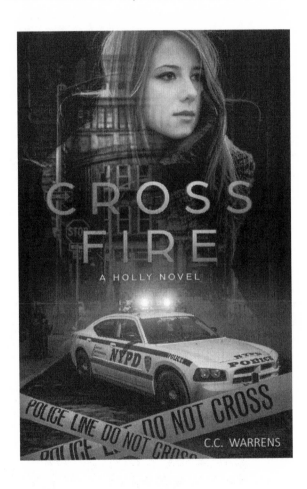

Made in the USA
Lexington, KY
30 April 2018